Full Figured:

Full Figured:

Carl Weber Presents

Brenda Hampton

and

La Jill Hunt

www.urbanbooks.net

Urban Books, LLC
78 East Industry Court
Deer Park, NY 11729

Who Ya Wit Copyright © 2010 Brenda Hampton
Seven Year Itch Copyright © 2010 La Jill Hunt

ISBN- 13: 978-1-60162-325-6
ISBN- 10: 1-60162-325-9

First Mass Market Printing November 2011
First Trade Paperback Printing July 2010
Printed in the United States of America

10 9 8 7 6 5 4 3 2 1

This is a work of fiction. Any references or similarities to ac-
tual events, real people, living, or dead, or to real locales are
intended to give the novel a sense of reality. Any similarity
in other names, characters, places, and incidents is entirely
coincidental.

Who Ya Wit

By

Brenda Hampton

Chapter One

I hated my job, but as bad as the economy was, I was pleased to have one. My boss, Mr. Wright, sometimes made me want to splash hot black coffee in his face, but other times he was cool to work for. I'd worked as his administrative assistant for thirteen years, and even though other opportunities at STL Community College became available, I somehow got complacent. Maybe because I knew the grass wasn't always greener in another department. I'd heard complaints from other administrative assistants who despised their bosses, so dealing with Mr. Wright just had to do.

Then again, maybe it was just me. I turned forty last month, my son, Latrel, had left for college this year, I'd been packing on the pounds, and my divorce from Reggie had recently been finalized. Needless to say, things were tough and never in my wildest dreams did I predict our marriage would end up as it had. We were high school sweethearts and had planned a life together forever. When Latrel was born, I was the happiest woman in the world. He and his father were very close, and over the years they'd gotten even closer. So close, that when Reggie started seeing another woman, Latrel knew about it but didn't say a word. I knew something was up, and when I would look him in the eyes I could tell that he was hiding something. He was so anxious to go away to college, and moving away from home had become his priority. Surely, I hated to put him in the middle of what was transpiring between me and his father, but I couldn't help but feel betrayed by both of them. Reggie's and my marriage had been on shaky ground for at least the last four years. His late nights at the office and constant trips out of town always brought about many arguments. It wasn't until I saw the infamous lipstick on the collar when I suspected something was up. I finally questioned him about my suspicions, and his response was quite surprising. He had come clean, admitting that he had fallen out of love with me and wanted his freedom.

To this day, I have flashbacks of that dreadful day, and even though it went down as one of the worst days of my life, I appreciated his honesty. No doubt, it was time to call it quits. We hung in there for another three months, but as soon as Latrel left for college, Reggie went his way and I went mine. I still love my ex-husband, but for him to renege on our vows as he had, I lost a lot of respect for him.

While sitting at my desk eating M&M's, I was daydreaming about my failed marriage and was attempting to type a letter for Mr. Wright that had to get distributed today. My fingers weren't moving fast enough for him, and when I heard him yell my name, my eyes rolled to the back of my head. I picked up my cup of hot black coffee and instead of taking it into his office with me, I sipped from the cup, smiling from my devious thoughts of tossing the coffee at him. Moving like a turtle, I placed the cup on my desk and straightened my gray fitted skirt that was glued to my healthy curves. I flattened the wrinkles on the front and made sure that the silver buttons were buttoned on my silk rosy-red blouse that squeezed my forty double-D's. Sometimes Mr. Wright complained about my attire. To him, for a full-figured woman I dressed too sexy, bringing unwarranted attention. And for anyone to stop at my desk to pay me a compliment, that was a distraction.

I considered myself to be a beautiful forty-year-old woman. I was confident about myself and even though my breasts weren't as perky as they'd been before and *some* cellulite was visible on my thighs, there wasn't much for me to complain about. Those things came along with the territory, and my two-times-a-week workout wasn't going to change a thing. My four-mile walk aerobics class helped me stay fit, but I had an addiction to sweets! Still, my body was proportioned well and what kind of man didn't want a woman with some meat on her bones? Reggie never had any complaints, but I had a feeling he traded me in for a woman who was half my size and age. It was his loss, though, and whenever I confessed my true age, no one believed me. My hair was healthy as ever and with the help of Pantene shampoo and conditioner, it gave me the feathery bouncing and behaving dark brown long hair I was aiming for. Halle Berry with long hair was written all over my face, but my body was thick like Toccara's from *America's Next Top Model*. Resembling Halle or having Toccara's body wasn't enough to spare me from losing the love of my life though. No doubt, I had to get over Reggie and it was a crime for a woman like me to feel so alone.

I slid my feet into the gray three-inch stilettos underneath my desk and made my way into Mr. Wright's office. He rubbed the wrinkles on his face up and down, massaging it with pressure. His cold blue eyes searched me over and a deep sigh followed as he extended his hand.

"Have a seat, Desa Rae."

I took a seat in the cherry oak leather chair that sat in front of his rectangular-shaped desk. Papers were spread out everywhere and his phone was buried somewhere underneath. I had attempted to organize Mr. Wright's office for him, but he was a serious pack rat. He hated to throw away anything, but some of the papers on his desk had started to turn yellow. I turned my eyes to the six smashed cigarettes in his ashtray. His office had a smoky smell covered with cheap Glade garden spray, and I hated it. I figured since he was under pressure, I was about to get an earful. I then looked at the round clock on his wall, seeing that I was ten minutes away from taking my lunch. Obviously, he needed to hurry up with what he wanted to discuss.

Mr. Wright peeled the black-framed glasses away from his face and then combed his fingers through his layered salt-and-pepper hair.

"I need a vacation," he yawned. "And when I get back, maybe my secretary—administrative assistant—will have all of my letters correctly typed for me, my office will be spotless and I'll never be late for an appointment because she remembered to tell me."

I had been through enough in my personal life, and for Mr. Wright to add to my misery wasn't going to benefit him in any way. No, I hadn't been giving this job my all, but he knew about my divorce from Reggie. He knew that my son had gone away for college and it seemed as if he wasn't willing to cut me any slack.

I repositioned myself in the chair and crossed one of my moisturized legs over the other. It was best that I kept quiet, and if I didn't have anything nice to say then I wasn't going to say it at all. I turned my attention to my chipped fingernail and thought about how badly I needed a manicure.

"Desa Rae," Mr. Wright said in a high-pitched voice. "Are you with me or is your mind floating somewhere else?"

With a blank expression on my face, I looked at Mr. Wright. "You asked me to take a seat, so I did it. You haven't required anything else of me, so I assumed my job was to just listen."

He threw his hand back at me and looked at his watch. "Would you mind bringing me a bagel sandwich with turkey, ham and cheese back for lunch? The deli shop on the corner has awesome sandwiches and you should get one too."

"My car really needs to be washed, so I planned to stop by a car wash. If you allow me a bit more time, I'll stop by the deli for our sandwiches."

"I'll allow you an extra fifteen minutes," he said, then handed me a Post-it note. "Before the day ends, there's a list of things I need you to take care of. It's not much, but if you have any questions about my requests, you can reach me by cell phone. After lunch, I'm leaving to spend the day with my wife. Today is our thirty-first anniversary and I've made special plans for us. Before you go to lunch, if you could call the florist and have some flowers delivered to my house, I would appreciate it."

I gazed over the Post-it note that specified minimal things for me to do, including finishing the letter I'd been working on and having it distributed. Mr. Wright had even drawn a smiley face on the Post-it, encouraging me to have a great day. I smiled and held out my hand. He inquisitively looked at it.

"What is it?" he asked. "You want more work to do?"

"Happy anniversary, but I need money for your bagel sandwich. You don't think I can walk in there and get it for free, do you?"

He chuckled and reached in his back pocket. "You're a fly young woman and you should be able to get whatever you want for free." He gave me a ten-dollar bill from his busted-up brown leather wallet. His credit cards had fallen out and so had his driver's license. I reached for it, holding it in my hand.

"At your age, Mr. Wright, what do you know about a woman being fly? Your grandkids aren't encouraging you to be hip, are they?"

"My grandkids are all a mess. They say I'm too old-fashioned, but I'm set in my ways. I'm appalled that they listen to rap music, and they drink and smoke pot too darn much for me. I can't tell you the last time I've seen any of them read a book, and my youngest grandchild, Katie, she's adapted a new gothic look. What's going on with these kids today, Desa Rae? It wasn't like that when I was growing up."

I stood up, wiggling my hips a bit so my skirt could drop to knee-length level. "Those days are long gone, Mr. Wright. Things have changed, and the best thing we can do for our children is be there for them."

He stood up too. His black slacks squeezed his waistline and his pot belly hung over his leather belt that was there to keep everything intact.

"Well, I'm not quite ready to accept this change yet. I'd love people to get back to their conservative values and start doing what's right for this country."

I felt our conversation getting political, but I couldn't help myself from going there. "With Obama being our president, you can count on change. Whether you like him or not, this country is moving more toward the middle and it will stay there for a long, long time to come. To me, he's what's right for this country and some of you older folks need to get with the program."

A die-hard Republican, Mr. Wright rolled his eyes and grunted. He reminded me of an angry Clint Eastwood, but I figured he meant no harm. Sometimes, though, by the things he said, he could easily be considered a racist. Then there were times that he seemed to simply care about people, no matter what color they were. He gave a lot of his money to charity, volunteered, and contributed an enormous amount of money to the college we worked for. His money helped many black students get scholarships and that was something about him that I couldn't help but to admire.

I followed behind him as he made his way to the door. His black leather shoes had scuff marks on them and his shirt could have been one size larger. For a man to have as much money as he did, when it came to his attire, obviously, clothes weren't his priority. He wore the same suit at least twice a week and his white shirts always looked dingy. He took frugal to a whole new level, but I guess spending money on clothes wasn't something he viewed as a necessity.

"I'm going to the men's room. Don't forget about my wife's flowers and I'll see you when you get back from lunch."

Mr. Wright flat-footedly walked away and I sat at my desk to call the florist. After I had a dozen roses sent to Mrs. Wright, I called to wish her a happy anniversary. She was one of the nicest women I'd ever met, and even though, at times, I hated to admit it, so was her husband.

The long line at the car wash made me very impatient. The workers were horseplaying around and seemed so darn unprofessional. One worker was on his cell phone cussing at his girlfriend and another was arguing with a white man about some spots the worker missed inside of his car. Lil Wayne's "Lick Me Like a Lollipop" was thumping through the loudspeakers and when I saw two females out of their cars shaking their asses, I was in disbelief. Of course, the attention they got delayed the workers even more. And after seeing numerous people waiting in line too, I was embarrassed. The hot sun was baking my body and my wet silk blouse was starting to stick to my skin.

I stood close by my car, only to reach inside for my glasses to protect my eyes from the sun's bright glare. As soon as I covered my eyes, my cell phone buzzed. I looked to see who it was and it was Reggie. The last thing I needed was to hear his voice, so I let the call go straight to voice mail.

"Sucker," I mumbled, tossing the phone inside of my tiny purse. I tucked it underneath my arm, abruptly walking inside of the car wash to speak to a manager.

"Can I help you?" the man behind the counter asked.

"May I speak to the manager?" I politely asked.

"Can I ask what for?"

I forced out a fake smile. "I prefer to speak to the manager about my concerns, if you don't mind."

The man twisted his thick crusty lips and walked away from the counter. Moments later, he returned, asking me to take a seat.

"The manager ain't here, but I got somebody else you can talk to."

I cut my eyes at him and wouldn't dare to take a seat in the lined-up blue chairs that had stains all over them. I could have easily gone somewhere else, but this place was close to my job. My Lincoln MKS needed a cleaning right here and right now. Time definitely wasn't on my side, and I knew that Mr. Wright was eagerly waiting for his bagel sandwich.

I gazed out of the huge smudged window at four black and two white men in darkblue jumpsuits sitting around doing nothing. The line with people waiting had gotten longer and some people started to leave. I shook my head and one of the workers had the audacity to look inside and blow me a kiss. My middle finger trembled by my side and I surely thought about lifting it so he could see it. My don't-mess-with-me expression said it all, but it wasn't enough to keep the man from coming inside.

"Is there somethin' I can help you wit?" he asked, entering the door.

I looked at his name stitched into his jumpsuit. "Bud, I don't think so. You look as if you're too busy to help anyone."

"I'm on my break, but for a scrumptious-lookin' cookie like you I'll—"

"Please don't do me any favors," I snapped. "There are people out there who've been waiting and waiting on your services. This is ridiculous and I can't believe I'm standing here trying to coach you into doing your job."

Bud's eyes damn near popped out of his head. "Another angry black woman," he spat. "Y'all need to cut *us* some slack. I offered to help, but you don't want it. You'd rather stand there wit yo' fine bitter self and attack . . ." My arched brows quickly shot up. This man didn't know anything about me to call me bitter. And his "angry black woman" comment sparked a major nerve. My middle finger rose and I was about to tell Bud to kiss where the sun didn't shine. Instead, I was interrupted by someone clearing their throat. My head snapped to the side and I witnessed an extremely attractive young man standing close. He immediately reminded me of Lance Gross, *Tyler Perry's House of Payne*'s character, Calvin. Due to the dirty blue jumpsuit he had on, he wasn't as clean cut as Calvin, but his dark and lovely smooth skin, thick dark eyebrows, and "lure me into your bedroom" hooded brown eyes nearly swept my feet from underneath me. His thin mustache was trimmed to perfection and so was the minimal hair that suited his chin. I hurried to gather myself, and when he turned toward Bud, I listened in.

"Are you finished with yo' break yet?" he asked.

"Almost. I just came inside to see if I could help out this lady. She seems upset about somethin', but I'm not sure what's up."

I looked at the name *Roc* stitched into Mr. Sexy's jumpsuit. "Are you the manager?"

He shrugged as if he didn't give a damn about my concerns. "No. But I'm in charge of things around here right now. What up?"

I dropped my head back and let out a frustrating sigh. All I wanted was a car wash, but instead I had yummy and dummy standing there as if I'd done something wrong. I tightened my lips to keep quiet and made my way to the door. Roc saw the smoke coming from my ears and hurried behind me.

"Did I say somethin' wrong?" he asked.

I kept on moving. My long hair was bouncing and my brisk walk implied that I would never, ever visit this place again. When I got to my car, I got inside and slammed the door. Roc stood with a confused expression on his face, and while rubbing his coal-black neatly lined waves, he squinted his eyes from the bright sun. I put my car in reverse, but couldn't go anywhere because another car was behind me. I hit my hand on the horn and couldn't believe how upset I was.

"Damn it!" I yelled.

Roc stepped up to my car, pressing his hands against it. He bent down and looked at me through the lowered window.

"Are you havin' a postal moment or what? Maybe I should back away from the car in case I get shot. You too dope to be as angry as you are, and if I've done anything to upset ya, hey, my bad."

I took another deep breath to calm myself. I'd been overreacting to a lot of things lately, but that was to be expected. I turned to Roc and zoned in on his straight pearly whites.

"Look," I said with frustration in my eyes. "All I want is my car washed. Is that asking too much? I'm on my lunch break and I have thirty-five minutes left."

Roc backed away from the door. "Come on, get out of the car. Leave it runnin' and I'll personally take care of you."

That was music to my ears, so I got out and let Roc get in.

"No offense," I said. "But your jumpsuit is kind of dirty. My seats are off-white and I'd hate for them to get any dirtier."

Roc pointed to his chest. "I thought that's why you were here? Ain't it my job to clean the out-side and inside of yo' car?"

"True. But you have grease on your jumpsuit. Right at your midsection."

Roc looked down, but it wasn't at his midsection. "Thanks for noticin'," he said and winked.

He got out of my car, standing tall in front of me. He reached for his zipper and our eyes were in a deadlock as he slid the zipper down, past the hump I'd already noticed in his pants. I felt so ashamed for getting myself worked up over a young man like him, but his sexiness was hard to ignore. He kicked off his black rubber steel-toed-boots and the jumpsuit came off next. Underneath he sported a white wife beater and jeans that hung low on his nicely-cut midsection. His arms were toned to perfection and he had tattoos on both of them. Still, his arms looked smooth as a baby's bottom, and how dare me stand there, gawking at him as if I hadn't eaten anything chocolate all day.

"I—if you don't mind, I'm going inside to suck up the air conditioner. Please come get me when you're finished."

Roc nodded and I made my way back inside, swaying my noticeable hips from side to side. I got a few whistles, and even though they were from Bud, I didn't seem to mind.

As Roc detailed the heck out of my car, I watched his every move through the window. His body was now dripping with beads of sweat and the thoughts in my head had gotten down-right nasty. I visualized my light-skinned legs resting comfortably on his shoulders as he pumped hard inside of me. I gave him head while he tongue tortured my tunnel in a 69 position. *Even Reggie couldn't do it like that.* I smiled . . . Roc smiled. I assumed he liked it rough, but then again, his voice had a romantic pitch to it. Yeah, he was a thug, but . . . *How old was he?* I thought about his age while biting my already chipped nail, trying to take back my outrageous thoughts. He had to be at least the same age as my son, Latrel, or maybe a tad bit older. I couldn't quite understand my immediate attraction to him, but maybe it was due to me feeling so alone. I chalked it up as him being a cute young man who was probably dating several attractive young women. Like the one with the petite figure who stood close by as he wiped my windshield. She wasn't giving him much breathing room, and by the evil stares she gave him, I could tell there was involvement. No doubt the competition looked steep, and if he was interested in women that small, I was way out of his league.

Roc tucked the dry washrag into his front pocket and reached in his back pocket for his wallet. I saw him hand over several bills, and afterward the young woman walked away. She sped off and he looked inside, focusing his eyes in my direction. I grinned, while taking a glance at my watch. Time was not on my side, so I left the building and walked over to my car.

"I'm just 'bout finished," Roc said, turning the rag in circles on my windshield. "Feel free to inspect it."

I walked around my car, silently admitting that he had done a pretty good job. When I noticed a tiny speck of dried water on the trunk, I called him out on it.

"Ooops," I said. "You forgot something."

He turned his attention to the trunk and looked at the dry water speck. "Are you serious?" He smiled, rubbing the tiny spot with a towel. "If you look hard enough, you might find more of those."

"I hope not. Besides, how much is this going to cost me? If there are spots on my car, then maybe you should consider offering me a discount."

He faced me and leaned his backside against the trunk. His arms were folded in front of him and bulging muscles were clearly on display.

"I usually don't offer peeps discounts, especially if the Roc personally takes care of them. But in this case, I got a better idea."

My hand went up to my hip as I felt the bullshit about to go down. "I'm almost afraid to ask about your idea."

"It's simple. What's yo' name?"

"Desa Rae. Why?"

"Dez, let me get yo' sevens so I can call you up and take you to dinner. How 'bout that?"

My eyes lowered to the ground, then connected with his. "Just for the hell of it, Roc, how old are you?"

Not holding back, he came out with it. In slow motion, I watched his thick lips spit out the number, "Twenty-four."

"How old are you?" he asked.

He was only five years older than my son! There was no way I could go there. "You know what . . . my age doesn't even matter. How much do I owe you?" I opened my purse, reaching for my wallet.

"The wash was on me. Now, to be fair, can you answer my question or did you just realize that this young man may be too much for you to handle?"

I tossed my hair to the side with my fingers and hurried to wrap up this conversation that was going nowhere. "I'm forty, Roc. Thanks for the free wash and you're right, you are too much for me to handle."

I headed to the driver's door and opened it. Once inside, I reached for my seat belt to strap myself in. Roc bent down to look into the window.

"Somehow, I feel as if I got snubbed." He pulled the wet wife beater away from his chest and wiped some of the sweat from his face. "I've been out here sweatin' and slavin' like a Hebrew slave for you and this is how you treat me? I see you got ghost when I told you my age, but if I told you I was thirty-one would you believe me? Better yet, would it make a difference?"

I couldn't help but smile at his attempts, and they definitely required a response. "No, it wouldn't make a difference."

"Why? 'Cause you lied about yo' age? You know damn well you ain't no forty. Thirty, maybe, not forty."

"I have no reason to lie to you, and if I had time, I'd show you my driver's license. I don't, so you'll have to take my word for it. Now, if you don't mind, I really need to get going."

"Can't say I didn't try," he said, shrugging and backing away from the car so I could drive off. I did just that, but couldn't help but take another look at him in my rearview mirror. I licked my bottom lip, biting into it.

Damn, I thought. *If he were only ten . . . fifteen years older.*

Chapter Two

Latrel was coming home for the weekend, and as usual, Reggie and I had been arguing over where Latrel would stay. After our divorce, Reggie had to give up our three-bedroom, two-bathroom ranch-style home that we'd stayed in for years. Latrel had a decked-out bedroom in the basement, so it only made sense that he would agree to stay with me. The decision was his, but when he opted to stay with his father at his condo in Lake St. Louis by the lake, I got upset.

"You don't love me, do you?" I asked with the phone pressed up to my ear.

"Mama, you know that ain't fair. I love you . . . a lot, but I want to check out Dad's new place by the lake. You and me gon' hook up. Besides, I want you to meet my new girlfriend."

"Girlfriend? That was quick, and shouldn't you be focusing on school and your basketball career?"

"Trust me, I am. I get lonely sometimes, Mama, and Tracie kind of been there for me."

My heart softened at the thought of him feeling alone. I definitely knew how that felt. "What time will you be here and where is Tracie going to stay?"

"I'll be there around noon and Tracie is staying with me. I already talked to Dad about it and he said it was cool."

"Oh, really? No wonder you don't want to stay with me. You knew darn well I wasn't going for it. If Tracie is coming with you, during the night she can either stay with me or get a room at a hotel."

"That don't make any sense. I already told you I talked to Dad about it and he cool. Why you over there trippin'?"

I was at work so I definitely had to keep my cool. Latrel and Reggie were always going behind my back making unjust decisions and it drove me crazy. "I'm calling your father tonight and we're going to discuss this. In the meantime, you'd better start making reservations at a hotel or leave Tracie in her dorm room."

"This is crazy, Mama. Are you saying that you don't trust me?"

I slammed my hand on my desk and pulled the phone slightly away from my ear. Once I was calm, I continued my conversation. "Tell me something, Latrel. Are you a virgin?"

"No. But what that got to do with it?"

"Strike one. Do you always use condoms?"

"S—sometimes. Mostly—"

"Strike two. Does Tracie take birth control pills?"

"I—I guess. I assume—"

"Strike three, my dear, and you're out! No, I do not trust you and—and at what age did you lose your virginity? This is something completely new to me, but I'm sure your father knows all about it."

I could hear Latrel sigh over the phone. "Huff and puff all you want to," I said. My feelings were hurt and my eyes started to water. I felt so excluded from his life and it hurt like hell. "I have to go. Mr. Wright is calling me."

"Mama, please don't be upset with me. I can tell you're upset, but just know that I do my best. I ain't perfect, all right? I didn't tell you about my first time 'cause I was confused about what I was going through and I thought I was in love."

"But you felt comfortable enough to tell your father?"

"I didn't tell him until much, much later. And that's because he asked me. You never asked me until today. Today is when I told you the truth."

I swallowed hard, wiping the tear that had fallen down my cheek. I hadn't had those kinds of conversations with Latrel and shame on me for putting all of the blame on him. "I'll see you tomorrow, okay? I love you and I look forward to meeting your girlfriend."

"Love you too, Mama. See ya tomorrow."

I slowly laid the phone on the receiver and got back to work. Thank God it was Friday.

It was almost noon and I was making lunch in the kitchen while running my mouth on the phone with my girlfriend, Monica. We'd been friends for as long as I could remember and whenever I was up, so was she. Whenever I was down, she was down too—vice versa. Monica had never been married and she loved to live the single life. She had two children, one who was in his second year of college and a daughter who recently moved to California to pursue her acting career. Monica had done a good job raising her children as a single parent, but she was never pleased with their choices. She sounded a lot like me, and as I sat at the kitchen table with the phone pressed up to my ear, we cracked up when she called her daughter Jade a joke.

"Now, that's not nice, Monica. That girl is doing her best and you should be proud of her."

"Oh, I'm very proud. But that doesn't mean she hasn't been working my nerves. That girl is rotten to the core and I don't know how she thinks she's going to gain her independence by moving to California."

"Well, just give her a chance, Monica. And you have no one but yourself to blame for spoiling those kids as much as you have."

"I couldn't agree with you more. Some parents are crushed when their children leave the nest, but for me, girl, I've been on cloud nine. You know I've been traveling and just getting out of this house that I've been cooped up in for so long makes me feel like a new woman. You should get your butt out of the house sometimes too. Life is too short and you've got to let your hair down and cut loose."

"Eventually, I will. I'm just so out of touch. Being with Reggie for all of those years was all I knew."

"I understand that, but Reggie isn't coming back no time soon. You need to go out and meet people. Every time you go somewhere you got men flocking all around you, but it's as if you look straight through them."

"I know, and at times I'm a little confused by that. I'm not what society considers a fit woman, and even though Reggie never complained about my weight, I do think he wanted me to lose weight."

"Are you crazy? To hell with society and there is no doubt in my mind that Reggie was satisfied with your looks all the way 'round. Y'all just had other issues. You are blessed with the curves that every woman should have, especially black women. I envy you and don't you be over there trying to cut back on nothing. If you lose one single pound, I'll hurt you."

I laughed, knowing my best friend was right. My divorce from Reggie was about him not being able to get it together, not me.

"Okay, Monica, you got a point. I'm cool with my looks, but sometimes surprised by the attention I get."

"I'm glad you got my point, and as long as you keep that big ole booty in shape and that waist-line perfected, you shouldn't have no problems meeting men."

"So, to hell with my brains, huh? Forget that I'm a wonderful woman who—"

"Yes, to hell with that, for now. Men aren't interested in those kinds of things, until they get to know you. Just make sure the inside, though, looks just as good as the outside."

We laughed, but agreed. Monica continued on, trying to convince me to stop staying cooped up in the house. I got up from the table to get a glass of water from the fridge.

"Where am I supposed to go?" I asked. "To a nightclub or something with you? Hell, I can't even remember how to dance and I wouldn't know what the latest dance was if somebody paid me to know."

"It's called the stanky leg."

I frowned and couldn't believe what she'd said. "Stanky what?"

"Stanky l-e-g."

"Not interested at all. If I had to dance at a club, I would probably embarrass the hell out of both of us. All I know how to do is snap my fingers and move side to side. That's as stanky as I'm gon' get." I did my side-to-side dance in the kitchen, just to make sure I still had it.

"Quit popping your fingers and think about going out with me tonight. Trust me, you'll have fun. Besides, by then Latrel will be with his father and you'll be sitting at home reading a book. How boring."

I told Monica I would think about it, and just as I was taking the homemade pepperoni pizza out of the oven, I heard the front door open. I stood with a big bright smile plastered on my face and waited for Latrel to make his way to the Italian aroma in the kitchen. When he stepped into the kitchen, as expected he was not alone. Reggie was with him and so was a young white girl. I was frozen in time. My smile vanished and my body felt as if cement had been poured over it. Monica was still running her mouth, and when she yelled my name, I snapped out of it.

"Girl, what's wrong with you?" she yelled. "Didn't you hear me?"

"I—I got to go. I think I've seen a ghost."

I hung up on Monica and wiped my saucy red hands on my apron. Latrel was so taken aback by my comment that he took Tracie's hand and left the room. Reggie's self-righteous butt looked at me with a forehead full of lined wrinkles.

"You were way, way out of line. You need to go and apologize to your son and his girlfriend right now."

I ignored his demand, untying the apron from behind me. "A white girl," I mumbled. "No he didn't."

Reggie cleared his throat. I didn't have time to encourage my thoughts of how good he was looking. His strong masculine cologne lit up the kitchen and he was always dressed at his best in casual attire. He rocked a peach polo shirt, a pair of off-white linen pants, and leather sandals. The Polo belt around his waist tucked him in nice and neat and his forty-one-year-old cut body was doing him major justice. Latrel looked a lot like his father, but was much, much taller. Reggie was bald, but kept his head clean-shaven. They both sported goatees, but Latrel had a head full of dark brown waves. And the only things that Latrel had inherited from me were my light-colored skin and almond-shaped eyes with upswept lifts at the corners.

"Hello to you too, Reggie," I said, washing my hands. "I didn't know you were coming with them."

"I wanted to call and tell you, but you know how our conversations can get at times. I'm not going there with you today, and for the last time, somebody may be in need of an apology."

I put my hand on my hip, giving my lips a slight toot. "And if not? What's going to happen?"

"Nothing," he said, walking away. "Nothing at all."

Reggie yelled for Latrel and Tracie to come upstairs. They did and he suggested that they all leave. Latrel gazed at me, waiting for a response. "I don't know what to say about you," he said. "What was all of that for?"

"You heard your father, Latrel. He's ready to go. I suggest you don't get left behind."

Latrel turned to Reggie and nodded his head. "I told you about her, didn't I?"

"Told him what? How I'd react to your girlfriend? If you knew, then why would you do something like this to me?"

Latrel stepped into the kitchen and looked down as he stood tall over me. Hurt was in his eyes and I had never seen him appear so serious. "When are you ever gonna back off and let me make my own decisions? I'm a grown-ass man, Mama, and you disrespecting me like some fool on the street you know nothing about."

I backed away from my son's aggressiveness. "Go, do you, Latrel. You have my blessings, along with my sympathy."

He shot me a mean mug and flipped the pizza tray off the marble-topped island. The pizza hit the floor and splattered on the hardwood. "I don't need your blessings or your sympathy," he yelled. "To hell wit it!"

Reggie stepped forward and put his hand on Latrel's heaving chest. Reggie then ordered him and Blue Eyes to the car and they left. I swallowed the huge lump in my throat and squatted down to clean up Latrel's mess. My head stayed dropped, as I didn't want Reggie to see the pain in my eyes from the hurt I'd just endured, compliments of *his* son.

Reggie held out his hand for mine. "Get up," he said.

I waved him off, and like always, I ignored him. He placed his hands in his pockets and jiggled his change.

"You know you brought this on yourself, don't you? For God's sake, Dee, why must you always make everything about you? Your son was so damn happy about coming here to see you, and since when did you start making comments like a racist? I'm speaking to you as his father," his voice rose. "Don't you ever treat my son like that again! If your beef remains with us," he pounded his chest. "Take your shit out on me! I can take it. Latrel can't. Now, he'll be at my place until Monday. Get yourself together and figure out how you're going to make this right."

As quickly as they came, they went. I had a headache out of this world, and after I cleaned up my kitchen, I took some Advil and went to my room to lie down. My thoughts of Latrel were killing me and my body felt as if somebody was sticking me with the tip of a sharp knife. I had always been the kind of person who reacted to matters too quickly. No, I wasn't enthused about Latrel being with a white girl, but maybe it was just me. Lately, I'd had hang-ups about everything, but something inside felt as if he was doing it because of me. He didn't want a woman who looked like his mother, nor did he appreciate all that I had done for him. He was moving in another direction, and as long as a woman didn't look like me, he was all good. I hated that about my son, and for him not to consider my feelings was gut-wrenching.

I was passed out until the loud ringing of the phone awakened me. My tired eyes were barely opened, but I managed to reach over and grab the phone.

"Hello," I said in a raspy tone.

"Girl, get your butt up," Monica yelled. I could hear her fingers snapping. "Have you made up your mind yet?"

I sat up in bed, rubbing my eyes. "Made up my mind about what?"

"About doing the stanky leg."

"Uh, no. No, I'm not going to no nightclub."

"Why not?"

"Because I'm still tired and I want to go back to bed."

"It is eight o'clock on a Saturday night. Who in their right mind is at home in bed?"

"Me."

"Well, not for long. I'm on my way to pick you up and you'd better be ready."

Monica hung up and I dropped the phone on the floor. I buried my face in the pillow, screaming loudly. I wasn't up to doing anything, but I knew how persistent Monica could be. She was definitely going to show up and it was in my best interests to be ready.

I showered and searched my walk-in closet for something to wear. It had been years since I'd been out to a nightclub and I couldn't decide on a black strapless minidress or my Jones of New York baby-blue pantsuit. I sorted through my accessories and when I came across my black and silver dangling necklace and silver bangles for my wrist, I decided on the mini. I slid it down over my hips and turned in the mirror to observe myself. My backside looked perfect, but my tiny love handles made my waistline look pudgy. I had a quick solution for that and found my corset that gave my waistline a slimming fit. *Awesome*, I thought, reaching for my Nine West black strapped heels with rhinestones. My feathery long hair was never a problem and the bouncing body that it had made me look and feel like a million dollars. I touched up my M•A•C gloss and makeup, then stroked my already long lashes with thick mascara. I was simply gorgeous and knew it.

***

The club scene had definitely changed since the last time I'd been. There were wall-to-wall people inside, some younger, but many who looked to be my age as well. It was a nice setting, though, and the music was a mixture of jazz, hip-hop, R&B, and even a bit of the blues. Monica and I lucked up on two bar stools that surrounded the huge square dance floor that was full to capacity. The disco balls were turning from up above and red, yellow, and blue lights spun on everyone. Monica sat next to me, snapping her fingers, while moving her hips in her seat. As usual, she looked nice. She was Vivica Fox all the way, and like me, for her, age was just a number. From being on the scene for so long, she definitely had rhythm, but had turned away several men who had already asked her to dance.

"If you're not going to dance," I whispered, "then why sit there in your seat shaking yourself, leading these men on?"

"Just because I get funky in my seat, it doesn't mean I want to get jiggy on the floor. I'll dance, just not right now." She pushed my shoulder. "What about you? Are you going to dance or what? You've been the rejection queen all night and I can't believe that margarita hasn't loosened you up."

"I already told you I can't dance and I'm not about to make a fool of myself. I will, however, have another drink because this one seems kind of weak."

Monica signaled for the bartender and ordered both of us another drink. This time she ordered me a cranberry cocktail and insisted on doubling up on the vodka.

"I bet that'll get your butt up and going," she said.

I wanted to enjoy myself, but my mind kept wandering back to Latrel and Reggie. I wondered what they were up to or if they were sitting around discussing me. I sat daydreaming for a minute, until my eyes came across someone intriguing. *It couldn't be,* I thought. I squinted my eyes to be sure. *Nah, he looks much too clean to be him.*

"Who you looking at?" Monica asked, interrupting my thoughts.

"Nobody. I thought I saw someone I knew."

Monica's eyes turned to where mine were and she zoned in at the three young men sitting at a table. "That is one fine, hunk of dark black-ass chocolate right there! He too young, but that brotha looks good."

"Which one?" I asked, pretending as if I didn't notice.

"The one with the gray tailor-made suit on and silk black shirt underneath."

"How in the heck do you know that brotha's suit is tailor-made?"

"Look at how it clings to his broad shoulders and arms. A man can't just go in the store and find something that fits him like that, trust me."

I kept my eyes on the man, trying to see if he was actually Roc from the car wash. When he got up from the table, he smiled at the men he was speaking to and that was all the confirmation I needed. I knew what seeing those pearly whites and dimples had done to me at the car wash and that same feeling came over me again. Monica and I both kept our eyes glued to him.

I played down my attraction. "I don't care too much for that skinny leg suit he's wearing. Latrel got one of those, but that's because his daddy got it for him."

"It's the style, Desa Rae, and that brotha has got the game and gone with it. Look at all the women checking him out. He like all that attention too. When he comes this way, ignore him. I don't want him to think he's all that, even though he definitely is."

We laughed and I watched as Roc made his way through the crowd. The bartender came just in time with our drinks, and with him standing in front of me, it was easier to pretend as if I didn't see Roc. Right after the bartender sat our drinks in front of us, Roc stepped forward and approached the bartender.

"Are you takin' good care of these two ladies?" he asked. I was floored. It was as if his entire demeanor had changed. His voice appeared more mature and the suit looked even better close up.

"I'm doing my best," the bartender replied.

"Good. Their drinks are on the house. Make sure they well taken care of."

Monica was grinning from ear to ear. Roc had to have had a twin.

"Thanks, but do we know you?" Monica asked.

"I don't think I ever met you before," he turned to me. "But I definitely met her."

"Roc?" I said, still a bit unsure.

He winked. "In the flesh." He looked at the dance floor. "Do you wanna dance?"

Monica quickly reached for my glass, taking it from my hand. "Yes, she would love to dance."

"Uh, no thank—"

I could barely get the word *no* out of my mouth before Roc took my hand and escorted me to the dance floor. Jay-Z's latest hit was playing and some of the female dancers were trying to drop it like Beyoncé. There wasn't a bone in my body that allowed me to move like her, so I did the norm and snapped my fingers while moving side to side. Roc, however, was all into it. He had his arms in the air, snapping his fingers. His suit jacket was open and his black silk shirt was hugging every single muscle in his chest. The lower part of his body was in motion and the women couldn't stop looking in our direction. I was so embarrassed that I didn't know how to work it like he was. All I kept thinking was . . . *God, this young man was sexy and it had to be a sin to create someone as well put together as him.*

Roc displayed his award-winning smile and turned around so I could check out his backside. I visualized my hands gripping his tight black ass and when I looked over at Monica, she was encouraging me to move closer to him.

What? I mouthed from the dance floor.

She rolled her eyes to the back of her head, gritting her teeth. *Move closer*, she mouthed back. I shook my head from side to side and she waved me off.

As soon as the song was over, I touched Roc's chest and told him I was done.

"So soon," he asked. "I can't believe you got me kickin' up a sweat again and gon' leave me hangin'."

I pointed to my shoes. "My feet are killing me," I lied, sparing myself the embarrassment of dancing through another song.

"A'ight," he said, taking my hand. I was shocked, and when he rubbed the inside of my hand with his finger, I pulled away.

"Thanks for the dance," I said, taking my seat next to Monica.

"Promise me another dance before you leave, a'ight?"

"Sure."

Roc walked away and Monica looked at me with a stunned look. "You really can't dance, can you? You had all of that man in front of you, and didn't have a clue what to do with him."

We laughed and I sipped from my glass. "I told you I couldn't dance. And if you expect for me to do all of those dance moves the women up there are doing, you're crazy."

"I didn't expect for you to do all that, but damn! Girl, you need to take some dance lessons. Forgive me for shoving your butt up there like that, but I at least hoped you would take advantage of him and get your feel on."

"I didn't want to come off as desperate. Besides, was my dancing really that bad?" I humped my shoulders and snapped my fingers. "I was kind of . . . you know, getting down a little bit, wasn't I?"

Monica held her two fingers close. "Just a tiny bit. Unfortunately, not enough to make that brotha remember a darn thing about you."

"I don't want him to remember me. A few days ago, I saw him at a car wash and he was trying to push up on me then. He's twenty-four years old, works at a car wash, and there's nothing a man like that can do for me."

"I beg to differ. There are plenty of things he can do for you."

I defensively crossed my arms. "Like what?"

Monica placed her hand on her chest. "You're my best friend, and even I can't muster up enough courage in my heart to tell you what *I* would do with a man that fine, sexy, energized, and interested." She placed her finger on the side of my temple and lightly pushed my head. "Use your brain, Desa Rae. Live a little and don't let life pass you by."

I knew Monica was right, and she had no idea how quickly my brain had been working. In my mind, I'd experienced many heated encounters with Roc, but wasn't sure if I was ready to make it a reality. The thought of him being an immature twenty-four-year-old was a struggle for me. What could being with a man like him do for a woman like me? The only thing he would be good for was sex, and since I was so darn horny, maybe that wasn't a bad thing at all.

***

One o'clock in the morning had come too quickly. Monica and I were having a wonderful time and neither of us could stay off the dance floor. The alcohol I'd consumed had my whole body feeling as if heat was running through my blood. My neck had beads of sweat on it and my vision was starting to blur. Neither of us were capable of driving home and we knew it. Therefore, when Roc came over and offered us a ride home, I couldn't decline his offer.

"What about my car?" Monica slurred while slowly getting into the backseat of Roc's SUV.

"You can come back to it in the mornin'," Roc suggested.

I wasn't as wasted as Monica, but at our age we knew better. I got in on the passenger's side and Roc closed the door behind me.

"Where do you live? And will it be okay if I drop off both of y'all at the same place? I have somewhere else I need to be."

I was grateful that Roc was even taking us home, so his comment about having somewhere else to be didn't bother me. With all of the women in his face tonight, I was sure he had plenty of choices. I gave him directions to my house and he used his GPS to direct him there.

"Did you have a nice time?" he asked while driving.

"Wonderful time," I said, staring out of the window.

"I could tell. I mean, you were out there sha-kin' yo' ass and everythang. I saw you and I noticed you picked up some numbers too. Too bad you can't dance, though, but you were damn sho' good to look at."

I turned toward Roc and smiled. "You weren't no Usher, you know. Until you can dance like him, don't go criticizing the way I dance."

"I ain't tryin' to be Usher. I'm me and I wouldn't trade me for the world."

"*Strangers in the niiiight*," Monica sung out from the backseat. She deepened her voice and made it baritone like Frank Sinatra's.

Roc and I both laughed. "What the fuck?" he said. "She really needs to get home and sleep off that madness."

I looked at the backseat, and just that fast, Monica was out. When I turned, I noticed Roc's sneaky eyes checking out my thighs that were clearly visible from the minidress I wore. I didn't say a word, but he knew he was busted. He reached for the knob on his stereo, turning up the music. As he rapped some lyrics, he nodded and tapped his fingertips on the steering wheel.

"That's the shit right there," he said.

No doubt, the loud music annoyed me. "Who is that?"

"You don't know who that is?"

"No."

"Young Jeezy."

"Oh, okay. But do you mind turning that down just a little bit?"

He lowered the volume and continued to look back and forth at me while nodding his head.

"You know what," he said. "You ain't gon' believe me when I tell you this, though."

"What's that?"

"I been thinkin' 'bout you. Just last night I said, damn, I sholl hope I see that Halle Berry look-alike again. I could've kicked myself in the ass for lettin' you get away without givin' me yo' sevens."

"It's Desa Rae, not Halle. And you didn't let me do anything. I chose not to give you my number because you're too young and I prefer not to date men who work at car washes. Bottom line, I don't give my *sevens* to men I'm not interested in."

Roc stopped at the red light and gave me a stern stare. "I don't work at the car wash. I was just helping out my uncle who owns the place. Same goes for the club you were just at, he owns that place too. Let me give you a lil' advice . . . I suggest you not judge a book by its cover and lighten up a lil' bit. And if you weren't interested before, are you interested now?"

"Are you still twenty-four years old?"

"Yes."

"Then, no, I'm not interested."

He forcefully put his foot on the accelerator and sped off. It was obvious that Roc wasn't used to rejection. When we got to my house, he had to carry Monica inside and lay her on the couch. I immediately rushed in the bathroom to use it, and when I came out, Roc was waiting for me by the front door.

"You don't know how much I appreciate this," I said, rubbing my forehead to soothe my headache.

"No problem. But if you appreciate me as much as you say you do, then you'd give me yo' sevens so I can call you."

My head was banging and I really didn't have time to stand at the door with Roc and deny him. In an effort to get him out of my hair, I reached for my purse so I could give him my business card. I wrote my *sevens* on the back and gave the card to him.

"Here, and please don't overuse my number. Don't be surprised if you start feeling as if you're wasting your time and I've told you once already that I'm too old for you."

Roc pulled his suit jacket back, resting his backside against the door. He slid his hands into his pockets, along with my card. "Prove it," he said. "Show me right now that you forty years old. If you are, I'll give yo' card back and you'll never see me again."

I reached in my purse for my driver's license and gave it to him. He looked it over, then gave it back to me. "Bullshit. That's a fake ID."

I smiled and shook my head at how cute and persistent he was. "Unfortunately, I don't have time to go get my birth certificate for you, but I do want my card back because we had an agreement."

He winked and reached in his pocket for my card. "My word, my bond," he said, giving the card back to me. He turned to the door and I unlocked it for him. No sooner than I could turn the knob, Roc eased his arm around my waist and pulled me close to him. He put my body right between his legs and moved his hips around, making sure I felt how excited he was down below. Our eyes stared at each other's hungry lips and his tongue went for the kill. His lips were soft like butter against mine and our tongues intertwined for at least a full minute. Like in my previous thoughts, I rubbed his neatly lined waves and allowed his hands to roam up my minidress to massage my ass. *You know better*, I kept telling myself. But then again, I told myself to *shut the hell up! Live a little, Desa Rae. Take this brotha to your bedroom and let him fuck away your misery. He's capable of doing it and to hell with Reggie. Reggie who? Don't you feel how hard his dick is? Reggie's dick never felt that big. Get it, girl. Go get that dick in you right now!*

Roc backed away from our intense kiss and I opened my eyes. Our eyes were deeply connected and tore at each other's soul. Thing is, neither of us knew where to turn next. *Fuck it,* I thought, reaching for his belt buckle. He touched my hand to stop me.

"My condoms are in my truck. Let me go get *some* and I'll be right back."

I nodded and opened the door for Roc. Since he had gone to get more than one condom, I predicted it was going to be a long, unforgettable night. I bit my nails as I watched him open the glove compartment to retrieve a box of condoms. He removed his jacket and laid it on his front seat. No doubt, he was geared to go and had already started to pull his shirt out from inside of his pants. I stood on my porch fidgeting and was fearful as ever. *Darn,* I thought. *Where were my chocolates? I needed a bite of something, but then again, my chocolate was right there in front of me. No . . . he was only twenty-four years old! What if Latrel was dating a woman my age? Wouldn't I be upset? This young man had a mother who I was sure wouldn't approve.*

"Roc," I said, halting his steps as he stepped onto the porch. "I'm sorry, but I can't. I apologize for misleading you, but this isn't a good time for me. My head isn't on straight and I'm not sure if this is something I really want to do."

Roc sighed and wiped down his face with his hand. "Damn, ma. You got me all worked up for nothin'? I ain't gon' force you into nothin' you don't wanna do, but why you makin' this so difficult? Age is a number and a number don't mean jack."

"I say that myself, but in this case it may very well apply."

"'Cause you think I can't please you, is that it? I promise you that I'm not yo' average twenty-four-year-old brotha out here, just tryin' to get in and out. Let me show you what I'm workin' with."

"I have a good feeling what you're working with, but just not tonight." I gave him my card again, just so he wouldn't feel as if I'd completely dissed him. "Keep in touch, okay?"

He looked at me with his hooded eyes, almost pleading for me to change my mind. "This shit ain't right," he said, tucking his shirt back into his pants. He stepped forward and left a sliver of breathing room between us. My nostrils took in his panty-dropping cologne and my thumping pussy was sending off signals of me being a fool. His lips touched my ear and his whispering words stuck in my head like Super Glue. "Tip one . . . I wanna fuck you badder than a mutha, ma, and I always get what I want. Two . . . you can be sho of that, so sleep tight on what I just said. Three." He took my hand, putting it down inside of his pants so I could feel his thickness. "They don't call me Roc for nothin'. I earned my name and you shouldn't be so worried about this twenty-four-year-old handlin' his business. I will and I intend to do so very soon."

Roc kissed my cheek and backed away. I watched as he got in his SUV and left. It was such a disappointment to see him go, but I knew that his words had much, much validity to them.

Chapter Three

For the last week and a half, things were awfully quiet. I assumed Latrel had gone back to school because I hadn't heard from him or Reggie. I was bothered that Latrel hadn't called me, but I had no intentions of picking up the phone to kiss his butt. That day, his tone rubbed me the wrong way and to toss the pizza on the floor as he had done was nonetheless disrespectful. As far as I was concerned he owed me an apology, not the other way around.

Reggie too. I'm sure he was boasting about the whole incident that took place and that gave him and Latrel a great opportunity to sit around and talk about what a terrible mother and wife I'd been. Realistically, both of them had the best of me. I put everything into my marriage to make it work and often gave my son too much. Everything backfired in my face, but I can't deny that I didn't someday see all of this coming. Reggie had the best wife ever, and how he ever found a way to fall out of love with me I'd never understand. Deep down, I knew there was someone else. He never said there was, but that's just something a wife knows. Still, I wished him and Latrel well. One day they'd realize how much I gave to them, but I hoped that by the time they woke up it wouldn't be too late.

It was a sunny day outside and the September heat was still going strong. I wanted to relax and clear my head, so I chilled out in the backyard while resting on my cushioned patio swing. A book was in my hand and a pitcher of lemon iced tea was on the ground beside me. A strong breeze blew in every now and then, and even though I hadn't had the money to take a vacation, the perimeter of my backyard would do. I laid the book on my chest and thought about the backyard parties Reggie and I used to have. He'd be firing up the gas grill right about now and Latrel would be running around in the backyard playing with his friends. The house would be packed with family and friends. When things started to take a turn for the worse, those kinds of days ended. Now, the backyard had become my place to pray, read, and think about where my life was headed from here.

The wind picked up again, this time blowing my yellow and white flower-print flimsy sun-

dress up like a balloon. I tucked the dress between my legs and got back to reading my book.
Just as I started to get into it, the cordless phone
rang. I looked to see who it was, but I didn't
recognize the number. Those kinds of numbers
meant bill collectors were calling, and since
Reggie was often late on his alimony payments,
some of my bills had to be put off. I ignored the
call, but when the phone rang again, I hit the talk
button.

"Hello," I griped.

"Can someone connect me to the prettiest
woman in the house?"

I hung up and got back to my book. I didn't
know who that was and wasn't interested in playing love games over the phone with a stranger.

The phone rang again. My book was too good
to keep putting aside, and because of these interruptions, the caller was going to get an earful.

"You have the wrong number," I yelled out.

"Dez, it's Roc. What's up?"

"Why didn't you just say so," I said, laying the
book on my chest again. I wasn't sure how I felt
about Roc calling me, but thoughts of our last
moment together had often played in my head.

"I thought you'd recognize my voice, but I
guess I didn't leave that much of an impression
on you."

"That was almost two weeks ago. I've forgotten about you since then."

He laughed and I visualized his dimples in full effect. "Well, let me stop by and refresh yo' memory. I was close by and wanted to call before makin' my move that way."

"I'm glad you did call first. I'm kind of busy. Maybe some other time."

He laughed again. "I knew you were gon' say that shit. I must be psychic or somethin'. And while I'm on a roll, I'm gon' make another prediction."

"Feel free," I said, tuned in.

"I predict that I'll be pullin' in yo' driveway in ten minutes. I just wanna drop in to see how you doin', but if you don't wanna be bothered let me know."

"Look, Roc. I was in the middle of reading a very good book. I've worked all week and I'm truly exhausted. If—"

"I like to read too. Check that out . . . we already got somethin' in common. Who would have thought that?"

I took a deep breath and sat up on the swing. This brotha just wasn't giving up and I didn't appreciate him pressuring me. "Fifteen minutes, Roc. You can stay for fifteen minutes, then you'll have to go. I have plans for this evening, okay?"

Roc hung up and I had no time to go inside and put on something I felt was more appropriate than the sundress I had on. No doubt, it made me look fat, but at least my breasts were held up by thick straps that rested on my shoulders. My hair had blown all over my head so I quickly straightened it with my fingers. I slid into my yellow flip-flops and made my way around to the front of my house. I hoped like hell that I wouldn't regret letting Roc know where I lived.

I could hear the loud rap music from another block over. Roc pulled in my driveway and he could tell by the look on my face that I wasn't pleased by the loudness of his music. He turned down the volume and looked at me standing on the sidewalk in my dress. When he got out of the car, he looked more like the Roc I'd seen at the car wash. His clothes weren't dirty, but he was casually dressed in jeans and an Ed Hardy t-shirt and cap. Clean white tennis shoes were on his feet, a silver cross dangled from his neck, and he sported a silver watch with a face filled with diamonds. He looked more like one of Latrel's friends, and I was concerned about him having money to buy a T-shirt and cap as expensive as Ed Hardy. The watch didn't look cheap either, nor did the diamond earrings in his ears. With that being said, he was still gorgeous as ever and the smile that he'd brought to my face hadn't been there all week.

He left his cap on the front seat of his truck and placed his hands in his pockets. "What's shakin, ma? You lookin' good as usual."

"Stop your lying, Roc. You know I look as if I've been in the house flipping pancakes or something."

We both laughed. "So, you got jokes today I see. Remember, though, I see way more than you realize," he said.

"Dressed like this, I hope so." I walked off and Roc followed me to the backyard. I offered him some iced tea and he accepted. We both took a seat at the table that was covered with an umbrella.

"You got a nice-ass yard," he said while drinking from the glass. "From what I saw, the inside of yo' house look nice too."

"Thanks. I do my best trying to keep up the place." I looked at the high grass that Reggie hadn't made his way over to cut. Even though we didn't live together, there were still some things he agreed to help out with, including the upkeep of the property.

"The grass is kind of high. Do you pay somebody to cut it for you?"

I really didn't want to get into a conversation with Roc about Reggie, so I lied. "Yes, but he hasn't stopped by lately."

"You want me to cut it for you? I don't mind. Besides, I think you like watchin' me sweat."

No doubt about that, I thought. "How much are you going to charge me?" I asked.

"Nothin'."

"Usually, when a man does something for free, he wants something in return."

"I got a lil somethin' in mind, but I don't think I'm gon' get lucky today. So after I finish cuttin' yo' grass, I'll settle for a kiss and be happy 'bout that."

My grass did need to be cut and there wasn't no telling when Reggie would show up to do it. Just like his alimony payments, they came when he was ready. I got the lawn mower from the garage and happily turned it over to Roc. If a kiss was all I had to give up, this task was well worth it.

Roc took off his shirt and displayed his washboard abs underneath. He pulled up his jeans, but I'd already seen his white and blue boxers. His baggy jeans looked so fresh and clean, I almost hated for him to mess them up.

"Are you sure you want to do this?" I asked. "I hate for you to mess up your jeans and your tennis shoes look as if you just purchased them."

"I'm good," he said, neatly folding his shirt, then placing it on the table. He removed his chain and watch, dropping them on top of his shirt. His eyes observed the huge yard, and before I knew it, he cranked up the lawn mower and got started.

I went into the house and got him some more tea, bottled water, and a cold, wet towel. It was awfully nice of him to do this for me and I appreciated it more than he knew.

I put the tea, bottled water, and towel on the table, and returned to my position on the swing. I started to read again, only to find myself taking peeks at Roc as he cut the grass in a diagonal pattern. His body was to die for. My erotic thoughts were back again and I had to get myself under control before I did something I figured I'd regret. I was so horny, though, and the last time I'd had sex was almost eight months ago. It was with Reggie, of course, and before that time, I could barely remember. Reggie had been the one I'd lost my virginity to and that was when I was seventeen years old. I had sex with one other person after that, and when Reggie and I got married, I had no other desires for men. He was all I needed and all I ever wanted. My attraction to Roc, however, was a new experience for me and I honestly didn't know how I'd handle it.

For the next thirty minutes, I managed to get back into my book. That was until Monica called and interrupted me. I couldn't help but mention that Roc was cutting my grass for me.

"I bet that is one Kodak moment to see," she said. "I'm on my way!"

"He'll be finished by the time you get here, and probably gone. Don't waste your time."

"Are you telling me you're going to let that man leave without—"

"Monica, you know me. I can't go throwing myself at him like that. I barely know him and he has yet to ask anything about me."

"Look, the less you know the better."

"What if he's some type of drug dealer or something? I mean, he be wearing all these expensive clothes, and from what he told me, he just be helping out his uncle. I don't know where this young man lives, who he lives with, where he works . . ."

"Does all that really matter? Stop talking like some high school chick worried about her reputation. You're a grown unmarried woman and just . . . just get you some, all right? I want details and do not let that brotha turn you out! Woman, up and represent for the forty-year-old woman. I remember you telling me how you and Reggie used to get down. Work your magic on Roc and tear the young thunder up!"

I couldn't help but laugh. I took another peek at Roc and tucked my hand between my thighs. "Girl, this is a shame. I can't believe what my eyes are witnessing. I wish you were here to see this."

"I wish I were too. I can only imagine and you are one lucky-ass woman. Tell me, did Reggie ever look like that while cutting the yard? Not!"

"Reggie ain't no bad-looking man, Monica. You know that."

"No, he's not. But he ain't no Roc either. Besides, forget about Reggie. Go do you and do it for me too. I gotta go, but be sure to call me later and let me know somethin'."

"Bye, girl, I'll call you later. Don't get your hopes up, though."

Monica laughed and hung up. When Roc turned off the lawn mower, I looked up. He was finished and the grass looked spectacular. He pushed the lawn mower up to the patio and reached for the bottled water. He poured the water on his face and it rushed down his chest as well. He used the towel to dry off. Afterward, he guzzled down the glass of iced tea and I was in a trance while watching his abs move in and out.

"Ahhh," he said, placing the glass on the table. "That was refreshin'."

I commented on the grass. "It looks nice and thank you so much for cutting it for me."

"No problem and it ain't like you had me out here plantin' flowers. I would've done it for you, but first, I would've planted that dress you got on or buried it."

I smiled at Roc and went up to him. "Insulting my dress will get you nowhere, and that comment caused you a major deduction." I got on the tips of my toes and pecked Roc's cheek. "There," I said, backing away from him. He held out his hands, but before he could say anything, his cell phone blasted with music. He looked to see who it was, and excused himself to take the call. He stepped a few feet away near my willow tree and all I heard was, "what's up, nigga."

Instead of listening in, I went back to the swing and took a seat. Roc soon ended his call, and I watched as he turned his phone on vibrate. He wiped his chest again, then came over and sat next to me on the swing.

"That sholl is a dope-ass dress you wearin'," he said, touching his chest. "And I truly mean that from the bottom of my heart."

We both laughed. "Are you tired?" I asked. "If so, you may want to go home and get some rest."

"You ain't gettin' rid of me that easy."

He laid sideways on the swing and encouraged me to lay beside him. "Come on," he ordered. "Let's read this book you been so into."

"You know darn well you don't be reading no books. Face it, you're just saying that to get close to me and impress me."

Roc took a glance at the cover and eased his arm around my waist. "I don't read those kinds of books, but I do read. I like self-help books . . . nonfiction, books like that. Now, lay down in front of me and get comfortable. Read the book to me and let me get into yo' head to see what kind of things you like."

I lay sideways with my back facing Roc and his arms comforting my waistline. He intertwined his legs with mine and I felt quite at ease. I started to read the book and at least twenty minutes into it, I could hear Roc's loud snores. His chest slowly heaved in and out, and when I turned my head slightly to the side, he looked so peaceful. I figured he was tired from cutting the grass, so I didn't wake him. I focused on finishing my book, but before I knew it, my eyes started to fade as well.

Roc's vibrating phone woke me, but he was still asleep. I'd felt his phone vibrating several times, but was too tired to move. The sun had gone down and the night was definitely upon us. We'd been asleep for hours and I couldn't remember the last time I'd felt this good being cradled in someone's arms. I almost hated to wake him up, but it was getting late and the caller seemed anxious to reach him. I moved around a bit, causing the swing to slowly sway back and forth. Roc stretched before opening his eyes to see where he was.

"Damn," he said, looking at the dark sky. "What time is it?"

"Late, but I'm not exactly sure about the time. You might want to check your phone to see."

He reached for his phone clipped to his jeans and pushed a button to check the callers. I saw his lips toot a bit and when he dropped the phone by his side, he obviously wasn't pleased about who the callers were.

"I can't believe time flew by like that," he said. "Why didn't you wake me? I thought you had somewhere to be."

I laid on my back and Roc kept his hand on my midsection. Our faces were extremely close and he looked down at me as I spoke. "I did have somewhere to be, but I changed my mind about going."

"Are you sure yo' man ain't gon' be mad at you for bein' a no-show?"

"Is that your way of asking me if I'm involved with someone?"

"Nope, I was just askin'. I didn't see no ring on yo' finger so I could care less if you got a boyfriend."

"FYI, no I don't. What about you? You got any girlfriends?"

"I shake, rattle, and roll sometimes, but you can believe that don't nobody excite me like you."

I didn't know what to say. It really didn't bother me that Roc admitted to having girlfriends, and at his age, what did I expect?

"You know what," he said, looking at my lips. "That sholl is a bangin'-ass dress you wearin'. I mean that mug—"

"Cut with the foolishness, Roc," I said, smiling. "You're only saying that because I backtracked on what I had planned for you. Sorry, you ruined it when you criticized my dress and that should be a warning for you to keep your mouth shut while you're ahead."

"Ha!" he shouted, then lightly squeezed my stomach. "Tell me . . . what did you have planned for me?"

I shrugged my shoulders. "I don't know. Whatever it was, I guess we both just have to miss out."

"See, you playin' now. It's all good, though. I see how you gon' do me."

Roc's lips were already close and he seemed so surprised when I lifted my head and initiated a lengthy kiss. "Mmm," he mumbled while indulging himself and circling his hand around on my hip. His hand went under my flimsy dress and when he moved his body between my legs, I bent my knees. My legs fell further apart and his hardness was right where I wanted it to be. My pussy was more than ready for him and I felt myself getting moist. Roc's hand kept touching my hip in search for my panties. When he didn't feel them, he halted our kiss.

"I knew there was a reason why I loved this dress so much. You ain't got on no panties, do you?"

I moved my head from side to side, implying no. Roc quickly jumped up, dug in his pocket for a condom, and removed his jeans. I laid there in doubt, thinking if I should allow this to happen. He was too young, but maybe I could get an orgasm and call it quits. I needed some kind of action in my life, and if Roc was willing to give it to me, what the hell? He returned to his position on top of me, and slightly raised my dress for easy access. He lifted himself a bit just to get a glance of my shaved pussy.

"Damn," he whispered while wetting his lips. "I wanna taste it, ma. Can we go inside? I need way more room than this."

I signaled no and reached down for Roc's at least ten-inch dick. Going inside of the house would waste time and it was not an option. "Work with what space you have," I suggested. "Be creative and don't keep me waiting."

Roc took heed and put it in motion. As soon as he cracked open each side of my walls, my mouth grew wide and I inhaled a heap of fresh air. With every thrust, I sucked in more air, letting out soft, pleasing moans. I kept telling myself that he was not a twenty-four-year-old man and his big dick was doing its best to prove it to me too. *Reggie is nowhere near this big*, I thought.

"This shit feelin' so *guuud*," he whined. "I need to get at it, though. Why you won't let me go inside and get at this pussy like I want to."

I basically ignored Roc's request. His package was feeling too good for me to pack up and go inside. At this point, releasing my grip from him would've been a crime. Instead, I massaged his black muscular ass, just as I'd imagined, and put my legs on his shoulders, making every bit of my dreams come true. I worked my body to the rhythm he'd chosen and my insides tingled all over. When Roc pulled my dress over my head and started in on my wobbling breasts, my body quivered even more. His lengthy chocolate dip into my cream made me crazy as ever. No, I didn't want to come yet, but I had to. The rush was there and I let it be known.

"Damn you!" I yelled with tightened fists. "I'm coming, baby. My pussy feels so good, but help it give you all it's got. *Pleeeze* help it!"

Roc picked up the pace and used his two fingers to turn circles around my swollen clit. It was rock-solid hard and he loved it.

"Shit!" he said, taking deep breaths. "I love this feelin', ma. You—you workin' with somethin' and a nigga lovin' the hell out of this."

Enough said, enough done. Roc got tense, his ass felt like I was gripping stone, and he tightened up all over. He kept toying with my clit, forcing my juices to ooze out quickly. I felt relieved and my body went limp. Following suit, so did his body. He laid on top of me, while the swing squeaked and swayed back and forth. I gazed at the twinkling stars, thinking about how I couldn't wait to tell Monica about this. More so, about how badly my pussy needed . . . wanted him. From the constant vibrating of Roc's phone, it was clear that somebody else was in need of him too.

Chapter Four

I was known for holding grudges, but I never thought I could go almost a month without talking to my son. This was the first time this had happened, and as many times as I had picked up the phone to call him, I always wound up hanging it right back up. No doubt, I missed talking to Latrel, but I couldn't get over the way he treated me, especially in front of his girlfriend and Reggie.

As for Mr. Wright, he had finally taken his vacation. I spent the entire week getting his office together. I cleared the papers from his desk, organized his files and cleaned his office until it was spotless. Admittedly, having him out of the office for the entire week was great. It was peaceful, and not to have him in the office yelling my name was the best. I had made progress, even though I spent many of my days taking personal calls. On Tuesday and Wednesday, Monica and I talked on the phone for hours. I took an extended lunch with her and we spent some extra time at the mall. I bought me two new outfits, some books, and therefore, I needed for Reggie to be on time with my alimony payment. He was late again, and for a man to own his own real estate company, I didn't understand the holdup with my checks. I tried to work with him on my payments, but his not paying me my money was putting me behind. Since our divorce, I had to make many, many cutbacks. I was so used to purchasing things when I wanted them and this was such a change for me. When I spoke to him earlier this week, he promised to throw in something extra. It was already Friday and I hadn't heard nothing from him yet.

Ever since my enjoyable night with Roc, I'd only spoken to him twice, within the last three weeks. We talked for hours, and I liked that he was a good listener and he didn't pry into my personal life. He continuously made me laugh and expressed his desires to see me again. I told him it would have to wait until this Friday. He was cool with that, especially since I agreed to make him dinner. I was just okay about seeing him again and I didn't want our friendship to turn into a relationship. He didn't seem to want a relationship either, and he proved that by only calling me in his spare time. He often seemed very busy and we never stayed on the phone for more than fifteen minutes. I viewed us as being nothing but sex partners and it was still a bit difficult for me to accept that I had sex with a twenty-four-year-old. That's why our meeting place could only be at my house and my house only. I didn't want to know where he lived, I never asked for a phone number to call him, and we could never, ever be seen in public together. Everyone would think I was out of my mind for being with him, and for now, this was a secret that I intended to keep. Yes, Monica knew what was going on behind closed doors, but she was the only one.

I'd thought about having a romantic dinner with Roc, but decided against it. I didn't want him to get the wrong idea, so I put the candles away and placed the china back into the cabinets. It was already 6:45 P.M. and he was expected to be here by 7:00. I had also changed my mind about cooking dinner, and instead I called a Chinese restaurant to order some food. I wasn't sure what kind of food Roc liked, but nobody could refuse the special fried rice that came from the Chinese restaurant in my neighborhood. The lady informed me that the order would arrive within the hour.

I had just enough time to get comfortable in my canary-lace boy shorts and tank shirt combination. I covered up with my cream cotton thigh-high robe and slid on my matching cotton house shoes. I was at home and there was no need for me to get all jazzed up for Roc. As far as I was concerned, he didn't give a care about what I wore. He proved that the last time he was here.

It was five minutes to seven and I was getting my MSNBC political fix on. Keith Olbermann was just about to deliver his special comment of the night when I heard the front door open. My heart jumped to my stomach and I rushed toward the front door to see who it was. Reggie met me while coming down the hallway.

"What are you doing here?" I asked, tightening my robe.

"I came to drop off your check."

"You could have called, Reggie. I don't like you popping up like this."

"Since when," he said, following me to the kitchen. "It ain't like you were doing anything."

If only you knew, I thought. And according to my clock on the wall, he had to go because Roc would soon be here. There was no way in hell I wanted Reggie to know about what I'd been into. He would use this as another excuse to degrade me and I didn't want him in my business. Since our divorce, he'd kept his social life a secret and it was only fair that mine was kept a secret as well. That thought was short-lived and when the doorbell rang, he glanced at me, already making his way to the door.

"Are you expecting anyone?" he asked.

"Uh, no," I said, quickly following behind him. I looked through the living room window and saw Roc's SUV in the driveway. *Oh, shit! How can I get out of this. . . .*

Reggie swung the door open and Roc stood on the porch, looking every bit of his age. I stood behind Reggie and saw a cold look in Roc's eyes that said I'd better come up with something fast. He looked pissed, but before he could say a word, I quickly spoke up.

"Jeremy, Latrel is still away at school. He told me if you stopped by to give you his address and phone number so you could reach him."

Reggie moved aside and I invited Roc in. At first he hesitated, but I gave him a look as if cooperation was needed. "Come into the kitchen. I'll write his number and address down so you can reach him."

Reggie extended his hand. "Jeremy, I'm Latrel's father, Reggie. Nice to meet you."

"S—s—same here," Roc said. We all went to the kitchen, and in a panic I searched the kitchen drawer for a pad and pencil. I found it and scribbled a quick note to pass to Roc. *Please bear with me,* I asked. *My ex-husband stopped by to bring me some money. He's leaving soon. Make small talk with me and don't leave. Sorry.*

I gave the note to Roc and he read it. He put it in his pocket. "Thanks for the info, I'll call him tomorrow."

"You're welcome," I said, smiling. "In the meantime, how are your parents doing? I haven't seen them in a while."

"My mom's doin' good. My father just got out of the hospital, but he doin' okay now."

Reggie was too busy looking through the refrigerator, but he soon closed the door with a beer in his hand. "Here," he said, putting the check on the marble-topped island. "I have to run and I'll give you a call tomorrow. We really need to talk about this thing with you and Latrel, okay?"

"Sure."

Reggie looked at Roc. "Nice meeting you, Jeremy. Take care and when you talk to that knucklehead son of mine, tell him to give his father a buzz."

Roc nodded. "Will do, sir. No doubt."

I walked Reggie to the door and was relieved to see him go. This time, I locked the door and connected the chain. As soon as I turned around, Roc stood behind me.

"Lying for you like that gon' cost you big-time. Why you ain't just tell that nigga what was up and be done with it?"

"Because I don't want him to know my business, that's why."

"Why should he care? If he yo' ex, I don't understand what's the big deal."

I got a little frustrated because I didn't want to talk about Reggie. "Look, Roc, I didn't know he was coming and that's all there is to it. I appreciate you not making a scene, but there was no way for me to prevent that from happening."

"Yes, it was. If y'all divorced, tell that muthafucka he can't be comin' over here when he get good and ready to. That's how you put a stop to that shit."

Roc stepped into my dark living room and sat on my micro-suede mahogany sectional. I couldn't see much of his face, but I knew he wasn't happy about the situation, or possibly jealous.

I stood with my back against the wall in the living room and folded my arms.

"So, I guess you're upset with me, huh?" I asked.

He leaned back on the couch, laying his arms on top of it. "Nope, I ain't mad. I don't get mad over no shit like this. Besides, all we gon' be good for is fuckin' each other so why should I trip?"

"What makes you say that? Was it something I said—"

"No, it's just somethin' I know. You don't seem as excited 'bout me as I am 'bout you and that's on the real."

"I'm very excited about you, but I just ended my marriage and I'm not looking to seriously hook up with anyone."

Roc didn't say anything so I walked into the living room and stood in front of him. I still didn't see those pearly whites and all I witnessed was the coldness in his eyes.

"If this is going to be a problem for you—"

"Where my food at? I don't smell no dinner cookin', no nothin'. I guess you lied 'bout that too?"

His attitude was working me, but since I felt bad about my situation with Reggie, I remained calm. "I didn't have time to cook, but don't think that I forgot about feeding you. I ordered Chinese and it should be here shortly."

"I don't eat Chinese food, so you may as well have forgotten 'bout me"

Roc wasn't letting up with his attitude. I knew how to change things around and I made a move to do just that, starting with turning on the lights. I opened my robe and tossed it on the couch next to him. I then straddled his lap, placing my arms on his shoulders. The cheeks of my butt were poking out of my boy shorts and one strap of the tank top I wore hung off my shoulder, revealing my hard nipples. Roc's eyes searched me over, but he continued to sit there like a bump on a log.

"I promise that I haven't forgotten about you," I said. "As a matter of fact, I can't stop thinking about what happened between us. I was glad that you called, and now I'm glad you're here."

"That's right, clean yo' shit up," he said. His phone caused an interruption, and yet again the loud music played.

He looked down at the phone attached to his casual shorts. "Get up," he ordered. "I need to see who this is."

I got off his lap and he looked at his phone. He put it back in his pocket and stood up. "I'm gettin' ready to bounce."

"So soon," I said, totally upset that he was leaving. I sighed and combed my hair back with my fingers. "What about your Chinese food?"

"I told you I don't eat Chinese food."

He stepped toward the door and had no sympathy for the saddened look on my face. He was looking so good in his khaki shorts that showed his toned calves and smooth legs. There was no way I could let him leave and I had to think of something fast.

"Before you leave," I quickly said. "I bought something for you. Wait right here."

Roc put his hands in his pockets and stood by the door. I walked off, moving my curvaceous hips and leaving my boy shorts high above my cheeks. I didn't even have to turn around because I knew he was looking. Moments later, I returned with a white plastic bag that had a book inside.

"I was at the mall this week and thought about you when I saw this. Here."

He removed the book from the bag and held it in his hand. The smile I hadn't seen all night had finally shown up. "*How To Go Down on A Woman and Give Her Exquisite Pleasure*," he read. "Are you sayin' you think I need help with that?"

"All I'm sayin' is you admitted to reading self-help books and I thought you might enjoy it."

Roc snickered while holding a tiny smile on his face. I took this opportunity to speak up.

"Please stay," I asked. "I apologize about dinner and it was wrong for me to assume you liked Chinese."

He looked as if he was considering it, and kept his eyes on the book. "Come here, and for the record, I love Chinese food," he said. I stepped forward and he slid his arm around my waist. "I'll stay but you gotta promise me somethin'."

"What?"

"That tonight I can explore all of yo' body parts and do it in any room of this house that I want to. No denyin' me anything I wanna do and stop tryin' to run this show from here on out. What happens, happens and what's gon' be, gon' be. Let the chips fall where they may, a'ight?"

"Yes," I replied, looking into his serious eyes. He sucked my lips with his and backed me into the living room. I sat back on the couch and Roc kneeled between my legs. He placed the book next to me and reached for my boy shorts to remove them. I slightly lifted my butt and Roc pulled the boy shorts off my feet. His hands massaged my hips while rubbing them up and down my thick thighs.

"Sexy, sexy, sexy," he implied. "Thick and sexy, just how I like my women to be. I'm gon' make you mine and I can promise you that shit."

He pulled his shirt over his head and stood to remove his pants. His dick was so ready to enter me, but he dropped to his knees again, positioning my legs on his shoulders. His arms wrapped around my thighs and his face navigated between my legs. As soon as his tongue separated my tingling slit, he licked the furrows alongside my clit while holding my labia open with his fingers. He then licked me from front to back, as if he were enjoying a chocolate cherry ice cream cone. A major shock went through my body, almost convulsion-like. I trembled all over but kept telling myself to relax. Needless to say, Roc was tearing it up and my shaking legs couldn't stay in place on his shoulders.

"Oh, baby!" I screamed while squeezing the pillows on the couch. "I wasted my—my money on that book! I'm taking it back tomorrow, I promise that muthafucka going back tomorrow!"

Roc slid his tongue out of my pussy, leaving it overly pleased. He licked around his wet lips, tasting the flavored juices I'd provided. "You damn right you takin' it back tomorrow. I already read it before and in case you ain't noticed, I'm very skillful at what I do, when I get a chance to do it."

Roc got back to business and calling him skillful was putting it mildly. He was . . . the bomb and as we tackled almost every single room that night, he proved himself to be even more than that.

I wasn't sure, but I thought I'd heard the house alarm go off. One of Jill Scott's favorite hits echoed loudly in the background as Roc and I were sprawled out in my king-sized bed. I was in-between his legs with no clothes on and nothing but a dark blue 500-thread-count sheet covered our naked bodies. We were so exhausted from last night's events and my body was hurting all over. In a good way, of course, as Roc had completely shown his talents. Reggie's loving couldn't compare and I got a taste of what I'd been missing for all those years.

I stretched my arms and when I tried to back away from Roc, my body was too sore to move. I laid myself back on top of him, causing him to wake up. He rubbed my backside, still covered with the sheet, and lightly smacked my butt.

"You put it on a nigga last night," he confirmed. "I almost hate to ask, but what time is it?"

"Time for you to get your shit and get the fuck out of here!"

Roc quickly looked over my shoulder and my head snapped to look behind me. Reggie was standing in the bedroom's doorway with fury in his eyes. I had a loss for words and hurried to cover my entire body with the sheet. Roc moved to the side of the bed and stood up.

"What in the hell is going on here?" Reggie shouted.

"Hey, man, I was just leavin', but you comin' at me like she yo' wife or somethin'."

"And I'm not," I added. "Last time I checked, I lived here—alone. Now, what are you doing here?"

Reggie looked at me with pure disgust. "Are you that damn desperate to be fucking Latrel's friend? Or was that a lie too?"

I really didn't owe Reggie an explanation, but I knew he wasn't leaving until he got one. I didn't want to have this conversation in front of Roc and he wasn't too anxious to hang around either. He'd already had on his shorts and his shirt was thrown over his shoulder. He grabbed his keys from the dresser and walked over to me as I stood by the bed. He lifted my chin and kissed my cheek.

"Handle yo' business, baby, and the next time I come, I want that dinner you promised me. Don't be afraid to tell homeboy what's up and I'll call to check on you later."

I nodded and watched as Roc made his way past Reggie. They mean-mugged each other and Reggie had a hard time keeping his mouth shut.

"Is this shit some kind of joke? Are you kidding me, Dee? Is this the kind of nigga you want?"

Roc's face twisted up. "Nigga, you don't know me, and for the record, I ain't yo' son's muthafuckin' friend. Obviously, yo' time with Dez is up and she breakin' in new ground. Stop sweatin' her and stop showin' yo' ass up without callin'. There's a new sheriff in town and you can address me as Roc."

I saw Reggie tighten his fist, and as soon as he swung, Roc ducked. I rushed over to both of them, but not in time enough for Roc to pin Reggie against the wall with Roc's arm pressed into his throat. Reggie's hands were gripped on Roc's throat and they looked as if they were about to kill each other.

"Please, don't," I yelled while struggling to separate their arms. I in no way intended for this to happen and I pleaded with them to break away from each other. Roc looked at me, and seeing the hurt in my eyes, he backed away from Reggie. Roc gave him one last evil stare before walking away and moments later I heard the front door slam. Reggie lifted his hand in a backhanded position, causing me to slightly back away. He caught himself and gritted his teeth.

"I have never come this close to wanting to hurt you, Dee. I can understand you wanting to be with someone, but him? How old is that fool? You couldn't be serious?"

I stepped further away from Reggie, putting on my robe to cover up. This was one awkward moment, but what Roc said quickly came to mind—*Handle your business*.

"Reggie, who I see is my business, not yours. You have no business showing up at this house like you do, and I've been allowing you to get away with it for too long. In the future, you need to call before you come. There's a possibility that I may have company, and I do not want something like this to happen again."

Reggie looked as if he'd seen a ghost. My words must have stunned him, as he seemed to be frozen in time. I had never seen him look so angry and it was as if he couldn't find the right words to say. That was rare.

"I—I came over this morning to cut your grass. When I saw that punk's car still in the driveway, I knew something was up. No, it's not my business, Dee, but I can tell you this . . . you are making one big mistake. That gangbanger can't offer you a damn thing and how dare you fuck him in the bed I used to make love to you in!" His voice rose. "What in the hell is wrong with you?"

"In case you haven't noticed, my grass has already been cut." I pointed to my chest. "And if I'm making a mistake, I'll have to live with it, not you! For now, though, that gangbanger doing all of the right things. You saw for yourself, didn't you, and the way he's made me feel in such a short period of time is better than your sorry ass made me feel during the last several years of our marriage." I pointed to *my* bed. "That bed belongs to me and I damn well will fuck anybody in it that I want to. Now, if you don't mind, I have plans for this afternoon. Lock the door behind you and throw away your keys because you'll never be able to use them again. I'm having all of the locks changed, something I should have done when you walked out on me and started your new life of freedom. I've adapted to your theme too and now it's time for you to adjust as I have."

Reggie dug in his pockets for his set of keys and threw them at me like he was a pitcher throwing a baseball. I ducked, but the keys slammed into the window behind me and cracked it. He stormed out of my room, slamming the front door behind him. I dropped to the bed and combed my fingers through my hair, gathering the back of it in my hand.

Damn it, I thought. *How did I ever let something like this happen?*

Chapter Five

Being with Roc on Friday nights—and him staying the night—was becoming a weekend ritual. I was starting to enjoy his company more and had even agreed to let him take me out for the day. He raved so much about my dinner last night and wanted to show me how much he appreciated my efforts.

We got dressed Saturday morning and Roc was so enthused that I decided to leave my house with him. It was kind of chilly outside, so I wore a waist-length blue jean jacket and matching wide-legged jeans. A soft pink top was underneath and three-inch stilettos covered my feet. I put my hair in a neat ponytail, leaving a sway of bangs on my forehead. I locked the front door, only to run back inside to get my CD. I got in the truck and handed the CD over to Roc.

"Here, baby," I said. "Put this in your CD player."

He laughed, realizing that his kind of music wasn't going to do.

"What you got on here," he asked.

"Crank it up and you'll see."

Roc snickered and put the CD in. He turned up the volume, only to be hit with Patti LaBelle's "Somebody Loves You Baby."

"Hell no," he laughed, switching to the next song, Aretha Franklin's "Respect." "Next." He switched to the next song and Marvin Gaye's "Let's Get It On" crooned. "Okay, we gettin' there. I can do Marvin and I don't mind gettin' it on, especially with you."

Roc leaned in for a kiss and backed out of my driveway. "So, where'd you say we were going?" I asked.

"I didn't say. And don't be tryin' to squeeze it out of me either. I told you it was a surprise."

"I really don't like surprises, but I'm going to trust you on this, okay?"

Roc nodded, and Marvin had become too much for him. He ejected the CD and the truck vibrated as T.I.'s, "Whatever You Like" blasted through the speakers.

"Please, please turn that down. How are we supposed to talk if we've got to yell at each other to do it?"

Roc turned down the volume and leaned his gorgeous self a little closer to me. "I turned the music down, so what you wanna talk about?"

"For starters, did you enjoy dinner as much as you claimed you did?"

"Dinner was off the chain. I love steak and shrimp and you did the damn thing. Shit was seasoned to perfection, just how I like it."

"Good," I said, having much more on my mind. I was starting to really feel Roc, and at this point I wanted to know more about him. We'd talked about some things, but there was still so much about him I didn't know. Before I could get another word out, a car pulled beside us and a horn sounded. Roc turned his head and two females in the car waved at him. He nodded, then turned his attention back to me.

"Did you know them?" I asked. "You kind of played them off, didn't you?"

"No, I didn't know them and I guess they were just flirtin' with me."

"I assume that happens quite often."

"Yeah, but I could say the same 'bout you. I know you get approached by a lot of men, don't you?"

I shrugged. "I guess, but I never paid it much attention, especially since I was married for so long."

"Now that you ain't married no mo, are you just rollin' with me?"

I placed my hand on the side of Roc's face. "You and only you, snookums. As long as you keep satisfying me the way you do, I'd say there's a very rare chance of my status changing."

"Snookums? You are so full of shit," he laughed. "You be tryin' to play with my mind and make a nigga feel good, don't you?"

"I hope you do feel good about us, Roc, and I'm serious when I tell you how happy I am that I met you at the car wash that day."

"You wasn't singing that tune back then. That day you looked at me like I was some kind of fool or somethin'."

"No, I didn't. If you only knew what I was thinking that day."

Roc displayed a big smile. "Tell me 'bout yo' thoughts. I seriously wanna know."

I cleared my throat. "I'm too ashamed to tell you. Just know that I had a feelin' about us."

"So you knew I was gon' be hittin' that pussy like I wanted to, huh?"

"Is that what you call it? Why do you have to be so blunt about everything?"

Roc looked himself over. "'Cause what you see is what you get. I am who I say I am. I say what I feel and feel what I want." He touched my thigh and squeezed it.

"I don't have a problem with that, but didn't your parents teach you how to talk to people?"

"FYI, my moms died when I was three and my old dude been in the slamma for years. My uncle is the one who raised me, but the only thing he taught me was how to survive."

Our conversation was getting interesting and I was starting to step into the unknown territory I wanted to, without upsetting him. "How do you make money? I hope you're not telling me what I think you are, and if so, you can do better."

Roc rubbed the neatly shaven hair on his chin and kept his eyes on the road. He leaned away from me, signaling that he didn't really want to discuss this. "All I can say is it's not what you think it is. I'm just a mover and shaker in the family, but my hands are clean."

"Mover and shaker? Simplify that for me, please. I don't understand."

He stopped at the red light and looked over at me. "I move and I shake. It don't get no simpler than that, and if you can't figure out what that means then I can't help you."

I could tell he was irritated, but I pushed. "So, how much money do you make moving and shaking? And, what kinds of risks are involved?"

"There are risks involved in anything you do. As for the money, it's good, but it can always be better."

I defensively folded my arms. "Look, Roc. We're cool and everything, but you make this moving and shaking thing sound kind of scary. Should I be concerned about riding with you and being in your presence?"

"No," he said, picking up his vibrating phone. I knew he was avoiding our conversation and answering the call saved him. "Roc," he answered. "Yeah, you know I'll be at the club tonight, why wouldn't I? Right now I'm chillin' with this fine-ass woman, but she workin' a nigga nerves, you feel me?" He looked over at me, just to see if I got the hint. I didn't want to ruin our first day out together, so I chilled on the questions and saved them for later.

To avoid any more questions, Roc talked on the phone with his friend until we got to our destination. That's when he ended the call and opened the door for me.

"Come on," he said, reaching his hand out for mine. I took his hand, gripping it tight to get his attention.

"Listen, before we go inside, I need to say something," I said. He stared at me without a blink. "Please don't be rude and talk to your friends on my time. I know you did it to avoid any more questions from me, but if you want to continue this friendship, there are some things I need to know about you."

"I just told you 'bout my mother, old dude, and 'bout what I do. Don't blame me if you the one who can't put two and two together. And if you want to continue this friendship, then I suggest you chill out with that tone you bringin' and enjoy this day that I got planned for you, ma."

He kept my hand clinched with his and moved forward as if our conversation was over. Obviously, Roc was used to having his way and getting what he wanted, but sometimes a man needed to be put in his place. I squeezed his hand again, halting his steps. He looked stunned that I challenged him.

"Let me make a suggestion to you too. I'm not the one, Roc, and if you continue with your controlling attitude, this will be the last time you'll ever see me. Got it?"

Roc let go of my hand and I followed behind him as we walked into the spa. He confirmed my appointment with the receptionist and ignored me.

"She's here for the private ultimate package," he said. "How long will it take and tell us what it includes."

The friendly receptionist laid a brochure on the counter and opened it. "It takes about six hours and includes: a custom-blended facial, Swedish massage, pedicure, manicure, a mineral body wrap, haircut and style, facial makeover using our makeup, and lunch with fresh flowers. How does that sound?"

Roc looked at me. "Are you gamin' or what?"

"Are you going to stay with me?"

"I hadn't planned to."

"If you're not going to stay, then—"

"This is a place for women. I—"

"No sir," the woman interrupted. "You can stay too. We encourage men to stay, and they can assist with pampering their women too."

I wanted to ease the tension between us. This was a good opportunity. "Is he allowed to rub my back and feet too?"

"Yes," the lady said, massaging the air with her hands. "We'll show him how to massage you in all of the right places to ease your tension."

"Now, you know I have plenty of tension and how can you resist that?" I asked Roc.

He cut his eyes, but agreed to stay with me. I kissed his cheek and thanked him. "You're so sweet, snookums," I said. "When you want to be."

"Get yo' butt back in that room and change clothes. Just so you know, I'll massage your back but I'm leavin' yo' feet up to the professionals."

"And what's wrong with my feet? I have some pretty, sexy toes and feet."

"I won't say all that, and I can really only vouch for that pretty pussy—"

I quickly turned, placing my hand over Roc's mouth. "Would you watch what you say in here," I said, smiling, but whispering. "That lady probably heard you."

Roc moved my hand from his mouth. "I don't give a damn if she heard me or not. This shit gonna dig deep in my pockets and I should be able to say what the hell I want to up in here." He patted my ass. "Now, go get naked and let me have some fun."

I entered the private room and it was to die for. The room was dressed with soft lime green and beige decor. A private whirlpool for two was in the middle, supported by four surrounding columns. A steam shower was to the left, and a flat screen TV was on the striped wallpapered walls. In one corner was a tiny bar and two lounging chaises were nearby. Two flat beds lay side-by-side and candles were all over the place. The smell of freshly cut flowers lit up the room and they were placed in glass vases. The lady explained everything that was on display in the room, including the exotic oils, down to the bathing beads that promised our skin a silky-smooth feel. I was in awe and before leaving, she gave Roc and me two thick white bathrobes to get comfortable in.

"When you're ready for us," she said. "Pick up the phone over there and we'll come back in and get started. Have fun and enjoy yourselves."

The lady left and I was still in shock. Reggie and I had never, ever done anything like this and it proved just how complacent we'd become in our marriage.

"Did you expect for me to stay here all by myself?" I asked.

"Hell no," Roc said, reaching for my waist and bringing me to him. "I told you this was a surprise and I want you to lay back and enjoy yourself, a'ight?"

I put my arms on his shoulders, pressing myself against him. "Is that all you want me to do? I definitely thought you'd want more."

"I do. I wanna make you mine and also put a major hurtin' on that pussy when we get back to yo' house."

"I give up," I said, tossing my hands in the air. "But, I must admit that the way the word *pussy* flows from your mouth, it just turns me on."

"And every single thing 'bout you, Dez, turns me on. I'm steppin' in new territory and I'm workin' this as best as I can. Be patient with me, a'ight?"

I nodded.

Roc went for one of his juicilicious kisses, and like always, we were interrupted by his phone.

"Do me a favor," I asked. "Please turn that off. I want to enjoy every second," I said kissing his lips, "every minute," I pecked his lips again, "and every hour that I spend with you, without any interruptions."

Roc didn't put up a fight and went along with my request by turning off his phone. We changed into our robes and that day would be remembered as one of the best days of my life. You learn a lot about a man when you spend time with him, and thus far Roc had impressed me more than I ever would've expected.

Just as I thought the day couldn't get any more interesting, it did. Roc and I finished up around 4:00 P.M. that afternoon and he took me to a clothing store at Frontenac Plaza. My body felt amazing and my makeup was flawless. I believed in a man taking care of his woman, but even so I was somewhat uncomfortable with Roc spending money on me. He dropped almost a grand for our spa treatment and we were now standing in a clothing store where the cheapest thing was a belt for $300. The salesclerk had an off-white dress in her hand and twirled it around in front of us.

"Is this the one?" she asked Roc, but he looked at me. "Yes. Now go try it on so I can see how you look in it."

Only the Lord knew how uncomfortable I was with this, but in an effort not to disappoint Roc, I took the dress to go try it on. When I got into the fitting room, I looked in the mirror and asked myself, *Girl, what are you doing?* If Roc was shaking and moving drug money, then how could I allow him to pay for the spa treatment and for this dress? I looked at the hefty price tag of $1,060 and shook my head. I swallowed the huge lump in my throat and did my best to go with the flow.

The size fourteen to sixteen dress looked amazing on me and was high enough to show my thighs that Roc admired so much. It left one shoulder bare and had a long bell swinging sleeve. It stretched around my curves, giving my body a silhouette look. It was so very classy and made me feel sexy as ever. I put on the two-toned off-white and gold sexy heels the lady had given me and was ready to walk the red carpet. To see myself in the mirror look so glamorous; it helped ease the uncomfortable feeling I had inside.

I left the fitting room and stood close by Roc as he sat slumped down in one of the soft black leather chairs. By the blank expression on his face, I couldn't tell if he was pleased or not. He rubbed his chin and asked me to turn around.

"So, what do you think?" I asked, modeling the dress for him.

"I think you got it goin' on, that's what I think. How do you feel 'bout it?"

I shrugged. "I think it looks nice, but the price is—"

He quickly shot me down. "Don't go there, a'ight? You look damn good and this is what I want you in tonight."

I turned my eyes away from the oval mirror that was nearby. "Tonight? What's going on tonight?"

"Fun," he said. "Now, go take off the dress and let's go. We're already runnin' behind schedule."

Since I'd given Roc the opportunity to plan our day, I kept quiet. I started to make my way back to the dressing room, only to hear him call my name. I turned without a smile on my face. He walked up to me and lifted my chin. He pecked my lips and looked into my eyes.

"I feel like the luckiest man in the world," he said. "But you gotta trust me, a'ight?"

I nodded.

"Then, put a smile on yo' face. Show me how happy you are to be with me. I need love and compassion too. If that only consists of a smile, don't make it so hard to do."

"I am happy with you, Roc. It's just that all of this is new to me. I have concerns and you make me uneasy when you don't want to talk about them."

"There's a time and a place for everything. Now ain't neither. We'll talk, but like I said earlier, just enjoy yourself. Don't knock me for tryin' to—"

I placed my fingers on his lips and smiled. "Let me go change so we can go wherever you want to and have fun. And before I forget, thank you for everything. I've had an interesting and unforgettable day."

I kissed Roc, and for now nothing else needed to be said. The dress was in the bag and he'd dropped me off at home, insisting that I be ready at 9:00 P.M.

Like before, the club was packed as ever. Roc had a limousine pick me up and the driver escorted me inside to find him. He could be spotted a mile away, dressed in off-white from head to toe. His suit jacket was open, and with the silk shirt underneath being unbuttoned, it showed his nicely cut chest and abs. A silver diamond necklace hung low and laid against his shiny black skin. The waves in his hair flowed, his lining was cut to perfection, and so was his mustache. I honestly had never witnessed anything like him, and with all of the women hanging around him, they obviously hadn't either. Roc sat with his arms stretched out, resting on top of a circular booth for at least ten people. Bottles of champagne were in buckets on the table and white and black balloons were all over. A huge cake sat on another table, which was filled with a bunch of women and men. One man sat to Roc's left and a female sat to his right. She had whispered something in his ear, but since the music was loud, I didn't make much of it. I stepped up to the table and Roc's dimples went into action. Before I could say anything, a man walked up from behind and eased his arm around my waist. His aggressive touch caught me off guard.

"Baby, you wanna dance?" he asked with an alcoholic's breath.

"No, not right now," I said, trying to remove his arm.

He tugged at my waist, pulling me in his direction. "Come on, girl. Let's go set this shit off!"

Roc told the female next to him to move and rushed up to intervene. Even the man who was sitting next to him got up, and they both approached the man.

"Get yo' muthafuckin' hands from around my woman's waist. Nigga, are you crazy?"

The man took one look into Roc's furious eyes and then glanced at his friend, who stood with his hands behind his back. He quickly let go of my waist, defensively holding up his hands. "Damn, all I was tryin' to do was dance. Is that gon' cost me my life or somethin'?"

I put my hand on Roc's chest and our connected eyes got his attention. "He's right . . . he just wanted to dance. Is all of this even necessary?" I asked.

The man shook his head and walked away. Roc eyeballed him, then turned his attention to me. "He shouldn't have been touchin' and pullin' on you like that. Muthafuckas up in here know when somethin' belongs to me and a nigga like that should've known better."

"For the record, there's no ownership between us. Now, I'm here to have a good time and it would be nice of you to tell me the occasion."

He pecked my cheek and looked as if my comment bothered him. "It's my birthday," he said, before moving back into the booth. "Are you gon' stand there or sit down and join me?"

My mouth hung open. Why wouldn't he tell me it was his birthday? We'd been together all day and he hadn't said one word. I slid into the booth and sat next to him. "I can't believe you didn't tell me about your birthday. I could've gotten you something and I feel so bad allowing you to splurge as you did on your special day."

"Thus far, I've had a good day. And I plan on havin' an even better night, as long as you chillin' with me."

"I'm with you all the way, but what happens tonight depends on you. From what I can see, it looks as if you have an array of choices up in here tonight. Who's going to be the lucky lady?"

"Her pretty self sittin' right next to me and she's the only woman I can see bein' worthy enough of my time. Besides, I like her ass and ain't nobody up in here I'm feelin' mo than I'm feelin' her."

Roc picked up a glass of champagne and handed me one. He turned sideways and focused on me and me only. "I'm drinkin' to more excitin' days to come, how 'bout you?"

"I'll drink to that, as well as wishing you the happiest and best birthday ever. May God bless you with many more."

We clinked our glasses together and followed up with a lengthy kiss. No doubt, all eyes were on us and the setting had become a bit uncomfortable. Roc knew nearly everybody in the club and they knew him. The booth we sat at and the ones nearby were crammed with people there for his celebration. He was "nigga this" and "nigga that," "what's up muthafucka" to "I'll kick that muthafucka's ass." This was the immature side of him that I didn't like, but Roc was being himself. There was no way that a woman like me could change him, and I wasn't even sure if I wanted to.

Roc was tipsy and so was I. His attention had been on me all night and when he excused himself to go to the restroom, I was able to stretch out a bit. Before making it to the bathroom, I watched him being stopped a million and one times. Either it was to get hugs from females hanging all over him or it was to slap hands with some of his friends. There were two moments, however, that caused me to focus in. The club already had a dark setting, but I was so sure that I'd seen a female kiss Roc on his lips. She wiped off her lipstick and walked away. Another time was very noticeable, and that was when another woman slapped the living daylights out of him. His head jerked to the side, but before he could make a move, a man dressed in a black suit grabbed the woman by her arm. He dragged her through the club and she shouted words to Roc that I couldn't hear. The music was too loud to hear anything, but the action I had witnessed said enough. Roc avoided the restroom and opened another door, disappearing for a while.

After seeing what I had, I was ready to go. It wasn't like I hadn't expected Roc to be seeing other women, but this setting wasn't the one for me. I couldn't wait for him to return so I could tell him I was ready to go. As soon as that thought crossed my mind, I looked up and saw a man who resembled Roc in many ways. He was just as dark, had a shiny bald head, diamond earrings in his ears, and was dressed to impress in white. Two females were connected to his sides and everybody treated him as if Denzel Washington had just walked into the club. Taking a guess, I assumed he was the uncle who owned the club and the one who was responsible for raising Roc since he was a child. He stepped over to the booths, slamming handshakes with everyone in sight, including the young lady I'd been sitting next to and conversing with all night.

"Where baby boy at?" he asked the young lady.

"He went to the bathroom."

The man's eyes shifted to me. His head slightly turned and he cleared his throat. "I don't know you, do I?"

Before I could say a word, the woman next to me spoke up. "That's Roc's woman. She here with him."

"Say it ain't so," he said. He motioned his hand for the other two women to back off and they did. I couldn't believe how controlled some of these women were, or how this man and Roc seemed to have women in control. It was obvious where Roc had gotten his personality from.

Roc's uncle plucked the collar on his suit jacket and slid in the booth next to me. He held out his hand for me to shake it. "I'm Roc's uncle, Ronnie. He ain't tell me he was doin' it like this, and I would be ungrateful if I didn't tell you what a gorgeous-ass young woman you are."

"Thanks for the compliment," I said, returning the handshake. I swiped the feathery bang away from my forehead, feeling uneasy about Ronnie's closeness and stares. The whole time, he didn't take one eye off me, and when Roc came back to the booth, he looked high as ever. His eyes were low and redder than a cardinal. He smiled at his uncle and I could see just how much he admired him. They slapped hands, gripping them tightly together.

"Baby boy," his uncle said. "Happy Birthday, mane."

Roc nodded and couldn't stop displaying his whites.

"You enjoying yourself," his uncle asked.

"You better know it." He looked over at me. "So, I see you met the love of my life, right?"

His uncle took another opportunity to look me over. "I'm damn sholl impressed. You must've handpicked this one from Hollywood or somethin'. Red bone . . . thick and gorgeous as ever. She ain't from 'round here, is she?"

"Ask her," Roc said, making the woman next to me move. I sat between him and his uncle. His uncle put his hand on top of mine and squeezed it.

"You from here?" he asked.

"Born and raised," I said, immediately turning to Roc. "If you don't mind, I'm really ready to go."

He looked taken aback by my request. "We'll leave in another hour or two."

My voice went up to a higher pitch. "I'd like to leave now. I'm getting tired and . . . and have you been smoking something?"

His uncle made a move out of the booth. He looked Roc directly in his eyes, giving him an order. "Take care of that. Pretty women always mean trouble and she doesn't seem to be the exception." He looked at me and winked. "Nice meetin' you. Take care."

Roc downed another glass of champagne and ignored me. He laughed and joked with more of his friends, talked to more females and even suggested cutting his cake.

Cake or not, I was leaving. I scooted over to get out of the booth and he grabbed my wrist. His face scrunched up and his forehead lined with wrinkles.

"Where in the hell are you going?"

I snatched my wrist away and hated like hell to rain on his parade. I had definitely seen and heard enough that completely turned me off.

"I'm going home."

Roc released my wrist and tossed his hand back. I wasn't sure how I was going to get home, but I saw the limo driver who had taken me to the club earlier. I asked if he would take me home, and as soon as we made it to the limo, Roc came after me.

"Why you gotta ruin my birthday like this? I asked you to give me one more hour and you couldn't even chill and do that."

I pointed my finger at him. "You didn't ask me, you told me. I've really, really been trying to go along with this, but my patience is running thin. You're high as hell, you got females in there kissing all over you and what about the one who slapped you? Who the hell was she? I must thank her because she did exactly what I felt like doing tonight."

No sooner had I opened the door, loud gun-shots rang out in the background. Roc covered me and we both fell hard into the limo. I scrambled backward and Roc hurried inside to close the door. I could hear people screaming and heard cars skidding off the parking lot. Roc covered me again, and when one of the glass windows to the limo shattered, he tightened his body over mine.

"Shit," he hollered at the driver. "Hurry up and drive the fuck off!"

The limo's tires screeched and it sped off. My body was trembling all over and Roc looked down as I was still underneath him, shielding my ears from the constant sounds of gunfire.

"Are you okay?" he asked.

I couldn't utter one word and had never, ever experienced anything like this. I had only seen scenes like this in the movies, and never thought I'd witness a real-life situation like this one. I was so done with this mess and for those who chose to live this kind of life, they could have it! Roc kissed my cheek and rubbed his hand through my hair. He rose up and reached for my hand so I could sit on the seat with him. I shook my head from side to side, implying no. All I wanted was to be left alone and he knew it.

He immediately dialed out on his cell phone. "Ronnie," he said. "You a'ight?"

He paused. "Yeah, I'm good. I'm in the limo taking Desa Rae home." He paused for a longer time and I could hear his uncle's loud voice coming through the phone. "So, you know who it was?" He paused. "Aw, just some drunk fools with a beef shootin' at each other? Niggas know they be trippin'."

He continued to talk to his uncle, and as I said before, you never really get to know a man until you spend quality time with him. I had a whole new impression of Roc and it really didn't matter if he knew how I truly felt. As far as I was concerned, this was over!

Chapter Six

Monica had been out of town for almost two weeks, so I hadn't had a chance to talk to her about what happened at the club that night with Roc. I was back to cooling out at home, watching movies and reading books. I didn't mind doing so one bit, and after what had happened, I appreciated my boring life even more. I expressed my feelings to Monica over the phone, and she couldn't believe it.

"Girl, I can't believe those fools were clowning like that. I'd been to that club several times and nothing like that went down," Monica said.

"Well, it did and it was so, so scary. I saw my life flash before me and I was worried about Roc getting shot. I can tell he's used to that kind of mess and he calmed down like nothing really happened. After he dropped me off, I ran my butt into this house, tore that dress off me, and thanked God for sparing my life."

"Now, you overreacted. I never would have torn that dress, but I can honestly say that Roc would be history. The way you told me he carried on, I don't know what to say about him now."

"I don't either. He's really a nice young man, but we don't have much in common. I suspected that being with a twenty-four . . . five-year-old would be difficult, but that was quite the experience."

"Have you heard from him at all?"

"Nope. And I don't intend to either. He was more than upset with me, and for a man who's used to telling women when, where, and how, I think he got the picture that I'm not the one. People treated him like he was black Jesus or something and his bodyguards jumped at the sight of anybody looking at him too hard. I saw this one chick slap him and she was the same woman I'd seen at the car wash that day. I can smell the drama a mile away with that chick. The whole night was crazy and I couldn't believe I was sitting in the middle of all that mess."

"That's a shame, and some women know they be acting a fool over a man who couldn't care less about them. But what goes up, must come down. He was such a gorgeous and sexy young man. I had hoped you and him would kick it for a while. It seemed as if you started to live a little and I was starting to feel very happy for you."

"I thought so too, but things did not work out in my favor. I'm okay, though, Monica. No need to worry about me. When the time comes for me to meet the man of my dreams, trust me, I will."

A call interrupted, so I asked Monica to hold on. I was surprised to hear Latrel's voice on the other end, so I told Monica to call me back.

"Hey, Mama," he softly said. A mother knew her child, so I could definitely tell something was wrong. My stomach turned in knots.

"Hello, Latrel. How are you?"

"I'm okay. I just wanted to talk to you and apologize for my behavior."

"I needed to hear that, and I'm sorry for the way I acted too. I know you feel as if I'm too over-protective, but that's because I love you, honey, and I always want the best for you. I meant no harm in speaking that way about your girlfriend, but things about the past make me feel the way I do. I don't expect for you to understand, and I can't promise you that—"

"We broke up," he said.

The knot loosened in my stomach and I looked up and mouthed, "Thank you." I could tell Latrel was upset, but I wanted to stand up and do the stanky leg. Needless to say, the news put a smile on my face. His career was my only concern, and I hoped that it was his priority.

I held my stomach with relief and hated to lie to my son. "I'm sorry to hear about your break-up. What happened?"

"Out of nowhere, she started hanging around one of my friends and it bothered me. I asked her what was up and she said nothing. Then I find out from old boy that she had sex with him. I'm just so damn upset, Mama. I seriously thought she was the one."

Oh, no he didn't, I thought. "Well, she wasn't and you have so much to offer to the right woman when she comes along. I'd like to see you focus on your basketball career and I know you're still doing well in school."

"I'm doing great. I got a 3.5 GPA and that ain't bad for no freshman, is it?"

"Not at all, baby. I'm so proud of you and there wasn't a day that went by that I didn't think about you."

"I know, Mama, and same here. I wanted to call, but you know how stubborn I can get at times. I inherited that from you, so you can't blame me for that."

"No, you got that from your father," I joked, knowing that he'd gotten his stubbornness from me. "Have you spoken to your father lately?"

"Yeah, I talked to him the other day. What's this I hear about you shackin' up with a younger man? You had daddy hot and he couldn't stop talking about what happened."

I was so embarrassed. I knew Reggie hadn't given Latrel details, or had he? "Latrel, I was alone and your mother met someone who seemed like a really nice person. We're not seeing each other anymore, but your father shouldn't be out there spreading my business."

"Sorry it didn't work out. I don't care how old he was, and as long as he made you happy, I'm cool with it. I told Dad the same thing and he kind of got upset with me. But you can't control who you're attracted to or who you love. Who says people have to be a certain age to fall in love or the same color or different sex? I can't promise you that I won't fall in love with another white woman again, but whenever I meet somebody else, my concern is to make sure they love me back."

I smiled, realizing that Reggie and I had done a phenomenal job raising our son. Any woman would be lucky to have him, but I still had my preference. "You're right, baby. Cheer up for your mama, and when are you coming home again to see me? I miss you and we need to go somewhere and hang out together, okay?"

"Sounds good. I'll probably shoot that way in a couple of weeks. If you rekindle your relationship with your man, I wanna meet him."

"No, I won't be rekindling my relationship with anyone."

"Why not?"

"I'm too ashamed to tell you, but mainly because he's a mover and shaker."

"Straight up? Are you down with that?"

"Latrel, I don't really know what a mover and shaker is. But I do know that he wasn't the right person for me."

"From my recollection, a mover is someone who moves drugs from one city to the next, and a shaker is someone who shakes down niggas who stand in their way. Some people might have their own definition, but that's how I see it."

"I figured it was something like that, and you know your mama don't need that kind of drama in her life. Anyway, that's behind me now and you need to move on as well. Love you, Latrel, and I'll see you soon."

"No doubt."

Latrel hung up, and just for the hell of it, I danced around in my kitchen, pleased that I wasn't getting a daughter-in-law any time soon.

Mr. Wright had me running around the office like crazy. But the busier I was, the quicker time moved by. It was already 3:00 P.M. and in two more hours, I was going home. I was working on Mr. Wright's calendar for next week, and was interrupted by a call from the receptionist, telling me a package was waiting for me up front.

I was expecting FedEx or a UPS delivery, but it was a sweetheart bouquet from Edible Arrangements. The keepsake container was filled with fresh strawberries dipped in gourmet chocolate. A small teddy bear was attached to it with a card.

"This looks delicious," the receptionist said, handing it over to me. "You're so lucky to have a husband that cares."

Lucky was not how I felt, but surprised I was. I carried the package back to my desk and immediately read the card: *I'm really sorry 'bout what happened, but some things are beyond my control. When you wanna talk, call me. Roc a.k.a. Snookums.*

I couldn't help but smile, and it had been a little over three weeks since I'd heard from him. And for the first time, I had his phone number to call him. I held the card in my hand for a few minutes, contemplating on what I should do. I couldn't deny how much I'd been thinking about him, and how did he ever know that chocolates were the way to my heart? But the controlling man who I'd gotten to know so well, and the one who seemed to love living on the edge, wasn't

the one for me. I tossed the card in the trash
and inhaled the sweet chocolate melted on the
strawberries. I put one in my mouth and closed
my eyes as I thought about having sex with Roc.
No matter what had gone down, I couldn't shake
those memories of him being inside of me. His
sexual performance was the best and I thought
about the creative things he'd done while explor-
ing my body. While delving into the strawberries, I could almost feel his curled tongue circling
my clit, his lips plucking my nipples, and his long
fingers fucking me like a dick. Too bad things
turned out as they had and I knew it would be a
long, long time before I received pure satisfaction like that again. I backed out of my thoughts
and when I opened my eyes, Mr. Wright was
standing in front of my desk. I was so embarrassed, and it was a good thing that he couldn't
read my mind.

"That's a good-looking arrangement, Desa
Rae. But you really should be eating those strawberries in the lunchroom."

I swallowed the strawberry and wiped my
mouth with a napkin. "You're right, but I couldn't
resist. They look so good, don't they?"

Mr. Wright nodded and couldn't keep his eyes
off my strawberries. "Would you like one?" I
asked, giving him a napkin.

He smiled, reaching for two. "Why don't you get out of here for the day? It's Halloween and I know you're going to a party tonight, aren't you?"

"No, I'm not. I'm dressing up as a witch and giving out candy to the kids."

"A witch? You should be a princess or something. Witches are mean, and even though you may sometimes fit that classification, you'll still make a beautiful princess in my book."

I laughed at Mr. Wright's comment. I knew I'd been a force to be reckoned with lately, and calling me mean was putting it mildly. "Just for you, Mr. Wright, I'll be a good witch, okay? I promise to be nice to all of the children who come to my house, but they must do a trick before I give them a treat."

My Wright tossed his hand back. "Don't count on it. Back in the day, I had to turn flips or show some talent just to get one lousy piece of candy. These days, kids don't want to do nothing. All they'll do is show you their candy buckets and grab handfuls of what you have."

"I have to agree with you on that one. It'll be fun, though, and I'm looking forward to seeing all of the creative costumes."

Mr. Wright downed his strawberries and reached for two more before going into his

office, closing the door. I gathered my things
and left with the bouquet of strawberries in my
hand.

Thus far, my witch costume hadn't scared
away any of the kids. I took Mr. Wright's advice
and turned myself into a beautiful witch with
M•A•C lip gloss and shimmering makeup. My
pointed black hat allowed my long hair to show
and the black fitted dress I wore made me look
like *Bewitched* from the '60s. I had been treating kids all night, and during my downtime, I
sat in the kitchen watching reruns of *American
Idol*. The singers were pretty good, and when the
doorbell rang, I rushed to it.

"Trick or treat!" the kids yelled while bravely
standing in the drizzling rain that was about to
pick up. I had given up on asking the kids to do
tricks, and all they were interested in was getting
candy.

"Take as much as you want," I offered, trying
to get rid of my candy. It was getting late and after this bunch left, my porch light was going off.

Some older kids came on my porch, leaving
my bowl empty. I encouraged them to be safe in
the rain and turned off the light as they walked
away. *American Idol* was still on, so I removed

my hat, making my way back into the kitchen. No sooner than I pulled back my chair, the doorbell rang again. I knew I'd turned off the porch light, but sometimes the light didn't matter. I pulled the door open.

"Sorry, but I—"

Roc was leaned against my rail with his arms folded in front of him. He wore a black leather jacket and black denim jeans. A cap was on his head and his diamond earrings were sparkling in the dark.

"Don't think I'm stalkin' you or anything, but I feel bad 'bout what happened. I can't get that shit off my mind, ma, and I don't blame you for being upset with me."

"Look, there are no hard feelings, okay? Thanks for the arrangement today and the thought was awfully nice. Truth be told, though, if that incident at the club had never happened, I still don't think this would have worked out between—"

He quickly cut me off. "I disagree. It's like you already had yo' mind made up that we couldn't do this, so I was fightin' a battle, through yo' eyes, that couldn't be won. Give me another chance, a'ight?"

Another chance wasn't what Roc needed. Everything about this didn't feel right to me and I was doing my best not to come at him the wrong way.

"Before you say anything," he said. "Can I come in or you gon' let me stand out here in the rain and darkness."

I sighed, knowing that Roc wasn't going to like what I had to say. "You don't have to stand outside, Roc, and you can always leave. I prefer that you let this go and accept it for what it is."

He turned his head, looking away. I saw him take a hard swallow and it was so obvious that my rejection was not working for him. "Are you back with yo' ex-husband?" he asked.

I was somewhat taken aback by his question. "No, but this has nothing to do with Reggie and you know it."

"No, I don't know," he said, raising his voice. "I know he the reason why you being so uptight and shit. I know he why you bitter than a muthafucka and I know he the reason why you won't let another man come in and do what he failed to do."

Mentioning Reggie's name always brought out the worst in me, and for Roc to stand there and throw this mess in my face angered me. I wanted to slam my door in his face, but instead I gave him a big piece of my mind.

"You know what . . . some of that may be true, Roc, but you're the one who messed this up. I don't like men who shake and move. I can't accept a man who gets high and any man who thinks he can control women will never find a way to my heart. Maybe your other girlfriends accept that crap, but I'm not that kind of woman. You are wasting your time if you think I'm going to fit in and I guarantee you that will never happen."

The wind was picking up and from the blowing tree limbs and scattering debris outside, I could tell the weather was about to get ugly. Roc stepped forward to shield himself from the drizzling rain.

"So, in other words, yo' ex is standin' in my way, right?"

"You're not listening to anything—"

He cut his eyes and snapped. "I hear you, damn it! And I ain't even wanna do this to you, ma, but sometimes women be so fuckin' blind and don't recognize a good thing when it's starin'em right in the face. Yo' ex ain't shit, Dez, and he ain't thinkin' 'bout you. I'm the type of nigga who watches his back, and when that fool stepped to me at yo' house that day, I had to see what was up."

I was confused about what Roc was saying and this had nothing to do with Reggie. "What are you talking about? Why are you putting the blame on Reggie when he—"

Roc asked me not to shut the door and he ran in the rain to his truck. He retrieved an envelope, then handed it to me as I stood in the doorway.

"What is this?" I asked.

"Just open it."

I opened the envelope and my hands trembled while holding the pictures. Tears rushed to my eyes, and after seeing Reggie lip-locked in the pictures with a *skinny* Asian woman, it just broke my heart. Yes, I'd known he'd been seeing someone else, but at that moment, reality kicked in. I dropped the pictures, allowing them to scatter onto the porch. My tears kept falling, and I used my hands to cover my face. I felt Roc's arms wrap around me and he insisted, over and over, that the last thing he came over to do was hurt me.

"I'm sorry. I wasn't gon' show those to you, but I knew he had a hold on you that you needed to let go. Let that nigga go, Dez, and let's see what's up."

I sobbed even more, thinking about the hurt Reggie had caused me. This wasn't supposed to be how my life turned out. He wasn't supposed to be with another woman and I wasn't supposed to be left with an empty house to come to every night. I had bills that I couldn't even take care of, and my credit score had sunk to an all-time low. I had been living paycheck to paycheck and I had Reggie to thank for the ongoing turmoil that just wouldn't go away. My tears turned into anger, then passion for Roc as he embraced me in the doorway. I pulled away from him, hurrying to wipe my tears. Lord knows I hated for him to see me like this, but I couldn't help it. My chest heaved in and out as I stared at him without a blink. He hesitated to speak, looking very uneasy.

"Are . . . are you okay?" he asked. I didn't respond, but my flowing salty tears that rolled on my lips showed that I wasn't.

Roc backed me inside, but before he could close the door, I unzipped his jacket, dropping it behind him. I then pulled his T-shirt over his head and my hands touched his chest that I admired so much.

"Fuck me," I told him. "Please help me make it through this."

Roc took my hand, kissing the back of it. "I'm gon' help you, but not like this. Let's go lay down and—"

I was in no mood to go lay down and my aggressiveness showed just that. I ignored Roc's comment and reached for his belt buckle. His pants dropped to his ankles and I got on my knees in front of him. I didn't care that the door was still wide open, and when my hungry mouth went to work, neither did he.

"*Dezzzz, dammmn*," he said with a fistful of my hair. "Baby, stop. Come here . . . I gotta tell you somethin'."

The way Roc pumped in and out of my mouth, I knew he didn't want me to stop. It required both of my hands to stroke him and they were in an up-and-down fast rhythm with my soaking-wet mouth and tightened jaws. I felt the need to give Roc all of me. Reggie had me for many, many years and didn't deserve all that I'd given to him. How dare me hold back on a man who seemed so willing to be there for me when I needed him. From this moment on, I had no intentions of depriving myself. The concerns that I had about Roc had to be put off for another day. All I needed was for him to help ease my pain. For the moment, he was working out just fine.

Roc didn't want to come, so he backed out of my mouth, holding his ten hard inches in his hand. I removed every single stitch of my clothing at the door and laid back, offering him my throbbing pussy while in the darkened foyer. Roc did what he knew best, and as my legs fell apart, he went right between them. His peace sign separated my pussy lips, giving full exposure to my stimulated clit. While his fierce tongue worked me over, he used his other fingers to bring down my juices. Over the thunder and rain that picked up outside, I still heard my juices flowing. My back squirmed against the hardwood floor, as Roc demanded, required, and received my undivided attention.

"I love suckin' this pussy," he confirmed. "I missed this shit and—"

I wasn't up to hearing Roc speak and his words took time away from his immaculate performance. I rolled my body over, straddling my thighs over his face underneath me. Just as he'd entertained my mouth, I entertained his. I rolled my pussy around on his lips, making sure that he tasted each and every part of me.

"Damn," Roc shouted. "Work that muthafucka, baby! Do that shit, girl, I like how you puttin' that pussy in motion."

I tightened my thighs around his face, and as I neared coming, I backed away. I inched my body down to his hardness and prepared myself to give him the ride of his life. I kept a strong arch in my back, allowing my ass to do most of the jolting. It bounced up and down on him, but the tight grip of my insides caused him to blurt out even more.

He squeezed my hips, pumping himself into my awaiting wetness. "I knew yo' ass was holdin' back on me. Gi—give me all you got! That's right,

I want all of it! Turn around and work that ass in my direction."

I turned, giving Roc a clear view of his entrances to my backside. His hands separated my ass cheeks and I'm sure he had the best view in the house.

"Um, um, um," was all he could say. With each pleasurable stroke on top of him, he lifted my butt to the tip of his head, making sure that I felt every inch when I dropped back down. No doubt, I was in pain, but it was pain that I didn't mind being on the receiving end of.

"Ohhh, Roc," I whined. "Why does this have to feel so *guuud*? My pussy hurts, but you make it feel so good."

"I don't wanna hurt you," he said, halting his actions and moving me over to his side. Right then, the thunder clashed, bringing lightness through the doorway. Roc kicked the door closed with his foot and resumed his position behind me. Doggystyle made me feel him even more, and each time I moved forward, he pulled my hips back to him. I spewed nothing but dirty talk to him and he fired back. I gripped my hair tight, mustered the pleasurable pain, and dropped my head low.

"That's right, fuck it, baby," I said, heavily breathing from my raging heart beat. "Fuck this pussy however you want to. With a dick like this, you . . . you have my permission to do whatever you want."

Roc let out a snicker and took it to a higher level. He went from one position to the next, touching my body in all the right places and causing me to come six times that night. I had put on an impressive show myself, and if he had never experienced sex with another woman of my size before, then he now knew what some healthier women were capable of bringing to the party. A skinny and frail woman didn't have anything on me, and this was one time that I felt as if I had something to prove.

The lights had gone out because of the heavy rain. I lit one candle and we lay sprawled out in my bed with many silk pillows around us.

"I don't think I've ever had a woman shake, rattle, and roll on me like that. That shit was off the chain, baby, and I hope like hell I don't have to upset you again in order for you to put it in motion like that."

I chuckled a bit while rubbing Roc's chest. "I don't know what got into me. Seeing those pictures hurt like hell, and it was the first time I'd seen Reggie with someone else."

"Again, I'm sorry for the pictures, but I was just tryin' to do my homework. I can't take no chances with people I don't know, and that's why I had one of my boys check into it for me. He gave those to me, but I didn't want you to see them. I was gon' tell you 'bout that nigga, but I definitely didn't want to bring that kind of hurt to you."

I thought about the pictures, and in an effort to move on, I looked up at Roc. "Nobody could ever bring as much hurt to me as Reggie did. I don't want to talk about him and promise me that you will never bring up his name again."

Roc zipped his lips. "Case closed. But it wouldn't be wise for me not to recognize the reason I'm here. I know the hurt from that nigga bringin' you in my direction, but you ain't the only one dealin' with some crazy shit. I told myself that if you took me back I would lay *some* of my shit on the line. I'm diggin' you like a muthafucka, Dez, and if I could make some of my fucked-up situations disappear, I would. Thing is, though, I got people dependin' on me and I just can't slam the door in their faces. There are times that I want to walk away, but I can't. It ain't like I'm on no street corners or nothin', but from time to time, I do move *things* around for my uncle. Like always, he takes damn good care of me, and if I have to return a li'l favor, then I do it. That's why I work at his car wash and at the club. Some of his shit legit, but then again, some people's opinion 'bout what he do may differ."

I wasn't sure how to confront Roc about what he'd just admitted and the last thing I wanted was to be judgmental. I hadn't walked in his shoes and I understood how a young man like him could get so caught up with the money.

"I'm not going to judge you, Roc, but you've got to consider other options. You are a gorgeous young man and I know you can get a modeling gig anywhere. There are so many things I'm sure you're capable of doing and you just can't sit back and accept things for what they may be. I know what it's like for people to depend on you, but you've got to look out for yourself. You are living a dangerous life, and unless you do something about it, your situation will end like all the others. I don't want that for you, and the people around you shouldn't either. All I'm saying is challenge yourself to do better. Don't travel down the same road as your father, and his father or the rest of your family members. Break the cycle and start a generation that your family can be proud of. Remember, money isn't everything. How you make it is what defines us."

Roc kissed my forehead and was silent for a while. Moments later, he spoke up. "I hear what you're sayin' Dez, and I wish it were that easy.

Unfortunately, society requires you to have all these degrees to make money, and I dropped out of school in the twelfth grade. I have money to buy whatever I want, so changin' course don't make sense to me right now."

"It might not make sense to you now, but one day it will." I touched Roc's hair on his chin and lifted my head to kiss him. "If there's anything I can do to help you turn your life in another direction, please let me know."

He nodded and cuddled me in his arms. I had a feeling that going forward, he would impact my life in a positive way and I would do the same for his life.

The lights were back on, and after I took my morning shower, I headed downstairs to find something to cook for breakfast. My fridge didn't have much in it, so I reached for my milk, opting for a bowl of Frosted Flakes. Roc was still asleep, so I sat at the table and made a long grocery list. He hadn't mentioned any of his favorite foods, but with a body like his, I was sure his fat intake was minimal. I wrote down fruits, vegetables, and even turkey burgers that I was sure he'd like. I then thought about baking him a cake, just because of the one he didn't get to cut on his birthday that night at the club. I searched through my cabinets and came across a red velvet cake I'd promised to make for Latrel. I wound up making him a German chocolate cake that day, but never got around to the red velvet one. I wasn't sure when Roc would wake up or how long he'd stay, so I hurried to whip the batter and get it into the oven.

Thirty minutes had gone by, and when I headed to my bedroom to check on Roc, he was still resting peacefully. Nothing covered his naked body and sexiness was written all over him. I wanted to jump on him, but I figured I'd wait until his cake was finished. As I made my way down the hallway, I heard a vibrating sound coming from my living room. I noticed Roc's phone on the floor, and when I picked it up, it showed that he had nine text messages waiting. I thought about not looking at the messages, but that was just a thought. When I clicked the view button, somebody named Vanessa seemed pissed. Where in the fuck are you? she inquired. Yo' ass just up and disappeared and I'm gettin' tired of the bullshit! I know you with some bitch, and when she don't fuck you like I do, don't come running back to me! I looked at another message she'd sent and it read:

The clothes you left here are on fire, nigga! I don't need you anymore Roc and neither does your son.

I heard Roc cough, so I quickly laid the phone back on the floor. This was definitely not the kind of drama I wanted or needed in my life, and as a black woman, I felt as if we had to do better. I wondered why Roc hadn't mentioned anything to me about a son? The text messages frustrated me, but at his age, what in the hell did I expect? His baby's mama seemed very immature, and if she had to leave nine messages and refer to the father of her child as a nigga, then she didn't need him, nor did he need her. Roc had been spending a lot of weekends with me, and I wondered how much time he'd been spending with Vanessa and their son.

Just as I was putting icing on the cake, I heard my hardwood floors squeak. I quickly turned around and Roc was standing by the island. He stretched and before he could ask what time it was, I told him.

"It's almost noon," I said, standing in front of the cake to hide it.

"How you know I was gon' ask you that?"

"Because you always ask, like you have somewhere to be."

Unclothed, he made his way up to me. "What you tryin' to hide?" he said, wrapping his arms around me. "I smell somethin'."

I turned around to face the cake and Roc kept his arms around me. "Tah-dah! It's your birthday cake. I didn't have much to cook for breakfast, so I thought a cake would be nice."

Roc pecked his lips down the side of my neck, repeatedly thanking me. "You so sweet. And I mean that literally."

I smiled, carrying the cake over to the table. He sat in a chair while I stuck twenty-five candles inside of the cake and lit them. I started to sing "Happy Birthday," but he interrupted me.

"If we gon' have a for-real birthday celebration, then you gotta put on your birthday suit like me. I ain't feelin' the silk robe, and if you want to make this more excitin', you should get comfortable."

I had no problem getting naked with Roc, and allowed my silk robe to drop behind me. I straddled his lap in the chair while resting my arms on his shoulders. I looked into his eyes and seductively sung "Happy Birthday" to him. I ended with a lengthy kiss and asked him to make a wish and blow out the candles.

"I wish that you and me could kind of hook up and do the significant-other thing. But since you ramblin' through my phone and shit, maybe you think I'm taken by somebody else. Everything ain't what it appears to be and if you ever want to know 'bout me, all you gotta do is ask. Some things are open for discussion, then again, understand that some things ain't."

Roc turned his head and blew out the melting candles. How in the hell did he know I'd checked his phone? I wanted to ask about Vanessa and his son, but I knew my answers would come later. For now, his significant-other wish went in one ear and out the other. There was more that needed to be revealed and I wasn't about to set myself up for another broken heart. Instead of ruining the moment, I cut a huge chunk of the cake and told Roc to open his mouth. He did and I put half of the piece inside of his mouth, saving the other half for me. He chewed, nodding his head.

"Damn, that's good. So far, yo' ass can cook."

"My ass doesn't cook, I do. I'm glad you like it."

Roc gripped my ass and shook it. "My bad, yo' ass good for many other things I get so excited about. And that's on the real."

He swiped his finger across the top of the cake, removing a healthy portion of the white cream icing. "Do you know what I could do with this?" he asked. "I can make this taste so much better."

"My imagination is starting to run wild, and while we're in our birthdays suits, let's not let anymore time go to waste."

"You a hot ass somethin', ma. What the fuck I'm gon' do with yo' pretty ass? You got my young mind all twisted and shit. Why you tryin' to mess with a nigga's mind?"

I took Roc's hand, spreading the icing from his fingers onto my nipples. I knew he'd find other places to put it, but my breasts were a good start.

"You're a very smart man, Roc. And diploma or not, you've gained an enormous amount of knowledge from the streets. I in no way have your mind twisted and the streets have taught you how to play your game and play it well. For the record, I'm digging the hell out of you too. But we're going to approach this one day at a time. Like last night, the ball fell in your court. Today, it's in your court again. Right now, you're playing your hand correctly, but don't be afraid to face a new dealer. She's a force to be reckoned with, and unlike your baby's mama who is bringing you drama, my mind can't be twisted neither."

I knew Roc wanted to fire back at me, but my tongue went into his mouth to shush him. I then lifted his hand to my breasts, and once he started licking the icing on my nipples, that was all she wrote. His intimate belated birthday celebration went out with a bang, and Vanessa or not, I was sure there were many more days like this to come.

Chapter Seven

Latrel called, and instead of him coming home, he wanted me to come to his school for an awards ceremony. Due to his excellent grades, he'd been offered another scholarship to further his engineering career. He had already received a scholarship for basketball, but since college was so expensive, every little bit helped. I told him I would definitely be there, and that's when he informed me not to come alone. I asked why, and even though he hated to tell me, he admitted that Reggie was bringing someone with him.

I pretended as if the news hadn't bothered me, but it had. I wasn't sure if I'd be able to hold my peace after seeing him with another woman, but I had to be there for my son. As usual, I expressed my concerns with Monica and she always had a solution. That was to take Roc along with me and not go alone. She even offered to go, and since she was Latrel's godmother, that only made sense. I wasn't sure if Roc would be willing to go, or if I was comfortable with introducing him to Latrel. When I talked to Roc about it, he was all for it. According to him, we needed to get out and have some fun. He knew how I felt about going places with him and his lifestyle still made me paranoid. I figured a car ride to Mizzou College couldn't do much harm, so the three of us rode together in my Lincoln MKS.

We arrived at Mizzou three hours before the ceremony. I was nervous about Latrel meeting Roc, and on our way to Latrel's dorm room, I pulled Roc aside.

"I am really nervous about this," I said, facing him. I brushed the fine hair off his shoulders from his fresh haircut and touched the side of his smooth face. "Can you do me a favor?"

"What's that?" he asked.

"I know how blunt you like to be, but please don't mention anything about us having sex. Eliminate the "*P*" word and don't be so vulgar, please?"

Roc just stared without saying a word. Monica pulled my arm and told Roc to ignore me. "Please forgive her. She got issues."

"Obviously," he said, reaching for my arm. He turned me to face him and spoke sternly. "I need to get this off my chest. I am who I am and I don't put on no front for nobody. If you didn't want

me to come here, then you shouldn't have asked.
Your son is a grown-ass man and I'm sure he's
come across people more blunt than me. Chill
out and if you don't start none, then it won't be
none."

"He told you," Monica mumbled. I rolled my
eyes at Monica and turned my attention back to
Roc.

"I'm sorry. I didn't mean for my words to
come out like that and my intentions weren't to
offend you. It's just that my son has never seen
me with another man and I really don't know
how he's going to react."

Roc shrugged and winked. "All we can do is
see. Either way, I promise to be on good behavior."

We made our way to Latrel's room, and after
one knock, he opened the door. His face lit up
and we embraced each other.

"Hey, Mama," he said, kissing my cheek and
inviting me inside. He hugged and kissed Monica too and afterward, I introduced him to Roc.

"What's up, man," Latrel said, gripping Roc's
hand.

"Nothin' much. It's good to meet you. I've
heard a lot about you and congrats on yo' achieve-
ments."

"Thanks," Latrel said, patting Roc's back.

We all stepped into the tiny room that had two bunk beds, two computer desks, and one closet stuffed with clothes. Posters of Beyoncé, Ciara, Kim Kardashian and Keyshia Cole were plastered on the walls, but two posters of half-naked models bothered me. If that wasn't enough to disturb me, Latrel came to the door with no shirt on and a female was sitting on his bed. *Didn't he know I was coming?* I thought.

"Mama, Monica, and Roc, this is Jeanne," he said.

She stood up, giving us a quick wave. "I'm going back to my dorm," she said. "I'll see you at the ceremony."

Jeanne left the room, but not before taking a double look at Roc. *Hell, who wouldn't,* I thought.

"Who's Jeanne?" I asked, while observing Latrel's room. It was junky as ever and I hadn't raised my son not to take care of his things.

"She just some trick I'm trying to lay."

Monica laughed and Roc smiled. I didn't hear anything funny, so I folded my arms and addressed Latrel. "So that's what you're here for, huh? And when did you start referring to women as tricks?"

Latrel put his shirt on and walked up to me. He shook my shoulders and smiled. "Would you please take a load off and relax? I'm just playing, Mama, damn. Can't you take a joke? Jeanne is just a friend of mine, okay? And check this out . . . did you notice that she was black?"

I smiled and lightly punched Latrel in his stomach. "Yes, I noticed, but there was still something about her I didn't like."

"Now, why doesn't that surprise me?" he said.

Monica chimed in. "Face it, Latrel. No woman is ever going to be good enough for your mama. And when she sees all these condoms over here in this trash can, you'd better have a good answer."

I quickly made my way over to the trash can, and there was one used condom inside. Latrel hurried to defend himself.

"That does not belong to me. It's my roommate's and you can ask him when he gets here."

"Now, you know I don't believe that for one minute. If you're up here messing around like this, I don't understand how you're capable of getting good grades."

Latrel defensively held out his hand with a huge grin on his face. I could always tell when my son was lying and he was. "I—uh, don't—" He looked at Roc. "Man, help a brotha out, would you? They ganging up on me," he laughed.

"Hey, I got battered on the way up here. If I could help, I would. You know yo' mama be trippin' sometimes."

I playfully cut my eyes at Roc, then at Latrel. "Clean this room and we'll meet you in the auditorium. We still haven't checked into our hotel."

I kissed Latrel's cheek, and before we left his room, he pulled me back inside, closing the door.

"It's good to see you smiling again. You look nice and I love you," he said.

I hugged Latrel, telling him I loved him too. I knew he hadn't seen this side of me in a long time and I was starting to feel better about life in general.

We checked into the hotel, then rushed to make our way to the auditorium before the ceremony started. I took longer than expected to get dressed and I would be lying if I said seeing Reggie and his woman wasn't on my mind. It was, and I did my best to look flawless. I wore a strapless silk peach dress with hand-beaded crystal detailing above my healthy breasts. The dress hugged my curvy hips and butt, and secured my tummy to make it flat as ever. T-strap silver leather sandals with a three-inch heel covered my feet and my pedicure was in full effect.

Not one strand of my feathery long hair was out of place and my bangs swooped across my forehead. Roc was on point too. He wasn't as dressed up as I was, but the black ribbed cashmere sweater he wore clung to his muscular frame. His dark denim jeans were highly starched and had a crease that could cut. His squared-toed black leather shoes looked expensive, but not as much as the diamond watch he wore or the ones he had in his ears. No doubt, we made a very attractive couple and Roc kept his arm around me as we made our way into the auditorium. Monica took a seat to my left and Roc sat to my right.

"*Girlllll*, he is cutting up," she whispered low enough so Roc couldn't hear her. "You . . . you look nice too and I can't wait for Reggie to get here. That sucker's face gon' get cracked."

I'd been thinking the same thing. I could always count on Monica to put things in perspective. I paid her a compliment as well, and my best friend always knew how to dress.

Right after I saw Latrel sit up front with some of the other students, I turned and saw Reggie walk in with his woman. It wasn't the woman in the picture, because this woman was black. Honestly, the sight of them didn't bother me as much as I thought it would. The woman looked just okay to me. Her hair was short, she was a shade darker than me, and her body looked as if she worked out. She had on a simple black dress and a silver purse hung from her shoulder. Reggie was suited up in a gray pinstriped suit with a white shirt underneath. Admittedly, he looked nice too, but he had nothing on my Roc. I smiled about that, and when I turned back around, Roc was staring right at me.

"What is it?" I asked.

"Did I tell you how much I'm diggin' you in that dress?"

"Yes, you told me at the hotel, but you also told me you were digging my flowered dress I had on a while back too. I don't know if I can trust your word because we both know that dress looked awful."

"*Shiiit*," he said. "That one was even better than this one. The only difference is this one got that plump ass sittin' up just right. I can't get my mind out the gutter sittin' next to you." He looked down at his lap and slumped down a bit. "Look at my shit. It's tryin' to jump out of my pants and get to you."

I couldn't help but laugh and so did Roc. "I swear, you are so nasty," I whispered. "Why are we having this conversation right now? Sit up straight and I promise to take care of *that* when we get back to the hotel."

Roc cleared his throat and sat up. He moved closer to me, whispering his words. "I'm not in the market for no mother, and I can't sit up straight with a hard-on like this. If you keep that shit up, I'm gon' spank that ass hard when we get back to the hotel."

Again, my words just didn't come out the right way, but I was learning how to enlighten the situation. "I guess I'm in trouble, huh?"

"Big, big trouble."

I pecked his lips, which is something I hadn't seen myself doing in public. "I love being in trouble. Just make sure you have what it takes to discipline me."

Roc snickered and moved away from me. He slumped down even more, rubbing the trimmed hair on his chin.

The ceremony got started and I couldn't keep my eyes off Latrel. I was so proud of him, and when they called his name to accept his award, I got emotional. He thanked his father and me, gave thanks to the organization that gave him the scholarship, and spoke so eloquently. I knew my son would grow up and make something out of himself, and knowing so had put me at ease. Monica touched my hand and squeezed it.

"You did good," she whispered. "Keep up the good work."

I nodded, and when Latrel was done speaking, we all stood and clapped our hands. At that moment, I didn't give a care about Reggie or his woman, who sat a few rows behind us. I was thankful he'd given me a son that I could love, support, and appreciate for the rest of my life.

The ceremony lasted for at least three hours. A brief step show was included, as well as some young women praise dancing. It was beautiful, and when I looked at Roc, he seemed to be all into it. Especially with the steppers. I figured that being here was something new to him, but that was just a guess.

When the ceremony was over, we waited for Latrel in the lobby. Roc's hand comforted the small of my back and he occasionally let his hand roll over my butt. I didn't mind, especially since I could see Reggie from afar with his eyes glued to us. Monica warned me that he was coming our way, but I had already seen him.

Roc was next to me talking to a young man he knew from his neighborhood. And when Reggie got closer, Roc's hand lowered to my butt again. This time, I moved it up to my back. Roc smiled, and with his hand remaining where it was, he continued his conversation with his friend.

"Hello, Monica," Reggie said, ignoring me. "How are you doing?"

Monica was fake as ever, displaying a wide grin like she was so happy to see him. "I'm fine, Reggie. How are you?"

"Couldn't be better." He turned to the woman behind him. "This is my, uh, fiancée Yvette."

Yvette reached out her hand to Monica and they shook hands. "Oh, it's so nice to meet you," Monica said. I couldn't help but turn away from the fakeness and when Roc squeezed my butt, I looked at him. His dimples were coming through for me and the compliment his friend had laid upon me was right on time.

"Yeah, this my baby right here," Roc told the other guy. "I wouldn't trade her for nothin' in the world."

"I wouldn't either," the guy responded while looking me over. He slapped hands with Roc and walked away. No sooner than he had, Reggie tapped my shoulder.

"Do—do you mind if I talk to you outside for a minute?" he asked.

Before I could say anything, Roc spoke up. "She might not mind, but I do. Whatever you got to say to her you can say it right here 'cause she ain't goin' nowhere."

Monica cleared her throat and coughed. This was the wrong time and place, so I had to quickly speak up. "Reggie, I'm waiting for Latrel. You and I haven't talked in quite some time now, and I'm not sure why you're anxious to speak to me now."

Reggie eyeballed Roc and folded his arms. "You are really starting to bug the hell out of me. Now, I was talking to my wife—ex-wife—and you just can't keep that big mouth of yours shut. Why don't you go somewhere and play, young buck. You got all these young girls in here sniffing after your ass and I'm sure your dope money—"

I placed my hand on Reggie's chest and stood face to face with him. "Stop with the insults. We're here for Latrel and I'm not about to let you do this."

Roc pulled me away from Reggie. "Baby, don't waste your breath. That muthafucka just jealous and I would be too if I had an ugly bitch like his by my side. Let's go find Latrel so I can take Reggie's advice . . . go home and play. I got a magnificent pussy to play with, and I ain't got no beef with this nigga for rewardin' me with what used to be his," he laughed while looking at Reggie. "You fucked up, playa, now get over it."

Roc shook his head and walked away. Monica followed behind him and when I turned around, Reggie reached for my arm.

"Aside from the dumb shit he talking, I need to talk to you about some things. Once you get your bodyguard out of the way, call me."

I didn't say if I would or if I wouldn't. I walked away to see what was taking Latrel so long from leaving the auditorium.

Latrel and six of his friends finally came out into the lobby. I walked up to give him a hug, and again, expressed how proud I was of him.

"I know," he said, looking embarrassed as I rubbed his hair. Monica was teasing him too and Roc had jumped in to congratulate him as well. Latrel introduced us to his friends who he was going out with later that night.

"Y'all be careful," I said. "And please don't be drinking and driving."

"Are you going out with us too?" one of his friends asked. "You can be my date, and my friends would envy me for bringing a woman into the pool hall who looks like Halle Berry."

Latrel playfully grabbed his friend by the back of his neck and squeezed it. He looked at Roc. "Man, you want me to hurt him? I got your back if you want me to."

Roc smiled and spoke with confidence. "Nah, I'm good. He ain't got nothin' comin'. Only in his imagination."

The young man pointed to Roc, then to me. "That's you, dog? Dang you lucky."

Roc eased his arm around my waist. "I keep tellin' myself the same thang every day."

Latrel playfully boxed with his friend and when another one tried to push up on Monica, it was time to go and let them have fun.

"Honey, let me tell you something," Monica said. "Y'all better be careful trying to mess around with older women. You gon' get caught up and I'm warning you. We will get you into something you can't get yourself out of."

"That's what I'm hoping for," Latrel's friend said. They all laughed and bumped fists together.

I wanted Latrel to go say hello to his father, as I could see Reggie getting antsy from a distance.

"Listen," I said, giving him another hug. "Be careful and please don't stay out all night. We'll have breakfast in the morning, okay?"

He nodded, and after kissing Monica on her cheek, he gave Roc another handshake.

"Say, man, you wanna meet us at the pool hall tonight? All kinds of fellas be hanging out and the game coming on tonight."

"Nah, I'm gon' chill with my baby. Y'all have fun and don't do nothin' that I wouldn't do."

I turned to Roc, wanting to cool out with Monica for a while. I also wanted Latrel to get to know Roc a little better, so I made a suggestion. "Why don't you get the address to where they'll be and meet them there?"

"Yeah, man, come on," Latrel said, encouraging Roc.

Roc took down the address, agreeing to meet up with them later. We then left and headed back to the hotel.

Later that evening, Monica and I sat in the hotel's dining room eating a late dinner. Roc had several phone calls to return and he stayed in the room to make them. He was planning to meet up with Latrel and his friends, and when he entered the dining room, he told me he was getting ready to go.

"Okay, I'll see you later," I said. He leaned in for a kiss and a lengthy one at that.

"Wait up for me. Leave the clothes in the closet and make sure that pu—"

I covered Roc's mouth. "I know, okay? You don't have to tell all of my business to my friend, do you?"

"She already knows what's up." Roc looked at Monica and smiled. "Don't you, Monica?"

Monica bit into a piece of bread, playing clueless. "Whuu—What?" she said.

Roc laughed and put a hundred-dollar bill on the table. "Y'all full of shit. I'm outta here and that should take care of dinner."

I was just about ready to open my mouth, until Monica interrupted me. "Thank you," she said, picking up the money and placing it inside of her bra.

Roc winked at me and walked away.

Monica shook her head. "I gotta be honest with you about something, Dez. Roc is a mess, but I love, love, love the way he handles you. I knew you were about to give that money back to him, weren't you?"

"Yes, and you know why. And since you're loving him so much, I guess you love how disrespectful he can be? Roc is too blunt and he don't care where he is. He says whatever he wants, and to me, he should watch what he says around people."

"Disrespectful? Reggie was the one who was disrespectful. Roc put a check mark on his butt and I was so glad he put that fool in his place."

"How? By telling him that he was going home to play with my pussy? Now, you know that was too much."

Monica disagreed and we went back and forth debating the issue. Personally, I didn't like what neither of them said to each other. But Roc was with me and I didn't approve of him going at Reggie like that.

Dinner was delicious. Monica and I sat for hours talking about Latrel's accomplishments, her kids, Roc and Reggie. I had so much fun with my best friend and we definitely had to do this more often. We headed back to our rooms around midnight and I told her I'd see her at eight in the morning for breakfast. I headed to my room and just as I put the card in the door, I heard Reggie call my name. My head quickly turned.

"Wait a minute before you go inside," he said.

I sighed and leaned my back against the door. "What is it, Reggie?"

"Look, I'm sorry about what happened earlier, but I'm not going to apologize for saying those things to your boyfriend. All I wanted to do was thank you for being such a great mother to Latrel and tell you how proud I was of him today. I know you've dealt with a lot lately and I'm so happy to see you up and lively again."

"Thank you. And, I have to give you credit for being there for Latrel too. I applaud your relationship with him, even though, at times, I do be a little jealous of it."

Reggie laughed and we stood silent for a moment. "Are—are you staying at this hotel too?" I asked.

"Yes. Yvette and I are on the second floor. I saw you and Monica having dinner so I waited around so I could talk to you."

I bit my nail and looked down at the floor. I had never been uncomfortable when talking to Reggie, but for whatever reason, I was. "So, are you and Yvette really engaged? I heard you tell Monica—"

"No," he said. "I said that to upset you. Yeah, it was stupid, but you know what, I couldn't help it." He took my hands, held them with his, and laughed. "I hate to tell you this, but I am so damn jealous of your relationship with this fool Roc. It's like the shit is driving me crazy or something. Ever since that day I saw you in bed with him, I can't get it off my mind. Something about the way he touches you just makes me cringe. And the sad thing is, I can tell how much you like him. Do you really like him as much as I think?"

After all that Reggie had put me through, I told him exactly what he needed to hear. "Yes, I do like him a lot. To me, age is just a number and being with Roc isn't any different than being with you."

His voice slightly rose. "How can you say that, Dee? He still wet behind the ears and what does he have to offer you? I know the sex couldn't be all that great, and if it is, I know damn well he ain't better than me."

Reggie waited for a response. I hated to be the bearer of bad news, but why not? "Don't let his age fool you, Reggie, and I'm not going to stand out here and discuss my *daily* sex life with you. Let's just say that we were married for too long. There was another world out there waiting for me, and the new experiences have been more than I could have ever imaged."

He shook his head. "That's messed up. When we were married you would go weeks without making love to me. You never—"

I placed my finger on Reggie's lips. "I guess it's obvious why we're not married anymore. No need to look back, right?"

Reggie couldn't say a word. He took a deep breath and attempted to lean in for a kiss. I quickly turned my head.

"No," I said. "Never again. We're done."

"The thrill is gone," I heard Roc sing. He was pimping down the hallway, and from a short distance, I could tell he was drunk. "It's gone away." He walked up to us, looking directly at Reggie. I could smell the alcohol and I knew he was high.

Reggie shrugged. "Go do you, baby. If this is what makes you happy, hey, what can I do?"

Reggie walked away. "You can't do a damn thing," Roc added. I hurried to go inside and Roc followed behind me. He started taking off his clothes, but I sat on the bed, leaning back on my hands. I wasn't smiling so Roc knew something was up.

"Ahhh, shit," he laughed, standing naked in front of me. "My ass in trouble, ain't I?"

"Big trouble. Now, why would you go out with my son and get blasted like this? I thought you'd contain yourself, Roc. How could you embarrass me like that?"

"Ay, I did my best to contain myself, but yo' son and them had some shit that was fire! What was I s'pose to do?"

"Stop your lying. Latrel might drink, but he does not smoke weed. I know that for a fact."

"Okay, Mommy, if you say so." Roc leaned me back on the bed and started kissing my neck. "Mmm," he moaned. "Take your clothes off. Why you still got on yo' clothes?"

"Because I don't want to have sex and I don't like it when you're high like this. Why can't you stop messing with that stuff?"

Roc held himself up over me. "Okay, so—you don't like me when I'm high, you don't like when I speak bluntly, you don't like when my phone rings, you don't like the way I wash cars, you don't like me kickin' game at the club with my peeps, you don't like for me to slump in chairs. Damn, Dez, what do you like 'bout me? My dick? Is that all you like? I don't hear you complaining 'bout that muthafucka. Let's just stop hangin' out with each other, and whenever you wanna wet that pussy, call me, a'ight?"

Roc got up and went into the bathroom. He closed the door and I heard the shower come on. I knew he was tired of my gripes, but I couldn't help that some of the things he said and did bothered me. Was I supposed to keep my mouth shut about him getting high? Drugs were no good and if Latrel was smoking weed, I was going to kill him. There was no excuse and I couldn't wait to see him at breakfast in the morning. For now, I had Roc to deal with, and as mad as I was with him, yes, I did have a special place in my heart for his dick.

I removed my clothes and entered the bathroom. Roc was lathering his chocolate body with soap and was surprised to see me join him. I took the towel from his hand, giving him a thorough wash. Minutes later, he returned the favor, but promised that he hadn't forgiven me.

"I ain't playin', Dez, you ain't got nothin' comin'. You can't come in here, tryin' to seduce me and thinkin' I'm gon' make luv to ya."

I pressed my soapy wet body against Roc's, putting my arms on his shoulders. I pouted and spoke with sincerity. "I don't want you to make love to me. I want—"

Roc nodded. "You want me to fuck you, don't you?"

"Yeah, that's what I want," I whispered.

"Yeah?"

I nodded, rubbing my nose against his. "Yes, snookums."

"No," he said, smiling. "Can't do it."

"Why not? Am I the one in trouble?"

He backed me into the wall, leaving no breathing room between us. "Big, big, ten and a half inches of trouble."

"That deep, huh?"

"Unfortunately so."

"So are you going to punish me right here, or out there?"

"Oh, right here, baby. Definitely right here."

We kissed and Roc's hands felt so good rubbing all over my soapy body. He punished me all right, leaving me hanging high and dry. I couldn't get nothing out of him, and when he laid his head on my lap and went to sleep, it was almost three in the morning. When it was time to get up and go to breakfast, he opted not to go.

"I'm too tired," he grunted. "Tell Latrel I'll holla later."

I got dressed and left to have breakfast with Latrel and Monica. They were already in the dining area and I couldn't wait to ask Latrel about last night. He looked hungover too and I knew he would have given anything to stay in bed as well.

"Good morning," I said, pulling my chair up to the table.

"Hey," he mumbled. He gulped down his orange juice and rubbed his temples.

"You look just as bad as Roc did when he came in last night. Did you have fun?"

"Lots. Roc a pretty cool dude. Good choice."

"Somehow, I knew you were going to say that, especially since y'all seem to have a lot in common."

"Do we?" Latrel said, cutting into his pancakes.

"Well, not a lot, but enough to be concerned about."

"What is it that you're concerned about?" he huffed, giving me an irritated look.

"Your drinking, your drugs, and your numerous lady friends. Where do I start first?"

He shrugged and had the nerve to blow me off. "So what, I drink. And so what, I have sex. What you think I'm some kind of queer or something?"

"Latrel, did you get high last night?"

"I smoked *a* joint, mama. I didn't get high, but I did have *a* joint. So there, what's the big damn deal? Dad said you and him tried weed before, so—"

"Your father is a liar and you'd better calm your tone. You are never too old for me to jump over this table and slap some sense into you. You are here on a scholarship program and I have no doubt that your basketball career will take off. Sooner or later, they're going to test you for drugs, Latrel, and if that mess is in your system, your career goes straight down the drain. Don't ruin your life over stupid mistakes. I've heard of young black men going to jail, for years, being caught with one single joint in their possession. Consider this a warning, and it's coming from someone who loves you. Don't be a fool, but remember, you're the one who will write your life story, not me."

I pulled my chair away from the table and headed back upstairs to my room.

How dare Reggie tell him that I'd tried marijuana before, and . . . so what, a long time ago, maybe I did. I didn't like it, and therefore, never, ever tried it again. I knew Monica was calling me a hypocrite and I could hear her saying "how soon do we forget."

Chapter Eight

Unlike the last time, Latrel and I quickly settled our differences. That evening, I left the hotel with Roc and Monica, but received a phone call from Latrel, apologizing for his stupidity. He realized that doing drugs wasn't in his best interest, and promised me that he would not pick up another joint. I wasn't sure if I believed him or not, but he was the one who had to live with his choices.

I felt the same way about Reggie. After seeing him with Yvette, I knew it was time for me to get over my hurt and forget about what could have been. Yes, it was a true disappointment that our marriage had ended as it did, but what could I do if my husband didn't love me anymore? That's what he said, but I could see in his eyes that he was starting to realize his mistakes. I'm not sure if my being with Roc had Reggie looking at things a little differently, but I sensed that he'd regretted his decision. For me, it was too late and I had no intentions on ever looking back again.

I sat at the library for a few hours reading books and surfing the Internet on my laptop. I asked Roc to meet me there, but he was already about an hour late. When he finally showed, he seemed to be in a rush. We sat at the wooden table together and did our best to whisper.

"Do you have somewhere you need to be?" I asked.

"Kind of, sort of. Why . . . what's up?"

"I won't keep you, but I bought something for you."

I reached in my leather carrying bag full of books and gave Roc two books that I'd purchased for him. One was titled *A Complete Guide to Preparing for Your GED*, and the other was *Secrets to Becoming a Professional Model*.

"Listen," I said. "You don't have to jump into these right away, but just consider looking through them, okay?"

Roc flipped through the modeling book first, then lifted the other book. "You really tryin' ain't you?"

"Yes. I think you have major potential and I'd love to see you living your life to the fullest. Ever since that incident at the club happened, I've been worried about you. When the news comes on, I'm so afraid they're going to mention your name. You go days and days without calling me, and there are times that I fear I'll never hear from you again. Please don't take my gifts as an insult. Consider them given to you by someone who cares."

Roc sat back in the chair and folded his arms. "I know you care, but like I said before, I'm doin' me. I'm not interested in becomin' a model and a GED really can't do much for me. I mean, I was inspired by Latrel's success, but we come for two different backgrounds. He had you and yo' silly-ass ex husband, and I'm sure that made all of the difference for him. You don't even wanna know where I come from, but whether you recognize it or not, I do view my life as being successful. I got money, I take care of my kid, and I keep a roof over my head. What more do you think a nigga want?"

"Legitimacy. Stop living in a fantasy world, thinking you can live as you do forever. All I'm saying is that getting your GED can start open-ing some doors for you that may have otherwise been closed. You've got to start somewhere, Roc, and I can't think of a better time than now."

I reached in my bag again and retrieved some black-and-white professional photos of myself that I'd had taken almost twenty years ago. Some of the pictures were very provocative and many were not. In one of my favorite pictures, I was shirtless and my breasts were covered by my crossed arms. My lower half was covered with bikini bottoms and I wore high stilettos. I gave the pictures to Roc and he looked through them.

"Those were taken back in the day, but I gave up on pursuing my modeling career. I had plenty of offers from major modeling agencies, but Reggie insisted that he didn't want me to go that route. He promised to take care of me and insisted that I kept working to a minimal. I gave up everything for us, Roc, and became content with my marriage. Years later, here I am. I'm heavier, but I will always wonder where my modeling career could have taken me. I barely get by as an administrative assistant and I in no way envisioned the life that I now have. All I'm asking you to do is take care of Roc, and never be a fool for someone else. That shouldn't be so hard to do, should it?"

Roc kept looking at my pictures, then put my favorite one inside of his jacket and zipped it. I knew this conversation was too deep for him, and he really didn't have much else to say. "Look, I gotta go take care of some business," he said, standing up. "If I don't talk to you before Thanksgiving this Thursday, have a good one."

He leaned down to kiss me, but I backed away. "You can't kiss me in the library."

"*Shiit*," he said loud enough where the people at another table heard him. "Don't you know by now that I can do whatever the hell I wanna do, where I wanna do it and when I wanna do it?"

He tucked the books I'd given him underneath his arm and reached for my hand. "Come here," he said, directing me down one of the empty aisles. He turned me to face him and moved my bangs away from my forehead. He then reached in his pocket and tried to give me five one-hundred dollar bills.

"Here, take this money and go buy yourself somethin' nice. I don't want you strugglin' and to hear that kind of shit just makes me mad."

"No," I said, refusing to take his money. "I'll be fine, even though it may take some time for me to get on my feet. I'm a survivor, Roc, and that's what my mother always taught me to be."

Roc touched my bangs again, getting a clear view of my makeup-less face. "You are such a beautiful woman, Dez, and yo' body is sexier than ever. I know you're not insecure about it, and if you are, I sure as hell can't tell. The woman in those pictures look nice, but I like what I got in front of me. I don't deserve you, but I'm glad you stickin' with me. Nothin' means more to me than a woman who got my back. Rememba, I got yours too."

He leaned in again for a kiss, but this time, I didn't stop him. The kiss went on for quite some time and it was good to hear that Roc was just as comfortable with my healthiness as I was.

"Mmm," he said with approval. "I love the shit out of those lips. After I get finished with my business, can I come over tonight?"

"Why are you asking, you never do. And like you said, you do whatever you want, when you want to do it and wherever. I guess if I see you tonight, that depends on you."

Right then, his phone vibrated and after he looked to see who it was, he quickly kissed my cheek. "See you later," he said. I nodded and Roc jetted.

Roc never showed up that night, and since he told me to have a happy Thanksgiving, I didn't expect to hear from him until it was over. For years, I looked forward to Thanksgiving Day. Now, it was just another day to give thanks and a day to be by myself. Latrel was spending Thanksgiving with one of his friends, and since my mother had died almost four years ago, I really had no place to go. Monica had gone to visit her kids and I was so sure that Reggie had made arrangements with his family and his woman. It was times like this that being an only child really hurt. I always had Reggie and Latrel to spend the holidays with, but this year alone would be a first. When Latrel asked what I was doing, I lied, telling him that Monica and I had plans. I didn't want to cause him to change his plans, worrying about me. And when Monica asked what I was doing, I told her I was spending some time with Latrel. I don't know why I had been dishonest, but I decided to attend my pity party all by myself. I did, however, cook a small Cornish hen, some dressing, and gravy to go with it. I laid a comfortable blanket on the floor in my family room in front of the fireplace, and got some wine. I turned down all the lights and clicked on the television. Nothing that I wanted to watch was on, so I turned on the stereo, listening to one slow jam after the next. Patti Labelle's "Love, Need and Want You" was playing, and when the phone rang, I turned it down.

"Hello," I answered.

"Happy Thanksgiving," Reggie said loudly, as I could hear all the noise in the background.

I was surprised that he had called. "Same to you."

"Are you busy?"

"No."

"Are you alone?" I didn't answer, so Reggie cleared his throat. "I wasn't trying to disturb you, but I just wanted to call. My mother asked about you and she thought you'd stop by to see her."

"I thought about it, but I changed my mind. Be sure to tell her I said happy Thanksgiving. Tell the rest of your family I said so too."

"I will. Take care, baby."

I hung up and sipped from my wine. All of Reggie's family knew he'd been cheating on me, including his mother. I couldn't stand to be around any of them and I would've been embarrassed to show my face. I hoped he was having fun, and at least he called to wish me a happy Thanksgiving. I guess I should have been grateful, because he really didn't have to do that.

The Lifetime Channel had a good movie on, so I laid on my stomach while checking it out. I continuously sipped from my wine and left the volume on the stereo slightly up so I could hear it. All of my lights were out, but the fire still burning in the fireplace provided a comfortable and peaceful setting.

A commercial came on, and that's when I got up to refill my glass of wine. As I was in the kitchen, the phone rang again. This time it was Roc.

"What you doin'?" he asked. I could hear noise coming from his background as well.

"Watching television."

"Have you been at home all day, or did you spend time with yo' peeps?"

"I've been here," I said drily.

"Did you cook?"

"A little."

"Is there enough for me?"

"No. I ate it all."

"So, you mean to tell me you didn't save me nothin'?"

"Unfortunately not."

"Why, are you mad at me about somethin'?"

"Do I have a reason to be mad?"

"No, I'm just askin'. You sound as if somethin's wrong. Do you have company?"

"Is this twenty questions?"

"No, it's *To Tell the Truth*. Again, do you have company? If so, I can always check back with you some other time."

"Happy Thanksgiving, Roc. Good-bye."

I hung up. Yes, I was a little perturbed that Roc hadn't showed or called the other night like he said he would. I had been tuned into the news, and like always, expected to hear that something bad had happened to him. That was the first time he'd said he was coming and never did, so I tried to cut him some slack. As for today, it was almost 9:00 P.M. I guess my name was last on his agenda, but again, at least I was thought about.

I carried my wine bottle into the family room and resumed watching TV. The movie had gotten even better, and as it neared the end, my doorbell rang. I kind of knew who it was, but I could never be too sure. I tightened the belt on my black silk robe and teased my messy hair. I took one last sip from my glass of wine and went to the door. It was Roc, leaning against the doorway. He had a plate in his hand, covered with aluminum foil.

"Can I come in, or is that nigga still here?"

I opened the door wide, allowing him to enter. He looked spectacular in his casual dark brown leather jacket with fur around the collar and denim baggy jeans. A brown Inspired T-shirt was underneath and an arrowhead necklace that looked like it came straight from Africa was gripped around his neck. There were a fresh pair of leather Timberlands on his feet and he wasted no time in taking them off, along with his jacket. Like always, the T-shirt hugged his muscles, showing off the numerous tattoos on his arms.

"How did you get rid of him that fast?" he persisted.

"Did I tell you there was someone here when you called?"

"No, but you sounded like there was."

I threw my hand back and went back into the family room. Roc followed, putting the plate in his hand on a table.

"You got it awfully damn cozy in here. House all dark, fireplace burning, music playin', wine-glasses on the floor." He reached his hand underneath my robe, feeling my bare ass. "Panties off and shit. What the hell been goin' on with you?"

I ignored Roc and laid back on the floor. I turned on my stomach, picked up my glass of wine, and focused on the television. He immediately laid on my backside, holding himself over me in a push-up position.

"Are you gon' talk to me or what?" he asked.

"Only when you start talking what I want to hear. Thus far, you're throwing false accusations at me and I'm not interested."

Roc dropped his heavy body on mine, pressing down so I couldn't breathe.

"Can you talk now?" he joked.

I tried to push him backward, but couldn't. "Get up," I strained. "You're too heavy."

"What's that? I can't hear you. What you say?"

I was defeated and when I told him I seriously couldn't breathe, he moved over next to me. "That's what yo' bad ass get. Don't be tryin' to ignore me."

I turned on my back, looking over at Roc. "For your information, I've been here all day by myself. I've been watching television and ate a little something before you came."

"Why didn't you go visit your family?"

"Because the family I did have was Reggie's family. My mother died a few years back, and my father died when I was nineteen. I told you before that I was an only child, so—"

"You should have told me you was gon' be by yourself. I would have come over earlier."

"It's okay. If you haven't noticed, I don't mind being by myself."

"I noticed. You stay in the house too much. I don't think I ever met nobody as secluded as you."

"I haven't always been like this. Things changed and—"

Roc rubbed my stomach while looking down at me. "Are you depressed? Maybe you should see somebody about how you've been feelin'."

"I don't know. I just think it takes time to heal, that's all." I touched the sexy trimmed hair on his chin. "Either way, I'm glad you're here and thanks for coming."

"You knew damn well I was comin'. I seriously thought you was over here slappin' bodies with some nigga."

"And if I was, what would you have done?"

Roc smiled. "Yo' ass would have been in trouble."

"Big trouble?"

"Yeah, eleven-inch trouble."

"I thought it was ten-and-a-half inch trouble?"

"You thought wrong. I'm still growing . . . wanna see?"

"Nah," I teased. "Not today. Some other time."

Roc started tickling me and my stomach was killing me from laughing so hard. My robe had slid open, exposing my left wobbly breast and hard nipple. Roc wasted no time putting his tongue in action. His hand was creeping down between my legs, but when I heard Beyoncé crooning "At Last" on my *Cadillac Records* CD, I interrupted him and stood up.

"I love this song," I said. "Turn off the television and slow dance with me, okay?"

Roc stood up, laughing. "You know you can't dance."

"Whatever. Then just hold me."

I turned off the television, upped the volume on the stereo and Roc had no problem holding me in his arms. My head rested against his chest and we slowly moved from side to side. I took in every word that Beyoncé sung and felt as if, at last, my lonely nights were over. In my head, I played back the moment I'd met Roc at the car wash, to the first time I'd seen him at the club. The night of his birthday was still fresh in my memory, and so was the first night he'd entered me as we had sex on my swing. At this moment and time, I was falling for him. His age no longer mattered and all I wanted was to be with the man whose heart I could feel beating just as fast as mine. One song ended, and another one played. We remained in the same position, having very little to say. The fire had even stopped burning in the fireplace and when the room turned pitch-black, I still wasn't ready to call it quits.

"What are you thinking?" I asked Roc.

"Let's see . . . where do I start?"

"You can start wherever you want to."

Roc backed away from our embrace, holding my hands together with his. "I got a lot of shit goin' on, Dez. But make no mistake about it, nothin' compares to bein' right here with you. It's like I'm in another world, tryin' hard to do somethin' different. When I get back to reality, sometimes, my shit be so fucked up. I don't wanna take you into that world, baby, but it's almost impossible not to. There's no way for me to have it both ways, and I'm afraid of losin' this. How can I not lose this, travelin' down the road I am? The closer we get, you gon' make me choose and I don't know what the fuck to do. All I know is you ain't here for nothin'. And it ain't no fuck thing either. I love that pussy, but it ain't just that, trust me."

At first, I had no response for what Roc had said. I reached up to touch his face and felt the need to share how I felt in the moment. I wasn't sure if it was my loneliness making me feel this way, or my possible desperation to have any kind of man in my life. Roc continued to ease much of my pain and my feelings for him had increased. "I—I feel myself falling in love with you," I admitted. "And anything I can do to make your life simpler and peaceful, let me know. That's the only reason I'm here. In the meantime, all I ask is that if you tell me you're coming to see me, and you're unable to make it, just call to let me know. That way I won't worry so much about you, okay?"

"I promise. But I want you to do me a favor too. Let me take care of you, a'ight? I know you don't approve of the way I make money, but no matter where it comes from, it spends the same way. Also, stop stayin' cooped up in this fuckin' house. Let's get out and do somethin'. Wherever you wanna go, I'll take you. I don't give a fuck if it's to the gym or to Japan, let's go. All you gotta do is say the word."

"I'll think about it, okay? But as far as the money is concerned, you're asking me to accept what you do. I don't say much about it, but I can't accept your contributions. I know you mean well, but this is something I have to stand my ground on."

Roc kissed my forehead and our lips soon met up. Moments later, we returned to our position on the floor. I felt something good stirring between us, and even the sex between us felt . . . different. I wasn't even disappointed that he hadn't said the "*l*" word to me, and I in no way wanted him to say it unless he meant it. For Roc, that would take time. I didn't know yet if I would allow him that time, but I continued to be patient. I was having fun and so was he. The empty void I had was being filled by a man I never thought could do it, and for that alone, I was grateful. Roc stayed with me for two days after that night, and when he left, I hated like hell to see him go.

Chapter Nine

When Christmas came, I spent the day with Monica. We cooked a bunch of food and took it to her family's house. Latrel stayed away again, and this holiday, I didn't hear from Reggie at all. I didn't hear from Roc either but on Christmas Eve he stopped by to bring my presents. One was a diamond curved journey pendant in white gold and the other gift was several sexy pieces of negligee. I thanked him for the gifts, and instead of telling him that I would never wear them, I tucked the necklace and negligee far away in the back of my closet. In return, I gave him a shirt and tie, a personalized fourteen-karat gold dog tag pendant and a sentimental key to my heart message in a bottle. I addressed the personal message to Snookums, and like always, encouraged him to strive for the best. He told me he had plans to spend Christmas with his son, and also mentioned working at the club. Working the club was his plan for New Year's as well, and he did his best to get me to come. I refused. Spending my New Year's at home was where I wanted to be. I couldn't complain because Roc had stuck to his word about getting me out of the house. We started going out to dinner a lot, checking out the latest movies together, working out, and even had a road trip planned to Las Vegas. Everywhere we'd gone, Roc was known. He had to be the most popular person in St. Louis, and we could barely eat dinner without being interrupted by someone he knew. That included females, but as long as Roc didn't disrespect me when we were together, I was fine. I had some concerns with his son's mother, Vanessa, but thus far, she hadn't said anything to me. She continuously rang Roc's phone. She'd been stressing the hell out of him about their son, and she left some of her personal belongings in his truck so I could see them. As a woman, I knew what her intentions were, and just as I knew about her, I was sure she'd known about me. I wasn't sure if they lived together or not until Roc invited me to his penthouse apartment in downtown St. Louis. He said it was one of the many places he called home, and I must admit, his place was laid out. Disapproving of his lifestyle, I definitely didn't stay long, but long enough for me to realize that whatever he was into, the shit was deep. I could smell the money in his rooms, and the whole place was decorated with some of the finest contemporary furniture that only a rich man's money could buy. His penthouse was spacious, and had not one, but three floors. Everything was neatly in place and if it hadn't been for the walk-in closet I'd seen filled with Roc's clothes and tennis shoes, I wouldn't have believed he lived there. Too, the books I'd given him were on the floor next to his bed, and I was happy to see that he'd delved into them. I was pleased not to see anything belonging to a woman, but I did notice several pictures of his son, and I assumed, baby's mama. The black-and-white photo he had taken from me at the library that day was on the front of his stainless steel double-door refrigerator. He claimed that he had to see my pretty face every morning, and said that seeing the picture motivated him. He kissed the picture, something he said he'd done every day, and when I told him he was full of it, we laughed and left.

The day of our road trip to Vegas, Roc came to get me in a rented RV. Needless to say, it was laid out as well. It had everything from a compact kitchen to a spacious bedroom in the far back. Flat-screen panel TVs were in both spaces and the bed was dressed with a paisley printed blue and gold bedding ensemble. Plush pillows were on the bed for comfort and two reclining chairs were included in the room for extra relaxation. Roc jumped on the bed, putting his hands behind his head.

"We 'bout to have some fun up in this muthafucka. My man up there got the wheel and we ain't got nothin' but hours and hours of time on our hands."

I lay on the bed next to Roc, resting my head on his chest. "Yes, hours to catch up on some sleep and read some of my books."

"*Shiit*. I hope you ain't bring none of those books with you 'cause you damn sho ain't gon' be readin' them. As for sleep, you'll sleep when I do and that ain't gon' be no time soon."

I poked at his chest. "So, let me get this straight, you got everything planned out already, huh?"

"Yep. Been thinkin' 'bout this vacation all week. You may as well get naked right now 'cause it's 'bout to go down in here."

"What's the rush? Like you said, we got hours and hours and—"

Roc reached for a pillow, hitting me with it. "Oh, no you didn't," I said, picking up one to hit him back. We went back and forth, hitting each other with pillows, and unfortunately one of them busted, spreading feathers everywhere.

"Awww," he said, grabbing my waist, luring me back on the bed. "Look what you did?"

"Damn, am I in trouble? I guess this means I'm in trouble again."

"Big trouble. Eleven-and-a-half-inch trouble."

"Growing again, huh?"

Roc reached for his belt to remove it. "You wanna see?"

"Nah, I wanna feel it. Let me be the judge on how big I think it's getting."

"You ain't said nothin' but a word."

Roc wasted no time *showing* me how big he'd gotten. I had never fucked so much in my life, but I could never get enough of him. He couldn't get enough of me either, and I was always required to step up my game. After one lengthy ride on top of him, he turned my sweaty body to the side, plunging into me from behind. My right leg was being held high, separated from my left one, which remained straight and relaxed on the bed. Roc entered my juiced-up dripping wet hole, while stroking my perky clit like a violin to bring more pleasure. He plucked my heavy nipples, and I sucked in major air, unable to keep my mouth closed.

"Whu—What is it with this pussy?" he inquired. "Why yo' shit gotta be so good like this?"

I turned my head sideways to suck in his awaiting lips. "It's your dick, baby. Your good dick just brings out the best in me."

"Well let me keep on bringin' it."

He let go of my leg, turning me flat on my stomach. My legs were squeezed tightly together and Roc slid into my tightened butt cheeks. He dropped his head on my back, letting out a deep sigh of pure satisfactory relief.

"Ahhh, this shit feels good. Don't move yet, okay?" he said.

I wouldn't dare move. With my legs closely together, his ongoing inches of hardness was killing me. I requested that he proceed with ease, and he honored my request. I then hiked my butt in the air just a little, gripping the sheets as he navigated in and out of me from different angles. My eyes were closed and all I could think about was how Roc was delivering all of the right moves to make me his. He lowered his head, pulling my hair aside to place continuous wet kisses on my shoulders and upper back. His rhythm stayed on point, until he stopped and called out my name.

"Yeah baby," I said raining cum, and softly moaning from his sensational kisses.

He nibbled on my ear, whispering, "I love you, a'ight? I don't say that shit too often, but when I do, you betta know that shit is real."

I kept my eyes closed and nodded. I knew Roc and I were dealing with something special, but I was in no way sure about trusting his words.

It was so easy to say something like that being caught up in the moment, and it was important for me to hear those words when we weren't. He lived in another world that I really didn't care to know much about. I did, however, know that other women revolved around in that world, and the possibilities of him truly loving any woman were slim. My thing was, show me love, don't tell me. And until he was willing to let go of his other life, the only thing he was showing me that he enjoyed having his cake and eating it too. For now, things were okay, and I felt no need to turn up the pressure. I wasn't really sure how I felt about my growing feelings for him, but I was optimistic that we'd grow in a positive manner.

According to Roc, we had almost eight more hours to go until we reached Vegas. I was tired from my ongoing workout and took a moment to catch a nap while lying on a pillow on his lap. He sat up watching television and when his phone rang, it woke me from my sleep. I kept my eyes closed, continuing to lightly snore because I figured Roc could see me through the many glass mirrors in the room.

"Speak," he said. He paused for a moment, but I couldn't make out a word that the other person was saying. "Just tell them muthafuckas to be patient, I'm on my way. When I get to the hotel room, I'll call you." He paused again. "Ronnie, you know better than I do that them niggas anxious. I got this shit under control and it's gon' bring great rewards." Ronnie kept talking, then Roc spoke out again. "Nah, I ain't with her, I'm with Desa Rae. I almost had to cut that bitch before I left, and I'll talk to you 'bout that shit when I get back." He paused. "Yeah, I'm good. My dick hurt," he laughed. "but I'm good. Baby girl been workin' this muthafucka out." It was Ronnie's turn to speak again, and I heard laughter. "All I can say is she got yo' nephew wide open. Yo' playbook failin' a nigga bad over here." He laughed again. "Yeah, I know. That's what I'm afraid of. Like I said, though, I'll get at you when I arrive in Vegas."

Roc ended his call and I still pretended to be asleep. I knew damn well this Vegas trip wasn't planned so he could make one of his runs. If so, our trip was about to get ugly. I continued to lay on his lap, and after a few more minutes, a familiar smell hit my nose.

I lifted my head, just to be sure. Yes, Roc was inhaling the smoke from a joint and continued to suck it in.

He could barely get the word *what* to come from his mouth and talked like he had gunpowder in his throat. "Why you lookin' at me like that?" He swallowed, holding the joint with the tips of his fingers.

"I'm stunned," I said, shaking my head. "I can't believe you would do that in front of me, knowing how I feel about it."

He laid the joint in an ashtray beside him. "Damn, Dez, I wasn't doin' it in front of you. Yo' ass was sleepin' and after all that sex, I needed somethin' to relax me."

I sat up straight, having no smile on my face. "There are certain things that I'm not going to tolerate. Your weed habit is one of them. If you don't put that mess out, then we're going to have a serious problem on our hands. Your baby's mama won't be the only *bitch* you'll have to cut, and if there is one ounce of cocaine or any kinds of drugs on this RV, I'm turning your ass in to the police." I threw the covers aside and got off the bed.

Roc responded with "Fuck you" and took another hit from his joint.

No lie, he caught me off guard. My face scrunched up, big-time. "What did you say to me?"

He got off the bed and stood over me. His fiery eyes stared deeply into mine, and he clarified what he'd said, gritting his teeth. "I said, fuck you! You ain't my muthafuckin' mama. I told you 'bout that shit, and rule number one . . . don't you ever threaten to call the police on me. Two, if you start actin' like that bitch back at home, you will be treated like her. Three, you just ruined my fuckin' day. Don't say shit else to me and when we get to Vegas, feel free to take the first flight back home."

So much for optimism. Roc went into the bathroom and slammed the door. I got dressed and spent the remainder of our drive to Vegas sitting at the circular booth in the kitchen. As soon as we got to Vegas, I took his advice. I called a cab that took me to the airport and left. Roc went on to handle his business, and just like me, there was nothing else left to say. I had seen an ugly side of him and there was no way for me to deal with that kind of behavior.

There was a delay at the airport, but I got home early Sunday morning. I had already taken a vacation day for Monday, and I truly needed the extra day to clear my head. I could have kicked myself for putting my guards down, and deep down, I knew what kind of man Roc was. *Had I been in denial?* I thought. And what made me think that a man like him would change because I wanted him to? I was hurt by what had happened, and I couldn't stop thinking about his angry face that stared at me with disrespect.

After I showered, I sat on my bed to check my messages. Latrel and Monica had called, trying to find out how my vacation was going. I didn't feel like talking about it, so I waited to call them back. I had three other messages, one from a bill collector and the other two were from Roc's baby's mama, Vanessa. She left a number for me to call her back, insisting that it was *now* time for us to talk. I wasn't sure how she got my number, but I knew a woman had her way of finding out things. I had no desire to speak to her, so I deleted her messages. Besides, her tone was shitty and I wasn't going to take orders from a woman who I considered to be very childish. She'd have to get her answers from Roc, but I was sure his response would be full of lies.

Due to the short work week ahead of me, I got in bed early that Monday night. My eyes were tired from reading and I put the book on my nightstand so I could go to sleep. Almost simultaneously, the phone rang and there was heavy knocking on my door. I carried the cordless phone in my hand, but before answering the unknown call, I went to the door to see who it was. When I opened the door, it was Roc. I immediately answered the phone, and the first response I got was, "Ancient-ass bitch, what's up with you and Roc?"

"Hello," I repeated, looking at the pissed look on Roc's face.

"You heard me. I got his son and you ain't never gon' take my man from me."

"Good luck with that," I said, handing the phone over to Roc.

He curiously looked at it, then put it up to his ear. "Hello," he snapped. I could hear Vanessa blasting him through the phone. He hung up, and when it rang again, he looked at the caller ID. He showed it to me, and why did Reggie's name and number flash across it? Roc threw the phone into the wall, shattering it into pieces.

"What the fuck up with you?" he yelled with a pitbull mug on his face. I could see how irate he was, and I did my best not to go there with him.

"We're not going out like this, Roc. I swear I'm not going to do this with you. Why don't you leave and come back when you've calmed down."

"Why, 'cause that nigga called to tell you he was on his way?"

"No, I don't know why he's calling. Maybe—"

"Maybe my ass! You ain't stopped fuckin' with him so quit yo' lyin'."

I couldn't bear to see him so angry and he wasn't going to stay another minute in my house. I spoke as politely as I could. "You're not welcomed here under these conditions, Roc. Please don't do this to us. You're going to ruin what we have."

He pointed to his chest. "I'm gon' ruin it? Nah, yo' ass ruined this shit when you talked about callin' the police on me! I thought you had my muthafuckin' back? How you gon' say some shit like that?"

I held my lips together, trying to muffle my words. I could see that the wrong move would set him off and this was a dangerous position to be in.

He was persistent with getting me to respond, and obviously, was used to the back-and-forth, fight-me-then-fuck-me drama.

"Answer me, Dez!"

I remained stone-faced, until Roc pulled the back of my hair, shoving me into the living room. I stumbled to the couch, where I fell face forward. I hurried to turn around and used my kicking feet to keep him at a distance.

"You're a real man, Roc. Is this the kind of shit in your uncle's playbook!" I yelled.

"And then some," he said, trying to grab my swinging legs. I did my best to disable him by kicking between his legs, but to no avail. Roc's strength was too much for me to handle. He gripped the back of my neck, while holding my face down on the couch. He used his other hand to tear at my panties, promising to give Reggie his sloppy leftovers. I wanted to cry so badly, but I didn't want to give him the satisfaction. How could the man who just told me he loved me the other day, treat me so ill. Without a condom on, he plunged deep into me, pounding my insides hard. So hard, that when I felt the wetness between my legs, I didn't know if it were my juices flowing or blood. Like a thief in the night, he busted me wide open, taking what did not belong to him. Did I consider it rape? Possibly, but as he questioned me about stopping, I encouraged him not to. I had to be out of my mind to feel anything for Roc, but there was something about the way he made me feel that I couldn't control. I squeezed my eyes, taking deep breaths to soothe my excruciating pain. *This couldn't be happening*, I thought. *Why would he do this to me?* Roc continued to tear into me like a hammer being slammed against a piece of meat. He finally let go of my neck and I felt him come inside of me. He slowly pulled out and a gush of his juices ran down my inner thighs. He breathed heavily, slowing it down with each breath. I eased myself away from him, rushing to the bathroom to clean up. I turned on the hot water and quickly got into the shower. First, I wet my face, just so Roc wouldn't see the many tears that had fallen.

I then scrubbed between my legs, and there was some blood that came onto the rag. I knew Roc would come into the bathroom, and when he did, it was filled with steam. I couldn't even look at him, so all I did was stare at the wall in front of me without saying a word. He slid the glass door aside, then stepped into the shower facing me. His clothes were on, therefore, allowing them to get wet. He rubbed my wet hair back and wrapped his arms around my trembling body.

"I am so, so sorry. I know you ain't tryin' to hear this, but I've been goin' through so much shit lately and . . . and I never meant to take my problems out on you. My uncle Ronnie been on my back, the cops been snoopin' around, and I don't need to tell you what's been goin' down with me and Vanessa. I wasn't goin' to Vegas to deliver no product. I had plans to meet with some of Ronnie's partners about some future possible connections, but that's it. Other than that, the trip was 'bout you and me. You my peace of mind, baby. I need that shit, ma. When you said you'd call the cops on me, I didn't know how to handle it. I do my best to avoid jail, Dez, and I'm fearful of a woman who start talkin' that kind of shit. How I know you ain't Five-O? I trusted you and I felt like you would betray me."

I still hadn't said a word, and at this point, I didn't have to. My psychotic look said it all and Roc knew that it was time to leave me alone.

"*Dezzzz*," he pleaded while touching my chin. I snatched my face away from his touch. "Baby, don't do this. I know you, ma. You gon' stop messin' with me, ain't you? Do—don't do that and I promise I'll never hurt you again. I promise . . . my word, my bond."

I looked up at Roc, blinking the constant dripping water from my eyelids. "Please leave," I whispered. "I ca—can't do this with you."

"Baby, please don't say that. I'll go, but not for long. Anything you want me to do, I'll do it! I give you my word that nothin' like this will happen again. I'll stop smokin' that shit, and if you want me to stop movin' and shakin' I'll consider doin' that too. I'll stay right here with you, just so you can keep yo' eyes on me. I ain't lyin' to you, baby. I need this shit between you and me. I fucked up, but I'm willin' to make it right."

Roc wasn't listening to me and was so determined to have his way. I honestly didn't know what to do or where to turn. I wanted him out of my house, but he was so on edge. I'd thought about calling the police, but that would have made matters worse. Instead, I stepped out of the shower, wrapping myself with a towel. I laid across my bed, thinking about all that had happened. I knew I would never forgive Roc for what he'd done, and it broke my heart that this had come to an end. I cuddled the pillow next to me and several tears fell onto it. Roc removed his wet clothes, and after he dried himself, he wrapped the towel around his waist. He got in bed behind me, pulling me close to him.

"I'm leavin' in the mornin'. I wanna spend what may be my last night with you, holdin' you in my arms. Trust, you've grown on me and I did my best not to bring my drama to you. I'm gon' make some changes and only 'cause I care for you like that. You'll see, yeah, you definitely gon' see."

I closed my eyes so I wouldn't see and mustered up enough courage to remain in bed with a man who I had lost all respect for. Morning couldn't come soon enough, and I hoped and prayed that it would the last time I'd ever see Roc's face again.

Chapter Ten

After all of the flowers, the apologetic cards, the ongoing phone calls to tell me how sorry he was, the unexpected visits to my job and to my house, and even the water in his eyes that I'd seen the other night as he'd pleaded for forgiveness on my porch . . . I still wasn't moved. This had been going on for at least a month and Roc was driving me crazy. Finally, after not hearing from him for a couple more weeks, it seemed as if he'd backed off. I was okay with that, and my life had started to feel normal again. I got my phone number changed, not because of the phone calls from Roc, but because of the calls from his woman. She and her girlfriends were playing on my phone, and it frustrated me even more that I'd gotten myself caught up in some foolishness like this.

I stopped at the bank on Friday, then headed for Target to pick up a few items. The March weather was playing tricks on us in St. Louis, and one day it was chilly and the next day the sun was shining bright. Today was kind of in-between. The sun was coming through for us, but it was a chilly forty-eight degrees outside.

We'd had casual day at work, so I had on my off the shoulder fuchsia sweater, my fitted jeans, and black leather high-heel boots. Pantene had my hair on point, and it was full of everlasting body. While in Target, I reached for a cart and rolled it around to find some of the items I needed. I stopped in the lingerie section, looking for a new bra, then picked out a few simple cotton nightgowns to bum around the house in. Just as I was heading to look at the pots and pans, someone caught my eye. I saw him in the concession stand with his back turned and arms folded. He was talking to two young women who were standing in front of him, grinning ear to ear. Why wouldn't they be happy? He wore jeans stitched in black-and-white and Nike body-fitting long-sleeve shirt looked dynamic against his dark chocolate skin. A black belt held up his pants and fresh black tennis shoes covered his feet. A Nike gym bag was on the floor next to him, and it appeared that he'd just come from the gym. The chicks must have said something funny, and when he turned his head sideways to blush, he also laughed, showing those addictive pearly whites. For sure, it was Roc and when he put the gym bag on his shoulder and covered his eyes with some dark shades, that was my cue to get back to shopping. I did watch him walk away from the concession stand and his fineness demanded attention. It was as if he was moving in slow motion, and looked as if he belonged in a rap video. The two women at the concession stand kept their eyes on him, several of the cashiers had turned their heads, and the women at customer service were nudging each other too. I took one last look, and when his head turned in my direction, I rolled my cart into the aisle. I picked out a new set of pots and pans, got some towels for Latrel, and couldn't leave without my toiletries. I wanted to look for another book to read, but I changed my mind. The cashier bagged my items and once the transaction was finished, I headed out the door. No sooner than I stepped outside, I saw Roc leaned against the trunk of my car. His arms were folded and his legs were spread far apart. I rolled my cart right up to him, politely asking him to move so I could put my items in the trunk. He lifted the shades from his eyes, resting them on the top of his head. A book was on my trunk, and when I looked at it, it was the study guide for his GED.

"Check this out," he said, holding the book in his hand and turning to a particular page. "I've been doin' some studyin' but I'm confused about somethin'. Do you think you can help me with this problem? You seem like a pretty smart lady."

I popped my trunk, putting my bags inside. When I closed it, Roc pointed to the book. "Are you gon' help me? I just need to know how to do this, that's all."

I knew what he was up to, but I took the book and held it in my hand. He stood behind me while looking over my shoulder. "The one right there," he said pointing to a mathematical equation. Honestly, I tried to figure it out, but couldn't. And the longer I stood, the closer Roc got to me. "You look nice," he whispered in my ear. "Can I get yo' sevens again?" I quickly turned around, closing the book.

"You'll have to check in to this on the Internet or hire a tutor. I've been out of school for too long and I've forgotten how to do a lot of that stuff."

"Why can't you tutor me? I'll pay for your time."

"I just told you I didn't know how to do it. You'll be wasting your money."

I walked away, heading for my car door to get inside. "Wait—wait a minute," Roc said, coming up to me. He handed me a large envelope.

"I hope this isn't some more stuff about Reggie. I really don't care, Roc, and—"

"No, trust me, it's not. It's somethin' I want you to look at. I need yo' help with that too."

I shrugged and opened my car door. "Sure."

Roc held the door so I wouldn't close it. "Can I come over tonight?"

"For what?"

"'Cause I miss you, ma. I wanna make love to you and my dick ain't been right since you've givin' up on it."

"You got all these women out here throwing themselves at you and I doubt that your dick has been deprived. It never has been, nor will it ever be. My only problem is, how dare you *take* sex from me and not use a condom. I don't know who Vanessa has been with, and I have not a clue how many women you've had sex with since you met me. In case you haven't inquired, our city is high ranked when it comes to STDs. I've been thinking a lot about that night you hurt me Roc, have you?"

"I think about it every single day. I wish like hell I can take it back, and you ain't got to worry 'bout me givin' you no disease. I stay strapped up, baby."

"So, are you honestly telling me I shouldn't be worried? Are you saying that you're 100 percent safe? Was I the only one giving you head without a condom? I doubt it, Roc, and damn you for putting me at risk."

"Why you bringin' up all this shit? Did I give you somethin'?"

"Not sure. But I got one hell of a discharge. I'm going to the doctor next week, and when I find out what's going on with my body, you don't want to be anywhere near me. Just leave me alone, okay?"

Roc really didn't have much else to say. I left the parking lot and pulled over at a nearby gas station to look inside of the envelope he'd given me. There were several pictures of him inside, all taken by a professional photographer. I smiled, looking through them one by one. Roc was absolutely gorgeous and he had definitely missed his calling to become a model. I truly hoped it wasn't too late for him and I was pleased that he'd taken the photos. There was a note included and it read:

Do me a favor and pass these on to some of your connections. Let's see what's up and thanks for yo' encouragement. I need you, baby, now more than ever. I thought a Christian woman like yourself was taught to forgive. You are a Christian, aren't you? PS. Can a nigga get his picture on the fridge?

Kiss me in the mornin' and just to let you know, I still kiss you every mornin' too.

Love, Snookums.

I laid the pictures in the seat next to me and let out a deep sigh. *Why did Roc have to take us there that day?* I thought. I wanted him erased from my memory, but with him showing up all the time, that was so hard to do. I had to forget about him and maybe my doctor's appointment would be just the jump-start I needed. I hoped there was nothing wrong with me, but with Roc being approached by so many women, I doubted that he was able to turn many of them away. I'm sure his young mind said "have at it" and I could only imagine what he'd been doing. I was so angry with myself for thinking I, and maybe Vanessa, were his only sexual partners. Still, I felt protected because we always used condoms. I silently prayed that everything would be okay, and until my appointment came, I knew I'd be on pins and needles.

Monday had come too fast. My appointment wasn't until Wednesday, and now I couldn't stop going to the bathroom to urinate. I wasn't sure what was going on and I hoped my condition wasn't brought on by a sexually transmitted disease. I was so mad at Roc and I couldn't get focused on doing my work while sitting at my desk.

Around noon, Mr. Wright called me into his office. He asked me to close the door, and after I did, I took a seat in front of his desk. Closing the door meant something was serious so I listened in.

"You've been here for almost fourteen years, Desa Rae, and I've been here for almost thirty. I got a call today from my boss, and unfortunately, they're eliminating my job. As you know, the economy is weak and it's definitely had an effect on us all. If they're eliminating my job, I guess you know they'll be eliminating yours too. I was told that we'll have no more than three months to find another job, and after that, we're out."

I sat there in disbelief. I had too many bills to pay and why did this have to happen to me now? I knew a lot of people had lost their jobs because of the economy, but it never dawned on me that I would be affected. Thank God my house was paid for, but I had to fork out a pretty penny each month for my Lincoln MKS and other bills. I had already made numerous cutbacks and really couldn't figure out how I could possibly make ends meet.

"I don't know what to say, Mr. Wright. I mean, what can I do? I have bills to pay, and ever since my divorce, I've relied on my paychecks from here. Is this final or did your boss say it was up for discussion."

"Unfortunately, Desa Rae, it's final. You can start to apply for some of the other positions around here, but many of those are being cut too. I'm sorry, and I know how difficult things have been for you. You'll get some money from the college, but not much. You can always draw your unemployment and maybe you do need to take some time off work. For a while, you seemed pretty upbeat. Then all of a sudden, things started to go back downhill. I've been keeping my eyes on you and you worry me. I know this news doesn't help in any way, and I'll do whatever I can to help you through this."

I was more than disappointed. I didn't have what one would call, plan B. I didn't have one with Reggie, didn't have one with Roc, and now this. I sadly looked down at my lap, while fiddling with my fingernails. "So, what are you going to do, Mr. Wright? Aren't you worried about this as well?"

He leaned back in his chair, placing his hands behind his head. "I was going to retire in a few years anyway, so I consider this an early retirement. My wife and I have always put away for a rainy day, so we'll be fine. If you haven't already, you should start doing the same. These jobs are never promised to us, and even after years and years of service, they can all go down the drain. Unfortunately for us, that's exactly what happened."

I thanked Mr. Wright for everything and left his office. And as soon as I got back to my desk, I went online to check out some of the other positions available at the college. After almost fourteen years of not needing a job, I had to update my résumé, so I sat at my desk doing just that. I also checked out other job opportunities online and jotted down a few that I was interested in. My head started to hurt so I downed two aspirin and headed for the bathroom. My urine just kept on flowing, but the discharge had lightened up a bit. Under enormous pressure, I splashed water on my face and rubbed my temples. My life sure was getting shitty, and for a forty-year-old, I expected it to be so much better. God promised not to put any more on me than I couldn't bear, but I had my doubts. I felt as if I was at my breaking point and the stress was unbelievable. Yes, I'd brought some of this on myself, but a lot of it had been put on me by some of the people in my life. If push came to shove, I'd have to ask Reggie for a job at his business and pretty much go from there. It was the last thing I wanted to do, but it was still an option.

When I got home that evening, I sat in the family room, searching for more job opportunities on the Internet. I occasionally sipped from my glass of wine and ate on the cheese and crackers that were next to me. Because of my situation, I'd gotten up enough nerve to call Reggie, just in case I needed him.

"Something has to be wrong. You haven't called me since—"

"I know. I've been busy and I haven't had time to reply to any of your messages."

"That's why I stopped leaving them. I was calling about your alimony payments, and I hope you've been getting them in the mail."

"Yes, I have. And thank you for being on time, it really helps."

"No problem. So . . . what's been up with you? You still hanging out with you-know-who?"

I was not about to tell Reggie the truth. "Sort of. We've been cooling out for a while because I've been so busy with work. My job is coming to an end, and Mr. Wright's been having me kind of busy."

"What? You're losing your job?"

"I'm afraid so."

"Dee, I'm sorry to hear that. You know I'll do what I can to help you, but the housing market hasn't been doing well either. I had to lay off

some folks, but I just sold one of my rental prop-
erties. Years ago, it was worth $145,000 dollars.
I had to sell it for almost half of that. You know
you got some money coming from that, and
when the deal is finalized, I'll make sure you get
it."

"Thank you. I can use all I can get."

"Well, look at it this way . . . the house is paid
for and you'll always have a roof over your head.
If there's one good thing we can account for during our marriage, it's that we had sense enough
to pay off our home. Don't get me wrong, there
were a lot of good things about our marriage, but
that was one of the smarter moves."

I nodded, and since Reggie was making cutbacks at work, I changed the subject. "I agree.
And while we're on the subject, if there were a
lot of good things in our marriage, how did you
manage to fall out of love with me?"

My question must have caught Reggie off
guard. I rarely questioned him about his decision, and when he asked for a divorce, I in no
way fought it. I didn't understand why I was asking now, but I guess a part of me wanted to know
why I was having such difficulties with men.

"Let's just say that you did your part, but I
didn't do mine. We got married at a young age,
Dez, and I always felt as if I was missing some-

thing. I wasn't proud about it, but I starting cheating on you and basically had no regrets. I may have fallen out of love with you, but I loved you enough to end it. I couldn't go on living that way, and you didn't deserve that."

"Why do men cheat, Reggie? Give me your honest opinion and maybe it'll help me understand things a little better."

"To sum it up, fear. I always had this fear of being a man, taking care of my wife and being there for my son. There was something inside of me, and it's still inside of me, where I can't get the concept of fully committing myself to a woman and being all that she needs me to be. See, this wasn't about you. We're not together and I'm still dealing with this. Most men have that same fear, but they won't admit it. I know that I will not be 100 percent fulfilled until I find a woman who is capable of helping me overcome my fear. Will that ever happen, I don't know. But my hat goes off to the men who've overcome. There's a certain aura about those men, and they tend to live some of the happiest and most fulfilled lives. Look at our president . . . he's a good example. I wanna get there too, baby, but unfortunately, I'm not there yet."

"So, I didn't help you overcome your fear."

"No. And even though you put everything you did into our marriage, I cannot answer why that fear of mine never, ever went away. It's something about me, Dez, which I have to figure out. I got six months to do it, and I'll be giving this marriage thing another shot."

I wasn't sure that I heard him correctly. "Did you say you're getting married again?"

"Yeah. I—"

"But you just told me that you haven't overcome your fear."

"I haven't. But I can't let that stop me. I gotta try."

"Reggie, you're going to wind up back in the same situation. Is Yvette the lucky one this time, or the Asian woman you've been seeing? Lord knows who else."

"It's somebody else. You haven't met her, but we've been dating for about a year."

I couldn't believe what Reggie was telling me. He was all over the place and I hoped like hell that Latrel wouldn't wind up like him. And even though his news was a surprise, my failed marriage was starting to feel better as time went on.

"Congrats. You know I wish you well."

"Same here."

We ended our call and my headache was going even stronger. I headed for bed and slept like a baby.

***

The day of reckoning had finally come. Thus far, my week had delivered major setbacks and the news about Reggie getting married had me on edge. I was so angry, and when I thought about all of the years I'd put into my job, I was upset about that too. I was definitely on a roll, but did my best to prepare for this moment.

I sat on the examination table with my hands clinched together, praying that everything would be okay. During the examination, my gynecologist talked about STDs and wanted me to get a HPV test. She had me nervous as hell and I started to bite my nails one by one. I envisioned Roc having sex with many women and wanted to kill him for what he'd done to me that day. No doubt, my insides hadn't felt right since then and I had to face the fact that something was up.

Finally, my doctor came back into the room, exposing a smile on her face.

She pulled up a chair beside me, crossing her legs. "I'm sorry it took me so long, Desa Rae, but the office is pretty crowded. I've sent your specimens out for lab work to be done, but in the meantime, sweetie, you're going to have yourself a baby."

Now, I know I didn't hear what this woman had said. My face scrunched up and I shook my head from side to side. "A what? No, I'm not pregnant. There's no way. I just got off my period, and haven't been sick or anything."

"The tests revealed that you are. You said yourself that you've been having headaches, you're discharging and urinating a lot. Women have many different symptoms, but all of those apply. It's possible for you to have your period and still be pregnant. Eventually, that should stop or began to get lighter."

"But Dr. Gray, I am forty years old. How could I—"

"It is very realistic for a woman in her early forties to have babies. Some women wait until then. I recommend that you increase your exercise a bit and give up on eating so much chocolate," she laughed. "At this point, I don't see this pregnancy being a huge risk for you. You gotta keep your stress levels down, though, and like any woman, I know how much the changes in your body concern you."

I dropped my head into my hands and closed my eyes. "Trust me, my body is the least of my worries." God, why are you doing this to me, I thought. Are you punishing me for something I did? What?

For a while, I stayed and talked to my doctor about my options. I had always been against abortions, but being faced with a situation like this, I wasn't sure what I'd do. I left her office more worried than ever, and with me losing my job, how could I even provide for this baby? Besides that, I didn't want to do this alone. I had to restore my relationship with Roc, and I couldn't believe how lonely I felt without him around. I missed having fun, and my boring life made me feel as if I were getting older. No, he was in no way perfect, but our baby needed a father. I had doubts about what kind of father he would be, and the more I thought about it, he was on my shit list for putting me in this predicament. I should have taken my butt back to the office that day, instead of going inside of that car wash complaining. Or I could thank Monica for dragging me out to the club that night. The moment I saw him again, I knew he would serve some kind of purpose in my life. Good or bad . . . I wasn't sure yet.

It was Friday, and I had to motivate myself to get up and go to work. Since Mr. Wright had hit me with the news about losing my job, I really didn't want to be there. Basically, I had no choice, and each time I touched my belly, I knew I had to keep it moving. The incident with

Roc took place in late January, so I figured I was almost two months or a little more. I had an appointment set up with my doctor for an ultrasound and that would give me an idea as to when to expect my baby. Since the doctor had hit me with the news, I hadn't been getting much sleep at all. I hadn't told anyone yet and I wasn't even sure how Latrel would feel about having a sibling. I wasn't sure about telling Roc anything, and the last time I'd heard from him was when we were at Target that day. I guess our discussion about STD's scared him away, because he sure hadn't reached out to me since then.

As the end of the day neared, my assumption about Roc was short-lived. The receptionist transferred a call to me and it was him.

"Is the verdict in yet? Am I in trouble or not?" he asked.

"Big . . . gigantic, massive, gargantuan, colossal trouble."

"Ah, shit. That bad, huh?"

"I'm afraid so. Tell me this . . . how many women did you have unprotected sex with when you were with me? I really need to know the truth because you may have to contact a lot of people."

He was silent for a moment, then spoke up. "I—I, uh, shit I ain't have unprotected sex with nobody. I had sex with three, four, maybe five women, but nothin' was on the regular. Those were stick-and-move situations and I was always strapped up. Why you puttin' me on the spot, though? We ain't never make no commitments, did we? I don't see how you got somethin' and you might want to call up old boy."

"No need to because I hadn't gone there at all. You know I'd only been with you, and for the record, if all of those women gave you head, you could still have something, you know?"

Roc's response was delayed again. "A'ight, stop with the lecture. Did I give you somethin'? Man, you got me over here feelin' like shit. I don't know what to say."

"Yeah, I got something. And it's something I can't get rid of."

"Herpes?" he shouted.

"Nope. Why don't you do me a favor and start asking around? Maybe one of your multiple sex partners can tell you what it is."

"Dez, don't play with me. I'm coming over to-night. I don't care what you say and you gon' tell me what the fuck is up."

"Good, I look forward to seeing you. When I leave here, I'm stopping at Schnucks and I should be home by six."

Roc hung up and I couldn't help but laugh. I was so sure numerous phone calls were being made.

Traffic was crammed, and by the time I made it to Schnucks, it was already five o'clock. Because of the baby, I had to be even more health conscious than ever. I had already made my grocery list, which started with the fruit and vegetables section. I picked up two bags of mixed fruits and made my way over to the packages of lettuce so I could make a salad. As I sorted through them, I felt someone rub my butt, causing me to quickly turn around. It was Roc and I instantly let out a sigh of relief.

"Are you stalking me? Every time I turn around, you're there."

"Nice ass, and hell no I ain't stalkin' you. Didn't you tell me you were comin' here?"

"Yes, but I also told you to meet me at my place, not at the grocery store."

"I was already in yo' hood, so why wait?"

I rolled my eyes and got back to my shopping. Roc followed me around, throwing things in my cart as well. He even tossed in several boxes of condoms.

"Can't forget those," he said.

"Yeah, right. I'm not convinced."

He laughed. "You should be. Now, what you gon' cook for me tonight? How 'bout some of those steaks and shrimps you cooked that day?"

I stood in the frozen food section, looking over the Hungry Jack dinners. "I'm not cookin' at all tonight." I put one of the dinners in the cart. "You can eat this."

"No thanks," he said, putting it back. He went right to the meat and seafood sections to get his steak and shrimps. "I'll cook these for me and you ain't gettin' nothin'."

I tossed my hand back at him and went into the cereal aisle. I contemplated on Special K or Froot Loops. "Which one?" I said, folding my arms in thought. Roc grabbed both boxes, including a box of Apple Jacks for him. The same thing went down in the ice cream section. I couldn't decide on chocolate or strawberry. I know my doctor told me to cut back, but if she thought I was going to give up my chocolates, she was crazy. If anything, I had to commit to spending more time at the gym.

Roc put both containers of ice cream in the cart and added a gallon of black walnut ice cream. I looked at the full cart and snapped my finger as I turned to him.

"Say, I forgot to ask, did you get a chance to find out about what we discussed earlier?"

"No. And we ain't gon' talk about that up in here. Keep switchin' that ass up and down these aisles so my dick can keep smilin'. It damn sho ain't contaminated, and like I said before, you might wanna start diggin' those skeletons out of yo' closet."

I had one more aisle to go to, and I was sure Roc would be able to assist me with this one. I stood with my hand on my hip, scanning over the numerous rows of baby food, formula, and pampers.

"Let's see," I said as if I were in deep thought. "What kind of formula do I—"

"What you drinkin' baby formula or somethin'? Or you tryin' to hook up one of yo' friends?"

"No, nothing like that." I picked up a can of formula, turning it to read the label on the back. "Yep, this would be for newborns," I said, putting the can into the cart.

I looked at Roc and smiled, but he seemed clueless.

"What?" he said. "What's wrong?"

"Nothing."

I picked up a bag of newborn pampers and whistled as I tossed them into the cart. "Do you think those will work? If anything, I just hope they're affordable," I asked.

Roc shrugged his shoulders. "Shit, I guess they'll work. And affordable for who, you?"

"No, not me, you."

I looked into Roc's eyes again, but this time he stared back. His hands went up to the back of his head and he turned around. "Ohh, shit! How could I be so stupid!" He swung around to face me. "Earlier you said that you got somethin' you can't get rid of. You fuckin' with me in this baby aisle and shit—Dez, baby, please tell me. You pregnant?"

Roc was so loud and I now figured this was a pretty bad idea. It was too late to change my mind, so I slowly nodded. He tightened his fists and turned back around. "Hell, yes!" he shouted as if he were Tiger Woods putting the ball in at the eighteenth hole for the win. "Fuck yeah, ma!" He swung back around to face me. "Why— when—why you fuck with me like that? Baby, I've been goin' through some shit all day, and this the kind of shit that brings happiness to a nigga! Yes!"

I hadn't gotten a chance to say anything, and it was interesting to watch Roc express himself. He picked up several bags of pampers, throwing them into the cart. "Hell yeah I can afford this shit. And then some. I ain't gon' argue with you 'bout this either and my li'l nigga will have nothin' but the best."

Problem numbers one and two had already arose. I was sure there were more to come, but I wasn't going to accept Roc's money to take care of our baby, and my child was not going to be referred to, especially by his father, as a nigga. For now, he was so happy and I wasn't going to steal his joy.

"What's wrong?" he said, easing his arm around my waist. "Are you okay?"

"I'm fine. I'm just glad to see you so happy, that's all."

"I'm ecstatic," he assured, then licked his lips. "Ca—can I kiss you right now? I know you still got some issues with me, but I promise you—"

I wasn't up to hearing broken promises, so I leaned in to kiss him. Admittedly, I enjoyed our kiss together, and his soft lips felt perfect against mine. We were known for having lengthy kisses and this particular one was not cut short. My eyes were closed and when Roc held the sides of my face, that's when I opened my eyes.

"You changin' my life for the best, ma. I love you for that shit and I know my baby gon' have the best mother in the world. It gon' have a good daddy too and I know I gotta start makin' things right. I'm workin' on it, but give me some time, a'ight?"

"I plan to. But please don't disappoint me, okay?"

Roc nodded and we headed to the cashier, along with all of the things he'd put in the cart for our baby.

"Say man," he said to a white man standing in line with us. "She havin' my baby. I just found out and that shit tight, ain't it?"

The man gave Roc a pat on his back and smiled at me. "Congratulations. That's good news."

I cut my eyes at Roc, and as the cashier waited on us, he announced the news to her as well. "Yeah, she just told me and I got a li'l shorty on the way," he said, pulling out a wad of money to pay for the items. His hand could barely stay gripped around the stash.

The lady smiled at both of us. "I'm sure the two of you will have a beautiful baby. Do you know what it is?"

"No," I said. "Not yet."

"Please," Roc intervened and spoke with confidence. "Trust me, it's a boy."

"Well, whatever you have, congratulations and he seems like he's going to be a great father."

I hurried to leave, and as we were putting the groceries in my trunk, Roc stopped another person. "Say man," he said. "Let me talk to you for a minute."

"Roc, please stop it," I said. "You're embarrassing me."

This time he cut his eyes at me and went on to tell the man about his "baby on the way." Once again, the man congratulated us, smiling and offering us his blessings as he walked away.

"I mean, why don't you just get a marker and write it on your forehead so everyone can see it," I suggested.

"And why don't you just shut the hell up, get yo' fine self in the car, and go home to cook my food. I got some other things in mind too, but that'll be discussed in mo details later."

When we got back to my place, Roc helped me put up the groceries and insisted on me cooking his food.

"Please," he begged. "I can't cook like you."

"I said no, Roc. I'm tired and if you'd like for me to throw something in the microwave for you, I'd be happy to do it."

He shrugged and stepped up to me. He then lifted my chin and pecked my lips. "Who needs food when I can eat you? It's been months and months since I last tasted you and I'm ready for my full-course meal."

I held up two fingers, easing up one more. "Two . . . maybe three months. It's been taken too long for you to get it together and how could you stay away from me for so long."

"I've been comin' at you with everything I got. You the one been dissin' the hell out of me."

"Sorry, and I hope I'm not in trouble. Am I?"

"Yeah, baby. Big, massive, gargantuan . . . my dick wanna get into you right now trouble. It can't go another day without you and you gots to let me put it in motion."

"And if I don't, will you take what you want?"

He rubbed his finger along the side of my face. "Never, never again. That shit will never happen again and my word, my bond."

"What about all this stickin' and movin' you've been doing? What's up with that?"

"Baby, I'm done. I ain't 'bout to lose you again and that shit gon' cease."

I pushed. "What about Vanessa?"

Roc swallowed hard, thinking about what to say. "What about her?"

"I mean, she made it clear that I could never have you. What do you think?"

"Fuck her, ma. You don't need to worry yourself 'bout her. My shit with her under control, a'ight?"

"It better be. And if she gets my number again, I'm dealing with you, not her."

Roc nodded, but I could see straight through him. There was more left to this story, but when it all came to a head, he'd have to deal with it. He unzipped the back of my fitted skirt and it fell to the floor, along with my panties. He lifted me high on the kitchen's island, standing between my separated thighs. My legs fell in place on his shoulders and when his tongue divided my slit, I sucked in my stomach.

"*Ssss*—so, we back in action, huh?" I moaned.

Roc was too busy making me his again, using his fierce tongue to turn circles inside my pussy. An electrifying shock transmitting through my body caused me to spew dirty, but stimulating, words at him. I rubbed his waves, only to eject my juices into his mouth shortly thereafter. His hooded sexy eyes made contact with mine and his dimples went on display. "You damn right we back in action. And we gon' be in action for a long while too."

Roc had spoken the truth. For the next few days it was all about me and him. He'd turned off his phone. I ignored mine and there were no interruptions. It was funny how I never thought I could feel so connected to him again, but there I was enjoying every moment, every stroke, and every compliment that he'd given me. Basically, I had my man back and I was, no doubt, elated about it.

Chapter Eleven

I had plenty of vacation time left, so I took two weeks off from my job. Monica and I shopped our butts off and Reggie was right on time with the money he'd gotten from selling his property. Monica had taken some vacation time too and just so we could relax from all of the walking we'd done, we stopped at Houlihan's to get a bite to eat. I plopped down in the booth, laying all of my bags next to me.

"My feet are killing me," I said, removing my strappy sandals.

"Mine are too," Monica said, following suit. "I hope my feet don't stink, and if they do, too bad."

I laughed. "Now the last thing I need is to be smelling your funky feet while I'm eating. If you have any concerns about them stinking, please keep your shoes on."

We laughed and got comfortable at the booth. Monica kept her shoes off, but I didn't smell a thing. The waiter was right on time with our menus, and after we ordered I called home to see if anyone had called. There were no messages, but I was expecting to hear from Roc about our getaway at Monica's parents' cabin in Branson, Missouri. He viewed it as a boring camping trip and joked about "a nigga from the hood" being in such a place. According to him, he hated insects and if he was bitten by one, or if he saw a snake, he was going to kill me. He still hadn't gotten back to me yet, but when I reminded him about the intimate and romantic time we could have, he said he'd let me know. I closed my phone and Monica was eyeballing me.

"Roc, right?"

"Yes. I was trying to see if he'd called. Remember, you're the one who told me to let down my hair, have fun girl, and don't break your back trying to ride him."

Monica laughed. "I did, didn't I? But, I didn't tell your butt to go get knocked up by him. Now that I didn't say."

I rubbed my hand on my belly that wasn't showing much yet. "No you didn't, but I feel good about this. I never wanted Latrel to be an only child like me, and I know this baby will bring me so much joy."

"I know it will too. I'm so happy for you, and I'm jealous that Roc didn't have his eyes on me first. I don't know what to say about him, Dez, but I can tell you one thing . . . that brotha got swagga. He's an original and I have honestly never come across anything like him. Girl, I would be going crazy with a man like that in my life. He'd have to screw me everyday and I wouldn't let him out of my sight."

"Oh, trust me, I've been like a horny li'l freak around him. Every time I look at him, I envision dirty things to myself. Like I said before, his sex is dynamic and I don't even think about Reggie's butt anymore."

Monica put up both of her hands, high-fiving me from across the table. "That's what I'm talking about. Good-bye madness, hello sunshine. I'm glad he's history and thank God for Roc. Now, what's been up with these silly bitches calling your house?"

"They haven't called since I got my number changed, but his baby's mama was about to drive me crazy. I can't stand foolish women like that, and let's be real, Roc ain't just putting it out there for her and me. He admitted that there had been others and I'm not sure how to deal with it."

"Yeah, that's tough, but he's a young man, Dez. A young, fine, sexy, wealthy, in-control black man that many women are bound to dig their claws into. You really can't do much about that, but how in the hell did you get pregnant? With a man like him, you've got to protect yourself and condoms are a must."

I couldn't agree more with Monica. And since I hadn't told anyone about the incident that had happened that day, I had to come up with a lie. "We were having sex one day, and the condom slid off. I was so caught up in the moment that I didn't ask him to stop. If you don't follow the rules, there are always consequences."

"You're right. But, I don't see it as a bad thing. I'm glad about the baby, and if that crazy bitch of his start messing with you, you let me know. We'll have to go back to our Sumner High School days and show this chick what we're all about."

"She don't know, do she? Girl, we used to cut up! I can't believe you had me fighting with all those girls and what about the time they surrounded your mother's car?"

"I ran them bitches over! They were jealous of us, especially since we had all the boys. You were stuck on Reggie, but that didn't stop the boys from chasing you."

"No, it didn't. But those were the days. I loved Sumner High School, and if I have to travel back down that road in dealing with Ms. Vanessa, I sure in the hell will. Now, I won't fight her, that's silly, but she will definitely know that I'm not the one to mess with."

Monica nodded and lightly pounded her fist into the palm of her hand. "I'll teach her a lesson or two. Age is just a number and if she keeps it up, she'll be on her back covered in dirt. Have you ever seen this chick?"

I thought back to the night of Roc's birthday party, as well as to the day I'd seen him at the car wash. "I'm really not sure, but I think I have. Twice."

"How does she look?"

"She's a really pretty girl, but her mouth is foul, which makes her ugly in my book. The woman I saw looked very materialistic, and I'm sure Roc is taking good care of her shopping needs. I could see her breaking a nail, screaming Roc's name like she done lost her mind."

We laughed.

"So, he got a gangsta bitch, huh?" Monica asked.

"I'm not sure what a gangsta bitch is, but—"

"A ride-or-die ho. She gon' ride it out with that negro until she die or he die. One or the other. And a woman like you don't mean nothing to her, and you will not take anything that belongs to her. I'm sure she's protective of him and you need to find out more about her because, the more I think about it, anything could happen, especially with you being pregnant."

"I've been keeping my eyes and ears open. I'm definitely not going to allow someone like her to upset me, and her dealings are with Roc, not me. I told him to handle his business with her, and it's up to him to make sure she doesn't overstep her boundaries."

"Roc may not have any control over her, then again . . . I take back what I said. He got control, and then some. I don't believe there's a woman in this world who can tame him, and unfortunately, that includes you."

"I won't disagree, but taming him is not what I want to do. I got other things in mind and you'll soon see what they are."

Monica tried to get me to tell her what I meant, but there really wasn't any secret. I wanted the best for Roc, and now that I was pregnant with his child, my mission to get him to change his life around had picked up steam.

I had one more week left for my vacation, and Roc and I were on our way to Monica's parents' cabin in Branson, Missouri. He'd been complaining about insects since we left, and while we stopped at Waffle House to grab a bite to eat, I assured him that we would be safe.

"I can't believe you're making such a big deal about insects. Enlighten me . . . what's up with that? Or are you aiming to ruin another one of our vacations together."

"I ain't aimin' to do nothin'. I don't do this kind of shit, and settin' up tents and all that mess for these white folks. If you ever lived in the projects, then you'd know what the big deal is 'bout insects. When you got roaches runnin' all around the place, in yo' food, crawlin' on yo' ass, then you'd know what I'm talkin' 'bout. Evidently, you had that silver spoon hangin' out yo' mouth and don't know what's up."

"We're not going to be setting up any tents and the cabin is really nice. You'll like it and if any insects or Freddy or Jason come out to get us, I'll protect you, okay?"

"If Freddy or Jason come fuck with me they gon' get shot." Roc pointed to his truck. "I got that nine millimeter in there, and after I fire those eighteen rounds in that ass, game over. I bet people won't be going to the movies to see them no mo'."

"Is it necessary for you to carry a gun around?"

Roc chewed his waffle, staring at me like I had asked a stupid question. I returned the stare, waiting for a response. When his cell phone rang, he broke our trance and answered. I wasn't sure what was up with him, and if the insects had caused him to have such an attitude, maybe it was in our best interest to head back home. I thought about making that suggestion, but for now, I kept my mouth shut.

Roc had been talking to Ronnie and he was on his way to meet us at the Waffle House. When he got there, he seemed upset that Roc was leaving and even his attitude rubbed me the wrong way.

"All I'm sayin' is I need for you to handle somethin' as soon as you get back. Are you sure you'll be back by Friday?" Ronnie asked.

"I got you," Roc said, looking across the table at Ronnie, who had taken a seat next to me.

"Nigga, I know you got me, but I wanna make sure this gets takin' care of. If you too busy rollin' with yo' bitch, hangin' out in the wilderness, then I'll get somebody else to handle it."

I pulled my head back, looking at Ronnie. "Excuse me? I'm sorry, Mister, but you don't know me well enough to call me a bitch. And even if you did—"

Roc touched my hand and could see the fire in my eyes. He quickly intervened. "Hey, Ronnie. Cool out with that shit, man. I told you I'm gon' handle it and no need to disrespect my lady. I ain't never let you down before, so there ain't need for yo' concern, right?"

Ronnie sucked his bottom lip. "Talk to me, baby boy. I hear you. I'm just a li'l paranoid 'bout some thangs, that's all. I need you focused right now, and you know what's been goin' down." He nudged his head in my direction. "Is she the one carryin' *our* li'l nigga?"

Roc squeezed my hand, as a cue not to say anything. He knew me all too well.

"Fa' sho," Roc said. "And I can't wait 'til he get here."

Ronnie turned to me again. His eyes cut me like a sharpened knife. I returned the look and did not break my stare.

"Congrats, li'l mama. You've made yo' way up to the winner's circle. I hope you survive."

Ronnie got up, slamming his hand against Roc's. "Have fun, my nigga, and leave yo' phone on in case I need to get at you." He pounded his chest and Roc did it back. "Much love, but handle that for me, a'ight?" I noticed his eyes cut in my direction and I was steaming inside. Roc could tell that I was, and as soon as Ronnie left, he had the nerve to ask if I was okay.

"No, I'm not. But I have a feeling that what I say or how I feel doesn't matter. Just do me a favor, all right? Don't ever refer to your child as a nigga and please see to it that I'm never around your uncle again. As you can see, we don't click."

"Ronnie was just being Ronnie. I can't change no grown-ass man, Dez, and it ain't my job. We talk that way all the time, and he meant no harm referrin' to our baby as a nigga. It's how we do it and—"

I had enough and couldn't help myself from raising my voice. "Stop makin' excuses!"

I scooted out of the booth, making my way to his truck so we could leave. A few minutes later, Roc came outside and stood in front of me.

"Why you gettin' all hype about this? I thought we was 'spose to be havin' some fun this week? You need to calm down and stop lettin' tedious shit upset you."

He kissed my cheek and opened the door so I could get in. I in no way felt as if I overreacted, and for Ronnie to call me a bitch was one of the most disrespectful things I'd ever witnessed. I waited for Roc to correct him, and even though he somewhat did, I felt as if it wasn't enough. I told him just that as we were on our way to Branson.

"What did you want a nigga to do? Jump up and knock the muthafucka upside his head? Would that had made you feel better? I asked him to cool out and he did."

"If you say so, Roc. I don't expect you to fight with your uncle and the last thing I want is to come between the two of you."

"That ain't gon' happen," he assured me. "Ronnie my nigga and I owe that man my life."

Enough said and enough done. This thing between them was even deeper than I thought and I'd be a fool to keep pouncing on something that was beyond my control.

When we arrived at the cabin, Roc got out of the car, looking around as if something was going to jump out at him. He wasn't lying about his gun and he pulled it from underneath his seat, tucking it into the back of his pants. I shook my head, making my way to the door. When we got inside, Roc was completely shocked— then again, so was I. The 3,350 square foot cabin was built with high log walls, giving it much support. There were three fireplaces, one in the kitchen, bedroom and family room, all made of stone. The country kitchen was spacious as ever and the arched glass windows gave view to the hundreds of trees in the forest. A custom-made balcony surrounded the entire back of the cabin and it had two levels. In order to get to the upper level, we had to climb the spiral handmade log staircase that looked down into the sunken living room on one side and the great room on the other. The cabin was lit up with handcrafted wooden lights and some were made from deer antlers. The cherry colored hardwood floors creaked as we walked on them, but some of the floors were covered with tweed round rugs that matched the decor in every room. Simply put, this place was fabulous. It was not only cozy, but quiet. I had only been there on one other occasion with Monica and that was a long, long time ago. She'd said that her parents had redone the cabin, but I hadn't expected to walk into nothing like this. No doubt, Roc's penthouse was banging, but even he was impressed.

"I told you this was nice," I said, slightly pushing his shoulder.

He nodded, continuing to look around. "Yeah, it's tight. I might have to hook up some shit like this."

I didn't want to give him any ideas about spending his money, so I asked him to unpack our suitcases. The bedroom was decked out with wrought-iron furniture and had a comfortable looking king-sized bed. The tub in the bathroom was an old-fashioned claw-foot white tub, more than big enough for me and Roc. I couldn't wait to sink my body into it and before I could get the words out of my mouth, Roc had already suggested it. He wrapped his arms around me as we stood in the doorway.

"We gon' have a good time, a'ight?" he said.

"With no interruptions?" I asked.

"No interruptions." He reached for his phone to turn it off. He then tossed it on the bed, already luring me back to it.

"Wait a minute," I said. "I gotta pee."

"Nah, that's just that pussy tinglin' 'cause I'm tryin' to get in it."

"Trust me, soon enough, you will."

We kissed, and after I used the bathroom, I went downstairs to make us some sandwiches. Roc had stayed in the bedroom and when I got back upstairs, he had made himself comfortable. He was laid across the bed in his boxers, paging through his GED guide. The pages were ruffled, so I could tell he'd been using it. I was impressed.

"So, I see you've been making use of that, huh?"

"Yep," he said, not taking his eyes off the book. "I told you I would."

I placed the tray of food on the bed, and after we ate and drank some wine, I turned on some soft music. We talked for a while, but then Roc got back to his book. I left him alone and laid next to him, reading mine.

It had gotten dark outside, but the cabin was lit up like Christmas. Roc had fallen asleep and so had I. When I got up, I went downstairs to turn down some of the lights, then went back upstairs to start my bubble bath. I wanted Roc to join me, so I put on the black sheer lace hipster panties I bought, with a matching embroidered, cleavage-boosting sheer bra. It had pink silk ribbon straps and a tiny pink bow sat in the middle of my chest. I stood at the side of the bed, calling out Roc's name. He lifted his head, but squinted his eyes. When he saw me, his eyes opened wide.

"Damn," he said, rubbing his eyes. "You look good in that shit, ma. Where the negligee that I bought you, though? I ain't seen you in it yet."

"It's at home. I'm going to wear them, but I wanted to wear this today."

"Good choice," he implied.

I turned, sauntering my way to the bathroom and swaying my hips from side to side. I could feel the air on my butt cheeks and I suspected that Roc's eyes were all into it. I stopped at the doorway, leaning my back against the door. I put my index finger in my mouth, sucking the tips of it.

"Are you going to take off your shorts, or shall I?"

Roc removed his shorts and placed a condom on his manhood that flopped out long and hard. He stood in front of me, aiming his goodness right between my legs. I widened them and he pulled the crotch section to my panties over to the side. He found home, lifting me higher to seek comfort. I held onto his neck, rubbing and soothing the back of his head. I expressed how much I wanted things to work out between us and reminded him that our hot bath was waiting.

We finished our quickie and then resumed in the tub. Water and bubbles were splashed everywhere, and there was nothing sexier than Roc kneeling between my legs, with water and soap dripping down his jaw-dropping black body. My hands roamed every inch of him, squeezing his muscles when I got a chance. At that moment, I wanted to thank Reggie for divorcing me. If I could give him an award for doing so, I most certainly would.

For the next several days, Roc and I got along well. Basically, I had one of the most enjoyable times of my life, and he admitted to the same. I knew he had to get back home before Friday, and as soon as he turned his phone back on, which was early Thursday morning, it rang like crazy. One call after the next interrupted our time together, and by early afternoon I had to say something. Besides, he had been all into studying from his GED guide, and I was in the middle of quizzing him.

I sighed, dropping the pencil on the table. "Come on now, Roc. Let's get finished with this. Can't you ignore your phone and I don't know why you turned that thing back on."

He held his hand up near my face. "Cut it off," he said to me, then answered his phone. "What up?" he yelled to the caller. "Yeah, man, I'll be back sometime tomorrow. Why you niggas keep callin' me?" He paused for a long time. "So, it's goin' down like that, huh? Y'all should have taken care of that shit, and I recommend payin' them fools off. Check with Ronnie to be sure, but I'm sure he'll be down with it." He paused again. "A'ight, get back at me."

Roc ended his call, and all this talk about "handling" business was making me ill. I graded the test quiz he had taken and laid the error-free paper in front of him. "Excellent," I said. "You've been doing your thing and I'm proud of you. I hope we're not wasting our time and—

Oh my God . . . his phone rang again! I got up to walk away and he grabbed my arm. He still answered his phone, and after a few minutes of griping to Ronnie, he told him he was on his way back. He looked at me, still holding a grip on my arm.

"Look, you haven't been wastin' yo' time and neither have I. I asked you to be patient, and I need you to do that shit for me. Now, we gotta go. Unfortunately, somethin' requires my immediate attention and we gotta cut this short."

This week was too good to be true. I swallowed the lump in my throat and did my best to face reality. "Is this what I signed up for? Tell me, Roc, will it always be like this? I need to know because I think I'm fooling myself, hoping and wishing for something better."

Roc stood and delivered a clear message, not with his mouth, but with his eyes. "If you hopin' and wishin' for somethin' better than me, then go find it. I am who I say I am, and if you don't like it, bounce. You're startin' to work a nigga nerves, Dez, and I've been dealin' with that shit for too long. Silence yourself sometimes, and if it's the baby that's got you all worked up, I can deal with that. But I got a feelin' that you like fuckin' with me and that shit seriously gotta stop."

Roc walked off to gather his belongings, and I thought, *never again*. This was the last time I'd recommend quality time away from home and my efforts didn't seem to be getting me anywhere.

Chapter Twelve

Finally, I told Latrel about the baby and he was ecstatic. I wasn't sure how he'd take the news, but he really was pleased that I had moved on with my life. Of course, he broke the news to Reggie, and when he came over that day, I thought the police were banging at the door he hit it so hard. Like always, we argued up a storm and Reggie told me that he never wanted to see me again. He called me a disgrace, and before he left, he had the nerve to suggest that I would pay for what I'd done. Now, what in the hell did I do to him? He was the one who happily ended our marriage and moved on with his other women. He had told me he was getting married, so why was it any of his business that I was having a baby with Roc? I couldn't understand men for nothing in the world, and they always wanted to have their cake and eat it too.

I had been going through my ups and downs with Roc too. He claimed working at the club had been keeping him real busy, but I didn't know what to believe. He always tried to make things right by showering me with gifts, or taking me somewhere so I could get out of the house. I did appreciate his efforts, but just last night, his silly little girlfriend got my number again. This time, she was calling to tell me how many times Roc made her come the other night. She kept putting emphasis on the child they had together and wanted me to know how much Roc loved her dirty drawers. I listened to her message on my voice mail thinking, that if he loved her so much then why in the heck had he been spending so much time with me? Why was he constantly underneath me, showing and telling me how much I meant to him? Now, I wasn't no fool and I was well-aware of what was transpiring behind my back. I knew the deal with Roc and based on what he had shared with me about his past, the word *love* didn't belong in his vocabulary. To me, he didn't even love himself, and if he did, he would focus more on getting himself together. I was doing my best to be there for him, simply because I had hopes that he would change for the better. Lord knows I was pulling for him, but I couldn't deny that his behind-the-scenes situation was starting to work me. I had warned Roc about Vanessa calling my house. I had enough to worry about with the baby and my job, and I definitely didn't need the extra pressure. Last week, when Roc had taken me to the park for a picnic, I noticed her makeup bag full of M•A•C cosmetics, purposely left in his truck. Roc had stopped at the gas station and I dumped it right in the trash. Another time she'd left a pair of her panties tucked nice and neat right by the passenger's side door. I'm sure they were for my eyes only and I kicked those on the ground as well. She wanted me to know about her so badly, but I already knew. Roc didn't have to say a word and his lies about the whole situation angered me. From day one, Vanessa had been in the picture and she wasn't going anywhere because he didn't want her to.

Like clockwork, Roc called to say he was on his way. It was a late Friday evening and I couldn't wait to discuss my concerns about the ongoing stupid phone calls. I had been on edge since then, and while in the kitchen, I splashed water on my face so I'd calm down. Being pregnant had me feeling as if I were angry at the world, and I knew this kind of feeling wasn't healthy for the baby. I took deeps breaths and brushed my hair back into a ponytail. I still had on my workout clothes from earlier, which were my fitted dark blue stretch shirt that showed my midriff and my stretch pants that matched. I looked in the mirror, and couldn't believe the gap that had grown between my legs. No doubt, I had Roc to thank for that. My belly was just starting to poke out some, but if I sucked in my tummy, it wasn't that noticeable yet. I turned sideways to be sure and was glad to see that my body wasn't out of whack.

Several hours had gone by, and Roc hadn't made it there yet. I gazed at my watch and it was almost midnight. I made him promise to always call if he was going to be late, and this situation seemed kind of odd. He knew how much I worried about him, and I figured the last thing he wanted to do was worry me at a time like this. I called his phone, which is something he made me do since I'd been pregnant, but I got his voice mail. I dialed again and the same thing happened.

When one o'clock came around, I tried to find the late news in St. Louis, but didn't have much success. I then got on the Internet to see if *STL Today* had any updates, but I came up empty. I was about to go crazy, and that's when my phone rang. I rushed to it and Roc was on the other end.

"Say, baby," he said in a scratchy voice. "Somethin' happened and I'm at the hospital."

My heart sunk right into my stomach. A knot felt as if it tightened around it and all I could say was, "Where are you?"

"Barnes Jewish. . . ."

I hung up, got in my car, and headed to the hospital.

As soon as I got there, the parking lot was packed with cars and the emergency-room entrance was filled with people. I was a nervous wreck, and when the double doors came open, I rushed straight to the check-in station.

"I'm looking for Rocky Dawson. Could you tell me where to find him?"

The woman pointed to the huge gatherings of people in the waiting room. "Have a seat over there. The doctor will be out in a minute."

There were too many people in the waiting area and too much confusion. All I wanted to know was where I could find Roc. "Have a seat over there," the lady repeated. "I promise you the doctor will be out to talk to everyone shortly. FYI, he'll be okay."

I released a sigh of relief and walked over to the waiting area. I saw some familiar faces from the club, but the most noticeable was Ronnie. He was cussing at somebody on the phone, acting a fool. Several men stood by the soda machines, some were by the television, and some hung out by the bathrooms. As for the women, I noticed the woman I'd sat by at Roc's birthday party, some women I had never seen before, and the woman who had slapped Roc at the club was there with, of course, his son on her lap. She was also the woman in the pictures at his penthouse, and all I could do was take a deep breath to prepare myself.

First, I headed for the bathroom, just so I could check myself. One of the men whistled at me, but I ignored him. I looked in the mirror, teasing my bangs on my forehead. All I could do with my ponytail was redo it, so I did. I refreshed my makeup just a little, but had no intentions of overdoing it. My workout ensemble was hugging the thick curves in my body, so I was glad about that. I left the bathroom with my purse tucked underneath my arm. As soon as I stepped out, the same man who whistled at me grabbed my hand.

"Say. You don't remember me." I looked again and it was Bud from the car wash. There was nothing like seeing someone I knew, or knew of, to get me to relax. Bud had my attention.

"Yes, I do remember you. Are you still at the car wash?" I joked. "I hope not."

He laughed and I did my best to be nice, just to get some answers. He told me Roc had been shot in the upper shoulder and said that two men had tried to rob him. When I asked if anyone knew who they were, he nodded and expressed that they'd already been taken care of. I pretty much had come to that conclusion, and with the numerous gangsta like, ride-or-die folks in the waiting room, Bud didn't have to convince me. I looked at Ronnie sitting in one of the chairs and noticed the women and men sucking up to him. Now he had Roc's son on his lap, and I had to admit, he was one of the cutest kids I'd ever seen. Vanessa was representing too and she looked even prettier close up. I noticed a heart with Roc's name in the middle tattooed on her leg. And, just as I had expected, she had a Coach bag by her side, a diamond necklace was blinging from her neck, and her manicure was in full effect. *I'm Roc's woman* was written all over her, but was she prettier than me? Nah, not at all. I wasn't sure if she knew who I was, so I decided to let my presence be known. I excused myself from Bud and walked between the two rows of chairs that faced each other. Ronnie was only two seats away from Vanessa and there just happened to be an empty chair directly across from them. I plopped down in the chair, crossed my legs, and looked over at Ronnie.

"Hey, Ronnie," I said, letting Vanessa know that I knew . . . some of the family. "How are you?"

He threw his head back without saying a word. He kept punching Roc's son in his chest, knocking him down. Roc's son was laughing, punching him right back.

"Don't hit him hard like that, Ronnie," Vanessa said with attitude. "Y'all be playin' too much."

"Be quiet. He ain't no punk."

Ridiculous, I thought. *If it were my child, I'd get up and knock the hell out of him.* I picked up a magazine from the table next to me and opened it up. I pretended to be occupied, but I could see Vanessa checking me out from head to toe. I closed the magazine, then looked at my watch as if I had somewhere to be. I then pulled out my cell phone and dialed out to no one.

"Hey, Monica," I said. "I'm at the hospital now. Bud says that Roc will be just fine. I haven't had a chance to talk to Ronnie yet, but I'm still waiting to see Roc. When I got his call earlier, I rushed right up here. He sounded as if he needed me and you know how I am about my snookums. He was supposed to come over, and I knew something was wrong when he didn't show up." I paused as if I were listening to someone on the other end. Vanessa was taking in every word I said. I rubbed my stomach and moved around in the chair like I was uncomfortable. "No, the baby is fine. Roc knows better putting me under all this pressure and I'm going to hurt him as soon as I see him." I chuckled a bit. "Yeah, we're going to do that too." I chuckled again, then told "my girl" I had to go. I closed my cell phone and Vanessa couldn't wait to put on her show. She stood up, just so I could see her shapely backside and breasts, flaunting it all in my face. She stood right in front of me, stretching her leg so I could see the tattoo on it. To complete her show, she held out her hand, loudly calling for her son to take it.

"Come on, Li'l Roc," she said. "Let's go get a soda. You should be able to go see yo' daddy in a minute."

She cut her eyes at me and walked off. It was so funny how a woman had so much crap to talk over the phone, but when you got face-to-face with them, they always had very little to say. I left my seat and waited for someone to buzz the emergency room doors open so I could sneak into the room where Roc was. The atmosphere was not my cup of tea and my only purpose was to see Roc.

I peeked into many of the closed-curtained rooms, and when I found the one Roc was in, there were two doctors in there with him. One of them left, and when I peeked into the room again, Roc saw me. He winked, giving me a slight smile. I slowly walked into the room and the doctor looked at me.

"I'll be another minute or two," he said. "Are you his wife?"

"Maybe," I replied.

"Yeah," Roc softly fired back.

We smiled at each other and he looked so, so tired. His entire left shoulder and part of his arm was wrapped in bandages. It looked uncomfortable. His eyes looked as if he had been heavily sedated and the doctor told me they removed the bullet during surgery. He said with a bunch of rest and pain medication, Roc would be fine.

The doctor left and I got closer to the bed. I held his hand with mine, kissing his knuckles "Are you okay? Why do you worry me like this?" I asked.

"It wasn't my fault those fools tried to rob me. I was sittin' in my truck at the light, thinkin' 'bout yo' ass and those niggas came out of nowhere."

"What were they hoping to get? Money?"

"Yeah, they tried to take my bank, but they ain't even notice my boy drivin' in the car next to me. Shit happened so fast, and next thing I knew, I was shot. The bullet caught my ass in the shoulder, and I was like, damn. At first, I didn't know where that muthafucka had hit me. I saw all that blood and started prayin' my ass off. I thought about you and my baby, my son, and . . . it was fucked up, ma."

I placed tender kisses inside the palm of Roc's hand and closed my eyes. I knew this could have been a lot worse. "I'm just glad you're okay. If something happens to you, I'd probably go crazy."

"Nah, don't do that. I'll be a'ight and I'm thankful that it wasn't my time to go yet."

"Me too," I said, leaning down to kiss his very dry lips. Our tongues added a little something extra, and I felt so relieved that he'd be okay.

"Listen, I'm not going to stay because you have many people waiting out there to see you. Let's just say it's *crowded* and I want to prevent any more confrontations. I'll call to check on you, but please call to let me know when you're going home. I want to help you get better any way I can."

"You gon' take care of me, is that what you're sayin'?"

"I always do, don't I?"

Roc snickered. "Hell, yeah. I can't complain."

I slightly turned to make my exit. "Bye Snookums," I said. He kissed his hand and blew his kiss in my direction.

I could barely make it to the curtain before he called my name. "Yes," I said, making my way back up to him.

"Come here, let me whisper somethin' in yo' ear."

I leaned down, putting my ear close to Roc's lips. "That ass lookin' real good and I hate like hell that I missed out tonight. I had a surprise for you too."

I turned my head, and was now face-to-face with him, breathing in his words. "You want to tell me now or save it for later?" I asked.

"Now," he whispered. "I took my GED test today. I'm positive that I did real good, but the results won't come back for a few weeks."

Honestly, I wanted to cry. Maybe a GED wasn't a big deal to some people, but for Roc to even put forth the effort to do it, it truly meant the world to me. If anything, it proved to me that he wanted to make some changes in his life and that's all that mattered.

"I'm so happy for you," was all I could say while continuously pecking his lips. "Things are going to get so much better, just wait and see."

As soon as Roc spilled the words, "All because of you, things will get better," his son came into the room. So did Vanessa and I couldn't help but take an extra peck on his lips. Afterward, Roc turned his attention to his son.

"What's up, man," he said smiling. He reached out his hand and his son gave him five. I said good-bye to Roc again and he winked. I ignored Vanessa on my way out, walking right past her. And just as I got ready to leave the hospital, that's when she called after me.

"Excuse me," she repeated at least three times. I kept on walking as if I didn't hear her and didn't stop until I got to my car. Then I quickly turned around.

"May I help you?" I asked.

She folded her arms, and tooted her lips. Much attitude was on display, and with that, she wasn't getting much of anything else from me.

"Are you supposed to be pregnant by Roc?"

"Are you supposed to be Roc's woman?"

"Twenty-four hours a day, seven days a week. You can count on that."

"Well, if you're his woman, then I suggest you go inside and discuss your issues with him. And if you've committed yourself to him twenty-four hours a day, seven days a week, then you have a serious problem on your hands. He's not with you for that many days and hours, and I know that for a fact because he's with me. Stop calling my house, little girl, and grow the fuck up."

I got in my car to leave, but not before she called me every name she possibly could. Even one of the ladies from inside had to come outside to calm her down. She gave me a devious stare and I waved good-bye to her as I drove off.

***

No doubt, things were looking up. I'd gotten a new job as executive administrative assistant working for the VP at another college, but I wasn't going to make a transition until my current position ended. I wanted to send a message that I appreciated the fourteen years they'd given me and leave on a good note. Mr. Wright agreed that it was the right thing to do, and the only thing I was sad about was not being able to work for him. Recently, I confessed that I hated my job, but the truth of the matter was it was my responsibility to make things better and that enabled me to appreciate my blessings even more.

Roc had been out of the hospital. He'd spent numerous days at my house and some days at his. He'd even started going to church with me on some Sundays and I was so grateful for the change I was starting to see in him. Not once did he mention anything about what had gone on between me and Vanessa, but I was sure—positive—that he'd gotten an earful from her, especially about the baby. But, as usual, he kept quiet. He was just that kind of man, and he knew how to play his hand. Bringing up Vanessa's name would require him to discuss his relationship with her, and he wasn't going to do it. If he did, I knew he'd lie his butt off so why waste the time? In my heart, I knew Roc cared for her and their son kept him tied to her. I felt as if he cared for me too, but caring for me just didn't seem like enough. I turned my focus on getting him to see that there was a more prosperous, legitimate life out there waiting for him. Maybe then, he'd view his future as I did. He had gotten the news that he'd passed his GED test and we celebrated that day like none other. I cooked dinner for him, had balloons all over the place, and gave him a keepsake personalized frame that he could put his certificate in. Sex was on the agenda that night and Roc continuously told me how grateful he was for me. It was my goal for him to start seeing the light, and that had been my intentions for as long as I could remember.

Summer was back in action and the weather in St. Louis was doing its thing. The sun was shining bright as ever, sizzling at ninety-six degrees. People in my neighborhood were outside washing cars, taking walks, swimming in their pools or jogging. I was standing on my front porch waiting for Roc to come get me, as he'd offered to take me to the park. My belly was sprouting out enough where anyone could tell there was a baby inside. I continued to work out and cutting back on the chocolates were the best things I could've done for my body. My hair had grown even longer, and for the day, I took the easy way out, putting it into a ponytail. My maternity white shorts were knee-length and the turquoise shirt I wore criss-crossed over my healthy breasts, loosing up around my stomach. My turquoise sandals had a tiny heel, displaying my freshly done pedicure.

I could hear the music, but the loud zooming sound is what confused me. When the yellow Lamborghini with tinted windows pulled in my driveway, I wasn't sure who it was. That wasn't until the side door flipped up and Roc got out. He was dressed down in some baggy khaki shorts, a black wife beater, and black leather tennis shoes. It looked as if he'd gotten more tattoos on his arms so I moved closer to take a look.

"What you think?" he asked.

I searched his arms, but there wasn't anything new. "I think you look gorgeous," I said, smiling.

"Nah, I mean 'bout the car. Do you like my new ride?"

"It's nice. I can't wait to see how fast this thing goes," I said sarcastically. "I'm sure you're going to show me."

Roc laughed, flipping the door so I could get in. He got in, covering his eyes with dark shades.

"How are you supposed to see with those dark shades on and these tinted windows?"

"Trust me, I can see. Just make sure yo' seatbelt is on."

I made sure it was fastened and Roc took off. The Lamborghini was moving fast, leaving nothing but dust behind it. I hung on for dear life, and as Roc swerved in and out of traffic, I asked him to chill out.

"Baby, you can't drive slow in no car like this. It kind of takes over. You wanna drive to see what I'm talkin' 'bout?"

"No, but your foot is the one controlling the accelerator. Lighten up, okay?"

Roc cooled out a little, but when we hit the highway it was all over with. He took it to the limit, zooming past other cars like a NASCAR driver. I just kept my mouth shut, as the last thing I needed was for him to turn his head toward me and start fussing. It was best that he kept his eyes on the road.

I was relieved when we got off the highway, but nervous when we had to drive through the city. Everybody was looking into the car, trying to see who it was. Several cars paced the sides of us, and I wasn't sure what was going to go down. Each time, Roc sped away from the cars, and when he finally parked the car at Forest Park, I dropped my head back on the headrest, thanking God for my safe arrival.

We got out and started to walk the trail. My arm was tucked into Roc's and we moved at a slow pace.

"It's hot as hell out here," he said. "I'm only walkin' for an hour today, after that, I'm outta here."

"Fine with me. As long as you stop on the way home and get me some frozen yogurt."

"It's your time to buy me some. I paid last time."

"I got you, you know I do." We walked silently for a moment and I could tell he had something on his mind. So did I. "Since you got your GED, what's next?" I asked.

"I've been thinkin' 'bout takin up a trade or goin' to a community college. Ain't nothin' in stone yet," Roc said, moving his shades to the top of his head. He squinted from the sun shining in his face. "But, listen, I need to tell you somethin', Dez."

Whenever Roc was willing to tell me something, I worried. My stomach had already rumbled. "What's up?" I asked.

"A few weeks ago, Ronnie got arrested. He was released on bail, but he gotta go back for his trial."

I wanted to jump for joy, but played down how happy I was that this man would possibly be away from Roc and out of his life.

"I'll be called to testify on Ronnie's behalf, but things may get a li'l tricky."

"What do you mean by that? I mean, if Ronnie had done something wrong, you can't perjure yourself and lie for him. That would put you at risk and possibly come back to haunt you."

Roc stopped in his tracks and turned me to face him. "There's a plan, and all I gotta do is follow through with it. I hate comin' at you like this, but I don't really have any choice."

I had a frown on my face and didn't like where this conversation was going. "What are you talking about? Please stop beating around the bush."

"What I'm sayin' is, I gotta do some shit you may not like. It'll all be worth it in the end, and I'll be free from this shit once it's done."

I stood stone-faced, looking into Roc's eyes with tears welling in mine. I felt the bullshit about to go down.

"Baby, don't look at me like that. You breakin' my heart, but I gotta do this. I owe Ronnie my life and you don't know what that man has done for me."

"What do you have to do? Tell me and stop—"

"I gotta take the fall. The only way he gon' get out of this is if I do it. Ten years, baby, that's all I gotta do."

"Are you kidding me!" I yelled. "Ten years! You are willing to do ten years—I can't believe this shit!" I turned around, abruptly walking back to the car. I smacked away the tears that fell from my eyes and Roc rushed after me.

"Dez," he said, grabbing my arm to halt my steps. "Ten years ain't much. I can get out on good behavior and may be lookin' at even less than that."

My mouth dropped open, and if I had a gun, I would have killed him. "Can you stand there and say to me that ten fucking years in prison is not that much! How can you say that, Roc, when by the time you get out I'll be in my fifties. Your baby . . . oh God," I cried harder, unable to control my tears. "Your baby will grow up without—"

I gasped, holding my stomach. This was too much. Roc pulled me close to his chest and did his best to soothe my pain. Nothing in life prepared me for this moment and how in the hell did I manage to let something like this happen?

"Don't do it," I cried more with every deep breath I took. "Please don't do it."

Roc didn't say anything else. He knew, as I did, that he wasn't going to change his mind. On the way to my house, we didn't stop for frozen yogurt because I didn't want to. And when we got to my house, I got out of the car, not wanting him to come inside with me. There was nothing else left to be said, and through my eyes, Roc had chosen Ronnie over me and his child.

I went to the bathroom to wipe my tear drop stained face clean. My eyes were red and I wished like hell that what he'd told me was in a dream. It wasn't and it was time to face reality. I had fooled myself into believing that Roc could be better than what he was. He was walking away from all the progress he'd made and what a waste of time it had been. He knocked on the bathroom door.

"Do you want me to stay or go?" he asked.

"Do what you want!" I said.

"I wanna stay, but you act like you don't want me around. I'm dealin' with this shit too, Dez, and the last several weeks of my life ain't been no picnic. I had to tell you what was up, and if I didn't say nothin' you would have been mad at my ass for not tellin' you."

I sniffled, wiping my noise with Kleenex. "Is there anything I can say or do to get you to change your mind? Please, Roc, tell me. If you won't do it for me, do it for your baby. What about your baby? He or she will need you and I can't do this by myself. Don't do this to us. Think about the baby, okay?"

"Open the door. I can't talk to you like this."

I opened the door, falling into Roc's awaiting arms. "I already thought about all that you sayin' Dez, and you know how much I wanna be there for my baby. The police are willin' to let some of this shit slide, only if they get me or Ronnie to do the time. If not, he'll be looking at twenty or thirty years. I can't let that shit happen. That nigga took care of me when I was a baby. If I didn't have him, I would've been dead. You gotta understand why it's important for me to do this and I hate like hell I'm bringin' this kind of hurt to you."

"When is his trial? How soon—"

"It starts in a couple of weeks. Until then, I'm gon' spend as much time with you as I can, but I gotta get busy tying up some loose ends too. Let's pace this one day at a time, and I don't want to spend these days arguin' with you or with you bein' upset."

Roc was right. His mind was made up and what good did my being upset do for me? It did nothing but add to my hurt and made me even sicker.

***

Roc had been busy "tying up his loose ends" and as the days and nights ticked away, I was getting more scared by the minute. I couldn't stop crying and was on an emotional roller coaster. Whenever Roc came over, I put on my game face for him. I knew he was worried as hell about going to jail, but he played it down as if it didn't bother him. That was until we talked about it one night, and after he came clean about some of the things he and Ronnie had done, a tear fell from his eye. I was crushed and it made me fight even more to try to turn this mess around.

I wrote letters to Ronnie's attorney, the prosecutors, and even to the assigned judge, in an attempt to clear Roc's name. No one had replied, but when I got another interesting letter, I dropped back on the couch in my living room and started to read it. Months ago, when Roc had given his professional photos to me, I sent his pictures to some of the connections I had made when pursuing my modeling career. One of the modeling agencies had inquired about Roc's pictures and forwarded them on to a well-known beverage maker and upcoming clothing-line establishment in New York. They wanted Roc to call right away and this could be his chance and the opportunity he needed. Excited, I rushed over to the phone to call him. His voice mail came on and I left a message for him to call me back. An hour had gone by, and I was so anxious to talk to Roc that I snatched up my purse and left.

Other than that one time, I had never gone to his penthouse before, but I was going there today. I had to prove to him that there was a way out of this and that the doors were opening for him to come in.

It took forty-five minutes for me to get to Roc's penthouse in downtown St. Louis, and when I got there, I rushed to take the elevators to the seventh floor. I could hear the loud music coming through the door, and paused before knocking. I wasn't sure what I was about to get myself into, but Roc had to change his mind about going to jail, and do it fast.

I knocked, but no one answered, so I knocked again. My knocks got faster and harder and that's when Roc pulled the door open. The look on his face said it all—I wasn't supposed to be there. He was shirtless, high as hell, and his jean shorts hung low on his waist, showing his boxers. The loud rap music continued to thump in the background and marijuana smoke filled the air. I could hear people talking and much laughter as well.

Roc appeared to have seen a ghost and my presence wasn't enough to put a smile on his face. "What you doin' here?" he asked. He attempted to close the door, but not before somebody pulled on it to open it wide. I figured it was Vanessa, but instead, it was another young woman. I hadn't seen her before, but just like me and Vanessa, she was very pretty.

"Who is this?" she said, sipping from the straw that sunk into her tall glass of Long Island tea.

"Gon' back inside. And don't be walkin' up to my door unless I ask you to."

The chick rolled her eyes at me, gave her lips a toot, and walked away. Before Roc shut the door, I could see his uncle Ronnie in the background, a few more fellas, and even more women.

Roc folded his arms, cocking his neck to the side to stretch it. "What's up, ma?"

I wasn't about to shed one tear about this, and it took everything I had to hold back my feelings inside. I swallowed hard, blinking my eyes.

"So, this is how you do it, huh?" I asked.

He shrugged. "Sometimes. Even more so lately. Now, why you here?"

I gave him the envelope, placing the contact letter on top. "They want you to call them. I hope like hell that you do, but the ball is in your court. You may not get another opportunity like this,

Roc, and it would mean the world to me if you would take it."

Roc read the letter and nodded his head. I thought he would smile, but he didn't. All he said was, "I'll call them."

"When?"

"Soon."

The door came open and Ronnie walked out, closing it behind him. He gripped Roc's shoulder. "I'm gon' run to my car and get some mo blow. You a'ight? This bitch ain't out here causin' no trouble, is she?"

My hand trembled, and before I knew it, I swung out my hand, landing a hard slap across Ronnie's face. "You lowlife son of a bitch," I yelled. Roc grabbed my waist and Ronnie grabbed my neck, squeezing my jawline. He reached for his gun tucked behind him, placing it on the side of my head. I was beyond nervous and could feel the beads of sweat forming on my forehead.

"Man, don't you do that shit!" Roc yelled. "Put that muthafucka down and cool the fuck out!"

Ronnie continued to hold his grip on me and the gun. "Nigga I told you to get this bitch under control, didn't I?" He shoved my temple with the gun. "The only reason you gon' live 'cause of that nigga you got growin' in yo' belly. If you wasn't pregnant I would blow yo' fuckin' brains out for touchin' me."

Roc reached for the handle of the gun, moving it away from my head. He kept his arm around my waist, backing me away from Ronnie. He released his grip from my neck and turned to walk away.

"By the time I get back up here, her ass betta be gone. If not, I may change my mind 'bout killin' her. Do the right thing, baby boy, I'll be right back."

Roc let go of my waist, and punched the door with his fist. "Why in the fuck did you just do that? I can't believe this shit!"

My eyelids fluttered, and I thanked God for sparing my life again. I walked past Roc, making my way to the elevator.

"Dez," Roc repeatedly yelled. I kept on walking. "Come back here!"

I got on the elevator, looking out at him by his door with his hands pressed against it. He could keep his double life, and after finally seeing what was going on with my own eyes, I couldn't continue to be a part of this. This chapter in my life was now coming to a halt and it had been written in stone. Roc turned his head toward me, connecting our eyes once again. The elevator door slowly closed, validating a near end of what we had shared.

Chapter Thirteen

It was three days into Ronnie's trial, and the only reason I'd known that is by keeping up with the news. Him and his posse, including Roc, had some heavy things going on, including money laundering, racketeering, possession of illegal drugs with the intent to sell, and even murder charges against Ronnie that apparently weren't going to stick. The prosecutors were determined to get Ronnie on anything they had, but just by keeping up with everything that was going on, I could tell their case would be sloppy. Numerous people were arrested, and every day the news mentioned individuals who had been arrested for their connections to the crimes. I just knew I'd see Roc's face on TV, but I never did.

The night before Roc was expected to testify, I couldn't sleep at all. The baby kept moving too and I turned from side to side, trying to get comfortable. Around midnight, I got out of bed and went into the kitchen to get some orange juice.

I stood drinking it, with thoughts of Roc heavy on my mind. I hadn't talked to or heard from him since that day at his penthouse, and I wasn't even sure if I was going to Ronnie's trial. A huge part of me still wanted Roc to change his mind, and I knew if he'd see me, maybe, just maybe, he would come to his senses. I had no idea if he'd called the modeling agency back or not, but I hoped that tomorrow brought about more good news than bad.

I turned off the kitchen light, but heard a squeaking sound coming from my backyard. I cautiously walked to the door, and when I pulled it open, Roc was outside on the porch, sitting on my swing. He was smoking a cigar, but put it out with his foot before I walked up to him. I sat next to him, gathering my robe to close it. Yes, I wanted to slap him, curse him and order him to go home, but my heart went out to the man I'd had very strong feelings for. I could tell he was going through something deep and I felt no need to argue about the things I had witnessed at his penthouse, or about the double life he had apparently been living. Tonight, I would be there for Roc, but tomorrow he needed to be there for me. I took his hand, clinching it together with mine.

"Are you worried?" I asked. "I know that's a dumb question, but—"

"Yeah, I'm worried. That's why I'm here. I need peace and I always knew I could get that with you."

"Then why didn't you knock to let me know you were here?"

"I was goin' to, but I wanted to chill out here first."

I stood, trying to pull him up from the swing. "Come on, let's go inside."

"Nope," he said, not making a move.

"Why? Because I'm in trouble?"

Finally, he smiled. The whites came out and so did the dimples. "Hell yeah, you in trouble. Big . . . twelve-inch trouble. Can I make love to you?"

As much as I wanted to, I couldn't. It was now time for Roc to stop making me promises and show me that he was serious about changing his life around. "No, I don't want to go there tonight. We have some things that need to be resolved, and you know exactly what they are. The last thing I want to do is bring more stress upon you, so let's just go inside and enjoy our night together." I took Roc's hand, but he still didn't budge.

"Nah, let's stay right here," he said. "We can play back the day when it all went down, and maybe I can persuade you to change yo' mind."

"But you complained about not having enough room. Remember?"

"Yeah, but I've gotten much more creative since then too."

Roc remained on the swing, and I stood in front of him. I cradled his face with my hands, and he laid the side of his head against my stomach. "So, this may be it, huh?" I asked. "It doesn't have to be, and remember, the choice is yours. Tell them about Ronnie, Roc. Free yourself and tell them everything you know. They want him, not you."

Roc directed me back on the swing, lying behind me like when the first time he entered me. "I don't want to talk about tomorrow, okay? This night is for you and me, ma, that's it. Now, lay on yo' back so I can kiss my baby."

Since I'd been pregnant, Roc had been making me open my legs so he could "kiss his baby." This night was no different as he placed tender loving kisses on the outside crotch of my panties because I wouldn't remove them. Normally, he'd kiss my coochie lips, telling the baby how much he loved *him*. And even though things didn't go as he had planned that night, my kisses were all that I could offer him. I lifted my head, giving him juicy, unforgettable kisses throughout the night, telling him how I managed to fall in love with him. The way I felt now, there was no more denying my feelings.

"Who you wit Roc? Tell me, who exactly are you with?"

"Wit you," he assured. "I love you too and I'm stickin' wit you."

Tomorrow would surely tell if there was validity to his words.

The courtroom was packed with people, and I had just gotten there in time to find a place to sit. The normal crew was in full effect, and there was no doubt Vanessa would be there too. She was, but thank God she had sense enough to leave their son at home. She kept turning her head looking at me, and I was glad that my belly was now showing. I wore a beautiful white linen maternity dress and my hair was thick and full. Several black long beads draped from my neck and my Nine West Jamil open-toed sandals really set me off. Roc left early in the morning, and I hadn't seen or talked to him since then. He told me he had to meet with Ronnie's lawyers, and I prayed that everything went well. Before he left, I begged and pleaded with him again to do the right thing, but he never gave me confirmation. His embraces and continuous kisses to my forehead worried me. And before he left, he told me everything would be okay.

I sat biting my nails, waiting for things to get started. Every time Vanessa turned to look at me, I looked in another direction. I wasn't there to confront her, I was there for Roc and that's what was important. Ronnie had made his way into the courtroom and so had his lawyers. The prosecutors had been working their case for the last three days and now it was his lawyers' turn. When the judge came in, everybody stood. My legs started to shake a bit, but calmed once I sat down. Roc hadn't come in yet, but as soon as things got settled, Ronnie's lawyers didn't waste no time calling for their first witness. The first person they called was Roc. He came through the double wooden doors, dressed in a navy blue suit. A lighter blue shirt was underneath, closed tight by a silk tie. His hair was flowing with waves and his lining was done to perfection. He had toned down the diamonds, but did have one in his left ear. Everyone in the courtroom turned to take a look, and as he passed by me, he turned his head slightly to the side and winked. I watched as he made his way up front, and even though I couldn't see if he'd made eye contact with Vanessa, her smile at him implied that he had.

Roc was sworn in, then took a seat on the witness stand. From the beginning, and question

after question, Roc defended Ronnie. He almost
made him seem like an angel, but everyone knew
that was a bunch of bullshit. I was kind of happy
by the way things were going until the prosecutor got his chance to cross-examine. That's when
things took a turn for the worse. The prosecutor
yelled for Roc to "man up" and encouraged him
not to perjure himself anymore than he already
had.

"I want the truth!" he yelled, darting his finger
at Roc. "The whole truth and nothing but the
truth! With that," he said, turning and pointing
to Ronnie, "that son of a bitch goes to jail!"

I eased forward, uncrossing my sweating legs
that had started to tremble. My eyes were glued
to Roc, and after he glanced at me, his eyes shifted to Vanessa for a second. He then looked into
his lap, clearing his throat.

"I—uh," he paused, taking a swallow. He looked
up, cocking his head from side to side to stretch it.
He then looked at Ronnie and he slowly nodded.
"Ronnie's not the one who's been behind all of
this."

I moved my head from side to side, tightening my lips to muffle my words. He took another
glance at me and I mouthed *no*.

The lawyer opened his jacket, arrogantly placing his hands into his pockets. "Then who is re-

sponsible, Mr. Dawson? You? Somebody's got to pay for these crimes, so tell me, will it be him or someone else?"

"It's gon' be me," Roc admitted. "I've been the mastermind behind all of this and it should be me, not Ronnie."

The courtroom erupted with noises, but none louder than the judge slamming down his gavel. With each loud thud, it felt as if he was slamming it into my heart. I deeply sucked in the air around me, trying not to faint. *How could he?* I kept thinking. I stared at him, hoping that he would make eye contact with me again. He did and I immediately had flashbacks of meeting him at the car wash, the club . . . our intimate moments from the swing, to the cabin. Talks, and movies . . . our lengthy walks in the park, the day I told him I was pregnant, to the late-night dinners we shared. I hoped he was thinking what I was and through the look in my eyes, I wanted to transmit our times together. Out of all those times together, though, last night stuck in my head like glue. I asked Roc who he was with, and he said, "me." Today revealed what I expected all along. Roc wasn't with me or in love with me. Fortunately, the same went for Vanessa. He was with Ronnie, and the love Roc had for him was worth giving up his freedom.

Following the plan, Roc confessed to the prosecutors all that he'd done. The entire courtroom took in every word he said and so had the judge. He called for the bailiff to arrest Roc and the courtroom turned into chaos. Vanessa wailed out loudly, dropping to her knees in tears. Some other people were crying, but many were left shaking their heads. Ronnie was leaned back in his chair with his hands resting on the back of his head. Roc stood tall, and without a blink, his eyes stayed on Ronnie. He put his hands behind his back, and for the last time, his eyes shifted to me. He winked again, and I got up, leaving my seat. I shed not one tear and didn't dare to look back. *Damn him*, I thought. *How or why did I ever allow somebody like him to come into my life?*

The answer to my question came only a few months later. I gave birth to a five-pound, six-ounce baby girl. While going through my divorce with Reggie, I had asked God to take away my lonely nights and remove my pain. There were many mountains to climb and much pain to endure, but when my daughter was born, he gave me everything I had asked for and more. Latrel had been coming home from school more often, just to spend time with his little sister and me. Nothing in the world meant more to me than being with my children, and me making sure they fulfilled all of their dreams. I was overwhelmed with happiness when I saw the two of my children together and my family couldn't have turned out any better.

Roc had been writing me for a little over a year, getting no response. I kept all of his letters and I was rarely moved by anything he said. He begged me to come see him, and wanted me to send pictures of myself and his child. I did neither and struggled with going to see him because I still had feelings for him. I didn't even consider going to see him, until he or someone sent me his framed GED. He told me it belonged to me and wanted to make sure that his daughter knew all about him. I hadn't a clue how Roc knew we'd had a daughter, but when it came to him, he had his ways.

The following week, I made arrangements to go see him. Latrel was home, so our daughter, Chassidy, stayed with him. Before leaving, I lifted my baby girl above my head, wiggling her around so I could get her to laugh. She laughed, having dimples just like Roc. Her eyes belonged to him too and so did her smile. I'd shopped her baby pictures around for modeling gigs, and had already gotten numerous responses. I tucked in my purse the pictures of her eating baby food, as well as the one with her laughing while playing with toys. The one with her in pampers was my favorite, so I put that one in my purse as well. No doubt, she inherited a gift from her parents, and I wanted to make sure she didn't miss her calling.

I sat on the cold bench, waiting for Roc to come out. I was a year older, and my full figure was still going strong. After the baby, I had lost a measly four pounds but that was just fine with me. I didn't want to look too sexy for Roc, and the casual khaki skirt and jacket I wore seemed right for the occasion. I crossed my legs, looking at the high arches on my feet and my mid-heel pumps. When the door opened, I quickly looked up and there stood Roc. A guard was behind him, but he stood at the door. Dressed in a blue oversized shirt and baggy jeans that cuffed at the bottom, he made his way over to me with a smile.

"It's about damn time," he said, sitting across from me. "I thought you'd never get here."

I spoke softly, as seeing him always did something to me. It hurt like hell that all I could do was hug him, but could do none of the things I'd dreamed of doing over the year. "How have you been? In your letters you seem fine, but—"

"I'm good, but I can always be better, you know? I miss doin' me, and this place don't allow any of that."

"I'm sure it has its limitations and you are definitely not the kind of man who plays by the rules."

Roc laughed. "That's puttin' it mildly. Ronnie makes sure that I get some special privileges in here, so I work with what I can."

The thought of Ronnie made me cringe and I instantly got quiet.

"So, where my pictures at? I know you brought me some."

I had to be thoroughly checked before coming in, and the pictures of his daughter had been placed in a Ziploc bag. "This is Chassidy," I said, handing the pictures over to him. "She's a baby model and has a really bright future waiting for her."

Roc grinned from ear to ear while looking at the pictures, seeing himself in her. "Damn, she gorgeous," he said. "I had no doubt she'd be this pretty and we did good, didn't we?"

"Yeah," I said, nodding. "Latrel told me to tell you hi too, and the two of them spend a lot of time together."

"Tell that nig—tell 'em I said what's up. Reggie ain't been snooping around, has he, or are you gon' hang in there and wait for me?"

Roc put his hands behind his head, waiting for an answer. The guard reminded him to keep his hands on the table so he could see them.

"No, Reggie hasn't been coming around and I've been pretty content by myself."

"But you ain't answer the second part to my question . . . are you gon' be there for me when I get out of here? I've been readin' a lot . . . even been reading some of those damn books you read. It be some freaky shit goin' on in them books, and no wonder yo' ass stay horny. I also been talkin' to a brotha in here 'bout how I can earn myself another degree. I already started to sharpin' my skills and you'd be surprised 'bout all I've been doin' in here."

"Are you willing to do those things when you get out? That's the question. I can't make you any promises, Roc, and unfortunately, I can't keep coming back here seeing you like this. I am still so angry for what you cost us, and I don't know when I'll be able to completely forgive you."

Roc looked down at Chassidy's pictures. "Sounds like I'm in trouble?" He smiled.

I laughed. "Big-ass trouble!"

"Well, it's a good thing that trouble don't always last too long. I'm gon' get out of here, ma, and I comin' for you. I ain't gon' make you no promises 'bout what I'm gon' do, and I know I just gotta show you what's up."

"Whatever you do, do it for yourself. Now, I gotta get back home. Latrel is heading back to school tonight and I told him I wouldn't be long."

Roc nodded and reached out to touch my hand. "Take care of my baby and keep sending me pictures. I still got that one of you that was on my fridge, but I want more. These niggas in here goin' crazy over that picture of you, and I still kiss that muthafucka every mornin' I wake up. I miss rockin' my pussy to sleep and I sometimes go crazy 'cause I can't get at it. I appreciate everything you done for me, Dez, and no matter what you think, I have a special kind of love for you in my heart. This shit was destined and it couldn't have turned out any other way. It was time for me to pay the piper and so be it."

I saw things much differently than Roc did, but didn't say what I felt. To me, he had a choice. Many doors opened for him, but he chose to close them. Opportunity after opportunity presented itself, but Roc had a mindset that the world he lived in was set in stone by those who came before him. According to him, his mother, father, and Ronnie had set it all up for him, leaving him very little options. He had options, but settled for what he thought was best. This time, his best wasn't good enough for him, for me, or for his children. His decision affected many lives, and there was no way for us to go back and turn back the hands of time.

The guard allowed Roc and me to embrace. He even threw in a lengthy kiss, implying that it was one of his privileges. We stood forehead to forehead, searching into each other's eyes.

"Take care, Snookums. I'll write you back and keep in touch."

"No doubt. When you get home, do me a favor. Look in yo' garage, by the lawn mower, okay? I got a surprise for you and I want you to keep it."

I nodded, and after one final kiss, Roc left the room.

I was so happy on my way back home, and was glad that I'd gone to see him. It gave me closure and that was truly something I needed. When I got back home, Latrel was in the yard playing with Chassidy. I kissed the both of them, then went to the garage to see what Roc had left.

While searching, I found a black leather briefcase tucked away in the corner. I flipped the locks and it came open. Inside was money. There were stacks and stacks of one-hundred dollar bills, and I couldn't even imagine how much money it was. I knew it was enough money where I could quit my job and live off of it for the rest of my life. I could travel the world . . . pay for Chassidy's education. Roc had put a note inside, telling me that he was saving this money for a rainy day.

I knew this day would come and I want you and my child to have everything you need.

Love, Snookums.

I kept the note, but closed the suitcase tight. *Didn't he get to know me at all,* I thought. I rushed outside, telling Latrel that I would be right back. I knew he had to drive back to school tonight, but I had to do this. I drove like a bat out of hell to Roc's penthouse, and just my luck, Ronnie was standing outside talking to several men. Some kids were nearby on a playground playing and many young men were outside playing basketball. I parked, making my way up to Ronnie with the briefcase in my hand.

"Don't start none, won't be none," he said.

"Go to hell, Ronnie. And I want you to know that this shit ain't over just yet. I'm going to do everything in my power to make sure you pay for what you've done to Roc and your downfall is definitely coming."

I flipped open the suitcase and several guns were aimed at me.

"Hold it down," he ordered.

"This belongs to you."

I tossed the suitcase high up in the air and all the bills came tumbling down like rain. The young men playing basketball chased after the money, and so did the kids from the playground. I headed back to my car, not knowing if a bullet was going to catch me from behind or not. I heard Ronnie mumble "stupid bitch" and he yelled for his men to get as much of the money as they could. I sped off, closing one long chapter in my life, happily waiting for the next.

Latrel was home for the summer and was now in his junior year at college. He was doing well in school and I couldn't be more proud. Reggie was glad that his son was doing well too, and even though we both felt the same way, unfortunately, our friendship never did rekindle. He was so upset with me for getting pregnant by Roc, and according to Reggie, each time he saw Chassidy it just broke his heart. I was sorry to hear that, because my heart was fulfilled. He was the one already planning for a second divorce and it was so funny how things had managed to turn around.

I told Roc that I would keep in touch that day, but our conversations were here, there, and far in-between. I had at least a hundred letters from him, but he'd gotten minimal from me. I wanted so badly to forgive him for taking the fall for Ronnie, but as I watched Chassidy get older, without having him in her life, I couldn't get over what he'd done. It wasn't like Roc would have been the perfect role model or anything, but to me, he could have changed his life around and tried to be there for his daughter. He was starting to prove that he wanted to do it, but the grip that Ronnie had on him was hard to break. In knowing so, I washed my hands clean and did my best to never look back.

I could hear Latrel outside playing with Chassidy in her rubber-ducky blow-up swimming pool he'd gotten her. He had the music up loud, but I could hear the water splashing, along with her laughter. I was in the kitchen preparing dinner and had bent over to remove the croissants from the oven. I burned my hand, immediately snatching it away from the hot pan.

"Ouch," I yelled, placing the tip of my tongue on my finger to cool it. I opened the pantry closet, looking for my oven mitten to use. The back door came open, and I heard Chassidy calling for me.

"Here I come, sweetie," I said, looking for my mitten. "Latrel, turn that music down a little and did you turn off the water outside?"

He didn't answer and when I stepped away from the closet to see why, I got the shock of my life. My heart picked up speed and I blinked several times, just to be sure. I saw those dimples that I figured I'd never see again. Those pearly whites were still going strong and the man whom I craved for was still clean-cut as ever. Roc balanced Chassidy on his shoulders, while she bent down pecking the top of his head.

"Daddy's home," he said. "I told you I was gon' do this, didn't I? Question is . . . Who you wit, Dez? You still wit me or wit some other nigga? Tell me what's up?"

I swallowed, speechless as ever. I hadn't a clue how I would answer his question, and a huge part of me thought this day would never, ever come.

Seven Year Itch

By

La Jill Hunt

Acknowledgments

First, as always, I would like to thank God for his continual and steadfast blessing. For everything, Lord, I say thanks.

To my daughters: Alyx, who has grown into a beautiful, young woman; Kamaryn, who continues to strive in everything she does, and Kennedey, who keeps me laughing and entertained. I don't know what I would do without you all.

To my family, for their support.

To my friends Yvette Lewis, Chenay Cuffee, Anisha Holmes, Monica Simon, Monteal Cuffee, Nakea Murray, Shantel Spencer, Joycelyn W. Ward, Saundra White, Scott Ward, W. Jermaine Roach, Tasha Price, Robin LeBron, Leslie Dickey, Tamara James, and Rosnette Hayes. Thanks for being there for me.

To my literary twin Dwayne S. Joseph, I am so proud of you and can't wait to see *Eye for an Eye* blow up. Do your thing, D!

To my agent, Portia Cannon for enduring the headache that comes with that responsibility.

To Trevis L. Brown, for trusting me with all that you are, and loving me with all that I am. I love and thank you, Bae for believing in me, and all that WE can make happen.

To Urban Books, again, thank you for another opportunity to release the DRAMA.

For my fans and readers, for all of the e-mails, messages, and support of all the DRAMA I write. Thank you, thank you, thank you!

To anyone I may have forgotten, believe me, it wasn't intentional. Insert your name here _____ and know that I thank you too.

Feel free to hit me up at MsLajaka@aol.com or on Facebook or Myspace.

Prologue

Am I dead? I can't be dead; my head hurts too bad for me to be dead. If I were dead, I wouldn't feel so shitty. Oh God, I wish I was dead rather than feel like this.

Avery tried opening her eyes, but the brightness of the sun peeking through the window caused her to quickly shut them. Without a doubt, this was the hangover of all hangovers. Her stomach flip-flopped and she tried to suppress the wave of nausea rising. She could tell by the feel of the bed and the scent of the room that she wasn't at home, that was for sure. The question was, where the hell was she and how the hell did she get there? Everything seemed to be a blur. She remembered attending the company gala at the Pavilion, and then someone suggested they all go for drinks afterward. She recalled being at a bar, then arguing with someone—that was it. The more she tried to remember, the worse she felt. She was definitely going to be sick. Slowly sitting up, she spotted a doorway opening to a bathroom and she rushed inside, barely making it to the toilet before vomiting.

I may not be dead, but I'm dying, she thought as she leaned her sweat-drenched face against the cool porcelain of the toilet. *I can't believe this, I never get drunk. What the hell was I thinking?* Before she could think of an answer, another wave of nausea overcame her and again she vomited for what seemed like hours.

"Are you okay?"

If she would have had the energy, Avery probably would have been startled out of her mind. Instead, she just glanced up to see him standing in the doorway, holding what seemed to be a glass of water and a towel. Instead of answering, she just closed her eyes. Moments later, she felt his arms around her, lifting her off the floor, something few guys were able to do considering her stature. But he seemed to have no problem picking all 232 pounds up and carrying her back to the bed that she had crawled out of.

"Thanks," she murmured, pulling the covers over her body. She felt too bad to even be concerned about the fact that the only thing she wore was a bra, camisole, and her panties.

"Here, drink some of this," he said. "You don't need to get dehydrated."

Avery sat up to take a sip of the water, praying that it wouldn't come back up. "What time is it?"

"Almost one," he said, handing her two small tablets. She hesitated before taking them.

"They're just aspirin, Avery. That's all," he said, smiling. "What the hell is wrong with you?"

"I don't know," Avery replied. "I just don't feel right. Like something's weird."

"It's called a hangover."

"No, I've had a hangover before. But this is different."

"Different how?" He frowned.

"Like, I can't remember anything from last night. Everything is all fuzzy."

"Avery, I hope you don't think I did anything to you, because I swear, I didn't," he quickly told her. "You called me from some bar downtown and when I got there, you were in the corner waiting for me. You passed out in the backseat as soon as you got in the car. You didn't have a purse, a cell phone. I didn't know what to do. I called Tabitha, she didn't answer, so I just brought you here. When I put you in the bed, you were dressed; you must've taken your own clothes off. I ain't do that. I didn't touch you."

Their eyes met and she became lost in his piercing gaze. His dark eyes told her things that she knew he felt, but dared not say to her, out of respect for her, and their friendship. She wondered if her eyes told him the same things. They were friends, nothing more and she knew she could trust him.

Avery shook her head at him. "I know you didn't."

She knew her body, and could tell that nothing sexual had taken place, which was a relief. And she also wasn't surprised when he said she had taken her own clothes off. Avery didn't get drunk very often, but when she did, stripping her clothes off was one of the side effects. Once, in college, she had taken all of her clothes off in the middle of the dorm hallway. That was one of the reasons she didn't drink to the point to where she was inebriated.

"I just wanna make that clear," he said.

"But where is my purse and stuff? Was I robbed?"

"I don't think so," he answered. "You called me from your cell. You probably left it in the bar."

Avery tried to remember, but it was too fuzzy. She took another sip of water, "Why the hell can't I remember anything?"

"Hey, lay back down for a while. We'll figure this all out when you're feeling better," he told her. "I'll check on you in a little while."

"Thanks," Avery said, drifting off to sleep. As much as she wanted to figure out what all had transpired last night, she wanted to go to sleep even more.

Three hours later, Avery woke again. This time when she opened her eyes, she had energy enough to sit up without feeling as if the world was spinning around her and she was going to puke her insides out. She still had a slight headache, but it was bearable. She felt better. Until she realized that she hadn't been home, hadn't called home, and her man was probably worried to death about her. She pulled herself together, took a quick shower and graciously accepted a T-shirt and a pair of baggy sweats to wear home. The twenty-minute ride to her house was mostly silent with the exception of the Anthony Hamilton CD playing. She was grateful for the silence, not knowing what to expect when she got to her house. She tried calling Duke, but didn't get an answer and left him a message saying she was on her way home. When they got to the neighborhood, she glanced over to see his reaction. He had to be wondering why a single, educated female making over sixty thousand dollars a year lived in a neighborhood as pitiful as the one she did.

She directed him to pull into the driveway directly behind her Maxima. As soon as he did so, the screen door opened and Duke walked outside. The frowns in his face were so deep Avery could see them from where she was sitting. She knew he was pissed, and that was understandable. She would be pissed too if he had done the same thing to her.

"Time to face the music," she said, shrugging.

"You gonna be all right?"

"Of course," she told him, "Believe me, his bark is worse than his bite."

"Still, maybe I should walk you to the door and help you explain what happened," he offered.

Avery paused before opening the car door. "I don't even know exactly what happened or how to explain it. I'm good, really."

Before she could stop him, he opened his own car door and hopped out. "What's up, Duke."

God, please don't let Duke act a fool out here, Avery prayed, quickly getting out.

"Hey, baby," she said, putting her arms around him. Duke stiffened, causing her to pull away quickly. "Did you get my message?"

"Yeah, I got it," he said, still staring at Kurt.

Avery looked down at her clothes and realized how crazy she must look in the T-shirt, sweats, and black stiletto heels with her hair standing all over her head. "It's a long story, believe me."

"Hey, the important thing is you're home and you're safe, right, Duke?"

"So, you spent the night with *him*?" Duke finally spoke.

"Yeah," Avery answered.

"Interesting," Duke said.

"Only because she called me," Kurt said. "She was wasted and needed a ride."

"You called him instead of calling me," Duke said, sounding more like a statement rather than a question.

Avery tried to remember whether or not she called Duke. Just as she was about to speak, a blue BMW pulled in front of the house. All three of them turned and watched as the door opened and Demi stepped out.

"Demi, what are you doing here?" Avery was surprised.

"I brought your purse and phone that you left at the bar," Demi said, passing Avery the small black clutch purse, then said suspiciously, "I'm glad to see you made it home. When Duke called your phone last night, I told him you left with a friend and I would make sure to bring your things over this afternoon."

Avery glanced over at Duke and saw the anger in his eyes. She knew what he had to have been thinking, especially after Demi telling him that. But none of it was making sense. She reached in her purse and took out her phone, scrolling through her call history. *What the hell happened? Come on Avery, think. . . . Try. . . . Remember. . . . the party . . . the bar . . . Demi. . . . Duke. . . . Demi. . . .*

Suddenly, as if a dark veil was lifted, it all became clear. Avery's breathing began to become labored and without thinking twice, she attacked.

Chapter One

Six Months Earlier

Avery sat in the driveway watching the rain hit the windshield of her car. She had been waiting fifteen minutes for it to stop, or at least slack up enough for her to run into the house. But it seemed to drag on and on, much like her day. As if Mondays weren't bad enough. Since Duke hadn't gone to the grocery store like he had been promising to do for the past three days, Avery had been forced to fight the first-of-the-month crowd at the Food Zone on the way home. After dealing with screaming toddlers throwing temper tantrums in the middle of the aisles and their loud, non-attentive mothers who were so busy yapping on their cell phones to even care that their kids were acting like misbehaved brats, then waiting in line for thirty minutes, Avery discovered that someone had politely helped themselves to her wallet. She knew she had it when she arrived at the store because she had double-checked it to make sure she had her Food Zone discount savers card. *Those sorry, thieving bastards*, Avery thought as she looked around the store for the culprit. Everyone near her looked like they had a reason to, and could have lifted her wallet and they all seemed to purposely be avoiding her looks. *This is why I hate this neighborhood. Gangbangers, hoochies, and ghetto dwellers who are too trifling to go to school, get a job, and do something with their lives. Instead, they would rather steal from people like me who work hard for what they have.* Without her wallet, she was forced to leave her items in the basket and go home. As soon as she walked out the store, the sky seemed to open up and cry, the same way she wanted to. She thought about calling the police, but there was no point. First of all, she doubted that they would even show up in the middle of the hood, and second, the culprit was probably so far gone and had already taken the twelve dollars in cash she had inside, bought the drug of their choice, and was already high as gas.

Avery hadn't always felt this way. Growing up, Coleman Village had been home for her. The small neighborhood of brick row homes was a close-knit community where everyone had looked out for one another. But over the years, it had diminished and become drug and gang infected. The streets she had rode her bike along when she was a kid no longer felt safe and it was often featured on the nightly news as the backdrop for the latest murder, gang war or crime wave. The only reason Avery stayed was because her boyfriend, Duke, had no desire to leave. If he had his way, he probably would be buried right in Coleman Village.

The sound of thunder clapped so loud that it caused Avery to jump. Duke's car was gone and the thought of being inside, alone, caused her to worry. The auto-parts store where he worked closed an hour ago, and he hadn't mentioned going anywhere when he got off. She reached for her cell phone and dialed his number for the fifth time since leaving Food Zone, and for the fifth time it went straight to voice mail. *Where the hell is he?* she thought. She shook her head and willed herself the energy to run from the car to the front porch. The cold rain did nothing to help the lock, which was now slippery, in addition to already being tricky.

"Damn it!" she shouted into the darkness, "I hate this fucking house!"

Finally, the light clicked and the door finally opened. Avery froze, hearing voices coming from the back room that they used as a den. *Great, that's all I need, to walk in on some damn burglars.*

"So, Ms. Crawford, tell me what you don't like about yourself?" a man's voice asked.

Avery breathed a sigh of relief. After locking the door, she walked in and saw a familiar scene from *Nip/Tuck* on the plasma TV screen, which Duke had obviously left on. She also noticed that he also left a huge bowl of half-eaten cereal in the middle of the coffee table and his Timbs and a pair of socks in the middle of the floor. Not having the energy to clean up his mess, she headed straight upstairs to their bedroom. Clicking on the light, she immediately saw that Duke had left a mess there as well. His sweats and wife beater were thrown in the middle of their unmade bed. In the bathroom, his razor was laying on the sink along with a wet rag. Again, Avery pretended the mess didn't exist. She took a long, hot shower, cleared a path in the bed, and climbed under the covers. Just as she was about to close her eyes, she spotted her computer bag and statistics book on the nightstand.

"Shit, my homework!" She sat up. It was well after eleven and she didn't even have the strength. Unable to hold back the tears she had been fighting all night, Avery lay back down and cried. This is not how she wanted to live her life. This is not what she worked hard and sacrificed for. *Four years of college, almost two years of grad school, twelve hours at a job I don't even like, a home where I don't even feel safe, and a man who seems to be gone more than he's home. Why am I dealing with all this bullshit? Why?* She knew the answer better than anyone. She dealt with it because she was in love.

"So, are you saying this is my fault?"

"I didn't say that," Avery snapped as she got dressed. The clock read 6:40 and she had to be out the door in the next twenty minutes if she was going to make it to work on time. The "no tardy" policy at her job, Jennings International, was one that wasn't taken lightly. Management was always looking for something to say and although she was rarely late, she wasn't in the mood to have to answer to anyone.

"But that's how you're acting. Like I was the one that stole your wallet," Duke grumbled as he rolled over and lifted his head. One of his turn-ons was watching Avery get dressed in the mornings and normally she would give him a show, but she wasn't in the giving mood this morning, that was for damn sure. Instead, she took her pantsuit into the bathroom and slipped it on. By the time she came back into the bedroom, she was fully dressed and Duke was now sitting on the side of the bed. Avery couldn't help but notice the slight glance of disappointment on his face. *No peepshow for you, boo*, she thought as she grabbed her laptop and book bag, then headed out the door.

"So, you're not even gonna say anything to me, Avery?" Duke whimpered.

Avery paused then turned around slowly. "You need to go to the grocery store. We're out of milk."

She had barely made it onto the interstate when her cell phone began ringing and Duke's name and picture appeared on the screen. It took her ignoring his calls five times before he realized she didn't want to talk. She sent him a text telling him she would call when she got to work and he responded with a quick I Love u. Normally, it would have put a smile on her face, but after the night and morning she had, she wasn't feeling any love. Her phone rang again, and this time, she saw that it was her coworker, Tabitha.

"Hey, girl," Avery greeted her, "I'm glad you called."

"You should always be glad that I call," Tabitha said. "Not too many people have that honor. I'm at Starbucks."

"Thank God," Avery sighed. The thought of much-needed caffeine waiting on her when she got to work was almost enough to make her feel better.

"And can I get a tall mocha latte, no foam," Tabitha said.

"No, wait,"Avery interrupted her. "Venti, with a double shot of espresso."

Tabitha repeated Avery's order to the barista, then remarked, "A double shot? Wow, someone must've had a hell of a night. Sex or studying?"

"Neither," Avery answered. "And I'm gonna need for you to let me into the building."

"Damn, you *are* having a rough morning. You left your badge too?"

"No, someone stole my wallet last night at the grocery store."

"Aw, Avery, that's jacked up. Did you cancel all of your credit cards?"

"They weren't even in my wallet; my check card and credit cards were at home in my checkbook, which was at home. All they got was my license, my insurance card, my work badge, and a measly thirteen dollars and some change," Avery told her. "They would've come out better stealing the damn four-hundred-dollar purse."

"Probably some low-life kids," Tabitha told her. "At least they didn't get your plastic."

"No, but it was still frustrating as hell, and I have to go get a new license. I'm gonna leave early and go take care of that, if they'll let me. You know how funny-acting they can be at times."

"If they give you any problems, just let me know. I'll pull some strings and see what I can do," Tabitha laughed.

"Yeah, like you got it like that," Avery chuckled. "Hell, they hate you as much as they hate me up in there."

"Not the guys, only the females, and that's because they are intimidated by our brains, beauty and most of all, our breasts!"

That really made Avery laugh. Tabitha was five feet two and a size four on a good day. They were total opposites. Whereas Avery's cup size was clearly a triple D, Tabitha's may have been a B. And although both women dressed better than anyone else in the entire five-story building, Tabitha's wardrobe only consisted of the color black and high heels. Avery loved her bubbly, petite, blond coworker who smoked like a chimney, although every week she swore she was quitting. How the two of them became such great friends, Avery didn't know, but working beside Tabitha made her days go by faster and the job a little more bearable.

"And what breasts are you speaking of, Tabitha?" Avery asked, "Surely, you must be referring to mine."

"Mine too, you jerk. Yours may be larger, but mine have more perk!"

"Okay, you do have a point," Avery agreed. "Just have your perky-ass breasts at the door when I get there and let me in. I'll be there in ten minutes."

"Not a problem. I'll be there in five."

Chapter Two

"Ladies, we have a department meeting this morning. You need to report to the conference room at nine-fifteen," the department secretary said as soon as Avery and Tabitha arrived at their desks.

"What's this about?" Avery asked, looking at Malcolm, who was their other coworker whose cube was between theirs—thus the nickname they gave him: Malcolm-in-the middle.

"Don't look at me," Malcolm said, shrugging.

"Don't lie, Malcolm," Tabitha whispered, "you know everything that goes on around here. First of all, you're nosy as hell and second of all, don't front like you're not banging Kurt's sister, Sharice, who works on the fourth floor."

Malcolm looked at the two of them like a kid who just got caught with his hand in the cookie jar. He was a really nice guy who seemed to have no control over his libido, and so oblivious to how attractive he was that it made him an easy target for the vultures in the office. If it wasn't for Avery and Tabitha clueing him in on the gaming skeezers they worked with, he would probably be a father a hundred times over in the three years they all worked together.

"I swear, I don't know anything. And I'm not banging Sharice," Malcolm told them. "We're just friends."

"Yeah, that's what you said about Darla, and didn't she file a paternity suit against you not too long ago?" Tabitha folded her arms and nodded. "Granted, she filed one against several other dudes too."

"And don't forget about Lori from accounting," Avery said, nodding.

"The married chick that looked like a man," Tabitha snickered.

"Who brought you lunch every day," Avery said, "and bought you some pretty nice gifts too, I might add."

"Until her husband found out," Tabitha added.

"Don't hate because I'm the office mack." Malcolm rubbed his chin and struck a *GQ* pose.

"More like the office whore," Tabitha corrected him.

"What are you trying to say, Tabitha?" Avery asked, taking a sip of her coffee.

"I'm just saying that if he's screwing the director's sister, which we all know he is, he should, one, make sure he's wrapping it up, two, he should be able to get some inside information, and three, can you put in a good word for me because you know how much I am really trying to get with Kurt." Tabitha plopped herself on Malcolm's desk. Tabitha wore her love for black men like a red badge of courage, and she was not ashamed in the least. The fact that the black women in the office frowned upon a white woman having the hots for them didn't even seem to bother Tabitha. She didn't care and just shrugged it off by saying she liked what she liked.

"You are crazy," Malcolm laughed, pushing Tabitha off.

Avery's cell phone rang, and she quickly grabbed it. "Damn it, I forgot to put this on vibrate. Hello."

"I thought you were gonna call me when you got to work," Duke asked.

"I just got here, Duke. I'm still getting settled," she said, turning her back to Malcolm and Tabitha.

"I can't believe you had an attitude with me this morning."

Had? How about I still have one, Avery thought but instead told him, "I can't believe that I told you someone stole my wallet out of the basket at the

store and your reaction was to tell me it was dumb
to have my purse in the basket to start with? What
kind of shit is that, Duke?"

"I'm just saying. You know this neighborhood
ain't the safest, boo. You gotta be careful at all
times."

"Is that supposed to make me feel better?" Avery asked, "You're right, the neighborhood ain't
the safest, which is why I've been telling you we
need to move for months now."

"Here we go with that again," Duke grunted.
"Avery, you know I ain't leaving this house. Uncle Larry left me this house and as rough as this
neighborhood may be, it's still home. You grew
up here the same way I did. I used to run these
streets, you know that."

He was right, he did used to run the streets of
Coleman Village. Not only did he run the streets
on foot as a little boy, but as he grew older,
Douglas "Duke" Manning became one of the
biggest runners in the dope game. Flashy cars,
clothes, jewelry, and the women, he had it all,
until one day he spotted Avery Belmont working
at the recreation center as a counselor one summer. She was seventeen and had just graduated
from high school, preparing to leave for college
in a few months. Duke asked her out and she
declined. Not only did she tell him no, but she

warned him that the center was considered a school zone and if he got caught on the property with dope on him, it was an automatic ten-year sentence. Duke thought she was joking until he saw in her face that she was dead serious.

"What's your deal?" he asked her. "You think you're too good for a brother like me?"

Avery looked at him and shook her head. "No, not at all. I think it's really sad that a brother with as much potential as you doesn't even realize that you're better than this."

"I don't think so." He stared at her. "You're beautiful, intelligent, and sexy as hell. What could be better?"

"I think you got it twisted," Avery said. "It gets no better than me. You're too good to be in this dumb-ass dope game. You're better than that."

From that moment, Duke was in love. His boys and most folks in the neighborhood couldn't understand what he saw in the "smart, big girl" as most of them considered her. It took him almost two years for Avery to go out with him. And she did so only after he eventually got out the game and became legit. It was Avery who helped him get his GED and by the time she finished college, he had gotten a decent job working at Tangier and Sons Auto Parts and Service, right near the neighborhood. His Uncle Larry was proud of the changes his nephew made and he knew that it was all due to Avery. When he died, he left the house to both of them, along with his beloved Caddy, which Duke cherished. Everything seemed to be working out for the young couple; without having to pay rent, Avery landed a well-paying job at Jennings International and enrolled in grad school. But lately, things were becoming strained between them. Her job was stressful and so was school, and Duke put more money into the Caddy and electronics for the house than he did into paying the bills and contributing toward their future. The two of them just weren't on the same page— hell, they didn't even seem to be in the same book.

"Look, I have a meeting I gotta go to, Duke. I'll call you at lunch," Avery told him, then hung up. She stood up and rubbed her temples. "My head is pounding."

"Well, prepare yourself because this meeting probably isn't gonna make it any better. You need some drugs, Ave? I got Percocet, Darvocet, Vicodin . . ." Tabitha began digging in her purse.

"Does it bother you that the contents of your purse contain as many narcotics as the Walgreens up the street?" Malcolm asked.

"Hey, I look at it like being a Girl Scout, always prepared," Tabitha replied.

"Prepared would be having aspirin," Malcolm said.

The three walked into the already crowded conference room and sat down, with Malcolm being in the middle of them once again. Avery couldn't help but notice the excitement in his face when Sharice walked in and waved at him.

"And you don't have a clue about what this is about?" Tabitha leaned over and asked.

"No!" Malcolm hissed. "I promise, I don't know anything. If I did, I would've said something."

The room got quiet as Kurt Miller, their CFO and director, who also happened to be the brother of Sharice, walked in, followed by the department team leads. Among them was a woman whom Avery had never seen in the office, but looked vaguely familiar.

"Good morning," Kurt said. His deep voice seemed to echo in the room. As usual, he was impeccably dressed in a dark suit and power tie; his wavy hair cut close and his face shaven so smooth that Avery could tell, just by looking at it, it was soft to touch. His skin was the exact shade as the coffee she was drinking and he looked just as hot. She saw every reason in the world for Tabitha to want him—hell—if her own situation was different, she would want him too.

"Good morning," everyone mumbled.

"Well, I'm sure you're wondering what this impromptu meeting is about. So, I'm going to cut straight to the chase and let you all know that as of last night, there have been some organizational changes," he announced.

A unified groan went through the room. Avery, Tabitha, and Malcolm all looked at each other. They all knew that *organizational changes* was the company's key phrase for either someone getting fired or their department was being shifted to clean up some mess created by another department.

"This department will no longer handle marketing for the southeast district," Kurt continued. "That task will be transferred to another office."

And here comes the bullshit, Avery thought.

"This office will now be the site responsible for consumer client commitments."

Consumer client commitments? Yeah, right. That's just a fancy term for customer service. Oh, hell no. I did not bust my ass in college to be a customer service rep.

"This is ridiculous," someone behind them said.

Kurt cleared his throat. "With all of the changes and regulations with Homeland Security, some of our clients have fallen through the loop and it's caused somewhat of a company dilemma."

"What about customer relations? Isn't that their job?" someone yelled. "Why are we always the ones changing departments? I'm tired of doing everyone else's job."

"I know this is gonna be a little uncomfortable at first, but look at it as the faith the company has in you, in addition to it being job security. In addition, over the next month or so, there will be a staff reduction of approximately fifteen percent."

Avery was shocked; a company layoff was the last thing she expected. She couldn't afford to lose her job. Although Duke was working, she was the major breadwinner in the house, plus this job was paying her way through grad school. Avery looked up and saw Kurt pointing to the woman she thought looked familiar.

"I'd like to introduce you to Demi Hayes, the district manager for marketing. Starting today, you will report directly to Demi. I've assured her that you all are hardworking and she can count on you for results. Demi."

The woman walked up to the podium, barely smiling. She didn't even say hello before telling them, "We will make every effort to assist those affected by the staff reduction with possibly finding other positions within the company. We will also be offering early retirement bonuses for those who wish to take advantage." As she spoke, Avery tried to rack her brain and figure out where she knew the woman from. "There will be schedule changes, including nights and weekends for some of you. And as Kurt has already said, you all will report directly to me. I'm sure that that is understood and therefore, this will be a smooth transition for us all."

No one moved when Demi walked away from the podium and out the door. They all just sat in silence, not knowing what to do next.

Reduction of staff . . . nights and weekends . . . customer service . . . stolen wallet . . .homework and school . . .it was all too much for Avery to deal with and her head began to pound harder, her coffee cup was now empty.

Finally, Avery stood up and said, "I need some caffeine and the strongest pill you got, Tabby!"

"I need a drink," Malcolm said. "And a couple of pills myself."

"Fuck all that," Tabitha said, frowning. "I need a blunt."

Chapter Three

"I can't believe you found it," Avery told Mr. Niwab, the store manager who called her and told her right before lunch she could come pick up her wallet. She got permission to take an hour lunch and rushed over to Food Zone.

"It was behind some boxes of cereal. Someone must've stuck it back there," the Indian man said, nodding. "Check it, is everything there?"

"Everything but the cash," Avery said, seeing her license, insurance card, and work badge all sitting in place. "But, that's fine."

"It was probably some kids," he told her. "They come in here and steal all the time. Chips, soda, candy, it's ridiculous. We will be selling this place soon enough."

"Really?" Avery asked. She wasn't surprised by his announcement and she didn't really blame him at all. Then, she thought about the fact that it was the only store within a ten-mile radius and the only one the elderly people in the neighborhood could get to. For a moment, she felt bad.

"It's no longer worth it. The thieves are taking more than we are selling," he said. "I remember when we first bought this place from Mr. McGregor. He was excited because we bought it rather than the big chain that would come in and make all the prices higher. He wanted to keep it family owned."

"Mr. McGregor," Avery said. "I remember him."

"Yes, he was a nice man. But the young people here have nothing to do. No activities or anything to keep them busy, so they fall by the wayside and steal from us. No more, we are leaving."

"That's sad," Avery sighed. She said good-bye and headed back to work. She thought about the days she worked at the neighborhood rec center and the lives she tried to impact. It had closed down before she had graduated from college, when the city said that it no longer had the funds to keep it open. Funny, they seemed to have enough money to build new jails and parks in the suburbs. As she drove home, she looked around. It was hopeless and there was nothing she could do about it. As she headed out of Coleman Village and emerged onto the interstate, the sky seemed to brighten as if the world was a better place.

"That's great news, baby," Duke said when she called to tell him they found her wallet. There was something in his voice that wasn't right.

"What's wrong, Duke?" she asked.

"Man, they just told us that some investment company just bought the shop and the store. I can't believe this shit. Now some shirts and ties are gonna be in charge," he sighed.

"They're not laying off, are they?" Avery asked. She hoped not, especially with the possibility of losing her own job.

"Naw, they ain't say nothing like that. But you know they are gonna come in here and try to change shit," Duke replied. "I know Mr. Tangier ain't have nothing to do with this, it's his sons. Backstabbing bastards. Those spoiled brats don't know anything about hard work."

"At least you still got a job, baby. And maybe this will be better for you. A bigger company means better benefits, like health insurance and 401(k)," she told him.

"Man, I ain't thinking about that. I'll have benefits when we get married," he said. "Right?"

"Well, I guess," she said slowly. In a sense, he was right—he would have health benefits through her job, but Avery wasn't ready to get married. And more importantly, she wanted him to see the importance of having his own benefits.

"You guess? You guess what? You guess you'll marry me?" He laughed through the phone.

"If this is your idea of a proposal, it's pathetic," Avery told him, pulling into the parking lot. "But I gotta go, I'm back at work."

"Okay, are you working late?"

"Probably. I gotta makeup the extra time I took for lunch, and then they're probably gonna make us work overtime."

"Well, I love you and I'll see you when you get home." Duke said it so tenderly that Avery wanted to turn around, go to his job, and hug him tight.

"Love you too."

"I'm glad you got your shit back" he laughed, "And baby?"

"Yeah," she said.

"Don't worry. I'll make sure I go to the store and pick up some milk."

Despite having to work an extra two hours, the rest of the day went by quickly, mainly due to the back-and-forth banter between Tabitha and Malcolm, who provided plenty of entertainment between the massive number of calls from their shipping clients. Avery was surprised to look up and see that it was time to go home. As usual, they were the last ones on their floor to leave. They all packed up and she and Tabitha made a pit stop in the bathroom while Malcolm waited to escort them to their cars.

"So, do you think this thing between him and Sharice is really serious?" Tabitha asked from the stall.

"I don't know," Avery said. "It's too early to tell. I will tell you that I don't think she's the type to run game on him though, Tabby. She seems like a nice girl. You are so overprotective of him."

"Because he's so bloop-bloop sometimes," Tabitha said, "I have to be. He should be grateful. If it wasn't for us, he would be trapped by one of these office whores. You know they prey on his adorable, goofy ass."

"The same way you prey on Kurt," Avery teased.

They both came out of the stalls at the same time and washed their hands.

"I don't prey on Kurt." Tabitha closed her eyes and said dramatically, "I long for him."

"So, why don't you make a move?" Avery asked. It seemed as if Tabitha didn't have a problem with anyone knowing she was feeling Kurt except Kurt himself, which seemed crazy. "He's single."

Tabitha became serious for a moment. "I don't know. Maybe I'm kinda scared."

"Of what?" Avery frowned.

One of the stall doors opened, startling both of them, and out stepped Demi Hayes.

"Oh, sorry," Tabitha said, smiling. "We didn't realize anyone else was in here."

Demi looked Tabitha up and down and gave her an icy smile, which Avery could see was as fake as the gray contacts their new supervisor wore. "That's okay."

Avery pretended to be focused on putting her lip gloss on while sneaking glances at the petite woman. Her hair was a weave, but a damn good one. The contacts made her keen face even more catlike than it already was. Avery tried to picture in her mind what she might possibly look like with brown eyes. *I know this chick—I know I know her . . . Demi Hayes . . . Demi Hayes . . .* The only Hayes Avery could think of was a girl from high school who they called "Meaty," who was even bigger than Avery had been. A quiet girl who rarely spoke to anyone and kept to herself. Avery looked up in the mirror and their eyes met.

"Meaty?" Avery said before she could stop herself. Demi suddenly looked away and Avery realized she may have made her uncomfortable. She quickly tried to correct herself. "Demetrius Hayes, is that you?"

Demi glanced over at Tabitha and laughed nervously. "Well, I like for most people to call me Demi, but yes, Demetrius is my first name."

"Wow, you look so different," Avery said. "I mean, really, you look like a totally different person. I haven't see you since high school."

"Avery Belmont, from Coleman Village, right?" Demi asked.

"The very one," Avery said.

"I thought that was you," Demi countered. "I look like a totally different person and you haven't changed a bit."

Something about the way Demi said it made Avery a bit uneasy. She picked up her purse and said to Tabitha, "You ready to go?"

"Since eight this morning," Tabitha replied.

"It was nice seeing you again, Demi," Avery said, as they exited the bathroom.

Demi didn't say anything, just nodded.

"You knew her in high school?" Tabitha asked when they were on the elevator.

"Knew who?" Malcolm asked.

"Demi, our new supervisor." Avery shrugged. "We went to high school together."

"Was she an ice queen back then, because she sure seems like one now," Malcolm said, leaning against the elevator wall.

"Yeah, she was," Avery told them. "I guess some things never change."

And who is gonna love you like I do?

Avery knew something was up the moment she walked through the front door and heard Babyface singing. The smell of garlic and spices filled the air, which was a clear indicator that Duke was cooking. Slipping out of her jacket, she continued into the dining room and smiled at the candlelit table, perfectly set.

"Welcome home, boo." Duke walked up behind her and kissed her gently on her neck. "How was your day?"

"It started out rough, but it keeps getting better and better," she told him as she turned and put her arms around him. "How was yours?"

"Better, now that you're home." He leaned in and covered her mouth with his. Avery felt herself melting. The wetness of his tongue welcomed her and she indulged herself in his taste, moaning in the process. After all these years, kissing him still made her weak at the knees. His hand slipped under her shirt while the other one unbuttoned her skirt. The brush of his fingertips through the lace of her bra made her already hardened nipples even more erect. Avery ran her hand down his body until it arrived at the noticeable bulge in his sweats. It only took a few seconds for her fingers to make their way into his pants and wrap themselves around his thick hardness. There was no bigger turn-on for Avery than knowing she had the ability to make her man hard like this. She was still almost fully dressed and he looked as if he was about to explode at any moment. The more she massaged him, the bigger and harder his dick became and the hotter she got. She stepped out of her skirt and his free hand now reached between her legs, pulling her panties to the side. She stepped wider to give him more access to what he was searching for. When his fingers entered her wet center, she gasped and he lowered her onto the floor.

"Damn, baby," she said, staring into his eyes seductively, "We're not gonna eat first?"

"I'm about to eat right now," Duke said, sliding her body in front of his kneeling body and pushing her legs back. Avery closed her eyes in anticipation of the satisfaction she knew she was about to experience. Duke began pleasuring her with his mouth, slowly at first, with soft kisses between her thighs and all the way until his tongue plunged into the center of her waiting core. The sensation of him teasing her clit, while moaning and groaning as if it was the tastiest fruit he had ever eaten, was nothing short of a thrill for her. Avery arched her back and reached between her legs, rubbing his bald head. She tried with all her might to suppress the eruption she felt erupting.

"Baby, you've gotta stop," she told him.

"Mmm-mmm." Duke refused and began sucking with even more determination, his tongue reaching even deeper than it already was.

Avery gasped as she found herself caressing her own breasts. She loved her body; her full bosom, her thick thighs, every curve and crevice, to her was beautiful, which was why she was so in tune with what she liked, what made her feel good. Her body began to swerve against Duke as if his mouth was a song playing in her and she had to dance. Faster and faster, she moved and he played and just when she thought she couldn't take anymore, she felt his rock hardness now replaced where his tongue was moments before.

"Oh, damn," Duke moaned as he thrust into her. Their bodies now moved in natural rhythm, and he stared into her face as he told her over and over again, "I love you."

Avery watched him carefully as she tightened her walls around him and rocked her body. She knew she was driving him into a state of sexual intoxication, which she knew he loved. Back and forth, over and over, faster and faster until the both climaxed together. Duke collapsed on top of her, gasping. For Avery, laying there, was complete and total bliss. It was if she was exactly where she was supposed to be, exactly where she needed to be, and exactly where she wanted to be. She closed her eyes and smiled.

"That was incredible," Avery said, taking another bite of pasta. After another round of lovemaking and showering together, they had finally settled down to enjoy the meal Duke had prepared.

"You are incredible," Duke replied. "That's why I want you to have my baby."

Avery looked up at him as if he was as crazy as the statement he had just made. "Now that's funny."

"I'm not joking," he said. "I want us to have a baby."

"Okay, where is all this coming from, Duke?"

"What?" Duke frowned. "Avery, we've been together for seven years."

"Five," she corrected him.

"Well, I fell in love with you seven years ago. Just because your ass wasted two of them turning me down, doesn't mean they don't count. Anyway, you know how much I love you and you say we're in this forever. But, lately, every time I bring up getting married, or having a baby, there seems to be a problem. I don't like this vibe I'm getting. What's up?"

Avery stared at Duke. There was no doubt in her heart that she loved him. She couldn't imagine her life without him. The problem was the questions in her head. Five years ago, marrying Duke, raising a family, and living happily ever after sounded ideal. But now she wondered if that was enough. Duke was happy living in Coleman Village, working his regular nine-to-five. She wasn't.

"Nothing's up, Duke," she assured him. "I still want that. But now is not the time."

"Why not?"

"You know I've got so much going on right now. I'm working all these crazy hours, trying to finish school. Sometimes, I'm overwhelmed and it's just me and you, right now. I'm not ready for a baby, and neither are you. *We* are definitely not ready for a baby."

"Fine," Duke relented, and then told her, "I've got something for you."

"Duke," Avery sighed as he walked out the room. He always did this, bought her nice things for no reason. His spontaneity, although at times irresponsible, was part of her attraction to him. She prayed he hadn't gone off on a whim and bought a crib or a stroller since he was on a baby kick, and was relieved when he came back in carrying a familiar gold box with a black bow from her favorite store. She couldn't help but grin. For some men, the thought of being unable to shop for their women at Victoria's Secret or Frederick's of Hollywood may have been embarrassing. The fact that she was too much of a woman, so to speak, to wear La Perla or Dolce V in the bedroom didn't matter to Duke. He had no problem walking into Lane Bryant and searching until he found the sexiest Cacique lingerie he could find. She opened the box carefully and sifted through the tissue paper until she saw a sexy red and black lace corset with a matching garter and thong.

"Dinner was on me, dessert is on you." Duke winked. "I'll be right up after I clear this mess and clean the kitchen. And I want the Jessica Simpsons on, the black ones!"

It was after ten, and as much as Avery wanted to continue their romantic evening, she knew she had to catch up on the homework she had been neglecting. She not only had a quiz Friday night, but she also had a major project due, which she hadn't even started on.

"Baby," she said, "I can't. I gotta study and get some work done."

"What? Come on, Avery. Not tonight. Study tomorrow night."

"I gotta study tomorrow night too," she laughed.

"Fine, handle your business." Duke shrugged and began clearing the table.

Seeing the disappointment in his face, Avery stood up and pulled him to her, "I'll make it up to you, I promise."

"Don't start nothing you ain't gonna finish," he said, shaking his head. "Go ahead and get your study on."

Avery kissed him once more before she grabbed her box off the table and headed upstairs to face the dreaded schoolwork she had been neglecting.

Chapter 4

"Baby, do you remember Demetrius Hayes?" Avery asked the next morning as she got dressed. "Meaty?"

"Meaty? Played football? Hung out with Anthony Marshall and the crew?"

"No, Duke, that's Meachie," Avery laughed. "Meaty is a girl."

"Oh, yeah, lived on the other end of the block." Duke nodded. "The fat girl."

Avery turned and scowled at him. He knew she hated comments referring to a person's size.

"What?" he asked innocently. "You know what I meant."

"No, I don't, especially since some people may consider me a fat girl," she replied.

"You're definitely not a fat girl," Duke said, climbing out of bed and walking over to her. "You, my love, are plush."

"Plush?" she said, trying to suppress a smile. "What the hell?"

"What's wrong with plush? I like that. I've actually been saving that one for a special occasion to use it," he said, laughing.

"Not funny," she said, grabbing her clothes off the bed and pretending to head into the bathroom.

"Wait, did I say plush? I mean perfect!" Duke yelled.

"That's what I thought," Avery said. "Like I was trying to tell you, Meaty is my new supervisor at work."

"Word? Did she remember who you were?"

"Hell, baby, I barely recognized her. She so different."

"Different how?"

"Well, she's skinny, with long hair and gray eyes. Oh, and she doesn't go by Meaty anymore. She's Demi Hayes."

"Demi, how bourgeois." Duke shook his head. "So, does she seem cool?"

"I can't really tell yet," Avery said, grabbing her books and laptop. "She's only been there one day. Although she doesn't seem like she's gonna be the friendliest supervisor I've had."

"Believe me, I understand. I wanna see what's gonna happen when these bigwigs take over the shop. I'm telling you right now, Avery, if they come with some bullshit, I'm walking."

"Duke, you've been there longer than anyone else. You practically run the place. If they have any sense, they will come to you before making any changes. It'll be fine," she assured him. As confident as Duke was, certain situations still made him uneasy, especially when it came to those he felt were better educated or of a certain class.

Avery wanted to share with him all the possible changes going on at her own job, but there wasn't any point stressing Duke out without even knowing how the changes would affect her. *If they say I gotta work nights and weekends, I'll tell him then, not now.*

"Okay, baby, have a great day at work. I love you," she told him.

"You're taking your books to work?" he asked, pointing at her leather bag.

"Yeah, I'm gonna try and get some work done during lunch," she told him.

"Please, the only thing you're gonna get done during lunch is gossiping with your snow bunny and Malcolm X," Duke teased.

"And the only thing you get done all day at work is bullshitting with the guys in the shop about your latest Xbox game or who's beefing with who in the rap game, so shut up," she laughed. "Love you, gotta go, bye!"

***

The office was eerily quiet when Avery arrived. The usual hustle and bustle and morning chatter seemed to be missing.

"What's the deal with everyone?" she asked Malcolm, who usually got to work thirty minutes early.

"It seems as if the she bear has been going around marking her territory," he said, shrugging.

"Who the hell is the she bear?" Avery chuckled.

"He's talking about Demi," Tabitha answered. "She's been calling people in one by one, and giving them their fate here with the company."

"Great." Avery sat down in her chair and clicked her computer on. There were several e-mails from Demi Hayes already. One addressed the noise level on the floor and in the break room, which she felt was too loud and unprofessional. Another one even banned eating at the desk. *What the hell is this chick trying to do*, she thought as she read through them. "This is ridiculous!"

"Ah, I see someone has read their e-mails." Tabitha leaned back in her chair, showing off her perfectly tanned legs and put her feet on Malcolm's desk. They were the same Jessica

Simpson heels Duke wanted Avery to wear the night before: four-and-a-half-inch black stilettos. How Tabitha managed to keep them all day was beyond her. As far as Avery was concerned, the only place she would be wearing hers would be the bedroom.

"Excuse you." Malcolm pushed her off.

"So, Malcolm, what's gonna happen to us?" Tabitha asked.

"I don't know," he said. "I haven't really heard that much."

"Oh, you've heard something," Avery turned and said.

"And you better make it quick," Tabitha added.

He looked at his two coworkers and then said, "Well, like we already knew, they are basically trying to make this a customer service office. She bear has a customer service background and this whole thing is her pet project. From what I hear, she has a thing for Kurt and is doing all this to impress him. When she was in the northeast office, she had more grievances filed against her than any other manager, and then something big went down—I don't know what it was—and they sent her ass here."

"To torture us, probably," Tabitha hissed. "You said you knew this chick in high school. Was she a bitch back then?"

"No, she mainly kept to herself. They used to tease her a lot," Avery told them.

"I can believe that," Malcolm said. "She's not the cutest to look at, that's for damn sure."

"No, she used to be big, I mean, really big. Bigger than me," Avery whispered.

"Wow." Malcolm looked shocked.

"Okay, you're acting like Avery is Quasi-modo or something. What the hell?" Tabitha punched him.

"I'm just saying, she's on the small side, so I'm trying to picture her being big." Malcolm glanced over at Avery. "Your words, not mine."

"Whatever." Avery sat back. "They were really hard on her in school, for real."

"Well, it seems like her ass is taking it out on us, now," Tabitha told them. "And I didn't do nothing to her. I didn't tease her so she needs to back up."

"Like your little ass is gonna do something," Malcolm tea-sed her.

"Boy, please, she don't want no parts of this!" Tabitha stood up and posed as if she was Jay-Z.

The three of them cracked up until they were interrupted by Demi's stern voice. "I take it you three didn't get the e-mail regarding noise level on the floor."

"Good morning, Demi, we're fine. How are you?" Tabitha slowly turned and smiled at Demi.

Avery watched the two women stare at each other. Demi looked put off by Tabitha and Avery could tell Demi didn't know what to make of the tiny white woman standing in front of her.

"The noise level needs to be kept at a minimum," Demi informed them. "It can be disturbing to your coworkers and the clients on the phone."

"Well, none of us are on the phone right now because we aren't scheduled to be on the clock for another four minutes," Tabitha told her.

"With the amount of calls I'm sure you all will be taking, you won't have time to socialize, so I suggest you all get used to it." Demi turned her attention to Avery, slowly looking her up and down and turned back to Tabitha. "Tabitha, I'd like to see you in my office as soon as you clock in. And after her, then you, Mister . . ."

"Mosley," Malcolm answered.

"Not a problem," Tabitha told her. "I look forward to it."

When she walked away, Tabitha turned to Malcolm and said, "Well, I guess I'm next to enter the death chamber, then you."

"I'm good," Malcolm told her. "I'm gonna go right in there and throw some of this Malcolm Mosley charm on her."

"Well, we know his ass is gonna be fired," Tabitha said and once again, they all laughed.

"Shh," Avery whispered as she clocked in on her desk phone. "Y'all better chill before she comes over here and tells us we can't go to the bathroom!

"Well, wish me luck." Tabitha said, sighing.

"If you need backup, I'm right here," Avery told her.

"Thanks," Tabitha snickered. Just as she left for Demi's office, Kurt walked over.

"Good morning, just the people I need to see," he greeted them.

"Hey Kurt, what's up?" Avery asked.

"Where's Tabitha?" He motioned toward the empty desk.

"In with Demi," Malcolm answered.

"Uh-oh, well, when she gets back I need the three of you to meet me in my office. I have a special project for you all to handle," he said.

"Special project like Habitat For Humanity or something business-related, and if so, special project like we broke this and need you to fix it or Christmas party planning committee?" Avery folded her arms.

"In other words, is it a good project or a BS one?" Malcolm clarified.

"It's a good one, believe me," Kurt answered, looking around and then added, "You three have the highest performance levels in the district. I know what you're capable of and I need you."

"We'll be there," Malcolm assured him.

Kurt paused at Avery's desk and tapped her thick statistics book. "I took this class at Chrysler University last year."

"I'm taking it there now," Avery sighed.

"Dr. Brewer?" he asked.

"Yep," she answered.

"Killer teacher," he said, smiling. "I didn't know you were in grad school."

"Two more classes and I'm done," she said with pride.

"I'm glad to hear it." Their eyes met briefly, and then he said, "See you in my office."

Tabitha returned minutes later, "That bitch is crazy!"

"What did she say?" Avery could see that Tabitha was so angry, she was beet red.

"She says that my new schedule is Wednesday through Sunday, from one to nine!"

"Oh, hell no," Avery was shocked.

"And get this, she says that she's moving my seat immediately. She feels that she needs to break up the monotony and change the atmosphere in the office." Tabitha was almost panting. "I need a fucking cigarette."

"Calm down, Tabitha. You're not working some crazy-ass schedule and you're not moving," Malcolm told her.

"What, you're gonna get her to change her mind when you go in there?" Tabitha glared at Malcolm.

"I'm not going in there," Malcolm said, smiling.

"Why not?" Tabitha frowned.

"Well, we had a visitor while you were gone," Avery said. She told her that Kurt selected them for a special project and they had a meeting in his office.

"Damn right." Tabitha's attitude changed instantly. She began digging in her large black Gucci purse and pulled out a makeup bag.

"Tabitha, we don't have time for all that, boo." Avery took the bag from her. "We have to go."

"Okay, how do I look? Let me at least put some lipstick on. I can't go in there looking any kind of way," Tabitha said.

"Maybe if you would've had this same attitude before you went into Demi's office, you would've got a better schedule," Malcolm joked.

***

The three of them met with Kurt for nearly an hour, discussing the project and their responsibilities. They also had a conference call with the other marketing directors and by the end, they were all satisfied and excited about what they would be doing.

"Is everyone on board?" Kurt asked as they were about to leave his office.

"Sounds like a plan," Avery said, nodding. "Basically, it's the same thing we've been doing, only on a larger scale."

"Exactly," Kurt responded. "And I'm counting on the three of you to carry the load and make it happen. The same way you've been doing it."

"We can do that," Malcolm said, shaking his hand.

Tabitha looked like a kid in a candy store, but she didn't have too much to say.

He walked them to the door and just as Avery was about to leave out, he touched her shoulder. "If you guys need anything or have any problems, let me know. I mean that."

They were so close, Avery could smell the scent of his cologne, which she easily recognized as Aqua Di Gio. Duke wore the same thing, but it smelled slightly different on him, sweeter maybe. She could feel his eyes on her, and it took everything she had within not to meet his stare with hers. Instead, she quickly thanked him and followed her coworkers back to their desks.

There was an e-mail from Demi requesting to speak with her. Her first instinct was to ignore it, especially since she would no longer be reporting to her. Instead, Avery decided to do the right thing and went to talk to her.

"Come in," she heard Demi's voice call out after she knocked on the door.

Avery stepped inside and remained close to the entrance. "You wanted to see me."

"Avery, have a seat."

Avery sat in one of the two empty chairs in the small office. She looked around and saw that there were no pictures at all, just frames that held random quotes about success. It seemed so cold and impersonal. In Kurt's office there had been pictures of him and his family. Malcolm seemed especially interested in one of him and Sharice. But there were no family photos in Demi's office at all.

"I understand you have been selected to be on a special project for Kurt," Demi started.

"Yes, I have."

"Okay, that's good. I also see that your performance since you've been with the company has been nothing short of stellar. From what I hear, people have nothing but great things to say about you. That is wonderful."

Avery wondered where Demi was going with all of this. "I work hard and make it a point to exceed company expectations."

"I'm glad to hear you say that. This is a great company to work for, and there are several different directions your career can go here. I'm proud of you, Avery. We both know where we come from and the fact that we've made it this far is nothing short of a miracle. You know that. You're a smart girl, or you wouldn't have made it this far. Now, when it comes to your continued growth here at Jennings, I can play a vital role. And I want to see you continue to succeed." Demi's voice dropped. "Let me give you a bit of friendly advice: watch who you associate with. Sometimes, casualties of war are not those that are pulling the triggers, but those that are standing near the line of fire. Be careful."

Avery sat in silence for a few moments and wondered how to react. Demi seemed to be sincere in what she was saying, but at the same time, it sounded a bit menacing, as if it was a threat. She chose her words carefully.

"I appreciate your taking the time to share that with me, Demi."

"Anytime," Demi said. "And Avery, I'll be checking on you."

Avery didn't say anything as she stood and walked out of the office.

Chapter 5

Although she enjoyed working on the special project, it was still exhausting and they worked longer hours than ever. Sometimes, she was surprised at how late it was when she got home. Duke wasn't too thrilled about the time she was spending at work.

"Damn, Avery, this is getting ridiculous," he said one night when he called. It was after nine and she was still at the office taking care of some last minute paperwork.

"I'm getting out of here right now, Duke."

"I thought we were gonna hang out and do something tonight," he whined into the phone.

"I know, baby," she told him. "I'll be home as soon as I fax this shipping proposal off. It has to get to the client before I leave."

"You said the same thing the other night, and the night before that. I'm going to Petey's and win some dough," he grumbled.

"Duke, I'm on my way right now. I'll be home in less than an hour."

"I left something for you on the table," she heard him say and the line went dead.

She knew he was pissed, but there was nothing she could do about it now. For the past couple of weeks, it was as if she no longer controlled her life, but life controlled her. Her days were endless and tiring and her plate was full. Making time for Duke was a priority, and as hard as she tried to do so, he wasn't making it any easier for her. The nights she came home late, she had homework and studying, which she barely did. Duke had started hanging out at Petey's, the local pool hall, with his buddies and came home even later than she did, bragging about his winning. And as tired as she was, she still managed to find the energy to break him off in the middle of the night, when he needed it, and even granted him an early-morning quickie a few times.

Exhausted, she finally arrived home where indeed she found a large gift bag sitting in the middle of the table. She peeked inside and gasped as she pulled out a large Coach purse she had been eyeing for months. At the bottom of the bag there was a small card that read All my love, Duke. The bag must have cost him four hundred dollars easily, and probably all of his pool winnings.

"Oh, Duke." She almost started crying as she looked at it. After taking a quick shower, she made a bowl of noodles, settled at the computer, and prepared to e-mail her teacher. The topic for her project had to be submitted by midnight tonight and the final project was due in less than a month. For some reason, she couldn't get an Internet connection. "Duke must have this thing hooked up to the PS3."

Avery grabbed her laptop and tried again to connect to the Internet but couldn't. What the hell is wrong, she wondered and then she paused and reached for the rarely used house phone. Just as she suspected, it was dead as well. *Damn it, damn it, damn it!*

Avery thought about the conversation she and Duke had one morning last week before she left the house.

"Don't forget the phone bill is due, baby."

"I won't. I'll take care of it this afternoon," he promised. "I brought my A game to the table last night and made plenty."

"Just put the money in the account and I'll pay it," she suggested.

"I'll pay it, don't worry. Now go to work and have a great day. I love you."

What the hell am I gonna do? Calling Duke would be a waste at this point because there was nothing he could do. If the service was off, that meant he hadn't paid it in at least three months. *Shit*. She had to get to a computer and get to one quick. It was after ten and even the closest Starbucks was closed. Avery slipped on a pair of jeans and a top, slid her feet into a comfy pair of brown Uggs and rushed out.

The parking lot of the office was completely empty with the exception of a few company cars when she returned. She convinced herself not to be scared as she walked into the building and onto the elevator, checking the time. She immediately turned on the radio she kept on her desk to keep her company, logged onto her computer, and got to work on her thesis.

"Now that's what I call dedication."

Avery nearly jumped out of her skin. "Ahh!"

Kurt laughed. "I'm sorry. I didn't mean to scare you. I thought you saw me walk up."

Avery clutched her chest and tried to breathe normal. "No, I didn't."

"That doesn't look work-related." He pointed to her computer screen showing the business Web site she was using as part of her research.

"Um, it's not," she said, guiltily. "I guess I'm busted."

"Don't worry, your secret is safe with me," he said, smiling.

Damn, even his smile is dazzling.

"Are you sure? I wouldn't want the wrong person to find out and cause a massive e-mail to be sent to everyone about sneaking into the office after hours and doing homework."

"I won't mention a word to anyone, not even the she bear," he said, laughing. "So, what are you working on?"

"My thesis for business stats," she sighed. "It's due in about eleven—no, ten—minutes and I'm nowhere near having any idea about what I'll be doing."

"Mind if I check it out?" Kurt asked, reaching for Malcolm's nearby chair and laying his briefcase down.

Avery slid her body over and made room for him beside her, as he removed his suit jacket. She tried to concentrate on the screen as he read, but for some reason, she kept being drawn to him instead. He was clenching his jaw and squinting.

"Do you wear glasses?"

"Huh?" He looked over at her. "No, I don't."

She then asked, smugly, "Let me rephrase that. Do you need glasses?"

It was his turn to look guilty. "I have been told that I need some visual assistance, but I chose not to."

Avery shook her head at him. "Wow, you're that vain that you'd rather go blind than wear some glasses? They also have these new things they invented called contact lenses too, you know?"

"Tried 'em, but they made my eyes dry and kept falling out," he said as he typed. Avery stared at his perfectly manicured fingers as they hit the keyboard.

"LASIK surgery?" she suggested.

"I considered it, but I'm scared of needles," he said, still typing.

She laughed. "I don't think they use needles for that."

He stopped typing and turned to her. "You want me to have surgery in my eyes and you're not even gonna put me under? Now I really don't want it. Paper's done, check it out."

Avery leaned in to see what he added to what she had already written. It wasn't a lot, but it pulled her ideas together and made them flow smoothly. It was just the finishing touch that she needed. She quickly saved it, attached it to an e-mail, and sent it just in time.

"You are a lifesaver," she told him. "I appreciate this more than you know."

Kurt stared at her and said, "It was nothing. You had done most of the work already. I just jazzed it up a bit for you."

"Still, you helped me out," she said, shrugging.

"Well, you've helped me out too. All the work you've been doing around here doesn't go unnoticed, Avery. You mean a lot—I mean, to the department—I mean, the company."

The room suddenly seemed hot and Avery wondered if it was just her. For some reason, she wished she had chosen a better outfit to put on and done something to her hair. The buzzing of her cell phone was a welcome distraction for both of them. She knew it was Duke without even looking at it and ignored the call.

"Well, you're all finished here?" Kurt asked.

"Yeah." Avery nodded slowly.

"I'll walk you to your car. I wouldn't feel comfortable leaving you here all alone," he said, standing up.

"What are you doing here so late anyway?" Avery began gathering her things.

"Working," he told her. "I gotta stay one step ahead of she bear."

"I didn't know you guys were in competition. Aren't you both second-level managers?" Avery reached for her leather jacket.

Kurt helped her put it on. His fingers lightly brushed against her neck and a jolt of electricity went down her spine.

"We are, but Demi has this personal vendetta against all the managers on our team. It's as if she's out to get us or prove something to all of us."

"I don't think it's just you," Avery told him. "I think she feels she has something to prove to everyone, even herself. That's why she's the way she is." Avery thought about the way Demi was teased in high school and the physical changes that she had made.

"You may be right, but when it comes to people like that in business, you've always gotta stay one step ahead of the game. Which is why I'm here this late."

"Thanks again," Avery said when they arrived at her car. "Where are you parked?"

"Well, my car is in the shop so I'm driving a company car this week."

"Wow, being a manager does have its privileges." She unlocked her door and got in. "Us regular folks would have had to bum a ride or get a rental."

"I tell you what, the next time you need to bum a ride, call me," he said, smiling. "And hey, if you need any more help with your project, holler at me. I'm not trying to brag, but a brother did get an A plus."

"An A plus?"

"Okay, an A. But if they did give pluses in grad school, I would've gotten one."

"If you say so," Avery replied. "Thanks again and see you tomorrow."

"Drive home safely," he said and stepped back so she could shut her door. He turned and headed toward the nearby white Ford Focus bearing the Jennings International name and logo. *That is one fine man*, Avery thought as she watched him walk away. *But you already have a fine man at home,* her conscience reminded her. *Even if he can't remember to pay a damn phone bill or pick his cereal bowl off the table.*

"Where the hell have you been?" Duke asked as soon as she walked in the door. "I've been calling you for an hour!"

Avery remained calm as she walked past him and up the stairs into their bedroom. "Work."

"Bullshit, Avery! I know your ass came home and left. You opened the gift I left you on the table and look," he pointed to her outfit, "you took the time to change clothes and everything!"

"I was at work," she said, nonchalantly.

"Work? 'Til midnight? And you couldn't answer the damn phone?" he yelled.

"I was too busy working on my paper, which I had to e-mail my professor." She sat on the side of the bed and removed her boots.

"You couldn't do that shit from home, Avery? I don't know what the hell is up with you but—"

"No, Duke, I couldn't do that shit from home because the fucking Internet is off! So after working until nine o'damn clock and coming all the way home, I get on the computer and the damn Internet doesn't work, oh, and neither does the phone, which means the bill ain't paid."

Duke tossed his head back and closed his eyes. "Damn, I forgot. I'm so sorry, Avery. I meant to take care of that bill, for real. I guess I was thinking the Internet was through the cable company, not the phone company."

Avery reached into the drawer and pulled out a pair of sweats. Without even saying another word, she slipped them on after slipping out of her clothes.

"Avery?" Duke called her name, softly. She turned the light off and climbed into bed. He reached out for her and she pulled away. "I'm sorry, Avery. Come on, you know we don't go to bed mad. I love you."

Closing her eyes, Avery prayed that she would be in a better frame of mind to deal with him when she woke up, because right now, she wasn't.

Chapter 6

"Come hang out with us tonight, Avery," Tabitha pleaded. "You are becoming such a prude!"

"She does have a point. You haven't been out with us in a minute, Avery," Malcolm said as they returned from lunch the following Friday. "We're just going to the Jazzy Blues Café after work, nothing big."

"I wish I could, but you guys know I got class tomorrow. Not only that, but we have a test that I'm probably gonna fail even though I've been studying all week."

"If you know you're gonna fail it, then you may as well come out and get wasted," Tabitha suggested. "What do you have to lose?"

"You are crazy, Tabitha," Avery laughed. "As soon as this semester is over, I will be back in full effect, I promise."

"Oh my God!" Tabitha shrieked when they got to their aisle.

"What is it? Is it a mouse?" Avery stopped dead in her tracks. There had been rumors about there being mice on the floor below theirs.

"Girl, no," Tabitha laughed. "Look!"

Avery went to see what had Tabitha so excited. She was shocked to find a large vase with a dozen roses sitting in the middle of her desk.

"Damn, someone must really be in the dog-house and trying to work his way out," Malcolm said, smiling.

"Hmm," Tabitha said, reaching for the card. "Let's see who it could be."

"Step off, chick!" Avery pushed her back play-fully and grabbed the card. She couldn't help smiling as she read Duke's scrawly signature. Things between them had become increasingly strained since the Internet had gotten discon-nected. He didn't seem to understand why she was so angry over something so menial, and be-cause he didn't understand it, it made her even angrier.

"That is so sweet," Tabitha said, sniffing the flowers.

"Yeah, it is," Avery said, thinking maybe she had been a little hard on Duke the past few days. She picked up the phone and dialed his number.

"Yo'," he answered.

"Hey, you," she said. "You made my day."

"That was my goal," he said. "You like them?"

"I love them," she said, "But not as much as I love you."

Avery's computer chimed and she noticed she had an e-mail from Kurt. He had been working in another office for the past several weeks, but he remained in contact with her often via phone and e-mail. He had even helped her out with her homework a couple of times when he called her desk late and found her still there. Avery found that the more they talked, the more she enjoyed him. He was entertaining and comical, yet he had so much wisdom that he didn't mind sharing.

> Hey A:
>
> Just wanted to say hello and hope you're having a great day. Came across this info and thought you could use it for your project. Don't work too hard and enjoy your weekend. See you soon.
>
> K

Attached to the e-mail were three articles dealing with redeveloping diminishing neighborhoods and creating new opportunities for communities, the topic of her thesis that she had been working on tirelessly. The fact that he not only took the time to help her out with her homework, but he even thought enough to help her with the research for her project was impressive to Avery on so many levels. She knew as a manager, Kurt had a lot on his plate, especially with all of the changes and cutbacks going on with the company. Having someone truly care about the goal she was trying to achieve was a welcome change.

Hey K:

Thanks for the info. I def appreciate the help. Enjoy your weekend as well. Can't wait for you to get back!

A

Avery read the message over again, and wondered if the last statement was a bit much. She decided to change it to the team can't wait until you get back to the office and hit the send button.

"Baby, you still there?" Duke asked.

"Huh?" Avery's attention went from the computer to her boyfriend on the phone. She couldn't believe she had allowed the e-mail to distract her.

"I asked what time you're getting off tonight."

"Um, I'm not sure," Avery told him. "Why? What's up?"

"Nothing, I just thought we could maybe go out, get something to eat," Duke replied. "Maybe go to Jasper's."

Avery knew Duke was making a true effort for him to call and want to go out on a Friday night.

Normally, that was the one night he had reserved for his boys. Not only that, but he had suggested Jasper's, which was her favorite restaurant. And as much as she wanted to go, there was no way she could risk failing her midterm.

"Duke, I have a midterm tomorrow. I really gotta study tonight."

"You can't study after you eat, Avery?" Duke pleaded.

"How about I eat after my midterm," she offered. "We can go out tomorrow night."

"But the fight's tomorrow night," Duke sighed. "Los is having a fight party."

"You can't go to the fight party after you eat?" Avery teased. "I get out of class at four, Duke. We can go then."

"A'ight, Baby," Duke laughed. "That sounds like a plan."

"Okay, I'll see you when I get home."

"I love you, Avery," he said.

"Love you too," Avery replied, sitting back in her chair and sighing.

"What's wrong?" Tabitha asked.

Avery looked up and saw that her friend had walked back over to the desk. Avery minimized her instant message screen and hoped she hadn't seen anything.

"Nothing," Avery said. "Duke and I are going to Jasper's tomorrow night after I get out of class."

"Jasper's is my spot," Malcolm told them.

Avery's desk phone rang, saving her from any further questioning. "This is Ms. Belmont, how can I help you?"

"Avery, I know Kurt is out of the office, but I still need a monthly report for your team," Demi said.

"Yes, I know," Avery told her.

"Do you think it'll be ready by two, in time for the conference call?"

"It's ready now." Avery reached for report that she did last night after completing her homework.

"When you get a chance, bring it to my office."

"Sure," Avery replied. "I'll be right there."

"What the hell does she want?" Tabitha asked.

"The monthly report for the team," Avery answered, standing up. "She needs it for the conference call."

"Why is she asking you for it? Kurt's not even here." Tabitha frowned. "She's trying to set him up and sabotage this project. I can't stand her."

"She can't sabotage anything, the report's done and I already did it," Avery said, winking.

"You did?" Tabitha looked surprised and so did Malcolm.

"When?" he asked.

"Last night, after I finished my homework. Unlike the two of you, who chose to hang out, I stayed and worked," she teased and passed her the papers.

"Wow, girl, how long did you stay?" Tabitha asked, flipping through the report.

"Until about twelve."

"Now, I feel bad," Malcolm said.

"You should." Avery playfully hit him in the chest.

"This is really good, Avery. Hell, you should definitely apply to the JMDP next year," Tabitha said, passing the report back to her. "I'll put in a good word for you."

"Thanks, but I don't think so. That's your thing, not mine. School is enough stress, I don't need any more," Avery said, shaking her head.

"It's not any more stressful than what we are doing now. The only difference is we'll get to experience the same stress on a bigger corporate scale and from all departmental points of view. I can't wait!" Tabitha smiled.

"Damn, Tabitha, I swear, I hope you get in, because at this point I'm sick of hearing about it." Malcolm shook his head.

"I've prepared for this program for the past three years. I know it inside and out and my application is so tight, there's no way for them to decline it," Tabitha informed him. "And when they announce my name at the gala as one of the winners, Kurt will take me into his arms and whisk me onto the dance floor, declaring his undying love for me."

"I don't know about all that," Avery laughed. "You act like the cat has your tongue every time he comes around."

"I'm waiting for the right moment, that's all." Tabitha walked back to her desk and sat down.

"If I were you, I'd hurry and make a move. According to Sharice, Kurt has his eye on some new chick," Malcolm announced.

"What? Who?" Tabitha's voice shot up about three octaves and she turned red as a beet. Avery wondered the same thing.

"Some line level director in the southeast office, I think. That's why he's always there," Malcolm said.

"Wow." Tabitha looked deflated, then perked back up. "Oh well, that just means that I have to request to work in the southeast office as my first assignment, that's all."

"I love that air of confidence you have when Kurt's not around." Malcolm shook his head. "And what's gonna happen in the southeast office? You'll still be waiting on the right moment."

Avery joined the teasing. "Yeah, she's gonna be at his wedding, still talking about waiting for the right moment."

"You two are so not funny right now." Tabitha rolled her eyes at them.

"I don't understand what the problem is. You can talk to a million other guys. I used to think it was because he was a brother," Malcolm turned and said to Tabitha.

"No, that's not it. You've seen Tabitha talk to men of every age and nationality. The only shade she's worried about is the color of his money!" Avery giggled. She could see her friend losing the fight not to laugh. "That's probably her real reason for wanting to get into the JMDP, so she can scope out all the single, wealthy managers."

The JMPD was the junior management development program offered by the company. Each office was allotted one selectee each year and it was competitive as hell to get into. Employees worked on their applications one, sometimes two years in advance in hopes of being selected. Not only did it provide one-of-a-kind, hands-on training and a salary almost as large as the managers, but the perks were pretty good. Members got a company car, a corporate spending account, and VIP treatment at all the corporate-sponsored events.

"There's only one manager I want, and you know who that is," Tabitha retorted.

"I can't tell," Avery said as she snatched the report from Tabitha and headed down the aisle. "I'll be right back."

She got to Demi's office and knocked softly on the door even though it was open. Demi's desk was covered with what looked like spreadsheets and folders. She looked up and motioned for Avery to come inside.

"Have a seat," she told Avery.

Avery complied and sat in one of the two chairs. "Wow, looks like you're working hard."

"Always." Demi nodded and smiled. "That's what they pay me to do."

"I feel you," Avery told her.

"I see you've been keeping some late hours yourself. The project seems to be going well for you all."

"It is." Avery wondered if Demi called her into the office to dig for information on Kurt. If so, it definitely wasn't going to happen.

"I have to admit, I thought it was going to be a waste of company time and manpower, but based on the numbers I see so far, it's a formidable idea."

Avery didn't know how she was supposed to respond, so she simply said, "Thanks."

"I noticed a finance book on your desk. Are you in school?"

"Yeah, I'm working on my master's."

"That's great! I'm glad to hear that." Demi nodded. "So many of us don't realize the real value of a higher-level education. We think once we get a bachelor's, then we've achieved something."

Avery passed the report to her without responding.

"I mean, don't get me wrong, graduation from college is an accomplishment, especially for someone who's from where we grew up. But, it's not the be-all and end-all. There is so much more out there to learn, and explore and achieve."

"You're right," Avery had to agree. One thing she learned after graduating from college and getting a job, was that these days having a college degree was barely enough to get you in the door. She was glad that she had listened to her aunt, Carolyn, who encouraged her to get into a graduate program instead of Duke, who told her to take a break from school. "But if you don't have the right people in your corner telling you there is more out there, then you don't know."

"Yeah, having the right mentor is key, especially in the business world." Demi leaned forward and stared at Avery. "I'm sure you already know how important having the right people in your corner are and sometimes you have to go above and beyond to prove your worth. It's especially hard when you don't look a certain way or fit the physical mold that they want you to look. Believe me, I know, I've been there."

Avery frowned at her, wondering what she meant, but instead of questioning Demi's comment, she politely said, "True. Well, I know you have to get ready for the conference call and I have my own work I gotta get back to."

"Oh, yeah," Demi said, nodding.

Avery stood up and headed out the door.

"Avery," Demi said. "Have you considered applying for the JMDP?"

"I don't think I could handle that right now." Avery shook her head. "I have enough on my plate with school, not to mention working here. Not that I'm complaining."

"I know you're not complaining," Demi laughed. "I think you should consider. We need more of us in that program and you would really benefit from it."

"I hear ya," Avery said, nodding, "Besides, the deadline is next week. There's no way I could even complete the application. But, I will definitely consider applying next year."

"You can't run from opportunities, Avery, and sometimes, we even have to create them. You're from Coleman Place. You know life wasn't easy for us growing up, but not only did you survive, you thrived. The business world is no different," Demi told her.

"Thanks," Avery said and walked out. She considered everything Demi told her. Despite the bad-mouthing around the office and the complaints, she had always known that Demi's bark was worse than her bite. Avery felt that although it was a little strange, Demi's encouragement was probably sincere. *We have more in common than most around here*, Avery thought. *We're both successful, black women from the same neighborhood. She was just trying to inspire me.*

The remainder of the afternoon went by quickly and before Avery knew it, it was dark and the building was empty. She went over and over the study material for her midterms, determined to do well. She was confidant about two of her classes, but when it came to her business ethics course, she was afraid. No matter how hard she tried, she just couldn't seem to get it together. Her professor was cutthroat and no-nonsense, who not only put the fear of God in her when it came to passing his class, but made it damn near impossible to pass. To make matters worse, he was also the head of the MBA program. If she didn't get at least a B in his class, she would be placed on academic probation or worse, put out of the program. Feeling even less prepared than when she started studying, she put her head down on her desk.

"Didn't we talk about you burning the midnight oil in this place?"

Avery's head popped up and she stared at Kurt. "Didn't we talk about you sneaking up and scaring the mess outta me?"

"I wasn't trying to scare you, I was trying to wake you up," he said, smiling.

"I wasn't sleeping, I was praying. I have midterms tomorrow, remember?" she groaned.

"I remember," he told her, then walked over and closed her book. "You've been staying late studying all week."

She playfully pushed hit him on the arm. "Then you should be praying with me. And why are you here late, again?"

"I had to pick up some paperwork and some more items from my office," he said, then pointed at the roses. "Nice, someone must love you."

"Everyone loves me," she teased. "But they're from Duke, my significant other."

"Okay," he said.

"Yeah, he kind of misses me. My time has been kinda limited these days," she sighed and looked at the flowers.

"Sounds like you miss him too," Kurt told her. "Hey, relationships are hard enough without the stress of work and school, and sometimes you gotta make time."

Avery looked at Kurt and realized he was right. She had been so focused that she hadn't really been making time for Duke. "You're right, and I will, but no time tonight. I've gotta prepare."

"You're already prepared," Kurt told her.

"I have business ethics, and you know it's all essay!"

"You're already prepared," he repeated. "You wanna do well on your business ethics midterms?"

"Yes," she said, staring at him.

"Fine, I'll tell you. Don't think about your own answers."

"What?" Avery frowned.

"It's not about how you would answer the question. That's how Dr. Brewer gets you. Answer the question the way he would. Put the answers you know he wants. And we all know not only is he the most opinionated bastard, but he's not ethical at all," Kurt said matter-of-factly. "Answer as if you were him."

Avery couldn't help laughing. "That's crazy. But it's probably the most brilliant thing I've ever heard in my life."

"Believe me, it works." Kurt pulled her up out of her chair. "Come on, pack up. Go home, relax with your boo. Get some rest and you'll be fine. If you go in there all stressed tomorrow, you're gonna forget everything you've learned. Let's go, I'll walk you to your car."

Avery packed up her things and Kurt helped her put her coat on. As they were about to walk out, he stopped and picked up a box he had placed near the elevator.

"What's that?" she asked, noticing some picture frames and awards in the box.

"I told you I needed some items from my office," he said. "I just put them in the box to make it easier to carry them."

"Looks more like you're moving," she said, then thought about what Malcolm said earlier about him dating a manager in the southeast office. "So, things in the southwest office must be really good."

"About the same as here." He shrugged. "Same drama, different office."

"The environment there may be nicer," she casually mentioned.

Kurt looked over at her and said, "What do you mean?"

Avery hit the ground-floor button and stood back. "Nothing."

"I bet." Kurt shook his head and rolled his eyes. "A brother can't even do his job without people talking."

"Who said people were talking?" Avery giggled.

"Come on, now, I've been here longer than you have. What's the word?" Kurt gave her a knowing look.

"I don't know what you're talking about." Avery blinked, trying to look as innocent as possible.

Suddenly, Kurt leaned in close, his arm outreached. Avery gasped and held her breath, wondering what he was about to do until she saw his finger almost touching the stop button.

"What are you doing?"

"Talk or I will push it," he threatened, jokingly.

Avery pushed his hand away. "Stop playing before you get us stuck. You know someone got stuck on here a while back, and the chick had an asthma attack."

"Yeah, I heard," he said.

"She was stuck for over an hour and they counted her as tardy from lunch," Avery made sure to add. "Oh, but you're management, so you would probably agree with that decision."

"You're trying to change the subject," Kurt said. "Nice try, but it's not working."

"I'm not," she lied.

The elevator doors opened and they stepped off. He continued to try to pull the latest gossip from her but she was just as determined not to say anything. They were laughing loudly as they walked out the front door and then they stopped abruptly.

"Duke," she said, shocked to see him leaning on his car parked right next to hers, talking to Demi, who seemed just as surprised to see her and Kurt walking out together.

"I thought you were working late," Duke said, looking past her and directly at Kurt.

"I was," Avery started and was interrupted by Kurt.

"Until I told her to pack up and get out," he said, walking over and extending his hand. "Kurt, man, I'm one of the managers here."

Duke hesitated before finally shaking Kurt's hand. "What's up? I'm Duke, Avery's man."

Something about the way Duke said *Avery's man* made her cringe. She wanted to pull Duke to the side and say, *He already knows that, Duke, you don't have to point it out like you have something to prove.*

"Avery's told me about you. It's nice to meet you."

"When did you get back, Kurt?" Demi's eyes went from Kurt, to Avery, then back to Kurt, where they landed on the box he was carrying.

"A little while ago. I stopped by here to pick up some things from my office where I ran into Ms. Workaholic, here." He looked over at Avery and smiled.

Her eyes met his briefly, and she quickly looked away.

"I was just telling Duke that I'm trying to convince you to apply for the junior management program," Demi said.

"You should." Kurt nodded. "It's a great program and I think you'd really benefit from it, Avery."

"She's barely home now between work and studying," Duke responded. "You said yourself she's a workaholic."

Avery looked over at Duke and quickly replied, "That's what I told Demi."

"I can see your plate is pretty full right now." Kurt agreed. "But you should definitely apply next year after you've graduated."

"Well, we've already planned to start a family after she finishes grad school," Duke said, smirking. "I can appreciate your recognizing the talent that she has, though. Maybe since you all see what a valuable employee she is, instead of working her so hard, you'll maybe cut her some slack and a bigger check."

Avery was stunned. She didn't know whether to be embarrassed or angry.

Duke continued to stare at Kurt as he said, "You look real familiar. Do I know you?"

Kurt's cell phone began chiming. He took it from his pocket and said, "Well, I have to be going. Avery, don't work too hard and Demi, I will check you out Monday. Enjoy your weekend."

"I need to be going myself," Demi said. "Duke, it was nice seeing you again."

"You too, Meaty," Duke said.

After Avery and Duke were alone in the parking lot, she finally spoke. "You wanna go grab something to eat?"

"Naw, I'll check you later at home," he said.

Avery frowned at him, sensing his attitude. "Is something wrong?"

"Naw." Duke just shook his head. "I'm good. Go ahead and get in your car so we can go."

"Duke," she said.

"Go ahead, Avery," he said.

Avery turned to walk toward her car. Kurt beeped his horn as he pulled out of the parking lot and she waved.

Behind her, she heard Duke say, "I know that cat from somewhere."

Chapter 7

"You have one hour and thirty minutes to take the exam. Once you are finished and have turned it in, you may leave," Dr. Brewer said as he passed out the exams. Avery swallowed hard and closed her eyes as he approached her desk. She had been at school since nine in the morning and it was her last and final class of the day, and her last and most difficult midterm exam. All of the other professors had allowed open book or multiple choice tests, but she knew that would not be the case in Dr. Brewer's business ethics class. He was a beast and she had been dreading this moment all day.

Dear God, you have to help me pass this test. I know I've been saying this to you all week while I've been studying and preparing and cramming, and I'm pretty sure you've heard me, but just in case you were too busy, or the message didn't come through, or you need to hear it for the eight hundredth time, please God, help me pass this test.

Avery turned her paper over and glanced at the twenty-five essay questions and her heart pounded. *Relax, Avery, you can do this. Don't panic.*

"You know this info because it's second nature to you, you're beyond ready, just focus, relax, and give the answers you know Dr. Brewer is looking for," Avery heard Kurt's words in her head the same way he said them the night before. She picked up her pen and began to write on the paper. She didn't allow the fact that Duke barely made it home before the sun came up to distract her. She blocked out the image of him pretending to be asleep on the sofa and ignoring her as she attempted to talk to him before she left this morning. She fought the urge to say "fuck it" and walk out of class because she didn't feel up to this. And she wiped away the tears that had started to form in her eyes. Instead, she relaxed, focused, and patiently completed the exam. When she answered her last and final question, she finally glanced up, sat back, and sighed. She even found the energy to smile as she stood up and walked to Dr. Brewer's desk, satisfied that not only had she passed, but she had done well.

"Ms. Belmont?" his stern voice said as she gave him her test.

"Yes?" she asked.

"I reviewed your thesis proposal and found it quite interesting."

"Thank you, sir," she said.

"You may want to do some field research and include it with your project. You may find it to be very beneficial," he continued. "I look forward to reviewing your final work."

"Yes, sir," she thanked him and walked out, shocked at the fact that the professor who had the reputation of gaining satisfaction in failing students and smiling as he did so had not only complimented her, but offered a bit of advice. What had started out as a day from hell had actually begun looking up.

As she walked to her car, Avery took her phone out of her purse. To her surprise and disappointment, there was no call, message or even text from Duke. *I can't believe him. He knows how important today was and even though there was that nonsense last night, the least he can do is call.* Just as she was about to dial his number, her phone began to vibrate and she answered it.

"About damn time, I was just about to call and cuss you out!" she said.

"Wow! And what did I do to deserve a cussing out?"

Confused by the female voice, Avery double-checked the screen of her BlackBerry and realized her mistake. "Tabitha?"

"Yeah," she laughed.

"Girl, I thought you were Duke," she apologized.

"I guess I'm a major disappointment," Tabitha replied. "I called to see how the midterm went."

"It went well," Avery told her. "Really well. As a matter of fact, I think I aced it."

"I wouldn't be surprised if you did," Tabitha said. "So, come on, let's go celebrate!"

"I can't. Duke and I are going to dinner, remember?"

"I thought that was later," Tabitha said, "I wanted you to go look at this condo with me and then maybe grab a drink."

"Sounds like fun, Tab, but I need to get home," Avery sighed. "Thanks for calling to check on me, though."

"No problem. I'm glad you aced your test. I'm gonna have to get something special for you. Enjoy the rest of your weekend, Avery!"

"You too, Tabitha. I'll see you Monday," Avery said and hung up, then dialed Duke's number. At first, it went straight to voice mail, and she dialed it again.

"Hello," he finally answered.

"Hey," she said.

"'Sup?"

"You tell me," she said. "Do you want to meet at Jasper's or you want me to just come straight home and we ride together? I know you mentioned something about wanting to go to Los's fight party."

"Mmmph," Duke responded. "Oh."

Avery's hands gripped the steering wheel harder as she drove. She knew before she called him that Duke would probably still have an attitude, and she was prepared to deal with it. "Oh?"

"I forgot we had dinner plans, I guess," he said, nonchalantly.

"What do you mean, you forgot, Duke? You were the one who made the damn plans, remember?"

"You're right, I did. But, shit kinda changed last night—"

"What the hell do you mean, Duke? I swear, I can't believe you sometimes. All of a sudden, shit kinda changed last night? And if it changed last night, why the hell couldn't you mention it last night? Oh, I guess because your ass didn't come home until this morning. But, wait, I tried talking to you this morning before I left and you were too conveniently passed out to mention shit had changed then, right?"

"Look, Avery, I ain't gonna go back and forth with you over the phone, and you know that," Duke's voice escalated.

"Fine, we'll deal with this when I get home." Avery hung up before he had a chance to respond. She could not believe him. Instead of Tabitha calling and making sure she had done well on her test, he should have been the one calling. Taking her to dinner should have been the only thing on his mind, especially after last night. And even though she had nothing to apologize for, she had done so, just to be the bigger person, but did he appreciate that? No, he brushed her off and decided to go to the club instead of coming home to be with her. This was getting ridiculous and she was getting tired. They had arguments and fallouts in the past, but they always worked through them. Now, their tiffs seemed to be more frequent and harder and harder to overcome. But wait, she loved Duke, and she knew that their relationship was just being tested. She had a lot going on with school and work and he was dealing with a lot on his job. Avery reminded herself of what he meant to her, and calmed herself down. Fine, just because Duke didn't want to take her to Jasper's didn't mean they couldn't eat Jasper's. Avery called the restaurant and placed a to-go order, and picked it up. She stopped and picked up some candles and a bottle of wine from the store and by the time she made it home, she was in a totally different frame of mind and ready to makeup with her man.

"I'm telling you, if you think things are bad now, wait, they're gonna get worse."

"They can't get worse, we already working in hell!"

Avery heard the loud voices before she got in the door and she stopped dead in her tracks. Duke didn't mention he had people at the house. She put the bags on the floor and walked into the den, where she found Duke along with five of his friends, screaming to hear each other over the basketball video game they were playing and Tupac blaring from the speakers. Half-empty bottles of beer were scattered on the floor and the room was filled with cigarette smoke. Duke knew she didn't allow smoking in the house.

"Yo', Avery! What's up, baby?" Los, Duke's cousin, yelled when he saw her standing in the doorway.

Duke glanced up. "Hey."

"Hey," she said, then quickly asked, "Can I talk to you for a minute?"

Duke followed her into the bedroom and she counted to ten before saying anything.

"What the hell is going on, Duke?"

"Nothing," he said. "Los had some issues with his girl, so he asked could he move the fight party over here. I told him as long as he brought the food and the liquor, it was cool."

"So, you agreed to all this without even talking it over with me?" Avery snapped.

"I didn't think it would be a big deal." Duke shrugged and took a swallow of the drink he was holding. Avery easily recognized the green liquid as incredible hulk, a mixture of Hennessy and Hpnotiq, which he loved.

"Well, guess what, now you got some issues with your girl," Avery told him. "First of all, you made plans with me, then change them without saying anything. Then, you agree to have a fight party at our house without saying anything."

"Well, like I said, I didn't think it would be a big deal," he sighed.

"And who the hell is supposed to be paying the extra sixty bucks on the cable bill for this fight?" Avery asked.

"What?" Duke seemed confused.

"You know the fight ain't free. So, who's gonna pay the bill for ordering it?" Avery folded her arms. She knew by his reaction that thought hadn't even occurred to him. Next, he would probably accuse her of tripping, which was his way of ducking out of a situation.

"You're tripping," Duke said.

"Oh, really?" Avery shook her head as she watched Duke walk out the door.

Frustrated, she sat on the side of the bed and tried to think of what to do. She definitely wasn't going to stay home and listen to all that racket coming from downstairs. She didn't want to even be at home anymore. She dialed Tabitha's number and agreed to meet her at the mall. She jumped in the shower and changed into some jeans, a cute top, and her Uggs. As she was putting on her makeup, she could hear the guys laughing and talking.

"I told you shit was gonna change," Los laughed.

"Ain't nothing changed," Duke said. "I got this."

"Yeah, you think you got it," another guy teased. "The same thing happened with my brother's wife. She went back to nursing school and then shit changed. She started complaining about him and it was like he couldn't do anything right. Next thing you know, she's sleeping wit one of the doctors at the hospital she worked at."

"That's not gonna happen to us. I love my girl and she loves me. I got this," Duke said.

Avery couldn't help laughing. She was glad he wasn't feeding into the negativity his boys were throwing at him. They were all losers who were just jealous of her and Duke. None of them had girls who were as accomplished as she was and all of them had two or three kids that they could barely take care of. Misery loved company.

After she was dressed, she made a big deal out of going downstairs and into the den where they were all assembled. She walked right over to Duke and sat in his lap, kissing him tenderly and then saying, "Bye, baby. I'm gone to hang out with Tabitha. I'll be back later."

Duke seemed shocked, but a slow smile spread on his face. "Okay, baby," he said. "I love you."

Knowing all eyes were on them, she stood up and said, "I love you too."

"Damn, boy, I guess you're right," she heard Los say as she walked out of the house. "You got that, lucky bastard."

"There are hardwood floors throughout the downstairs, and Berber carpet upstairs in the bedrooms. The countertops are granite and the fireplace is gas," Bobbie, Tabitha's real estate agent said as she gave them a tour of the huge condo that Tabitha was looking at. Avery instantly fell in love with the place as soon as they entered.

"I'm thinking I like the place we saw last week," Tabitha said. "It seemed a little more chic."

"Well, this one doesn't have all of the amenities that the other one had, but this one does come with all stainless steel appliances and it's closer to your price range," Bobbie said.

"I will be able to afford the other one once I get accepted into the JMDP at work. I'll get a raise then. What do you think, Avery?" Tabitha asked, opening the closet door.

"I love it," Avery said, wishing she could buy it. It was exactly what she wanted. She could picture herself lounging in the living room, her home office set up in one of the extra bedrooms. The condo was perfect. *If only*, she thought to herself as she walked into the shiny new kitchen, *if only things were different*. Like, if only the decision was solely up to her, which, in some ways, it should have been. Especially since it was her income that paid the majority of the bills. If only Duke could see how nice the condo was.

"Maybe you should consider buying it, Avery. You've been complaining about your house for months now, and saying you want to move," Tabitha suggested.

"Is that so?" Bobbie asked. "Do you own or rent now?"

"I live with my boyfriend in a house that he inherited," Avery replied.

"Really? Where?"

Avery paused before answering. "On the east side."

"Okay, do you think he would be interested in putting the house on the market and moving?"

"I doubt it," she said. "He grew up in that house and if he has his way, he will die there."

The three women laughed. Although it seemed like a joke, Avery knew it was very much the truth, and deep down she was saddened. In some ways, she wondered if she too would end up dying in that house with Duke.

"Well, I can get your information and prequalify you. There's no harm in that," Bobbie suggested. "And there's no harm in having your own place, either. I mean, it can be an investment."

"You got that right. I don't know why she doesn't just buy a place. She works with me," Tabitha volunteered. "So there's no doubt that she can afford it."

Avery thought about the idea of possibly owning the condo and agreed to apply for the loan. After all, it was only an application. A prequalification. Bobbie was right, there was no harm in that.

"Okay, I'll apply." Avery shrugged and filled out the paperwork the agent pulled out of her leather briefcase. While she was writing, her cell phone rang. She saw that it was Kurt and she quickly answered.

"Hello?" It sounded more like a question rather than a greeting.

"Hey, Avery, are you busy? Is this a bad time?" he asked.

She glanced over and saw that Bobbie and Tabitha were engrossed in a conversation about marble versus granite countertops and she told him, "No, I'm not busy. What's up?"

"Listen, it's my parents' anniversary this week and I'm trying to come up with somewhere nice to have a small dinner party. Nothing extremely fancy, but really nice. Got any suggestions?"

Avery wanted to ask him why he called her of all people but decided to just go with the flow. "Well, you can always go to Jasper's."

"We go there all the time. No Cheesecake Factory, Bravo, McCormick and Shmick's. My whack sister, Sharice, has suggested all of those places. I want to go somewhere a bit nicer and different."

She thought about Steinhilber's, a new sea-food restaurant she wanted to try, but Duke had refused to go because they required a shirt and tie. It amazed her that he had no problem dressing up when it came to functions he wanted to attend, but when it came to something she wanted to do out of the norm, it was always a problem.

"You should call Steinhilber's. They are really elegant and I've heard the food is great. You have to make reservations, though."

"Oh yeah, I heard about that place. Thanks, Avery. Hey, how did the midterm go?"

"It went great. I'm confident that I passed."

"So, my advice worked?"

"Yes, it did. I owe you, big-time," she said, smiling.

"I'm gonna hold you to that," he replied.

She felt herself become flush and heat rising on the back of her neck. Had her complexion been lighter, there was no doubt she would be blushing.

"Let me ask you a question," she said. "Why did you ask me about a restaurant, of all things? Is it because I'm a big girl?"

"What?" He laughed. "No, Avery, I asked because I know that you have great taste, and I value your opinion, crazy."

"Okay, I was just wondering."

"Thanks again," he said. "I will see you in the office later this week, but you know I'll e-mail you and check in before then."

"I know," she said and hung up.

"Well, whoever that was put a smile on your face, Avery. You're red as a beet. Was Duke seducing you over the phone?" Tabitha teased.

Avery shook her head. "No, he wasn't."

Chapter 8

"You and Douglas Manning, I would've never put the two of you together," Demi said. She and Avery had arrived at work at the same time and parked beside each other.

"Yeah, they say opposites attract. I guess it's true." Avery smiled. "We've been together for seven years."

"He still looks the same," Demi said. "Fine as hell. Lucky you. Did you think any more about applying to the JDMP?"

Avery shook her head, wondering why Demi was so determined to get her to apply. "No. Why is my applying so important to you, anyway? I know how important mentoring is to you. Have you thought about mentoring Tabitha? She's applied twice and is dying to get into the program."

"Tabitha? Are you crazy? Why would I do that? I have no desire whatsoever to mentor her." Demi's eyes widened so big that Avery thought her gray contacts would pop out.

"Why not? Because she's white?" Avery was bold enough to ask as they walked into the building and entered the elevator.

"It's not about race, Avery. I told you I've been where you are and I want to help you to get where I am. If that's somewhere you would like to be. Tabitha doesn't need any help. And have you considered that maybe she's trying to sabotage your chance of getting ahead?"

It took all she had not to laugh hysterically. "Now that's crazy. Tabitha is my friend and she's encouraged me to apply to the JDMP too."

"Well, every time I hear her she's either trying to get you to go to some club instead of studying, or asking you out to eat or bringing you some sort of edible gift," Demi said.

Avery looked at Demi like she was crazy. "You are funny."

"I'm serious. Coffees and lattes, calorie-filled lunches and snacks. Let me ask you this, when is the last time she suggested that you all take a walk during lunch, or hit the gym after work. She goes to Pilates and yoga, but has she ever invited you?"

"No," Avery mumbled.

"Exactly," Demi said, with a satisfied look on her face. "But how many times have you all hung out at a restaurant? And did she order a complete meal, or just a salad?"

Avery thought about going to Bardo's, a tapas bar, after leaving the condo Saturday night and indulging in various appetizers while Tabitha nibbled on crackers and brie. She hadn't really thought about it until that moment. As ridiculous as it sounded, Demi might have had a point.

"Think about it," Demi said as they got off the elevator and went their separate ways.

Waiting at her desk was a small cake, decorated like an ace of spades, with the words *Congrats Avery, our Ace!* along with a card signed by Tabitha and Malcolm, who were smiling at her as she sat down.

"Thanks, guys," she said, placing the card on her desk. She appreciated the gesture, but somehow, it was tainted, mainly due to Demi's conspiracy theories.

"What's up, girl? Have you heard from Bobbie about your application?" Tabitha asked.

"What application?" Malcolm questioned.

"Avery fell in love with one of the condos I toured," Tabitha told him.

"Wow, Avery, that's what's up. And you thought Duke wanted to stay in that house forever." Malcolm leaned back in his chair. "Can you hurry up and cut that cake? A brother is kinda hungry this morning."

"Stop being greedy, Malcolm. That's why I got her a personal-sized cake, so she wouldn't have to share," Tabitha told him.

Avery looked down at the cake, and saw that although it was small, there was plenty to share. She wondered if Tabitha really did think she would eat the entire thing by herself.

"Did you see the e-mail about the gala next month? I can't wait. I already found the perfect dress at Nordstrom," Tabitha gushed.

"Are you bringing a date?" Malcolm asked.

"Are you?" Tabitha responded.

"Maybe," he said, shrugging.

"Stop fronting. We all know you're bringing Sharice," Tabitha laughed. "And who knows, I may have made my move on Kurt by then."

"I doubt that," Malcolm said. "Word on the street is he came and cleared his desk out Friday night. He's transferring."

"Oh my God, he's really leaving to go and be with that heifer in the southeast office?" Tabitha gasped.

"He did not clear out his desk." Avery shook her head, amazed at how fast rumors made their way around the office. "He came by and picked up some files, that's all."

"How do you know?" Tabitha frowned.

"Because I was here studying," Avery replied.

"Oh, that's right." Tabitha relaxed.

"He is working out of the southeast office, though. At least for a while," Malcolm added.

"Yeah, he is," Avery said, nodding.

"He'll be back here on Wednesday night, though, because it's his parents' anniversary and they're having a dinner party at some overpriced place." Malcolm informed them.

"You think anywhere without a drive-thru is overpriced," Avery laughed. She looked up and saw Demi staring at them. She looked down at the cake on her desk and tried to cover it, but she knew it was too late.

"Can you all keep it down a little?" Demi asked, giving Avery a knowing smile.

"Sorry, Ms. Hayes, we'll try not to be so pleasant in the office," Tabitha's voice dripped with sarcasm.

Demi didn't say a word; she just cut her eyes at Tabitha and walked away.

"That was mean, Tabitha," Avery told her.

"That bitch is mean," Tabitha replied. "I'm telling you, she's a snake and I don't like her. Have you noticed that she's always looking at you?"

"She's always looking at everyone," Avery said. "I think her contacts make her look that way. She's harmless."

"That's what you think." Tabitha turned and walked back to her desk.

Avery opened her e-mails and saw the company announcement regarding the gala. She was looking forward to attending the event herself. She had missed the previous ones because Duke didn't want to rent a tuxedo, but she had decided that this year she would definitely attend. She needed to start networking with some of the other company execs, especially if she wanted to apply for the JDMP in the next year. She needed to get a gown and some shoes, which she was sure Tabitha's shopaholic self would have no problem helping her find.

Later that afternoon, she got a call from Bobbie.

"Hey Avery, I just wanted to let you know that you are more than qualified for the condo if you're interested."

"Really?" Avery knew that she would qualify, but hearing it made it much more of a reality than she thought it was.

"Yep, and I have a couple of others that you may be interested in," Bobbie told her. Her phone beeped and she saw that it was Duke, so she ignored the call and made a mental note to call him back.

"Um, wow. I mean—" Avery didn't know what to say.

"Well, I know you're at work. So, call me later and we can go over a couple of things."

"Okay, will do," Avery told her. Her emotions were a myriad of excitement, joy, and nervousness. Her desk phone rang and she quickly picked it up. "Avery Belmont."

"What the hell is going on, Avery?" Duke's voice was so loud that she had to turn the volume down on her phone so others wouldn't hear him yelling.

"What are you screaming for, Duke?" she hissed.

"Because I'm pissed, that's why, in case you can't tell," he said.

"Pissed for what?" she asked, wondering what could have possibly happened to set him off. Things between them seemed to have been back to normal by the time she returned home Saturday night. She had even relented and gave him some after everyone had cleared out of their house after the fight was over.

"Is there something you need to tell me?" he asked.

She quickly tried to think of what he could possibly be referring to. "No, nothing."

"Then why the fuck did you just get a message from some chick saying that you're good to go on the condo? Huh?"

Shit, Bobbie must have called the house before reaching me on my cell phone. Avery hadn't mentioned the condo to Duke at all, not wanted to spark an argument between them. Now, it seemed as if she was going behind his back.

"Duke, it's not what it seems," she tried to explain to him.

"It seems that your ass is making plans and making moves without me, Avery. What's the deal?"

"There is no deal, Duke. Tabitha went and looked at a condo Saturday and I was with her," she said.

"I shoulda known it had something to do with that "Becky" from the job. I swear, it's like you're turning into a fucking Stepford chick since you've started working at that place a year and a half ago," he told her.

"You've been listening to your cousin too much, Duke, because you sound just as stupid as he did telling you that bullshit Saturday night," she whispered into the phone.

"If you don't wanna be here anymore, Avery, that's fine. Just be woman enough to tell me," Duke said and hung the phone up. She was livid. Duke knew that of all the things he could do to piss her off, hanging up in her face was the worst. She tried calling him back several times, but he ignored her calls. Sitting back in her chair, she tried to calm down enough to get some work done, but she knew that there was no way she was going to accomplish anything, not until she had this situation handled. She sent a quick e-mail to the department secretary and Demi, letting them know she was leaving work because she was ill. She knew that they would probably bitch about it, but she didn't care.

"What's wrong?" Tabitha asked as she grabbed her things and prepared to leave.

"Nothing, I've just got a migraine. I gotta leave," she told her.

"You need me to drive you home?" Tabitha offered.

"No, I'm good," she told her.

"Can I have your cake?" Malcolm asked.

"Malcolm!"

"What? She's leaving," he said.

"Sure, knock yourself out," Avery told him and hurried out. Cake was the last thing on her mind—saving her relationship was the only thing she wanted. She fought back the tears as she left the building.

"Hey, where's the fire?"

Avery turned to see Kurt waving at her across the parking lot. She slowed up enough where he could catch up to her.

"I'm leaving early," she told him. "Migraine."

Kurt looked at her strangely. "Man, I'm sorry. Wow, you don't look so good."

"Thanks," she said.

"I didn't mean it like that. I meant I'm concerned. Let me drive you home."

"No, I'll be fine," she said, "I just need to get home."

"Okay, well, can I call you later and check on you?"

In a sense, she really did want him to call, but she knew that things between her and Duke were bad enough as it was. The last thing she needed was for him to see Kurt calling her cell phone.

"I'm sure I'll be fine."

"Now that I think about it, I guess that's a bad idea anyway. Your man didn't seem too keen about meeting me the other night," he said, smiling.

"Exactly," she said. "What are you doing here? I thought you were working out of the southeast office."

"Things changed. Besides, it didn't make sense for me to fly out and then fly right back Wednesday. So, I stayed."

"I'm glad," she said before she could stop herself.

"Me too." He looked at her and again, she felt

the heat rising on the back of her neck. *Damn, how does he do that? What is it about him that makes me hot? He's not even my type. I don't go for shirts and ties, I go for jerseys and Timbs!*

"Well, I will see you tomorrow," she said and got into her car. As she drove off, she saw him out of her rearview mirror watching her. Knowing that Kurt was back in the office almost made her want to turn around and stay at work, but she knew she had a situation to handle and kept going.

Chapter 9

Avery pulled into the parking lot of Duke's job and prayed his car was there. She was relieved when she spotted it parked on the side of the building. She knew that if he was still at work, there was a chance she could talk some sense into him because Duke never clowned in public. He always said that he kept his dirty laundry at home where it belonged.

Stay calm, Avery, she told herself as she dabbed on her lip gloss and checked her reflection in the mirror. *You know you're the reasonable one and you're gonna have to make him understand that you didn't do anything to disrespect him. Remember how much you love him.*

"Hey there guys," she waved at Los as she walked into the auto parts store, "Is Duke busy?"

An unfamiliar, attractive black man in a shirt and tie standing near Duke's other coworkers looked up and smiled at her. "Well, hello there.

I'm sure he's not too busy for a beautiful young woman."

He is cute, Avery thought as she smiled back at him, noticing his green eyes. "Thank you."

Los shook his head as he picked up the phone and called Duke over the intercom system. "Duke, you have a visitor at the front."

A few seconds later, Duke strolled out and looked surprised to see her.

"Hey," she said, grinning, hoping he would be glad to see her.

His face was void of any expression as he simply replied, "Hey."

"I came to take you to lunch," she said.

He looked down at his watch and said, "It's after one o'clock, Avery. I went to lunch at twelve."

Avery knew that Duke pretty much came and left the store as he wanted to in the past. She thought he was trying to be difficult until she saw him glance over at the shirt-and-tie guy.

"New management, new rules," Los volunteered.

The man looked over at Avery and said, "Come on now, Duke. You know it's not even like that. If you need to take a few and go speak with this young lady, you can."

Duke looked like he wanted to snap, and Avery wondered if his disgust was directed at her or the shirt-and-suit man. Either way, he simply said, "I'll be back in fifteen. And for the record, I'm right in the parking lot and I'm not leaving the premises in case there are any questions or problems."

"I got you, Duke," Los made sure his voice was heard.

Avery followed Duke out into the parking lot and stood next to his shiny car. The custom paint job still looked brand new.

"Duke," she started to talk first. "You know I love you and I would never do anything to jeopardize what we have. What I don't think you realize is that everything I do is to benefit us. That's why I enrolled in grad school, that's why I work so hard, that's why I fuss so much. I want us to have everything we want."

"But I already have everything I want, Avery. I have you. That's all I need. You act like we ain't talk about all this. When I told you I loved you and wanted to be together, I did everything you asked me to do in order to make that happen. You told me to get out the game, I did. You told me to get a job, I did. You told me to stop hanging out and be there for you, and I am. And I did all of that out of love, because I love you. Do you know what I gave up for you? Now, all of a sudden, you done changed shit up in the middle of the game."

"But I haven't changed shit up, Duke," Avery told him.

"You have, sweetheart. You just don't realize it. Now, my house ain't good enough for you. I've been asking you to marry me for years, and you keep saying wait. And let's not even talk about when I bring up having a baby. I'm beginning to wonder if I'm good enough for you, for real."

Avery looked at him, shaking her head. "Duke, you know that you're the best thing that ever happened to me. When my mother died my senior year of college, you were the one that stood in and took care of me. My life wouldn't be as good as it is right now if it wasn't for you. And you're right, you did everything I asked you to do. You went above and beyond to prove how much you love me. But, it's like now that you have me, you're fine with that. I want to travel and do things, but when I mention it, you act like I'm all of a sudden trying to be bourgeois or something, and I'm not. Am I wrong for wanting to buy a house?"

"You have a house, Avery. What's wrong with our house?"

"It's nothing wrong with our house, Duke. But look," she pointed at his car, "your car was fine. It drove great, had the rims, the system, but you wanted to get a fresh paint job. Why?"

"So it would look better." He shrugged. "So, all of this is because I got my car painted?"

Avery shook her head. "No, Duke, it's not about the paint job at all. You're not getting what I'm saying. You wanted your car to look better. That's what I want for us. Our life is good now, but is there something wrong with wanting it to be better?"

"It is if it's never gonna be good enough. Let's say we get this dream house you've gone and picked out. What's gonna happen in a year? It's not gonna be good enough, then we're out looking for something better. That's not how I wanna live, Avery. I like our life now, we're happy. Well, I'm happy," he sighed. "And you were happy too until you started working at that place. Now, you can't even seem to stay outta that place. You barely even come home."

"Because I'm studying, Duke. It's just a quiet place for me to study," she responded without adding *and somewhere I don't have to worry about the damn internet getting cut off.*

"I don't know what you're doing. Your ass wasn't studying when I popped up there Friday night. What was I supposed to think?"

"I was on my way home to be with you, Duke," she explained for the hundredth time. "You popped up as I was leaving."

"Yeah, the broke brother popped up as you were leaving with the Brooks Brother, go figure," he laughed. "I gotta get back to work."

Before she could even respond, Duke had walked away and back into the building. Avery had too much pride to go after him. Instead, she sulked back to her car. At this point, Avery did have a migraine. Her head throbbed to the point that her face was starting to ache. She went home and crawled into bed without even taking her clothes off.

It was after eleven when Avery finally woke up. She sat up and listened for the blaring of the TV coming from downstairs, but it was eerily quiet. After going to the bathroom, she peeked out of the window and saw that Duke's car wasn't in the driveway. She checked her cell phone to see if he had called, but the only missed calls she had were from Tabitha and Bobbie. Not only had Duke not even come home, he hadn't even called to check on her. Avery quickly changed clothes, grabbed her laptop, and left. She didn't want to be there when he came home. She thought about going back to the office, but didn't want to chance running into Kurt or maybe even Demi. Instead, she drove to IHOP, thinking she could kill two birds with one stone: Feed her growling stomach and study for a while.

The restaurant was fairly empty when she walked in. She was seated at a table far in the back and ordered a hot tea, along with an omelet and a stack of pancakes. She ate her food and dug into her books, determined to at least get some studying done.

"Now what's a pretty girl like you doing all alone in a place like this at night?"

Avery looked up and saw the shirt-and-tie guy from Duke's job standing in front of her table looking very much like Terrence Howard. She smiled. "Studying."

"So, I see," he said. "Are you taking the bar soon?"

"No, accelerated MBA program," she told him.

"Just as difficult," he said. "We weren't properly introduced earlier. I'm Daniel Flanagan."

"Nice to meet you, Daniel." Avery wiped her hands on a napkin and stretched it out to him. "I'm Avery Belmont."

"The pleasure is all mine," he said. "Well, I'm not gonna disturb you. Nice seeing you again."

"You too," she told him, and then added, "I hope I didn't get Duke into trouble this afternoon."

Daniel laughed and said, "No, not at all. They act like I'm this Nazi manager who is out to get them, which I'm not. I'm pretty much a laid-back guy. They just like to give me a hard time, all the time."

"I can imagine," Avery said.

"They hate the fact that I was brought in to run the store, but what they don't realize is that I'm the best thing that could have ever happened to them. If I hadn't intervened, my uncle was going to sell to one of the large corporate chains and they would be out of a job. We all know how that goes," Daniel sighed. "They would have fired every last one of them and brought in their own employees. All I ask from them is to have a little work ethic and respect the job, that's it. But, I guess that's too much."

"It's all a learning process for them," Avery said. "They were used to running the shop and having their way, and now they got a real boss. I think what you did is commendable. I'm actually writing about that topic for my senior seminar thesis. You mind if I ask you a couple of questions?"

"Not at all," Daniel said, sliding into the booth and sitting across from her. For two hours, they talked about the ever-increasing problems within inner-city neighborhoods and solutions that could take place within the corporate arena to alleviate them. Daniel seemed to have as much passion about the subject as she did. She shared with him the desire to buy a home, but her reluctance due to her relationship.

"It's hard," Daniel told her. "You want more out of life, but somehow feel like you're betraying your past if you move on."

"Exactly." she nodded. "I love my neighborhood and the people. But, I'm starting to feel trapped. It's like all of a sudden, I feel like if I want to get ahead in life, I'm the bad person."

"You can't allow yourself to feel that way, though. If you do, you're gonna end up resenting your life, and becoming bitter. You've got to make choices to make yourself happy, and make them without regret. Despite whoever says or feels differently."

Avery looked up at him and knew who he was referring to. "But, it's not about just me."

"It is about you. You're the only person in your life that can make you happy. Listen to me; I've been where Duke and Los and the rest of those guys are. They're complacent. They're happy with just having a nine-to-five with enough money in their pocket to buy the latest video-game system and party on the weekends. That's why I can relate to where they're coming from," Daniel told her. "But, then I realized that life was too comfortable to me. I was no longer satisfied with having just enough. I wanted more; more out of myself, and more out of my life. So, I did more, I worked more, I achieved more. There's nothing wrong with wanting more, Avery. Hell, there's nothing wrong with expecting more from Duke. He's comfortable."

Avery was shocked at how a stranger could evaluate her situation and put things into perspective better than she could.

"Oh my goodness," she said, noticing the time. "It's almost two-thirty."

"Wow, I didn't realize it was that late—or should I say, early," he said.

Avery gathered her books and thanked him again for his time and insight. "I really appreciate it, Daniel."

"Hey, anytime. I enjoyed it," he said and passed her a business card. "If you need any more help, feel free to give me a call. And remember, there's nothing wrong with wanting more."

She picked up her things and hurried home, knowing that Duke would be worried. *He's not that worried, he hasn't called to check on me. He's probably not even home himself.*

She arrived home to find him fast asleep in their bed. She quickly changed into her pajamas and climbed in beside him, careful not to wake him. He stirred beside her and she eased under the covers. Her head hit the pillow and she closed her eyes, thinking that as soon as she drifted off to sleep, it would be time to wake up.

"Avery," Duke whispered into the darkness.

"Yeah." Avery's heart began pounding.

"I love you," he said, and pulled himself close to her, snuggling tightly.

Relieved, she told him, "I love you too, Duke."

"Then stop running away from me," he said.

Chapter 10

"I think you should get that one," Tabitha said.

Avery looked at her reflection in the mirror as they stood in the dressing room at Nordstroms. Finding the perfect dress for a size-four person like Tabitha was easy, but the perfect dress for a size twenty diva, such as herself, was a little more difficult. This was the first dress she had tried on when they arrived at the mall earlier, and now, after trying on six more in four other stores, she returned and decided to retry the black Adrianna Papell gown. It actually flattered her thick curvaceous body; the dramatic, deep-cut neckline was perfect and showed off just enough cleavage. It was classy and sexy all at the same time.

"Yeah, I like this one the best." Avery turned around and looked at her behind. "Maybe I can get some butt pads to make the back look as good as the front."

Tabitha laughed. "You have enough junk in your trunk, girl. As a matter of fact, you should donate some to me."

"Yeah, you are lacking in that area. I guess being a size two does have its disadvantages," Avery teased. "No junk in your trunk and no food in your stomach."

"I have food in my stomach. Heck, you're the one that's been starving yourself these past couple of weeks." Tabitha stood up and unzipped the dress.

Avery gently held the lace against her skin to keep it from falling as she walked back into the dressing room. Once the door closed behind her, she stepped out of the dress and looked at herself. She had lost weight. Not too much, but it was becoming noticeable, especially in her face. Even Demi commented on it a few days ago.

"Wow, you're looking good, Avery," she told her. "You been working out?"

"Nope, not at all, just working hard." Avery smiled and kept walking. She really didn't feel like hearing any of Demi's no-nonsense advice, critiques, and more importantly, cynicism. The truth was she had cut back. No more lattes in the morning, just hot tea. She started bringing her own lunch, and when they did go out, she was mindful about what she ordered. She even started walking outside during her breaks every now and then. It was surprising what a big difference the little changes in her life made. She even felt a lot better.

"Is Duke coming to the gala?" Tabitha's voice asked over the dressing-room door.

Avery took a deep breath and answered, "No, you know the gala isn't his cup of tea."

Even though she had expressed to Duke how important the gala was to her, he had flat-out refused to attend.

"I don't even like you working at that place. Do you really think I wanna pay to rent a tuxedo and hang out all night with a bunch of fake-ass folks that I don't know and don't wanna know?" he said, grimacing when she asked him for the fourth and final time.

"You know *me*, Duke, and that's all you need to be concerned with," she told him.

"I don't see you making an effort to hang out with me at Los's house, and you know all of us," Duke replied. "I asked you to come with me to his sister's baby shower and you didn't want to come."

"That's because I had class, Duke. I'm not missing class for a damn baby shower," she said, *especially for some seventeen-year-old chick that I don't even know.*

"And I'm not missing the basketball play offs for some gala I don't wanna go to," Duke said. "End of discussion."

Avery didn't mention it again. She just planned to attend without him. In her mind, she started planning to do a lot of things without him. She remained in contact with Bobbie, and even started looking at new construction homes on Saturdays when she got out of class. She hated to do it, but Duke's attitude was making it easier and easier for her.

She put the dress back on the hanger and after getting dressed, headed out to pay for it.

"Do you need shoes?" Tabitha asked.

"No, I'm good with shoes and a purse. I just needed a dress. Do you have everything you need?"

"Girl, I've been ready for months. I thought I was gonna have a date, but Kurt declined my offer."

"What? You asked him to the gala? You actually talked to him? I can't believe it." Avery smiled.

"Yeah, the other night at Steinhilber's," Tabitha said, smiling.

"Oh no, Tabitha, you didn't!"

"It's not what you think." Tabitha turned beet red.

"You're stalking him now?"

"No, Malcolm's wallet fell out in my car when we went to lunch, so I had to take it to him. Kurt was outside when I got there. But we did talk," Tabitha explained. "And I even flirted a little."

"I hope his date didn't see you." Avery gave the cashier her credit card.

"He didn't have a date. It was just him, his family, and Malcolm. He did buy me a drink at the bar though and it was nice."

Avery felt a twinge of jealousy, but brushed it off. *You have a man.*

"So, he knows you're interested at this point?" Avery asked.

"I'm sure he does. It's not as if I came out and said 'Hey, I wanna get with you'."

Avery gave her a knowing look. "Don't front like you haven't said that to a guy before. I've been there when you've done it, at a bar, mind you, while standing on the bar."

Even the cashier laughed at Avery's statement.

"Well, no, I didn't say that. And this time, I wasn't standing on top of the bar. I really just made small talk with him. Talked about the job— turns out he works out at the same gym as I do, so we talked about that." Tabitha smiled. "Then I brought up the gala and I asked if he had a date."

"And what did he say?" Avery took the now plastic-wrapped dress and draped it over her arm and thanked the cashier.

"He said no. So I asked if he was interested in one. And believe it or not, he kinda got excited. So, you know I thought I was in there. I smiled and said 'me'."

"Well, no subtleness there, huh?" Avery laughed. "Then what did he say?"

"He thanked me and said he was flattered, but he had to respectfully decline. Do you think he really has something going on with Demi?" Tabitha became serious. "I can't see him even being attracted to that toad. She looks like a bobblehead doll. A scary one, with those ugly contacts."

"You are so mean. I'm really thinking that there's nothing going on there. You can't listen to office gossip. You of all people should know that. Look at how everyone said that you were sleeping with Malcolm. That rumor circulated for years."

"Yeah, it did," Tabitha laughed.

"And that's all it was: office talk, assumptions, and lies."

"Well . . ." Tabitha said, guiltily.

Avery stopped dead in her tracks and stared at her friend. "Well what? It was just talk, right?"

"For the most part, it was. But, Malcolm and I did hook up a couple of times when we first started working there."

"What? Are you serious? When? Where was I? I can't believe this." Avery couldn't believe this was the first time she had heard Tabitha talk about this.

"I think you were still in training, a newbie, when we hooked up. I mean, it's not like we dated or it was serious. It was purely physical and out of that we became like the best of friends. We haven't slept together in years."

Avery was still in shock. "And neither of you ever said anything about it?"

"We don't talk about it, Avery. I mean, what? You think I'm gonna look over at him and say, 'Hey Malcolm, remember that time you came over to my apartment and did me on the living room floor'?"

"He did you on the living room floor?" Avery continued to be stunned.

"Yeah, and it was great."

"I don't even wanna hear any more! He's like my brother!"

"Okay, believe me, as soon as I saw how much of an office whore he really was, I stopped ASAP!"

"I can't believe you never said anything," Avery shook her head.

"I can't believe you didn't know," Tabitha giggled, then seeing that Avery was serious, she added, "I really thought you knew, Avery. I'm sorry."

Avery didn't know whether to be angry, disappointed or amused. On one hand, she felt that if Malcolm and Tabitha shared this deep-dark secret, what other secrets did they share between them? On another, she knew that if neither one felt the need to share the fact that they had, at one point, slept with one another, then it must not have been that serious.

"Well, what else have you been hiding?" Avery asked her.

"Um, well, you know Brinkman from accounting?"

"Yeah." Avery nodded, wondering what in the world Tabitha was about to say about the old, balding man who had a habit of belching at the most inappropriate times.

"I did him in the back parking lot one day after staff meeting," Tabitha looked down in shame.

"What? Oh my God, Tabitha! What the hell is wrong with you? That's so gross!" Avery couldn't help yelling. People in the mall stopped and stared at them.

Tabitha began laughing uncontrollably. "I'm just kidding, Avery. You know I would never do him. I do have standards."

"I used to think you did, but now I don't know. I mean, you did sleep with Malcolm."

"Malcolm is fine, and you know it. Hell, if you weren't so in love with Duke, you would be all up in his face the same way all the other single females in the office are."

"Including you," Avery teased.

"I was never in his face, he was in mine. But, now that it's all in the open, let me ask you a question. And I need for you to be totally honest with me." Tabitha became serious.

"What?"

"When the rumors started about Malcolm and me, people really started treating me different— some were even nasty. Now, Malcolm has slept with plenty of women in that building, more than you and I can even count. But when they thought it was me, it damn near caused an uproar. I even think that's why I wasn't selected for the JDMP last year. Why do you think that was?"

Avery knew exactly what Tabitha was getting at, and she knew there was no point in trying to sugarcoat the explanation. She had too much respect for her friend to lie, so she said straight up, "Probably because you're white. You know that."

Tabitha seemed relieved at Avery's answer. "I know, and you're right. But, do you think that's why Kurt declined my invitation?"

"Now that, I don't know," Avery told her. For some strange reason, Avery was relieved that Kurt turned down Tabitha's invitation. Not that she didn't want to see her friend happy, because Tabitha deserved someone special in her life; Avery just didn't want that person to be Kurt.

Now, you know you're wrong, Avery Belmont. How can you be so selfish? You have a man, why wouldn't you want Tabitha to be with someone as nice, charming, smart, attractive, and desirable as Kurt? Why wouldn't I? Wait, I know why. Because he's nice, charming, smart, attractive, and desirable and you want him for yourself.

"Hey," Avery said, walking into the bedroom and hanging her dress bag on the closet door. Duke was lying across the bed, flipping through a car magazine.

"Hey," he said, looking over at her. "What's that?"

"My dress for the gala." She removed it from the bag and held it against herself so that he could see it.

Duke looked up and nodded. "That's nice."

"Tabitha helped me pick it out," she told him, then, testing the waters, she said, "Guess what I found out today?"

"You're pregnant?" Duke's eyes widened.

Avery shook her head. "No fool, I'm not pregnant. Remember a while back when I told you about people saying Malcolm and Tabitha were sleeping together?"

"Let me guess, they were."

"Yep," Avery said, nodding, "Can you believe that? And I had no clue."

"That's because you're unaware," he said.

"What?" She frowned, "What's that supposed to mean?"

"You're innocent." He smiled. "Gullible, a square. I told you if people were talking about it, it was probably true."

Avery rushed over to the bed and playfully began wrestling with him. "I'm innocent? A square?"

"Yes, you are." Without warning, Duke flipped her over on the bed and straddled her, looking deep into her eyes. Avery wrapped her arms around him as he said, "That's one of the reasons I fell in love with you. You were a goody t wo-shoes."

They kissed for what seemed like an eternity, and in that moment, everything was right between them. Nothing else seemed to matter, not the job, not school, not Kurt, not the condo, and for the first time in a long time, Avery didn't feel as if she was constricted and confined to a world that she no longer wanted to be in, but was afraid to leave.

Chapter 11

The ballroom of the Omni Hotel was a perfection of blue and silver, the company colors of Jennings International. There was a band and a DJ, an open bar, and waiters offering endless trays of appetizers and flutes of champagne. It seemed as if the company wasted no expense. Avery had heard the tales of how elegant and extravagant that the gala was, and now she was experiencing it firsthand. She scolded herself for missing it in the past.

"Wow, Avery, you look gorgeous," Malcolm said.

"Wow yourself," Avery said, admiring her friend looking quite dapper in his tuxedo. "You clean up nice, friend!"

"Stop hating, I'm always clean," he said. "Man, you look amazing!"

"Well, I didn't know I looked that bad before," Avery laughed. She knew she looked good, she made sure of it. Her hair was straightened and pulled up into a perfect chignon, with soft curls framing her face. Her makeup was flawless, along with her nails and feet, thanks to the talented staff of After Effex, her favorite salon. Not only had Duke done a triple take when she passed him as she walked out of the house, but she could feel the eyes on her when she walked into the ballroom. For some reason, she felt as if this was her night.

"Naw, you know what I mean. Everyone knows you're pretty, Avery, but tonight, you really look like a model. A supermodel," he said, grinning.

"Now you're going too far." Avery shook her head. "But thanks for the compliments. Did you pick up the roses?"

"Yeah, I put them in the coat check," Malcolm said. "I sure hope they call Tabitha's name. If they don't, she's gonna go off, believe that."

"I know she is," Avery agreed. Earlier in the week, Tabitha had put a contract on the large condo she had been wanting, confident that after tonight, she would be the latest selectee for the JMDP and guaranteed a huge raise to help her pay for her new home. "I'm sure she's gonna get it, though. There's no one else who can beat her out for the spot."

"That's true," Malcolm said, nodding.

"Where's Sharice?"

"She's riding with Kurt. I think she wanted to arrive in his C Class rather than my Camry," he laughed. "But, it's cool. She'll be departing in it after this is over."

"I guess Tabitha isn't the only confident one."

"Don't you think I have every right to be?"

They turned to see Tabitha walking up, looking stunning in a black silk gown. If anyone looked like a supermodel, it was she. Malcolm gave a low whistle and Avery began applauding.

"Mah-va-lous, dahling, simply mah-va-lous." Avery kissed both sides of her cheek in a dramatic fashion.

"No, you are fabulous," Tabitha told her. "I told you that dress was perfect."

"Not as perfect as yours," Avery replied.

"Ladies, ladies, no need to argue. I can settle this right now, yours truly is the babe of the ball tonight," Malcolm told them. Tabitha playfully punched him in the arm and Avery tried to fight images of the two of them having sex out of her head.

"Shall we take our seats?" he asked, looping his arms thro-ugh each of theirs. They made their way through the crowded ballroom until they found their table. Avery scanned the crowd, noticing her coworkers and trying to see if she could spot Kurt. *He's probably going to be seat-*

ed at the head table, she told herself. *And he's probably going to be with his date.*

"Champagne?" one of the waiters offered.

"No thanks," Avery told him, then pointed to Tabitha. "She'll probably want some."

"No, none for me," Tabitha said, to all of their surprise. "I want to be sober when they call my name."

Malcolm shook his head in disbelief, then said, "There's Sharice. Let me go over so she'll see how good I look."

Tabitha took the time to introduce Avery to all of the company execs and key people she felt Avery needed to know. They circulated the room, speaking and making small talk until the program began. Mr. Jennings, the CEO, along with several other members of the board of directors, Kurt, Demi, and a few other managers, all took their seats at the head table. Avery could barely concentrate on the welcome speech Mr. Jennings gave because she was focusing on not staring at Kurt. Tabitha didn't make that task any easier, especially with her commenting every five seconds about how sexy he looked.

"I'll be right back," Avery said, standing up once the first half of the program was over and dinner was served.

"Where are you going?" Tabitha asked.

"To the restroom."

"I'll walk with you. I need to go to the bar."

"I thought you weren't drinking," Avery reminded her.

"I need something to calm my nerves," Tabitha sighed. "Just one martini and I should be good."

"Okay." Avery shrugged and they walked into the hotel lobby. "I'll meet you here."

"Cool," Tabitha said, nodding.

Avery walked into the bathroom and checked herself in the mirror, reapplying her lipstick.

"Avery, you really look nice."

Avery looked up to see Demi smiling at her, dressed in a slightly too-tight blue cocktail dress and matching heels. Her weave was slightly longer than normal in a mass of thick curls, and the blue and charcoal shadow she wore on her eyes made her gray contacts even scarier.

"Thanks," she told her. "You look really nice too, Demi."

"I love the gala. It's the best event the company has. The food, the music, the dancing, the decorations, it's all so magical. It's a privilege just to be a part of it all, you know what I mean?"

"Yeah, I do," Avery nodded. "This is the first one I've attended."

"Well, it won't be your last. You'll see what a difference tonight makes. You do realize the importance of being here, correct? Is Duke here? I don't recall seeing him at your table."

"No, he's not here," Avery told her.

"Well, I'm sure you'll have lots to tell him when you get home tonight. It's going to be memorable, believe me," Demi said, smiling.

"Yeah, I'm sure it is," Avery said, politely. "I'll see you later."

Avery eased out of the bathroom, and returned to find Tabitha, Malcolm, and Kurt chatting near the bar.

"Avery, you look amazing." Kurt grinned, looking her up and down. "Are you enjoying yourself?"

"Thank you," Avery said, smiling back at him. "And yes, I am."

"That's good," he said. She tried not to stare at him.

"I told Avery this is the event to be at every year," Tabitha said, nodding.

"She's right, especially if you're hoping to move up within the company or even change departments. But I know you're not trying to leave me, right?" Kurt teased.

Avery didn't know if he meant her personally, or them as a group and she was glad when Malcolm answered, "Naw, you know I can't go anywhere until I'm in good with the family."

"Well, at least you're honest," Kurt said, then added, "Well, let me get back to my seat before they start calling my name over the mic. I will definitely see you all later."

They returned to their seats just as the program resumed.

"Are you still nervous?" Avery leaned over and asked Tabi-tha.

"Not so much," Tabitha told her. "I'm thinking maybe I should have had another drink though."

"You'll be fine," Avery assured her.

"They'd better call my name," Tabitha warned.

Mr. Jennings began telling the history of the JMDP and how it became one of the most important programs within the company. He also stated how each year, hundreds applied and only a few were selected; one person from each of the seven district offices.

Avery glanced over to see Tabitha inhale deeply as she waited in anticipation. One by one, he called the names of the selectees, and they applauded them as they rushed on stage to receive the plaque that would undoubtedly change their lives forever.

"Our last and final recipient tonight is a special one, a candidate who has impressed others not only within her office, but at the district level. Her contributions to the staff has been exemplary not only to her peers and management, but to clients as well. After hearing about this young woman and the goals she has set for herself not only as an employee, but as a civic leader, as well, led to her being selected. She truly embodies what Jennings International strives to achieve" Mr. Jennings paused.

Avery reached over and grabbed Tabitha's hand, and her friend held her breath, sitting up in her chair.

"Ladies and gentlemen, our honorary selectee for the year—Avery Belmont."

Applause erupted in the ballroom, and Avery froze, not knowing what to do. This was not what was supposed to be happening and she didn't know why it was. She didn't even apply for the program, so how the hell was she selected?

"What the hell?" she heard Tabitha say.

"Yeah, Avery!"

"You go, girl!"

"Congratulations!"

People shouted and whistled. Avery remained in her seat, still shocked. *Don't just sit there, looking crazy. Get up and go! You'll fix this later.*

"Miss Belmont, you may come and get your award," Mr. Jennings laughed.

Avery's eyes met Tabitha's and she saw the hurt and betrayal.

"Tabitha, it's a mistake. It can't be right," she told her. "I'll fix it, I promise."

Tabitha didn't say anything; she just stared at Avery with tears in her eyes. Avery walked up to the stage and Mr. Jennings passed her the crystal plaque embossed with her name. She posed for the photographers who took pictures of her with the JDMP selectees. It was unbelievable. She looked over and her eyes met Kurt's. He beamed with pride. Her eyes then went over to Demi's, who was smiling just as hard. After several minutes, she was finally able to leave the stage and go back to her table. Maneuvering her way through the crowd of well-wishers, she saw that Tabitha was gone and she headed to the lobby.

Tabitha was standing near the bar, talking with Malcolm and Sharice.

"Tabitha," Avery said her name softly.

"Leave me the hell alone, Avery," Tabitha told her. "Now is not the time, for real."

"You know I didn't know any of this was gonna happen. I didn't even apply. I wanted you to win, and you should have. I'm gonna talk with Mr. Jennings and get things straight," Avery tried to explain.

"I don't even want the fucking position. I see now that the entire thing is rigged, it's fake. They pick who they wanna pick. It doesn't even matter if the person is qualified or not! Fuck Jennings International and fuck the JMDP bitches, including you!" Tabitha hissed, her eyes red from crying.

"Tabitha, come on. You know there has to be some sort of mix-up. Avery has been saying all along that she didn't want to be in the program. Besides the fact that she's your girl and would never do anything like this behind your back," Malcolm tried to reason with Tabitha. "She knows how much this meant to you."

"I do." Avery nodded. The fact that Tabitha called her *unqualified* stung, but she ignored it.

"Don't be like this, Tabitha," even Shanice tried to calm her down.

"Fuck you, Avery. Get outta my face, for real before I kick your ass! I'm warning you!" Tabitha's voice became louder and people started to look over at them.

"You need to excuse yourself from the venue right now, Tabitha!"

They turned to see Demi headed toward them.

Oh great, her ass is only gonna make matters worse.

"This doesn't have anything to do with you, Demi. Step off," Tabitha snapped.

"Excuse me? I beg to differ. This is a Jennings International event and it has everything to do with me. I'm sure you're disappointed in your not being selected, but so are a lot of other people here and none of them are acting as inappropriate as you are." Demi's anger could be seen in her eyes.

"What's inappropriate is how the hell Avery got selected and she didn't even apply?" Tabitha looked over at Avery and then added, "If you really didn't apply."

"I didn't," Avery told her. "Tabitha, I swear, I wouldn't lie."

"Avery, you don't have to appease her. You got selected and she didn't, end of story," Demi said. "Now, if you're gonna continue to make a scene about it, you really need to leave, Tabitha. And from what I understand, this isn't the first time you haven't been selected, so this really shouldn't be a big deal to you."

"Demi, you're out of line," Malcolm stepped between Tabitha and Demi. "You really owe Tabitha an apology."

"I don't owe her anything," Demi laughed. "And neither does anyone else around here. Contrary to popular belief, Tabitha is not all that. I don't care how many men she sleeps with in the office, including you."

"Demi!" Avery squealed and it was her that now stepped in between Malcolm and Demi. He looked as if he was about to swing on Demi.

"I think we all need to just walk away before anything else gets said," Sharice said, reaching and touching Malcolm's arm. He relaxed and took a step back.

"What seems to be the problem?" Kurt's voice asked.

"It seems as if Tabitha is having a hard time accepting the fact that she was not selected again this year," Demi told him. "And she's taking her anger out on Avery."

"Let me handle this, Demi, thanks," he said and after Demi walked away he turned to Tabitha and said, "Tabitha, that doesn't sound like you. What's the problem?"

"She didn't even apply and her ass got selected?" Tabitha yelled at him.

"First of all, you need to lower your voice." Kurt told her. "And Mr. Jennings said she was an honorary selectee. Her selection was based on merit. I really don't know the specifics. You know there are honorary selectees sometimes. Are you okay, Avery?"

Avery stared at him and said, "Yeah, I'm okay." He touched her arm and she became lost in his stare, and remained there until she heard

Tabitha's voice, "You've gotta be kidding me, right?"

"What's the problem?" Kurt asked.

"No problem at all," Tabitha said, then added, "No, wait, there is a problem. I quit!"

"What?" they all said at once.

"You all and Jennings International can go to hell. Now, there's no problem," she said and walked off.

"I'll get her," Avery said.

"No, let her go," Malcolm said. "I'll make sure she's good."

"I'll go with you," Sharice told her.

Once they were alone, Kurt grabbed her arm and escorted her to one of the nearby leather sofas in the lobby. She sat down, still confused by what was going on.

"I feel really bad," she told him.

"Why? You deserve to be selected."

"But, she's wanted this for years, Kurt. She worked hard for it," Avery told him.

"You did too, Avery. What makes you think your work is less valuable than hers? What you do within that company doesn't go unnoticed," he said, shrugging.

Avery looked up at him and asked, "Did you have something to do with this?"

"No, I didn't know anything about it. I was just as surprised as you were when they called your name. I was elated, but surprised nonetheless."

"She's my friend," Avery told him.

"And she'll get over this. She knows you didn't intentionally do this to hurt her," Kurt's voice comforted her.

"Hey, Kurt, there you are!"

"Man, you are late as hell." Kurt stood up. "You missed the entire program."

"I wanted to miss the boring part!"

Avery looked over to see Daniel, Duke's boss, walking over to them.

"Daniel, what are you doing here?" she asked.

"Avery Belmont, looking gorgeous as ever," Daniel said, beaming at her. "My boy, Kurt, here, invited me to this fancy shindig. I figured I could do some serious networking."

"You two know each other?" Kurt asked.

"Yeah, he's the manager at Duke's job," Avery told him.

"Wow, small world," Kurt said.

"Wait a minute," Daniel said, putting his arm around Avery. "Is this the chick you've been telling me about?"

For some reason, Avery felt very uncomfortable. At first, she thought it was because of Daniel's question to Kurt, until she realized someone was staring at her. She looked up to see Demi, standing beside Duke of all people, looking like a million bucks in a tuxedo.

"Duke," she stood up and rushed over to him. He stepped back before she could get to him.

"Damn, I thought I was surprising you but I guess I was the one to be surprised," he said.

"Man, it's not what it looks like," Daniel told him.

"It don't even matter." Duke shook his head. "It's all good."

"Baby, please listen to me," Avery pleaded, but Duke took off and was out the door before she could stop him.

"Avery," Daniel called her name.

"Excuse me," she told them, rushing out of the hotel. She searched the parking lot, and spotted Duke just as he was getting into his car. "Duke, wait!"

He looked over at her and got in without saying a word. Avery tried to run, but her dress and heels made it damn near impossible. She knew catching him was hopeless, which was probably a good thing, because there was a strong chance if she had gotten any closer, he would have run over her. She stood in the hotel parking lot, defeated and disgusted.

"Avery, are you okay?"

"I'm fine," Avery said to Demi, who seemed to appear out of nowhere.

"You're not fine," Demi told her. "Come on back inside."

"No, I'm leaving." She shook her head. "My head is pounding."

"Fine, we'll get you some aspirin. You don't need to leave, tonight is your night. Don't let anyone take that away. You should be celebrating, now come on," Demi replied. "Besides, you left your plaque."

"I don't want it," Avery sighed.

"That's crazy. Everything is gonna be fine. You can't just leave now. You do know all eyes are on you, especially right now. How would it look to Mr. Jennings, the board of directors, and everyone else if you just left? Be reasonable and think. Do you know how many people would kill to be in your spot right now, including Tabitha."

All Avery wanted to do was get in her car, go home and talk to her man, but instead, she followed Demi back inside and took a seat.

Demi said to Avery, "You look like you could use a drink. I'll get you one."

Avery pasted a fake smile on her face and thanked those who were still congratulating her. Inside her heart was aching. She reached into her small clutch and took out her phone, sending

Tabitha a text apologizing again and asking her to call.

"Here you go," Demi said, passing her a small tablet and a glass of champagne.

"What's this?" Avery asked, looking at the tablet.

"For your headache," Demi said.

"Oh, thanks." Avery swallowed the pill and drank the bubbly liquid. She felt her body relax and she even began enjoying herself.

Kurt and Daniel both came and checked on her, both making it a point not to mention Duke or Tabitha. Avery even dared to dance; once with Mr. Jennings at the encouragement of his wife, and twice each with Daniel and Kurt. *Demi is right, it is my night and I deserve to enjoy the moment. If Tabitha and Duke want to hate on me, let 'em!*

"So, some of the managers are heading down-town to the bar district when this is over," Demi yelled over Flo Rida rapping about shawty getting low. "You wanna come?"

Feeling completely euphoric, Avery nodded. "Sure, sounds like a plan."

She grabbed her plaque and purse, thanking Mr. and Mrs. Jennings again, and followed Demi out the door. Kurt and Daniel were standing outside the hotel when she passed them. "Hey, we're going clubbing. You fellas wanna come with us?"

"Cool, where?" Daniel asked.

Demi shook her head and told them, "This outing is strictly for the female execs— sorry, guys!"

A stretch limo pulled up in front and the driver opened the door.

"You guys got a limo?" Avery turned and asked them.

"Naw, not us," Kurt laughed.

"This is our ride." Demi pushed Avery inside and she nearly tumbled, laughing uncontrollably.

"Well, I'm glad y'all have a designated driver," Daniel said. "You girls be safe!"

"*Byyyyyeeeee!*" Avery called out as the door closed. She sat back on the leather seat and told Demi, "I'm really having a good time. I'm glad I didn't leave."

"I'm glad you didn't either."

"Where is everyone else? Aren't they riding in the limo?"

Demi shrugged and said, "No, they're just gonna meet us down there. They wanted to drive."

"Maybe I should drive too. My car is right there."

"No, the limo will bring you back to get it. It's not a problem," Demi told her as she sat beside her. She was so close that Avery could feel her thigh brushing against hers. Oddly enough, the sensation of her leg against hers seemed to be strangely pleasant.

"But what if I want to leave before you do?"

"We can leave together. It's no big deal." Demi smiled. "You really look amazing."

"Thanks, Tabitha helped me pick out the dress," Avery told her.

Demi seemed to ease closer and closer to her, and then, Avery felt her hand gently touching her face. Avery blinked, wondering if she was dreaming. Everything seemed to be hazy, but she felt wonderful. Demi's hand on her face was turning her on. Then, it was no longer her hand, but Demi's mouth slowly kissing her cheek, her lips easing their way to hers. Avery's eyes closed and her breathing became harder. She tried to tell herself to stop, but her body wouldn't listen to her mind and she found herself not only kissing Demi back, but enjoying it.

What the hell is happening. Avery tried to open her eyes, which were now closed. *Something's not right.*

Demi's hands were caressing her breasts and she moaned, "You feel so good, Avery. I've been wanting you for so long. Since high school. I know you didn't even know what I could do for you, the difference I could make in your life. But tonight, I showed you. I was the one who convinced the board that you deserved that position. And now, I'm gonna let you show me how much you appreciate me."

Avery Annalise Belmont, get yourself together right now and get yourself out of there. She felt the limo come to a halt and she saw that they were downtown. Avery pushed Demi's hands away and she snatched the door open and jumped out of the car.

"Avery! Avery!" She heard Demi calling her name, but she kept running ducking into a dimly-lit country-western bar and walking all the way to the back, praying Demi didn't see where she went.

Oh God, please help me. Duke, I need to call Duke. She realized that she had left her purse and cell phone in the limo. The loud music from the bar seemed to make her heart pound faster and she felt as if she was gonna pass out.

"Are you all right, lady?" a young waitress asked.

"I need a phone," Avery told her.

"Pay phone back near the bathroom," the waitress pointed.

"I don't have any money." Avery felt tears begin to form in her eyes.

The waitress must have known something was wrong, especially since Avery was dressed in an evening gown in a hillbilly bar. She reached into her apron and passed Avery a dollar in quarters. "In case you need to make two calls."

Avery thanked her and rushed to the phone booth. She dialed Duke's number and just as she suspected, he didn't answer. She hung up without leaving a message and the two quarters fell out of the coin slot. She dialed Tabitha and didn't get an answer either. She tried to think of anyone who could come to her rescue, and for some reason, an odd, vaguely unfamiliar number popped into her head. She dialed it and was relieved when the deep voice on the other line answered.

"Hello."

"Help me. You've gotta come and get me," she cried.

"Avery, where are you?" Kurt demanded.

She told him where she was and thanked God when she heard him reply, "I'm on my way!"

Epilogue

"This place is really nice, Avery," Malcolm said, carrying the last of her boxes and setting them inside the living room.

"Thanks, Malcolm," she said. "I really appreciate you helping me move in."

"Hey, it's not a problem," he told her. They had been at it since seven-thirty that morning and it was almost six in the evening. She knew he had to be worn out, because she was and she hadn't worked half as hard as he had.

"Where do you want this?" Sharice asked, carrying in a box of photos.

"You can put it on the table," Avery said. She walked over to the box and removed a framed picture of herself, Malcolm, and Tabitha taken on Valentine's Day the previous year. All three of them were dressed in red sweaters and jeans, and they all looked so happy. It was a great picture of a great time in their lives. Avery wished they could go back, but she knew they couldn't.

"Have you talked to Tabitha?" Malcolm asked.

"No, I haven't." She shook her head. She had tried to call several times, but she wouldn't answer her calls. She had even e-mailed her apologizing again and explaining what went down with Demi.

Demi—this was all her fault. And although she had been fired once Avery reported her for sexual harassment, the damage had already been done. If she had some way of proving that Demi had drugged her, she would have filed charges for that as well. That had to be the only explanation for her actions after drinking the champagne Demi had given her.

"I told her about your new place," Malcolm said.

"Really? I wouldn't even have this place if it wasn't for her." Avery smiled. "What did she say?"

"Not too much, but I think she was kinda happy for you."

"I think she misses you," Sharice told her.

"I miss her, that's for damn sure," Avery confessed.

There was a knock at the door and she hurried to answer it. "I got a visitor already?"

She opened it and was surprised to find Duke standing in the doorway with a gift bag in hand. "Duke?"

"What's up? Is this a bad time?"

"No, not at all. We're just finishing up," she said and opened the door so he could come in.

"What's up, Duke?" Malcolm gave him a pound. "This is my girl, Sharice."

"Nice to meet you," Sharice said, smiling, "Well, I guess we're done here."

"Yeah, we better get outta here before Avery remembers just one more box," Malcolm laughed. "Nice seeing you ag-ain, Duke."

"Yeah, same here," Duke said, nodding.

Avery walked Sharice and Malcolm to the door. "Thanks again, guys."

"No problem. See you at work Monday, boss," Sharice teased.

Her first assignment within the JMDP had been as a manager over Sharice's team. It was challenging, but fun.

"When you talk to my brother, tell him don't forget my birthday next week," Sharice whispered, making sure Duke didn't hear her.

Avery and Kurt had been hanging out from time to time. They were only friends, and Avery knew if she wanted it to be more, it easily would move into another level. She wasn't ready for that. He had mentioned it on more than one occasion. Her focus at this point was school and her workload, and becoming the best JMDP selectee the company ever had. In addition to her growing friendship with Kurt, she had also started hanging out with Daniel, who proved to be a viable source for her thesis.

"I can't believe you're here," Avery told him once they were alone.

"I can't either," he told her, then looking around, added, "This place is really nice."

"Thanks, that means a lot coming from you."

"This is for you." He passed her the gift bag. She reached inside and took out a Coach laptop bag.

"Oh Duke," she gasped. "It's gorgeous. You always know just what I want."

"I figured you would need it now that you're an executive and all," he teased her. "I never did get the chance to congratulate you on your new job."

"Well, it's never too late." She smiled.

"Does that apply to us too? Seven years is a long time, Avery."

She stared at him, reaching out and touching his face. She loved him. Always had, always would. She pondered the question in her mind. It had been seven long years. She was a different person then and a lot had changed. But, her love for him had remained strong. *Maybe, we still have a chance.*

"Only time will tell, Duke," she answered.

ORDER FORM
URBAN BOOKS, LLC
78 E. Industry Ct
Deer Park, NY 11729

Name: (please print):_____

Address:_____

City/State:_____

Zip:_____

QTY	TITLES	PRICE
	16 On The Block	$14.95
	A Girl From Flint	$14.95
	A Pimp's Life	$14.95
	Baltimore Chronicles	$14.95
	Baltimore Chronicles 2	$14.95
	Betrayal	$14.95
	Black Diamond	$14.95

Shipping and handling-add $3.50 for 1st book, then $1.75 for each additional book.
Please send a check payable to:

Urban Books, LLC

Please allow 4-6 weeks for delivery

ORDER FORM
URBAN BOOKS, LLC
78 E. Industry Ct
Deer Park, NY 11729

Name: (please print):_____

Address:_____

City/State:_____

Zip:_____

QTY	TITLES	PRICE
	Black Diamond 2	$14.95
	Black Friday	$14.95
	Both Sides Of The Fence	$14.95
	Both Sides Of The Fence 2	$14.95
	California Connection	$14.95
	California Connection 2	$14.95

Shipping and handling-add $3.50 for 1st book, then $1.75 for each additional book.
Please send a check payable to:
Urban Books, LLC
Please allow 4-6 weeks for delivery

ORDER FORM
URBAN BOOKS, LLC
78 E. Industry Ct
Deer Park, NY 11729

Name: (please print):_____

Address:_____

City/State:_____

Zip:_____

QTY	TITLES	PRICE
	Cheesecake And Teardrops	$14.95
	Congratulations	$14.95
	Crazy In Love	$14.95
	Cyber Case	$14.95
	Denim Diaries	$14.95
	Diary Of A Mad First Lady	$14.95
	Diary Of A Stalker	$14.95

Shipping and handling-add $3.50 for 1st book, then $1.75 for each additional book.
Please send a check payable to:
Urban Books, LLC
Please allow 4-6 weeks for delivery

ORDER FORM
URBAN BOOKS, LLC
78 E. Industry Ct
Deer Park, NY 11729

Name: (please print):_____

Address:_____

City/State:_____

Zip:_____

QTY	TITLES	PRICE
	Diary Of A Street Diva	$14.95
	Diary Of A Young Girl	$14.95
	Dirty Money	$14.95
	Dirty To The Grave	$14.95
	Gunz And Roses	$14.95
	Happily Ever Now	$14.95
	Hell Has No Fury	$14.95

Shipping and handling-add $3.50 for 1st book, then $1.75 for each additional book.

Please send a check payable to:

Urban Books, LLC

Please allow 4-6 weeks for delivery